LUNAR
DANCE

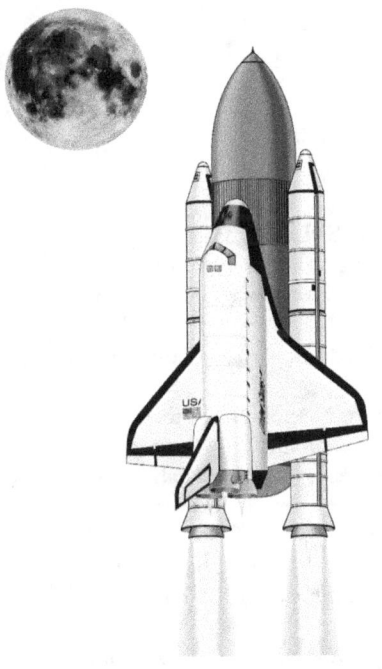

A novel by Robert Sapp

Sail Away Publishing Partners
Pensacola, FL 32526
www.robertsapp.com

First Trade Paperback Edition: December 2012

Cover image: NASA
Space shuttle graphics: NASA Dryden Flight Research Center

Library of Congress Control Number: 2012920162

ISBN: 0988543206
ISBN-13: 978-0-9885432-0-1

1 3 5 7 9 10 8 6 4 2

DEDICATION

To my wife Rhonda, who supported and embraced this silly notion of mine to write a novel.

To my brother Mark, my first reader, who enthusiastically encouraged me to continue with his repeated cries of "More chapters!"

To the heroes of my youth—those brave adventurers who willingly strapped themselves to rockets to expand man's horizons.

And finally, to star struck dreamers everywhere, who wish things had turned out differently.

PREFACE

I am a child of the space age. As a young boy, I covered the walls of my room with posters I received from the NASA public affairs office in response to the numerous letters I wrote requesting information about the space program. A large map of the moon hung above my bed, on which I carefully plotted each of the Apollo landing sites. I knew the name of every astronaut on every space flight, from Mercury to Skylab. I was excited about the future of space exploration, so full of unimaginable possibilities. It was a thrilling time to be a young child in love with science and adventure.

Somehow, things didn't work out the way we all expected. Whether through inertia, fatigue, or a simple change in priorities, it seemed we stopped dreaming the big dreams. The space program that so excited me and thousands of other young dreamers lost its focus, its glory, its glamour. And then one day, many years later, the shuttle stopped flying, and it was all just ... over.

This story is an attempt to recapture some of the spirit and excitement of that earlier time, when all things seemed possible. It's merely a work of imagination, but while writing it, it allowed me to once again feel for a precious few brief months the satisfaction and thrill of watching a group of audacious and determined men and women look upward and say, "We can do it." I hope that reading my tale brings you as much pleasure as writing it brought me.

Some scientists believe that we live in a multiverse,
composed of an infinite number of universes.
In it, every possible reality has its own existence.
The following events unfold in one such reality.

PROLOGUE

Quan Tran Lee waited impatiently for the climber to depart, his dive gear stuffed into the luggage bin under his seat. He would have normally taken a more leisurely and less expensive route, flying from Shanghai to Singapore in order to catch the main trunk of the Pan Asian elevator. Unfortunately, the markets had been very active this week, and he had been detained at the office and had missed his flight. With barely enough time to catch the bullet train to Hong Kong, he bought a ticket on the Southeast Orient elevator feeder root instead. It cost more and would mean a longer ride to orbit, but it would get him there in time to meet his friends for a drink at the Celestial Bar before catching their shuttle to the dive platform.

Glancing around the climber passenger compartment, Quan noticed that most of his fellow riders already displayed the blank expression indicating that they had jacked into the onboard infotainment system. *Why not*, he thought, *there's not much else to do for the next four hours.*

Scanning his thumbprint into the armrest's biometric sensor, he authorized the charge to his credit account. Opening the now unlocked compartment, he removed the temporal arch inside. Placing it on his head, he carefully adjusted it to ensure his visual cortex was properly stimulated. The scene before him vanished, replaced by an interactive menu system filling his entire field of vision. *Let's see. Not interested in news, I watch that all day from the trading floor*, he thought. *Looks like a few dozen people have linked up to play games. No, not that either, I just want to relax and enjoy the ride.*

Scanning now through the entertainment menu, Quan skipped the listings for the popular serial dramas and comedies. *Never had time to follow these, always too busy*, he thought. Flipping to the feature length productions, the motion of his eyes across the virtual screen causing the titles to rotate past, he paused. *Wait, here's something. I've been meaning to watch this—this is how it all began. Never had the time though, the ride from Singapore is too short. Let's see,*

1

three hours twenty minutes? Yes, this will work.

Quan confirmed the selection and settled back to enjoy the video drama. His visual field went dark, music swelled within his head, and the opening scene appeared before him.

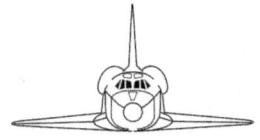

CHAPTER ONE

July, 1969

The screen door's hinges creaked loudly as Marta pushed it open, calling out, "Boys, it's happening!" into the still and steamy darkness. In from the warm Alabama night bounded her sons Alan and John, abandoning their pursuit of lightning bugs to observe the historic moment about to occur.

"Quietly now, don't disturb the grownups," she cautioned, as they pushed past her to rush to the living room and collapse in a sweaty heap in front of the television. Displayed on its screen was a ghostly, softly flickering black and gray and white image, showing the barely discernible shape of a person moving slowly backwards down a ladder. Seated around them was their father Carl Heinel, their grandparents Kurt and Annalee, and a collection of neighbors and friends.

"I almost can't believe this is actually happening," said Carl. "My God, if you had any idea how many things had to work exactly right."

"Hell son, most of my life we were told it was impossible," said Kurt. "I'm damn proud of you guys, you pulled it off!"

Just moments before, Carl had been intently praying, "Please God let it work!" as Neil Armstrong had climbed out of the Lunar Module and pulled a handle to release the stowage assembly Carl had designed, swinging a video camera into position. If the cable had broken or the latch had frozen or the connector on the camera had come loose, the world wouldn't be seeing the images that now had almost a billion human beings glued to TV screens around the globe.

From the TV, a voice said, "Ah, you had a good picture, huh?"

Another voice replied, "Ah, there's a great deal of contrast in it, and it's currently upside down on our monitor, but we can make out a fair amount of detail."

And for the first time that night, Carl was able to relax, the burning pit in his stomach turning to butterflies instead. "Thank you God!" he said quietly, as his wife Marta slipped into the seat next to him and reached out to hold his hand. As the apparition on the screen moved further down the ladder, everyone in the room unconsciously slipped forward to the edges of their seats, anxious to witness the moment that the men in the room, NASA employees or support contractors all, had worked day and night for years to achieve.

"And I'll step off the LEM now," came the voice from the moon. "That's one small step for man, one giant leap for mankind."

The cheers, shouts, and whoops of joy could have been heard at the neighbor's house, if the same scene hadn't also been repeated there. It was a small community in the northern Alabama woods, the German and American engineers, technicians, support personnel and their families that lived just outside of Huntsville. A small community that had played a large role in creating this historic event.

"Absolutely unbelievable!" shouted Kurt, choking back emotion as he pounded Carl on the back. "You did it son, you guys said you could do it, and goddammit you did it!"

But Carl's thoughts were elsewhere, already moving on to the next challenge, and the next, and the one beyond that. "This is just the beginning, Dad, just wait. Dr. Von Braun has such incredible plans! After we're done exploring the moon, we're going to Mars! And after that, the asteroids and Jupiter and the rings of Saturn!"

Standing as he spoke, Carl pulled Marta to her feet and wrapped his arms around her in a dancer's embrace. "We'll dance on the moon someday, my darling!" he said, twirling her gently, and then kissing her softly on the lips. She laughed at the thought, drunk with happiness. "I mean it!" he emphasized, reaching up to hold her face in his hands as he gazed lovingly into her eyes. "One day we will, I promise!"

The future was so incredibly bright on that warm July night in 1969. And not a person there doubted that it would all come true.

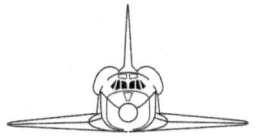

CHAPTER TWO

Two hundred miles above the Indian Ocean, shuttle Atlantis fired its orbital maneuvering system engines and began its hour long fall to Earth. Aboard the spacecraft, the crew tidied up the ship for landing and worked through the items on their reentry checklists.

After dropping for twenty-five minutes, Atlantis encountered the tenuous upper reaches of the atmosphere. Flares of hot plasma pulsed like lightning bolts past the flight deck windows, as a yellow-orange glow spread rearward from the nose. The crewmembers were awed by the power and energy of the hell-storm raging outside. As the ship was enveloped in a white hot mantle, everyone thought of the Columbia. Everyone said a silent prayer.

Encountering denser air, Atlantis' flight controls started to gain effectiveness, and it transitioned from spaceship to aircraft. The computers now flew it through a series of sweeping banks, bleeding more and more speed. Lower and slower Atlantis flew, throwing supersonic shock waves across the northern Gulf coast, finally becoming subsonic just minutes from touchdown. A human hand now assumed control, the commander banking the vehicle into a wide rightward turn to line up with runway 33 at the Kennedy Space Center.

Sinking rapidly toward the pavement below, still more falling than flying, the commander pulled up the nose to flatten the descent and gently kissed the long concrete ribbon with the orbiter's wheels. Atlantis sped down the runway balanced on its main gear, the nose wheel slowly, slowly dropping closer to the runway. Behind the vehicle, a parachute deployed to wrest the last bit of momentum from the enormous craft. With a solid thump, the nose wheel planted itself firmly on the concrete. As the commander applied the vehicle's brakes, the pilot, sitting to his right, reached up to release the parachute. In one of the few malfunctions in an almost perfect mission, it failed to separate from the orbiter. Finally, its fall from space complete, the vehicle smoothly coasted to a halt.

"Houston, Atlantis, wheels stop," announced the vehicle commander.

"Atlantis, Houston, copy that, congratulations on a fine mission and welcome home," came the reply.

The landing chute, still attached to Atlantis, gently drifted down to settle in a compact pile on the runway. As it came to rest, the thirty year history of the space shuttle program reached its official end.

***

The Honorable Will Daisy, representative of Florida's 15th Congressional District, looked around the floor of the Vehicle Assembly Building. A large buffet had been set up, and hundreds of NASA and Alliance Space Systems employees, those who had survived the layoffs so far, were milling about, eating and talking among themselves. *Incredible*, Will thought with disgust. *Last month you couldn't have brought a stick of gum in here, and now it's a goddamn diner.*

"Do you believe this?" asked Bob Brock, the *Orlando Guardian's* space reporter, who had driven over to cover the final shuttle mission.

"Well, this building has no real purpose as of today," Will answered. "Doesn't make much difference at this point, now does it?" he sighed.

"No, I suppose not," answered Bob. "So what's next for them?" he asked, nodding at the scientists, engineers and technicians scattered about the floor of the cavernous building.

"NASA might find something else for a handful of them. The majority will be officially unemployed in the next few weeks," Will stated bitterly. "The outplacement center has been open since spring, and we'll be holding a job fair soon." Shaking his head, he added, "Home Depot will be there. Home freaking Depot. Do you believe that? Some of these folks are PhD's in astrophysiology, and they'll be interviewing for jobs selling goddamn toilets."

"How long do you think before NASA is flying its own rockets again?"

"It takes five damn years now just to get a highway off-ramp built," growled the Congressman. "Designing an entirely new launch system? Anyone who thinks it will be less than a decade before we can do more than rent a seat from someone else is delusional. And you know what? That's too damned long to depend on the Russians."

"Some of the commercial launch companies are making good progress," Bob noted. "Apex's Dreamlifter is getting ready to fly a cargo mission to the space station, and there's talk of it being upgraded to carry passengers."

"You know what Bob?" Will said angrily. "The most capable manned orbital system in the world is sitting right out there on that runway. And shuttle will *still* be the best system in the world even *after* commercial launch arrives. And what do we do? Declare them obsolete. And all these people along with them," he said, gesturing at the assembled crowd. "A bunch of goddamn crap is what that is."

Behind the long buffet table, a large video screen showing photos depicting the history of the shuttle program suddenly switched to CNN. The screen now showed a podium bearing the presidential seal, while the ticker at the bottom read "President To Speak On Conclusion Of Final Shuttle Mission." The noise from hundreds of conversations diminished as people directed their attention toward the screen.

"So tell me about your work on the Shuttle Preservation Act," Bob asked.

"Well, as you know, the President had other budgetary priorities and killed off the Constellation program, leaving us totally dependent on the Russians," Will said, his contempt evident. "A year ago we had no options. But he took a shellacking in the midterms," he said, nodding toward the screen, "and became somewhat more reasonable afterwards. So my colleagues and I drafted a bill to put a freeze on NASA's plans to retire the shuttle. Rather than take these wonderful machines and stick them someplace for pigeons to crap on, we want to keep them here, maintained and ready to return to flight, if the need arises."

"A jobs program?" Bob volunteered.

"Yes, that, but also an insurance policy. Look, if the bill passes, we're going to be able to keep as many as a hundred of these folks employed. If we're smart about it, we'll also be keeping the core of a skilled workforce, because when the last of them leave, those skills are gone forever."

With a loud pop, the sound for the video screen was turned on, and everyone could hear the CNN anchor announcing the President's arrival. He stepped casually to the podium, greeted everyone, and then began his familiar left-then-right head bob as he read his prepared remarks from the Teleprompters. "Today, we reached the end of a long chapter in one of mankind's greatest stories ... "

Boos and catcalls echoed through the lofty volume of the VAB, drowning out the small amount of polite applause.

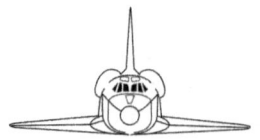

CHAPTER THREE

Juan Meneurez was one of the lucky ones. Once a senior space shuttle technician, he'd landed one of the few available jobs working on Apex Aerospace's Dreamlifter commercial cargo vehicle. Even better, he had managed to finagle a position for Manuel Ortiz, his friend and former partner.

Standing on an elevated platform beside the delta-shaped craft's open avionics bay, Juan plugged the cable of a handheld test scanner into one of the bay's diagnostic ports. Powering it on, he started his systems checks. *I wonder where that late-ass partner of mine is*, he thought.

Manuel's head popped up over the edge of the platform. "Dude, you started without me?" he asked in a hurt tone, as he finished climbing the ladder.

"Manny, where you been, man?" asked Juan.

"Human Resources called me at home, told me I had to stop on the way in to update my personnel file," Manuel replied, joining Juan on the platform. "Didn't tell me it was gonna take a freakin' hour, but there was a damn line. Sorry man."

"Yo, why can't you just admit you can't get your sorry ass outta bed!" teased Juan as he punched buttons on the scanner.

"True that, I was definitely draggin' ass this morning, but I did have to stop at HRO to sign a damn form. So how's it lookin'?" he asked, nodding toward the spacecraft.

"Same as yesterday, and the day before that," Juan said impatiently. "Don't know why they want these damn systems tested so much, but this'll be the last series. We're sealing it up and signing it off as flight ready when we're done."

Manuel picked up the test log clipboard from the adjacent safety rail to record the inspection results. "So dude, been meaning to ask you, how are you and Theresa doin'?" he asked casually, pretending to study the forms in his hand.

"Why you asking, man?" Juan said, looking up from his scans.

"Oh, no reason, just haven't heard much about you two in a while is all," Manuel said as he flipped through pages on the clipboard and made a brief note.

"Actually pretty good, man," replied Juan, returning to his tests. "We've been talking it out. Says she's done with that asshole Richard. She knows she screwed up, wants to make our marriage work," he added, as he plugged the scanner cable into another port in the bay.

"So listen man, I don't want to start some shit, but there was a truck parked in your driveway when I came in this morning," Manuel stated matter-of-factly, watching Juan's reaction from the corner of his eye.

Juan stopped what he was doing and spun around. "You saw that asshole's truck at my house?" he asked, exploding in rage.

"I'm just sayin', man. I was running late, and there was a pickup in your driveway when I went by. Couldn't say whose," replied Manuel with a shrug.

"I told her I'd kill that son of a bitch if I ever caught him with her again!" Juan exclaimed angrily. Violently yanking the scanner free from the avionics bay test port, the cable whipping about wildly, he threw it at his feet and started toward the platform ladder.

"Dude, where you goin'?" implored Manuel, attempting to block Juan's path. "Stay here man, it's not worth it, you'll get your ass fired ... "

"Shut the fuck up man, get the hell out of my way," yelled Juan, shouldering his friend aside. "If I find him at my house, I'm gonna fix his ass good, goddammit!"

Manuel could see the cold fire of jealous rage burning in his friend's eyes. Holding his hands up and backing away, he said, "All right, all right, do what you gotta do man. I'll try to cover for you." As Juan descended the ladder and rapidly strode across the floor of the maintenance bay, Manuel called after him, "But you're bein' a dumbass, man!"

Don't know what that stupid bitch sees in that Richard dude anyway, thought Manuel, turning back to the spacecraft. *Juan's a good man, he deserves better. Not his fault she can't keep her damn legs together*. He paused for a moment to assess Juan's progress with the testing of the craft's avionics systems. *Not that I wouldn't hit it if I had a chance*, he smirked. *That's some fine ass!*

Picking up the scan tool and scrolling through its internal log, Manuel could see that Juan had completed the systems checks. *Looks good*, he thought, picking up his clipboard and noting the results. After carefully forging Juan's signature as lead inspector, he signed again as second checker, and then closed and secured the bay. He never noticed the retainer latch that had sprung open on the ranging system control module when it had been hit by the flailing scanner cable.

Patting the side of the spacecraft, Manual said, "OK baby, looks like you're ready to go."

***

"Station, Houston, ready to proceed to the grapple point."

"Roger Houston, standing by," Eileen Coalwood replied. For the previous two days, Eileen had closely monitored the progress of the unmanned Dreamlifter vehicle from onboard the International Space Station as the ground controllers had put it through its paces. After successfully completing a series of orbital maneuvers, NASA deemed it safe to allow it to approach within range of the station's robotic arm, where it could be grappled and pulled aboard. From her position in the station's cupola with its many large windows, she had a fine view to photograph the craft's approach.

"Officially, we are not comfortable with this," she heard from behind. Turning, she saw Gennady Usarov, commander of the current station expedition, floating gently toward her.

"Gennady, you know it's good for the program," Eileen replied. "No one benefits from being completely dependent on a single launch provider."

"*We* benefit," he said. "My government is not yet convinced of the safety of this plan, allowing private spacecraft to approach the station." Then breaking into a grin, he added, "But I do not see any members of my government here at the moment, so you may as well conduct your experiment." Joining Eileen in the cupola and looking out at the Dreamlifter, he said, "If only those fools on the ground could coexist as well as we do up here, eh?"

"I know, wouldn't the world be a better place?" Eileen said with a smile.

"Well, I have work to attend to. Please let me know when the craft is holding at the grapple point," Gennady said, turning and drifting away.

"OK boss."

***

The Dreamlifter received the signal to approach the station. Scanning with its laser rangefinder, it compared the returned signal with the station's infrared signature, and computed a range. Determining the appropriate velocity vector, it fired its maneuvering thrusters.

***

"Houston, station, the vehicle is making its approach," Eileen reported, as she swung her camera into position. The spacecraft, bearing a strong resemblance to a small space shuttle, moved slowly and deliberately toward her.

***

Inside the Dreamlifter's avionics bay, the unsecured retainer latch on the craft's ranging system control module had allowed the module to work loose from its bus during launch. The maneuvers the vehicle had flown to validate its operation on orbit had jostled the module further, until the interface connector barely maintained contact. Now, as the craft accelerated toward the space station, the nudge from its thrusters rocked the module, severing its electrical connections and shutting down the craft's ranging system. The ship realized it was blind. As it had been programmed to do in such an event, it secured its systems, issued a cry for help, and awaited a command from the ground.

***

At Apex Aerospace's flight control center, an engineer noted their ship's call for help. "Control, we've lost LIDAR and infrared!"

"You mean we're blind?" the flight controller responded.

"Affirmative, we've got nothing for range measurement."

"Are you sure?"

"Yes, damn it, we need to abort the approach, now!"

The controller hesitated several seconds too long. "OK, this is an abort! Vehicle to station keeping. Get it stopped, now!"

***

That's odd, it should have started slowing by now, Eileen thought. Watching the Dreamlifter cross the grapple point threshold without stopping, she radioed her concern. "Houston, station, what's going on? This ship is getting pretty damn close up here. Wait, oh my God!"

***

The closing speeds were low, but the masses involved were large. The multi-ton spacecraft bulldozed into the station's Harmony node, opening a long gash in the module's thin aluminum hull. Then, receiving a signal from its ground controllers to halt its forward motion, it backed up and hit the station a second time, fracturing the mating ring between the Destiny and Unity modules. The station's atmosphere rushed into space, dooming the men and women aboard.

***

And with that, Theresa Maria Meneurez, through an illicit affair that had until then been of no particular importance to anyone not actually involved, indirectly caused the deaths of six souls, effectively ended NASA's manned space program, and destroyed the most expensive object ever constructed by mankind.

CHAPTER FOUR

The helicopter banked low over the sunbaked hills, bouncing in the columns of heated air rising from the scorched brown earth. Squinting in the bright midday light, Carl could make out a cluster of metal and block buildings ahead, randomly arranged around the margins of a long concrete runway. Near its midpoint sat a larger chrome and glass structure that looked as if it were poised to take flight.

"We'll be landing in just a couple of minutes," said the pilot over the intercom. "Please leave your headset on the seat, grab your gear and go when the door opens. We're not stopping, we need to make the lunch run."

"Understood!" Carl answered, not really understanding.

With a shuddering jolt, the helicopter lurched to a halt amid a thick cloud of brown dust kicked up by the rotors. Through the cabin window glare, Carl perceived the shape of a man rushing toward the aircraft. The door flew open, and he was assaulted by heat, dust and noise.

"Dr. Heinel! Welcome to Spaceport. Let me help you!" yelled the man over the whine of the turbine. Assisting Carl out of the cabin, both men then ducked and rapidly ran-walked away from the aircraft as it lifted off and spun away to the south.

"Where is he headed in such a hurry?" asked Carl as the dry brown dust started settling on his hair, face, and clothes.

"Look around Doctor—there's not a whole lot of lunch options here, except the gourmet place at the terminal. Mr. Armac figures he's in for the lease on the helicopter, so he might as well get his money's worth. We make a run to the airport in Las Cruces, and the delivery guy from Gino's Pizza is waiting with five large supremes to go. Beats the hell out of a three hour roundtrip by car. Mike Patrick, by the way, Roadrunner Rockets," he said as he reached out to shake Carl's hand. "Glad you could make it. Follow me!"

Mike led Carl to a nearby Jeep, its engine running. "I keep the A/C going full blast. A parked car can top a hundred fifty degrees out here in no time. Get in!" Mike quickly slipped behind the wheel while Carl moved more slowly into the passenger seat. The heat and the jostling from the helicopter ride caused him to feel every one of his 73 years.

"Thanks for coming out to meet with us," Mike said loudly to be heard over the sound of pebbles and sand pelting the underside of the Jeep as they sped away. "You Apollo guys are getting few and far between. We're lucky as hell to find you!"

"Last of a dying breed, I guess," Carl said sadly.

"Before you meet the gang, I want to show you something," Mike shouted. The Jeep skidded as he quickly turned right onto an intersecting dirt road and accelerated toward a distant building. "We're doing a firing to validate a new design. Should be lighting up any second now."

"You're an engineer?" yelled Carl, wondering about the young man he had only communicated with via email.

"No, I'm a coder—I write physics engines for the boss. This is really just a cool hobby for us, messing around with rockets. Our day job is running our online gaming environments. That's what pays the bills. But we try to spend at least one week a month out here doing shit we love."

The Jeep slid to a halt outside a lone cinderblock building emblazoned with a large "RRI" and a stylized image of a roadrunner spouting flame from its rear end. Mike threw open the driver's door, piled out as if ejected, ran around to Carl's side and yanked open his door.

"This way please, I think if we hurry we can catch the burn." Mike led Carl to a plain steel door with a sign that read "Static Test Control." Entering without knocking, he quickly ushered Carl inside.

A huge expanse of glass flooded the room with the glaring light of the inescapable New Mexico sun. A group of casually dressed young men and women sat in front of laptop computers, intently monitoring readouts. Looking outward, Carl recognized a large rocket engine test stand several hundred yards away.

"Luke, how long 'til the burn?" asked Mike of the only person standing. "I'd like to watch from outside if it's OK."

"We're just clearing our final safety hold, so it'll be two minutes," replied Luke Rungren, gazing through binoculars at the distant test stand. "Outside is fine, make sure you grab your PPE."

"Here, take these," said Mike to Carl, pulling safety glasses and earmuff-style hearing protectors from a bin. "Your PPE—personal protective equipment. It's way cooler to watch from outside, but it gets loud as hell! Follow me."

Carl once again scrambled to keep up as Mike led him to another steel door. "That was Luke, he runs the test center," explained Mike. "He'll want to meet you after the test."

Exiting the building, Carl found they were on a covered patio. It was still desert hot, but the overhead metal awning provided some escape from the searing sun. A clear acrylic barrier faced the distant test stand—obviously a safety shield to protect observers from whatever was about to happen.

Carl heard Luke's voice over the public address system. "This is Range Safety, we are go for static fire in two minutes. All personnel stand clear!"

"He's so full of himself!" Mike called out from next to the safety barrier. "Most days he coordinates tier 2 tech support for our online games, but out here, he becomes Gene freaking Krantz!"

"So this is the hybrid engine you referred to?" asked Carl as he joined Mike behind the shield.

"Yeah, this will be our first 'B' scale test. We finally got the 'A' scale working reliably, and we want to see if the design solutions scale to the larger size."

"Thirty seconds!" Luke announced.

"Better get ready," said Mike, tapping the hearing protectors Carl still held in his hands. "If you don't, you'll wish you had!"

"Ten seconds! Nine. Eight. Seven. Six. Five. Four. Three. Two. One."

A puff of smoke appeared from the object in the distance, followed by a bright orange flame. A loud shrieking howl reached them as the flame grew in length and brightness, its color changing from orange to yellow to iridescent white. The noise became a physical force—a deep seismic rumbling Carl could feel in his chest—accompanied by a horrendous shriek that stabbed at his eardrums through his earmuffs. For a moment, the rocket reached equilibrium, emitting a steady, constant flame and unwavering sonic blast. Then subtle signs of instability appeared. Pulses of orange and violet began to stream through the rocket exhaust, as the noise changed to a staccato beat.

Carl felt an uncomfortable pulsating pressure that made it difficult to breathe—a sensation similar to having a toilet plunger used on his face. Suddenly, an enormous yellow fireball engulfed the distant test stand, followed immediately by the concussion of a massive explosion. Large pieces of the former rocket spiraled lazily into the air trailing thin streams of black smoke. The metal roof above them rattled as smaller pieces of rocket, test stand, and desert floor rained down.

"God *damn* it!" yelled Mike, staring at the remains of the test stand. "That should have *worked*. That's going to *kill* our schedule!"

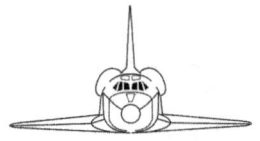

CHAPTER FIVE

Carl followed Mike into the small conference room. As they entered, the group of people seated in cheap plastic chairs around a folding table covered with pizza boxes stopped their conversation and looked up.

"Dudes, this is Dr. Heinel, the Apollo guy," said Mike. "Did you watch the test?"

"Yeah, we watched the live feed," replied the huge black man at the head of the small table, standing as he spoke. "Looks like we're pretty much screwed. Luke's team is already gathering up the pieces. Maybe we'll have some idea what happened before we head back to Dallas." Extended his hand to Carl, he said, "I'm Marcus Short, Dr. Heinel. I'm the Hot Wax team lead. Glad you could make it. Forgive us if we're a bit bummed, but we were really counting on today's test to keep us on schedule."

"Hot Wax?" asked Carl, looking up in puzzlement at the giant towering above him.

"Our hybrid rocket motor. We're experimenting with paraffin fuel. It's basically a big candle. Hot Wax. It sounded good over beer and nachos, so we've never bothered to change it!" grinned Marcus.

Carl's mind raced to recall anything he'd read about paraffin rocket motors. "They work," he muttered. "The theory is good, but undeveloped."

"Come again?" said Marcus.

"Sorry, I'm thinking out loud. Is ... is this what you wanted to see me about? To talk about paraffin hybrid motors? Because I really haven't done any work on them, my work was solid fuels and ... "

"No Doc, that's not why," said Marcus, interrupting Carl. "We want to pick your brains on the work you did on the shuttle solid rocket boosters. And we want to hear about Apollo."

"Yes, that's what Mr. Patrick mentioned, that you wanted to talk to me about Apollo. I'm not quite sure why, though. It's ancient history after all.

Wouldn't you rather discuss something newer? Maybe you should speak with one of the former Constellation engineers, perhaps? I know some good people that would love to do some consulting … "

"No Doc, we don't want to talk to any Constellation drones," said Marcus contemptuously. "Look, we're on a really ambitious schedule here. We need to do too much too fast with too little. Right now, we're getting our asses kicked, and we need help. You Apollo guys were rock stars. You did in a day what NASA takes a year to do now. What did they call them in that movie?" Marcus asked, looking over his shoulder at his comrades. "Steely-eyed missile men? That's what we want, Doc. A steely-eyed missile man! Are you a steely-eyed missile man?"

Carl blinked suddenly, not sure if the people in front of him were serious or crazy or both.

"OK Doc, sit down and we'll explain," said Marcus. "Want some lunch? There's plenty," he said, pushing a pizza box across the table. "Ever heard of the Low Cost Launch Initiative? The LCL One prize?"

"Yes, of course," answered Carl, recognizing the name of NASA's engineering challenge to private industry, part of their Centennial Challenge series. The goal was to significantly lower the cost of access to space. The company that could reduce launch costs to below $250 a pound would win an enormous prize and revolutionize the industry.

"Well, we're in it, Doc. We're in it big," said Marcus. "We think we've got the right idea. If we can build our 'C' scale motor, we think we can beat the EtherX boys and win the $200 million prize. And we need to win it, Doc. Those guys at EtherX have major coin behind them. Their owner Elton Funk rules online payments. This is pocket change to them. We're working on a shoestring, with the few million dollars Mr. Armac can squeeze out of our gaming revenue, and whatever sponsorships we can line up. We're all in on Hot Wax, Doc, and if we don't win, well, we're totally screwed."

"I see," said Carl. "I really don't understand though what it is you think I can do for you. I'm sure there are better people, more experienced people … "

"It's like this, Doc," explained Marcus. "Until the station disaster, all anyone was interested in was developing a commercial launch capability, to hell with the cost. Apex and EtherX were gonna own that market. NASA was even signing contracts with them for flights to the station. Well suddenly there wasn't a station anymore, Apex is gone, and there's no place for EtherX's Minotaur capsule to fly to. Now it's all about low cost, low cost, let's drive the cost down for commercial launches. And suddenly we're golden, Doc. Our big bet paid off."

"Big bet?" asked Carl.

"We could have chased every other wannabe launch services company down the liquid fuel path," Marcus answered. "But then Luke and his team had this idea. A fully reusable hybrid motor fueled by paraffin and liquid oxygen. Cheap and elegant, Doc. Cheap and elegant!"

"So ... ," Carl began, still struggling to understand where he fit in.

"So, Doc, if the goal is cheap access to space, then EtherX's multi-engine, liquid fueled, sort of partly reusable Raptor rocket costs too damn much!" Marcus explained.

"Uh-huh," said Carl, as confused as ever.

"OK Doc, two things," said Marcus. "First, our 'C' scale motor is being designed to use the same external casings as the shuttle solid rocket boosters."

"You're using shuttle components?" asked Carl, his eyebrow arching.

"It's all about cost Doc, it's all about cost," emphasized Marcus. "With the end of shuttle, suddenly there are a lot of spare parts sitting around doing no one any good. We've already talked to the manufacturer in Utah, and they're selling us a bunch of their tooling and equipment for salvage cost."

"I see," said Carl, finally beginning to understand what was happening.

"So we're going to buy all the second hand handling and servicing equipment we can get a hold of, adapt our paraffin fuel to those casings, and have one cheap-ass booster!" Marcus triumphantly exclaimed while slapping the table.

Carl stared at Marcus for a moment, his silence causing Marcus' smile to fade. "So because I did shuttle SRB design work, you think I can help you with your hot candle rocket," he stated.

"Hot Wax, Doc. Exactly," confirmed Marcus. "We think having you on the team will save us months, maybe a year, coming up with the designs to adapt our paraffin LOX system to those casings. And then there's the second thing," he added.

"And that is?" Carl inquired.

"The spirit of Apollo, Doc. The spirit of Apollo. You were there, Doc. You helped make it happen. No challenge was too big, no problem too difficult. You guys set an ambitious, audacious goal, and you pushed through, Doc, you *pushed through* until you made it happen. We need that spirit, Doc. I want you to inspire my team. I want you to show them what it means to be that steely-eyed missile man I mentioned. I have good people, Doc. Very good people. But I want them to be inspired. I want them to eat, sleep and breathe this project just like you guys did back in the day. Inspire them, Doc. Inspire them!"

Carl sat quietly, surveying everyone in the room, seeing the excitement reflected in their faces. Suddenly, a thought appeared—a thought Carl had put away years ago, never expecting to revisit, but now resurfacing as vividly as the day he first conceived it. He finally realized why fate had placed him in this room in front of these people on this day.

"Let me ask you a question," Carl said, continuing to scan the faces in the room. "Mr., Short is it?" he began, looking at Marcus. "What is it that truly motivates you?"

"What do you mean?" replied Marcus, now his turn to be puzzled.

"Launching cargo into space less expensively than your competitors," answered Carl. "Is that really what excites you about spaceflight? Your owner, Mr. Armac you say? Is flying cheap rockets what makes him want to get up in the morning and spend millions of dollars? Or is it really the spirit of adventure, the chance to do something truly amazing?"

"Still not following you, Doc," said Marcus, looking around at his team in confusion.

Carl focused intently on Marcus. "When I look at you, I see people who want to do something significant. Something that matters. Something that people will remember and talk about for years. What if I told you that you need to think bigger?"

"Go on," said Marcus, intrigued by Carl's tone.

"Ladies and gentlemen," said Carl, "what if I showed you a way to go to the moon?"

For a moment, everyone sat in stunned silence. Then they all began talking at once, some amused, some outraged, some laughing at the absurdity of the proposal. Carl sat back in his seat, his face serenely composed.

Finally, Marcus' voice cut through the chatter. "The moon, Doc? Seriously?"

"Yes, the moon," Carl replied. "I'm quite serious. You'll need your hot wax rocket. Several of them in fact. And a space shuttle."

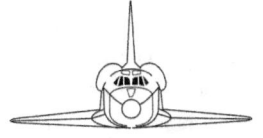

CHAPTER SIX

"The *moon*?" Tom Armac asked incredulously. "Is the man demented? Because I'm thinking he has to be completely freaking nuts!"

"No, boss, he was dead serious," replied Marcus. Marcus, Mike Patrick, and Luke Rungren were seated in a semicircle of papasan chairs in Tom's office at the headquarters of Altered State Software outside Dallas. They were there to report on the latest round of testing at Spaceport, but the conversation focused almost entirely on Carl and what they were referring to as "the proposal."

"So did you smell his breath then?" asked Tom. "Because if he's not crazy, then there has to be a bottle involved."

"Seriously, Mr. Armac, we thought the same thing at first," said Luke. "But after we quit laughing, he proceeded to tell us exactly how to do it. Claims he and a few of his old STS/Apollo friends worked it out years ago. Figured out how to do it with stuff already sitting around."

"And the weird thing, boss," added Marcus, "is that when he was finished, we all just sat there slack-jawed, because you know what? It could work. It sure as hell could work."

"So you're telling me that after years of development and millions of dollars of my money," said Tom, "we're this close to meeting our launch goals, and you want to shitcan the entire project and chase after this wild-assed notion?"

"That's what made the whole thing so cool," said Mike. "Within an hour of arriving, he'd figured out our entire program, introduced the proposal, and then showed how it actually helps us meet our launch goals. It's like, hey, we can build a cheap rocket and win LCL One, or we can build a cheap rocket, win LCL One, and go to the moon—which would you prefer?"

"Fine, let's just say for the sake of this discussion that I'm intrigued," said Tom. "Does this Dr. Heinel just happen to have a spare space shuttle parked in his *freaking garage?*"

Marcus, Luke, and Mike exchanged sheepish glances. "He says that's our problem," Marcus said with a shrug.

"Excuse me?" said Tom.

"He says if we want to do it, he'll show us how, but it's up to us to pull together the necessary resources," explained Luke. "But he gave us an idea on where to start," he added.

"Oh please, enlighten me!" said Tom, sarcastically.

"NASA's plan is to find good homes for the shuttles now that they're retired," said Marcus. "They basically want to sell them to the highest bidder—whoever pitches the best proposal for displaying them."

"So I heard," Tom said. "So what?"

"Well, there's this Congressman who's trying to get a law passed to make NASA hold on to them," said Marcus, "but the smart money says it'll never fly. They'll probably be coming up for bid before too long. Everyone pretty much knows that what they'll eventually end up doing is keeping one at the Kennedy Space Center, sending one to the Johnson Space Center, and probably give the last to the Smithsonian. Make them all tourist attractions."

"No shit," said Tom. "So what, we plan a clandestine mission to kidnap one, fly it to the moon, and then bring it back in the morning before anyone notices?" he sneered.

"No," said Marcus, "we make them a better offer."

Everyone sat uncomfortably in their extremely casual seats while the man who signed their paychecks glared at each in turn. Tom knew his people were no fools, and whatever this gentleman had told them had made believers out of them.

"Get him down here," Tom ordered. "I want to talk to this Dr. Heinel myself."

***

Mike stood in Love Field's main terminal waiting to meet Carl's flight from Atlanta. "Dr. Heinel, over here!" he called, spotting Carl entering through the arriving passenger's portal.

"Nice to see you again, Mr. Patrick," smiled Carl. "How have you been?"

"Great, Dr. Heinel, just great. Here, let me take that," Mike added, reaching for Carl's small carry-on. "Do you have any other luggage?"

"No, no, just the one," Carl said. "And please, call me Carl."

"Sure thing, Dr. Carl," said Mike. "This way, the car's in the lot across the street.

Carl and Mike exited the terminal building, stepping into the sauna that was Dallas in July. "My God, it almost takes your breath away!" said Carl, as they crossed the street and entered the parking garage.

"Welcome to Texas, Dr. Carl," said Mike.

"I used to come here often," said Carl, half to himself. "Houston actually, not Dallas," he added. "Business at the Johnson Space Center. But not in years now, not since I left NASA."

Mike opened the passenger door of his Lexus coupe and helped Carl get in, quickly pitched his bag into the trunk, and then dashed around to the driver's side and slid behind the wheel.

"No jeep this time?" asked Carl, recalling their first meeting two weeks previously and their wild ride across the New Mexico highlands.

"No, that was a company car, this is my *baby*," Mike replied, patting the black leather dash with one hand and navigating the parking garage exit ramp with the other.

Carl settled comfortably into the soft leather seat as they exited the garage and headed up the freeway on-ramp. Turning to Mike, he said, "Since we have some time, would you mind telling me a little bit about Mr. Armac?"

"Sure, what would you like to know?" asked Mike.

"Well, I found some general details about his history and background online," explained Carl. "I'd like to know a bit more about him as a person."

"Well, if you looked him up online, then you probably know he started out writing shareware games," Mike said, while changing lanes to merge left onto the freeway. "He decided to take his best ideas and start his own company, taking along some of his previous employer's top programmers."

"And they started Altered State Software?" asked Carl.

"Yes indeed. So the first thing you probably need to know is that Mr. Armac likes to control things," he added, looking at Carl. "He's not really *controlling*, like he's a tyrant or anything, just that he doesn't like it when other people have too much influence over him."

"I see," said Carl. *Good*, he thought to himself.

"So they hit a few homeruns with some innovative 3D games, and Altered State becomes a player in the industry," continued Mike. "But unlike other people, he refused to cash out when the buyout offers started coming in. That control thing, you see," Mike explained, glancing again at Carl. "Mr. Armac says he has no interest in managing someone else's dream."

"Yes, interesting," nodded Carl. He quietly contemplated this information for a few minutes, and then turned and asked, "So how did he get from there to building rockets?"

"Well, the company has made a pretty sweet profit," Mike answered. "Enough to let Mr. Armac indulge some of his passions. Personally, I think he was looking for a bigger challenge," he added, glancing again at Carl.

21

"But rockets? I can't really say for sure. But he's always pushing himself, pushing us, trying to take everything he does to the next level. It's like he has something to prove," Mike observed good naturedly.

Now that is interesting, Carl thought. *I can work with that.* "So how did you become Mr. Armac's propulsion systems expert?" he asked.

"Well, I code the physics engine for our games," explained Mike. "We try to make our virtual worlds as realistic as possible, which means the physics has to be right. Gravity, explosions, how things fall or interact with other things—they all have to be exactly right to make a believable world. It wasn't much of a leap from there to trajectories and orbital mechanics," he said, grinning. "And I've always had an aptitude for mechanical stuff. Our rockets are pretty simple devices, really, so getting my head around how they work was no sweat," he concluded.

"But no formal education?" asked Carl.

"Math and programming, but nada in engineering or aerospace. Making it up as we go along!" replied Mike.

"So then Mr. Rungren? He manages the test program?" asked Carl.

"Luke actually invented Hot Wax," replied Mike. "It was his idea originally. He pitched it to Mr. Armac three, four years ago when we thought we could grab a piece of the market for supplying NASA with trips to the space station."

"I see. And his background?"

"I think he went to Embry Riddle for a couple of years, so he's the only one on the team with some aerospace education. He came to us because of some flash animation work he had been doing. Short online cartoons. Mr. Armac liked them, met Luke, heard about his ideas for Hot Wax, and brought him onboard," Mike explained. "I don't think any of us would be here without Luke and his ideas," he added.

"Yes, I see," nodded Carl. "And Mr. Short? Which is an inappropriate name in my opinion. How tall is he, by the way?"

"Six foot five, two hundred eighty pounds," laughed Mike. "Marcus is one colorful dude," he continued. "Played ball for Auburn and actually had a pro contract for a few months before blowing out a knee in training camp."

"But he appears to be the person most responsible for running things," said Carl. "How did that come about?"

"He actually graduated from Auburn with a degree in computer science," Mike explained, "along with a minor in graphics and illustration. Mr. Armac wanted to explore development of a sports game, and thought Marcus seemed like a good resource."

"From sports games to Roadrunner Rockets?"

"We decided pretty quickly that Madden owned football games and we'd never get any market share," replied Mike. "But Marcus and Mr. Armac really hit it off. Marcus is like Mr. Armac's alter ego. Where the boss can be uptight, Marcus is laid back. If Mr. Armac gets too drifty, Marcus pulls him back down to earth. And sometimes Mr. Armac's people skills can be a little, well, let's just say we think he has a touch of Asperger's. Meanwhile Marcus is everybody's friend, and has outstanding coaching skills from playing football for years. Plus he has a natural talent for program management. He's the one who makes the team work like a team should."

"That's the impression I was left with," said Carl.

"Most of Mr. Armac's time goes into running Altered State, so he needed someone who could take RRI and run with it. That would be Marcus," he concluded. "And here we are," Mike announced, pulling into a front row parking spot before the headquarters of Altered State Software.

Carl looked up, noting the non-descript two story stucco office building in front of them, similar to ones found in any office park anywhere. "This is your corporate headquarters?" he asked.

"Not what you were expecting?" answered Mike.

"No, I suppose not," said Carl. "For some reason I had pictured mirrored glass, maybe a fountain, some granite or marble … "

Mike laughed, and then said, "Mr. Armac established a pretty pragmatic corporate culture. We have kick-ass computers, but he believes pretty buildings don't write better software," he explained. "It's a short drive to work, a quiet neighborhood, plenty of places to eat for lunch, the A/C works great and the roof doesn't leak, so anything else is just a waste of resources," he added.

Outstanding, Carl thought with a smile.

"Ready?" Mike asked, opening his car door to get out. "Our meeting's in ten minutes."

"More than you'll ever know," Carl said softly to himself, looking again at the building before him.

"Huh?" Mike asked.

"Nothing, Mr. Patrick. Yes, I'm quite ready," Carl said as he opened his door.

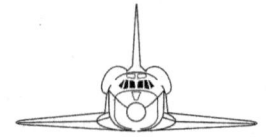

CHAPTER SEVEN

"Good morning, Dr. Heinel. Thank you for seeing us on such short notice," Tom began. "You made quite an impression on my team last month. I'm anxious to hear more about your very interesting proposal."

Carl looked around the second floor conference room that Mike had escorted him to. Everyone Carl had met at Spaceport weeks earlier was seated around the large oval conference table. Tom sat in the center of one long side, Carl facing him from across the table. An additional half dozen people who Carl did not recognize had also joined the group.

"I believe you know most of my team already," continued Tom. "In addition, I've asked several of our legal, engineering, and marketing people to also participate in today's meeting."

"Thank you for having me, Mr. Armac," replied Carl, attempting to use the exchange of pleasantries to probe his host's frame of mind.

"So, Dr. Heinel," said Tom, "you know Roadrunner Rockets is a bootstrap operation. We've yet to conduct our first launch with our Hot Wax system. And yet I'm told you believe that with your help, it's possible for us to not only succeed with winning the $200 million LCL One prize, but also take this team to the moon." Tom presented it as a statement rather than a question.

Skeptical, concluded Carl. "Indeed I do."

"I have to tell you, Doctor, that if this, *proposal*, had come from anyone else, we wouldn't have bothered to give you the time of day," explained Tom. "We're not the biggest or best funded commercial launch company in the arena, but we take what we do very seriously."

Skeptical, and somewhat hostile, Carl thought.

"But we did some research on you, Doctor," continued Tom, punching at the face of a tablet with his index finger and then reading from the screen. "Doctor Carl Heinel, Bachelor of Science in engineering from the

University of Alabama, 1961. PhD in aeronautics from MIT, 1964." He looked up at Carl. "Finished the program a year early," he added with a slight nod that may have reflected respect. "Thirty years with NASA, first with Project Apollo, where you did general spacecraft support systems development, then design work on the Space Transportation System, concluding as lead engineer for the STS solid rocket booster program." Tom laid the tablet back down on the table. "One thing I noticed is that your 30 year career was spread over 36 years, Doctor. Why was that?"

"Virtually everyone was laid off at the end of Apollo," explained Carl. "The public grew bored, the program was terminated, the final missions cancelled. I taught physics at Jacksonville Community College for four years, until I was offered a position with the shuttle design team. And then after the loss of Challenger, our program ground to a halt, and I was laid off again. It was voluntary that time—I had seniority, but we had a lot of young engineers that would have never weathered the layoff."

"I see," said Tom. "Well Doctor, as I said, if this proposal had come from anyone else, we would have summarily dismissed it as nonsensical. But you have enough credibility that we feel you deserve an opportunity to make your case."

"Thank you," replied Carl.

"So, the floor is yours, Doctor. Make your case," Tom stated, sitting back in his chair and folding his hands in his lap.

"I have a question first," said Carl.

"Please, go right ahead."

"It's never been clear why you reached out to me in the first place," Carl stated. "For the entire duration of my visit with your team at Spaceport, I never understood what it was that you thought I could do for you."

"That's very simple, Doctor," replied Tom. "We needed your name on the letterhead."

"I'm sorry?" Carl said, confused.

"Development costs for Hot Wax have exceeded our projections, Doctor," Tom explained. "We're attempting to obtain venture capital bridge financing to fund the company until we win the LCL One prize. Our advisors tell us our team, this team," he gestured to the people around the table, "while possessing the drive and talent, lacks the necessary *credentials* to be taken seriously." The touch of bitterness in his voice was clearly evident. "So we intended to add you to our design team and offer you a seat on the board."

"To increase your likelihood of receiving venture financing," concluded Carl.

"Exactly," nodded Tom.

"Not because of any specific contribution you thought I could make, but merely for my credentials?" Carl asked.

"Welcome to the business world, Dr. Heinel," said Tom with a shrug.

Carl was overwhelmed by a sense of worthlessness he hadn't felt in decades.

***

An hour into his presentation, Carl noticed a visible change in his audience's demeanor. Their initial skepticism was gone as the group challenged his assumptions, evaluated his responses, and recognized the feasibility of his proposal.

"This is the best part, boss!" Marcus excitedly exclaimed.

"So once the shuttle is on orbit, we face trans-lunar injection," continued Carl. "Shuttle carries two orbital maneuvering system engines, here and here," he said, using a laser pointer to highlight the OMS engines on the tail of the shuttle diagram projected on the conference room wall. "Using extended OMS propulsive burns on two sequential orbits, shuttle first elevates its apogee to achieve a highly elliptical orbit, and then conducts a gravity assist maneuver to achieve escape velocity and enter a Hohmann trans-lunar trajectory."

"A Hohmann trans-lunar trajectory?" asked Tom.

"It is the method requiring the lowest total energy expenditure," explained Carl. "It allows shuttle to reach lunar orbit using only the thrust of the OMS engines."

"Why is a gravity assist necessary?" asked a smartly dressed Asian woman to Tom's left, one of the new faces with whom Carl was unfamiliar.

"Because the OMS engines don't have sufficient thrust to directly boost shuttle into trans-lunar injection," explained Carl. "You will need to first elevate the orbital apogee to six hundred kilometers, and then on the following orbit, use the 'slingshot' of gravity assist to accelerate to escape velocity. It's actually a bit more complicated," he added, facing the young woman, "but that's the easiest way to explain it."

"OK, please continue," said Tom.

"Right. So at this point," Carl said, "the shuttle performs a propulsive OMS burn to decelerate into a highly elliptical lunar orbit, or HELO. This orbit would have a perilune, or closest point of approach to the moon's surface, of one hundred kilometers, and an apolune of approximately nine thousand kilometers."

"And why the elliptical lunar orbit?" asked the woman.

"Again, it's a matter of expending the least amount of energy," replied Carl. "Circularizing the lunar orbit would require a significantly longer deceleration burn than entering a HELO. This would require the shuttle to carry more OMS fuel. Too much," he added, "to allow us to do this at all."

"But the shuttle's OMS engines can't possibly carry sufficient fuel for all those burns," stated Tom.

"True, in their current configuration," confirmed Carl. "But we will modify the shuttle to carry additional fuel thusly." He nodded to Mike, who tapped his tablet screen. On the projected shuttle diagram, a pair of cylindrical tanks appeared and settled into the aft two-thirds of the shuttle cargo bay.

"And how much additional fuel would that require, Doctor?" asked Tom.

"Shuttle carries 360 cubic feet of fuel for the OMS engines," Carl said. "We will need an additional 8,000 cubic feet."

"And there's room for that?"

"Indeed. The diagram is to scale. The cargo bay is 10,200 cubic feet," replied Carl, smiling. "The fuel will fit with room to spare."

"But if you intend to transport additional fuel, why not use the shuttle main engines?" asked Tom. "They produce much more thrust than the OMS engines do."

"That is actually the mission profile we analyzed when I was with NASA," replied Carl. "We preferred that method, but then we had access to billions of dollars and thousands of engineers. There are two major reasons why this is the better approach now. First, what I'm showing you today is how to take surplus STS equipment and supplement it with your hybrid fuel boosters, your Hot Wax system, to cost-effectively reach the moon. Shuttle's main engines were not designed to perform the multiple restarts in space that would be required. You would have to completely redesign them—a very expensive and time consuming process indeed. The OMS engines, on the other hand, are the same engines originally designed for the Apollo service module. This mission profile is exactly what they were designed to do."

"I see," said Tom. "And the other reason?"

"As the external tank is exhausted launching shuttle into orbit," Carl said, "we would need to create a way to refuel the tank once on-orbit. And that would be one very interesting problem."

"Agreed," said Tom, mentally calculating the years of effort that would be needed.

"As the OMS engines are of an extremely simple design," Carl continued, "modifications to the shuttle will merely consist of the additional tankage and fuel transfer valves. And besides," he continued, smiling at the group, "there's a certain, *poetry*, in returning to the moon using the original Apollo engines."

"All right, I'm convinced," stated Tom. "How hard would that be to build, Viv?" he asked the woman who had previously questioned Carl. Turning to Carl, he added, "Doctor, Vivian Lee is our lead engineer for Roadrunner Rockets projects."

"It would just be some titanium fuel tanks and cylinders for helium and nitrogen, a few solenoid valves," Vivian answered. "We could have it done in a few months, once we had the shuttle engineering drawings."

Tom leaned back, nodding slightly as he contemplated the merits of Carl's plan. "OK," he said, "so we get to the moon. We won't want to go all that way just to make a few orbits and then come home. We're going to want to land. And obviously we're not landing the shuttle on the surface."

Carl smiled inwardly. *He's saying* "we" *now, not* "you," he thought. "Very true, we'll need a lander, obviously."

"So that's it then," declared Tom, pushing back from the table, the spell broken. "Now you're talking about an additional spacecraft that will have to be designed, built, tested—God knows how we'd even test something like that. And we certainly don't have the money for a project that size. Or are you proposing that we ask the Smithsonian for the loan of their lunar lander?"

"Wait for it!" Luke quietly whispered to Marcus with glee.

"That's actually one of the easier problems to address," stated Carl with a wry grin. "There are several payload laboratory modules that have been built for shuttle. Personally, I recommend ShuttleHab, although there are several of the older European Space Agency Spacelab modules that could work."

Mike again tapped his tablet, and another cylindrical module appeared above the diagram of the shuttle, and then dropped into the cargo bay just forward of the fuel modules.

"The ShuttleHab laboratory already contains the necessary environmental control systems," explained Carl. "With the addition of a small fuel cell as an internal power supply, the module would become capable of supporting independent operation for several days." Carl turned to face Tom. "It would become our lander."

Tom stared at the projected image for a moment, and then said, "That's fine Doctor, but I'm not seeing how you'd get it down to the surface and back again."

"Ah, well, we will attach a propulsion unit to the laboratory like so," said Carl. The projected image showed the lander nestled in the shuttle cargo bay. As they watched, the shuttle's robotic arm reached into the bay and removed a unit containing fuel tanks and a small rocket engine and attached it to the module's top. Four landing struts then extended upward from the corners of the unit, each containing a cluster of attitude control thrusters.

"As the shuttle approaches perilune, the lander will detach from the orbiter and fire its engine to descend to the surface," Carl explained. While he spoke, an animation showed the lander leaving the shuttle and landing on the surface. As it touched down, a space suited figure exited the lander and deployed a large Roadrunner Rockets flag. The audience erupted in laughter and applause.

"I added that last bit, Doctor Carl," said Mike, smiling proudly.

"Yes, I see that!" Carl replied good-naturedly. "So, to continue, after a day on the surface, the lander will boost back to orbit, rendezvousing with the orbiter at perilune, after which the shuttle will perform a propulsive burn to leave lunar orbit and return to Earth. As simple as that," he concluded, turning to face the audience.

"As simple as that," echoed Tom. "Viv?" he asked.

"The lander propulsion unit looks like the biggest challenge," Vivian replied thoughtfully. "We'd have to source a descent/ascent engine and the attitude control thrusters, but I have a pretty good idea what to use. The rest is just framework, tanks and plumbing. If there is actually a payload laboratory module that we can adapt, then we'd have to figure out a way to integrate the fuel cell power source. I know some people in the electric car industry who could consult, though."

"Mike?" Tom then asked.

"I could model it all in our standard physics engine to work out the orbital mechanics and propulsion solutions. Shouldn't take more than a couple of laptops to operate guidance control onboard the lander. Plus we could use the data to drive a simulator to practice the maneuvers. Plug in some virtual reality goggles and you'd think you were actually there."

"Luke?"

Luke gazed at the screen image, his brow deeply furrowed. "Mike, show me the shuttle diagram again."

Mike tapped his tablet a few times, and the projected image changed to the diagram of the shuttle.

"How much OMS fuel did you say the shuttle normally carries?" Luke asked Carl.

"Approximately 360 cubic feet."

"And what does that weigh, Doctor?"

"About ten thousand kilograms." Carl knew the question that followed. He had hoped to avoid the issue for now, while he was planting the seed.

"And how much additional fuel will those tanks need to contain?" Luke asked, gesturing at the projected image.

"Eight thousand cubic feet."

"That's what I thought you said," said Luke. "I've been thinking about this since you gave us the brief outline at Spaceport, Doctor. While I agree that there is room in the cargo bay for the additional fuel, that would turn out to be about," Luke punched at the screen of his phone briefly, "roughly two hundred and forty thousand kilograms. That's over half a million pounds, which is something like ten times the cargo capacity of the shuttle. And that doesn't include the lander, or the lander's propulsion unit. Doctor, I can't believe you're sitting here talking about launching the shuttle carrying over ten times the payload it's capable of lifting into orbit."

Everyone faced Carl, their expressions ranging from confusion to contempt.

"Doctor?" stated Tom, the implied request for an explanation hanging tangibly in the air.

"Oh, I never said we'd launch the shuttle carrying the OMS fuel modules," Carl replied, smiling at his audience with a quiet confidence. "Mr. Short, how did you describe the rocket you are developing when we met in New Mexico last month?"

"Doc?" asked Marcus, taken by surprise.

"One cheap-ass booster, I believe you called it," Carl continued, a twinkle in his eye. "The stated purpose of Roadrunner Rockets is to develop an inexpensive heavy-lift launch capability based on adapting your Hot Wax technology to STS solid rocket booster segments. I've looked at your design, ladies and gentlemen, and I believe it is sound. You're anticipating that your 'C' scale booster will produce four million pounds thrust, correct?"

"That's right," replied Marcus.

"Well, with the appropriate second stage, a pair of your boosters should be capable of placing 100,000 kilograms into orbit."

"That's the goal, and for less than $250 per pound," said Tom.

"Well, you will need to demonstrate that capability to win the LCL One prize for which you are competing. If memory serves me, that will require you to conduct two successful launches."

Tom nodded briefly, confirming Carl's conclusion.

"So gentlemen, on one launch, you place the first OMS fuel module in orbit. On the next, you orbit the remaining one," Carl explained. "You have to orbit something, after all."

"Luke?" Tom asked.

Luke stared intently at Carl for a moment, and then turned to Tom. "We're planning to launch an instrumented dummy payload on the first booster to qualify for the competition. We were hoping to find some paying customers for the second launch who would be willing to take a chance with their payloads in exchange for a big price break." He looked back at Carl. "But he's right, we could launch a fuel module on each flight."

"In any event, that is the heart of the matter," Carl concluded, changing the subject. "I've shown you the basic overview of how to take this team to the moon. I'm very interested in seeing what you do with the information."

Everyone paused for a moment, unsure of the next step. "All right then," Tom announced, "this apparently concludes our fun and games for today. Marcus, before everyone gets back to work, your team has had a couple of weeks to think about this. What did you decide?"

"Well boss, it's like I told you before. It's crazy, but when you see it all laid out, it sure as hell could work. We're not saying it's bet the farm time, but it's worth looking into."

"So what would it take at this point?" asked Tom.

"Well, we see this as a problem with four parts," replied Marcus. "First there's the technical part. That one's pretty obvious—what do we need to actually do this, and how do we go about getting it? Next would be the political part. As much as we'd like to dazzle the hell out of NASA with our audacity and have them bequeath a shuttle to us, truth is it's going to take some serious political mojo to get our hands on one. And without the shuttle, well, this is a just a big freaking waste of breath."

"I hear that," Tom nodded.

"Next is the personnel part. We'd obviously have to find a former astronaut crazy enough to help us fly the shuttle to the moon and then land on it, 'cause sure as hell no one here is going to be able to do it."

"I was already starting to think about that myself," said Tom.

"And finally, there's the financial part. Even though we're talking about cheap-ass boosters and off-the-shelf hardware, truth is, boss, this isn't going to be cheap. Not cheap at all. Instead of the LCL One prize money being our big payoff, we'd have to consider it just walking around money to get the ball rolling. So those four things: technical, personnel, political, and financial."

"You're overlooking something," said another woman, silent until now. "There's a legal component to this as well."

Tom looked at Nicole Ferry, his corporate lead attorney. "I think I know where you're going, but explain," he said.

"Say we get a shuttle," Nicole said. "I sense that we might be … let's just say less than completely forthright about our intentions for use of said equipment. So that's an area for concern—we'd have to be very careful to make sure we're protected. There's the whole issue of liability and indemnity, were one of our launches to hurt a civilian not associated with the program. Launch permits, reentry permits, dealing with the FAA and Homeland Security. Contracts with subcontractors. Non-disclosure agreements. And if we actually made it to the moon? What's the law say about that? Could we land there without permission? If not, whose permission would we need? Could we claim some portion of it as ours? If we brought anything back, would we be able to keep it, or would it be considered illegal contraband? I have no idea what the laws are regarding commercial lunar spaceflight."

"Nicole makes some good points," Tom said. "So obviously there's a legal consideration here as well."

"OK then boss, we have technical, personnel, political, financial, and legal considerations," said Marcus. "Hate to say it, but we probably need to explore the political part first, because if we can't gain clear title to a shuttle, we've got nothing and we all go back to building our cheap-ass booster."

Carl sat quietly observing the conversation taking place around him. Once a bold vision has taken flight, its death could be a demoralizing thing to witness. He had opened their eyes to the possibility of achieving something truly historic, and the notion of returning instead to something merely extraordinary caused a sense of gloom to descend upon the participants.

Tom thought for a moment, and then reached his decision. "Dr. Heinel, you do present an interesting case. While I'm not convinced it's possible, nothing we've seen tells me that it's impossible. I definitely think it's worth continuing to investigate." Turning to Marcus, he said, "Pick your teams, and be ready to brief me in a week on your findings." He paused for a moment. "Better make that two weeks," he added, remembering that everyone in the room still had day jobs supporting Altered State.

The meeting started to break up, as one last item occurred to Tom. "Dr. Heinel, one quick question before you go," he asked. "What do you wish to get out of this?"

Carl slowly smiled at Tom. "Oh, I very much want to go with you."

"To the moon, Doctor?"

"Yes, of course."

"I see," said Tom, nodding. "Well, I suppose that's only fair."

"And one other thing," added Carl.

"What's that, Doctor?"

"I wish to bring my wife with me."

All conversation in the room immediately stopped as everyone turned to look at Carl in astonishment.

"You've got to be shitting me," said Tom.

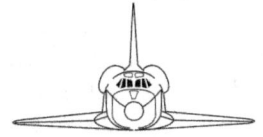

CHAPTER EIGHT

December, 1971

Carl sat alone in the hospital waiting room, numbly staring at his feet, contemplating the broken shards of what had been his life. How suddenly the world had changed that bright spring day of the previous year when his father Kurt had suffered a massive stroke. The weeks of torment that followed, watching the once proud and robust man reduced to having others feed and change him like an infant, had made his subsequent death seem a tender mercy.

Carl's beloved mother Annalee, devastated by the loss of her husband, had slowly dragged herself from the depths of depression and despair by finding delight in her grandchildren, Alan and John. Oh, how she had doted on them both! The pride she took in every "A" they earned in school. The elaborate event she made of each of their birthdays!

His boys, Alan and John. How amused everyone had been when he and Marta had named their two precious boys after astronauts. How impressed they had been when both men made time to attend their namesake's baptisms while in Huntsville inspecting flight hardware.

Carl could still recall every agonizing detail of the day the police officer had come to the door. Marta had answered the knock. He had heard her cry of anguish and the sound of her body collapsing on the floor as she sobbed hysterically.

It had been an accident. No one could be blamed. There was no one at whom to direct the anger. The delivery truck hadn't been speeding. The driver wasn't drunk. The front tire just *blew*, sending the huge vehicle careening into Annalee's car as she drove Alan and John home from their monthly visit to the barber shop. She loved taking the boys for haircuts. The boys loved the stop for ice cream that was always her reward to them for being so good.

The three closed coffins at the service. The car had burned. Those closed coffins, denying him and Marta the chance to say one last goodbye. No parent should have to bury a child. God should not demand that of anyone. Carl had begun doubting if there even was a God, for surely he couldn't be this cruel.

Marta was so strong. She received every grieving friend or relative with subdued grace, accepted every expression of condolence with quiet gratitude. But Carl heard her tears at night as she poured her grief into the darkness. Nothing he could do could lighten her soul.

Then, shortly after the funeral, her discovery of the lump in her breast. *How long had it been*, he thought, *how long since she came to me with the news? October. It was a year ago October. The boys were excited about Halloween.* Carl's gaze slowly lifted from his shoes and settled on the small Christmas tree, his only companion in the sterile white glare of the waiting room. *Christmas*, he thought, *it's almost Christmas. Just a little over a year.* Carl's breathe caught in his throat, as his chest heaved with an involuntary sob. He had spent that 14 months taking Marta to an endless succession of doctors, hospitals, treatments. He watched as the drugs took their toll, watched as she grew paler, thinner and weaker. Her hospital visits became more frequent, her stays longer.

"Mr. Heinel? Your wife is awake now, she's asking for you."

Carl's eyes regained focus as he slowly turned toward the voice. A nurse stood before him in a crisp white uniform, a look of concerned compassion on her face.

"Yes, thank you," he said. "I'll be right there, I just need a moment."

"Of course, sir. We'll be with your wife." She turned and softly walked away.

Too many goodbyes, Carl thought. *There have been so, so many these past two years.* The thought of another goodbye briefly reminded Carl of the envelope in his pocket. Slowly, he reached for it, pulling it from his jacket, opening the envelope, unfolding the form inside.

"Notification of Reduction In Force," Carl read again. A termination notice. The loss of his career—the only thing he had loved even a tenth as much as his family. *Too many goodbyes*, Carl thought again, returning the form to the envelope and placing it back in his pocket.

Slowly, as if in a dream, Carl stood and walked up the short hallway to his wife's room, gently tapped on the door, and entered. Inside, he saw the nurse who had summoned him gently wiping Marta's brow with a compress, while Dr. Thayer, Marta's doctor, made notes in her chart.

The nurse bent down and softly spoke to Marta. "Mrs. Heinel, your husband is here."

Marta laid in bed, so frail, the blue lines of her veins startlingly visible through the translucent parchment of her skin. An IV dripped fluids and morphine. Only morphine now, no longer any drugs, as her condition was hopeless. Carl knew every day could be the last, every visit his final one.

"Carl, are you here?" she called out weakly.

"Right here, baby," he answered. "I'm right here." Carl sat beside her bed and took her cold tiny hand in his. "How are you, darling?"

"I'm so tired, Carl. So tired," she sighed, breathing slowly.

"It's all right baby, the doctor is taking care of you."

Marta began to cough, first softly and shallowly, and then deeper and harder. The cancer had spread to her lungs some time ago.

"Oh baby," Carl cried, embracing his wife, attempting to will his strength into her. Dr. Thayer stood beside Carl and placed a hand briefly on his shoulder, and then reached past him to place a stethoscope under Marta's gown and listen to her body's struggle to live.

"It hurts, Carl. It hurts so much," Marta said between gasps for air.

"I know baby, I know." Carl paused, and then, gently stroking his wife's face, said the thing he never wanted to say. "It's time, baby. It's time to stop fighting. It's OK. You did your best. I'm so proud of you. It's time." Carl looked at the doctor, pleading with his eyes.

The doctor nodded, picked up a syringe and injected it into Marta's IV. "We'll make sure she's comfortable, Mr. Heinel, but I'm afraid it probably means she won't be awake again."

Marta's coughing began to subside and her face relaxed as the extra dose of morphine flowed through her veins.

"Carl, I'm not afraid anymore," she quietly spoke. "I'm not afraid anymore. I'm not afraid because I'm going to see my babies again. My babies … " she trailed off.

Fighting back his tears, Carl bent down and gently kissed her forehead. "It's OK darling, you rest now. Get some rest," he whispered.

"Carl?" she spoke softly, her eyes closed. "Carl, promise me something … promise me something before you go."

"What baby, what do you want me to promise?"

"Promise me you'll go to the moon, Carl. For us. Go to the moon like you promised. And dance. Think of me and dance."

Carl unconsciously reached for the envelope in his pocket, briefly touching it before taking his dying wife's hand a final time.

"I will, darling. I promise. I promise."

CHAPTER NINE

The team Marcus now called the Lost Boys was assembled in his office, waiting for Tom to arrive to brief him on their progress. Luke, Mike, Vivian and Nicole sat around the compact table Marcus had brought in, which had turned his office into a cramped and claustrophobic space. Tyler Allen, the most recent team addition, had the "seat of shame" squeezed between the water cooler and the corner of Marcus' desk. He had been brought over from Altered State Software for his marketing and sales experience, and hadn't yet earned his place at the table.

Marcus had covered his office walls with stick-on dry erase wallpaper, turning them into enormous white boards. They displayed project planning diagrams, concept maps from brain storming sessions, organization charts, technical illustrations, and one very large cartoon of a stick figure astronaut standing on the moon holding an RRI flag.

Tom Armac appeared in the doorway and surveyed the scene. Since tasking Marcus with this analysis, Tom had been buried with issues at Altered State, and this was his first chance to see the progress the team had made.

"OK, what do you have for me?" Tom asked, pulling out a chair and sitting down. "Is Doctor Heinel wasting our time trying to relive his glory days, or is there actually some possibility of making this work?"

Marcus was used to Tom's brusque manner. He knew what Tom lacked in tact, he made up in trust. He trusted his people to make good decisions, and he accepted what they told him at face value. Tom expected to make a multi-million dollar decision based on what he learned in the next hour. A decision to either commit RRI to pursuing Carl's proposal, or to thank him for his time and send him home with some nice parting gifts.

"Well boss, even with the long days, we could have used another week," said Marcus. "But I think you're going to like what the team has put together."

"The Lost Boys?" Tom asked, noting the title above a list of names on the left hand white board.

"Sure, we refuse to grow up, and we're trying to learn how to fly," replied Marcus. "And we're somewhat disreputable," he added with a grin.

"Cute. OK, whatcha got? Will it work?"

"First thing we did is run Dr. Heinel's numbers," said Luke. "He's dead on with his calculations. If you put the pieces together the way he outlined, you can indeed make it work."

"Good," said Tom. "I'd have been pretty damned pissed if he was just talking out his ass."

"No, apparently he earned that PhD," Luke observed, reflecting the team's contempt for credentials not backed by ability. "If we can get the bugs worked out of Hot Wax, validate it with a successful test of the 'B' scale rocket, and then hit our thrust target for the larger 'C' scale model, then it will do the job."

"So what are the remaining roadblocks with Hot Wax?" Tom asked.

"We need to get the damn thing to not blow up," said Marcus.

"Indeed," chuckled Tom. "That would be the preferred outcome. Are we making any progress there?"

"I spoke with Dr. Carl again yesterday," said Mike, "and he believes he might know what our current problem is, and has some suggestions on how to solve it."

"When will we know something?" Tom asked.

"If you'll authorize the expense, we'd like Dr. Carl to visit our plant at Spaceport again, see how we cast the rocket motor segments, and help with our next test series."

"You mean we don't have him onboard yet?" asked Tom in amazement. "Nicole, please put together a consulting contract for the Doctor. Non-disclosure agreement, no compete clause, all the usual stuff. Marcus, contact the Doctor and negotiate a suitable consulting fee. Within reason though. Tell him if this works, his ticket to the moon will be his performance bonus."

Both Marcus and Nicole nodded.

"Get that contract signed," Tom continued. "I don't want to lose this guy to a competitor. The idea might occur to him that we're not the only rocket company in town."

How 'bout that, thought Marcus. *From demented old man to key team member in two weeks!*

"And how about the launches for the shuttle OMS fuel modules?" asked Tom.

"If we get Hot Wax squared away … " started Luke.

"*When* we get it squared away," Tom asserted.

"*When* we get it squared away, the plan is to build a two stage launcher by using the 'B' scale motor as the second stage, married to a pair of the larger 'C' scale first stages. That should give us ample thrust to park the fuel modules in orbit while we launch the shuttle. Viv has been doing some preliminary design work on interstage units."

"And the fuel modules themselves," Vivian added.

"Any issues?" Tom asked.

"Nothing I can't handle so far," Vivian replied, "although we're nowhere near ready to start bending metal yet."

"How many rockets will we need?"

"At least five, three of the 'B' scale and two 'C' scale," said Luke.

"We really need to give these things names," said Marcus. "This 'B scale C scale' thing lacks personality."

"Another item for your list," suggested Tom. "So only five?"

"When we get a successful test firing on the 'B' scale motor, we refuel it, put it aside, and build two more," explained Luke. "When we get a successful firing on its big brother, we do the same, building one additional unit."

"Big Brother, I like that," said Marcus, writing it on the board.

"To qualify for LCL One," continued Luke, "we'll build a launcher using one Big Brother, and one, what, Little Sister?" he said, glancing quickly at Marcus with a smile. "That will give us a full systems validation test. We'll recover the Big Brother and refuel it. First OMS fuel module launch, we use two Big Brothers, and another Little Sister. We orbit the fuel module, win LCL One, pass Go and collect our $200 million prize. We recover the Big Brothers, and refuel them. Third launch, we use the Big Brothers again, and the last Little Sister. That puts both fuel modules in orbit. We recover the Big Brothers once again, refuel them, and use them for the shuttle launch. So start to finish, two Big Brothers, three Little Sisters."

"How long?" Tom asked.

"From the first launch until the shuttle goes up, four months," answered Marcus. "Maybe less if everything comes together well."

Tom pursed his lips. "That's going to require some damn tight coordination. I'm not too crazy about the risk either, having no surplus boosters. Let's factor in at least one more pair of Big Brothers. That way we can run some things in parallel. It might help us with our schedule if we get behind."

"Sure boss, it's your money," replied Marcus.

"Indeed," Tom replied. *And I have no idea how I'm going to pay for it all*, he thought. "OK, how about the lander?"

"Still trying to nail down specs on a ShuttleHab module," said Vivian, "but as it turns out, the company that built them is only three hours south on I-35. I'm driving down next week to meet their lead engineer. He seemed pretty interested in working with us, although I was kind of vague about our intent."

"OK, and what about the rocket engine you'll need for the lander's propulsion unit?" asked Tom. "And the maneuvering thrusters?"

"Well, we found the perfect engine, flight tested and ready for use," Vivian said.

"Excellent, what is it and how much?" asked Tom.

"An EtherX Wizard."

Tom immediately tensed up. "No way. No way in hell." Everyone in the room knew of the antipathy between Tom Armac and Elton Funk, owner of EtherX and RRI's biggest competitor for the LCL One prize. "I don't want that son-of-a-bitch to have any idea what we're up to, and I certainly don't want him to profit from it," Tom said.

"Mr. Armac, the engine is perfect. It's the right size, the right thrust, it's designed for multiple starts and can be throttled. It's like it was made for this lander. It will save us at least a year of development. Plus the price is right."

Tom glared at Vivian. She held his gaze, hoping she projected both competence and confidence.

"If you're serious about it, you'll do this," she said, casually lifting her coffee cup to take a sip.

After a long pause, Tom said, "All right, but you make damn sure he has no idea what we intend to do with it. If we pull this off, you tell everyone we built our lander out of a second hand Russian ICBM we bought on eBay and stripped for parts. I don't want them getting any credit."

Vivian choked out a laugh, spewing the mouthful of coffee she had just sipped. Everyone chuckled as Marcus scrambled to grab napkins from his desk drawer to clean up the mess.

"Ok, ok, enough of that," smirked Tom, reaching for a napkin. "So what's next?"

"Well, it looks pretty encouraging from the people side," said Nicole, who had taken the lead in the personnel search in addition to researching the legal issues. "NASA has trained almost two hundred people to fly the shuttle. Probably fifty of those were current within the last five years."

"So finding someone to pilot the mission isn't out of the question?" Tom asked.

"It doesn't appear that way," answered Nicole. "Same for technicians. The layoffs at the end of the shuttle program hit the Florida space coast hard. Unemployment is scary high, with no end in sight. Getting a team together to service the shuttle for launch should be achievable."

"OK, good. So what can you tell me about the financial side? How in hell are we going to pay for all this?"

Tyler cleared his throat briefly and scooted his chair forward so Tom could see him better between the heads of the people seated at the table. "Mr. Armac, I've kicked this around a bit, talked to a few friends, and you know what we have here?"

Altered State Software was a small enough company that Tom still recognized every employee. "What's that, Tyler?" he asked.

"A license to print money," Tyler replied, as if no further explanation was required.

"And how's that exactly?" asked Tom, annoyed by the answer.

"We're talking about going to the *moon*," Tyler said. "The first private, civilian, commercial moon voyage. Do you have any idea how many companies would want to be part of that?"

"Tyler, cut to the chase," Tom ordered.

"The first cell phone call from the moon," Tyler began. "How much do you think AT&T would pay to prevent Verizon from landing that deal? What's it worth to Oakley to have the first private moon walkers wearing their sunshields rather than Ray-ban's? What would Nike pay for their logo on the boots, shoes, whatever you wear on the moon? I'm telling you, Mr. Armac, they don't make a big enough armored car to carry all the money you could swing in sponsorships."

"OK, well, you might have something there," Tom said, considering the possibilities.

"And that's just the beginning," Tyler continued. "Do you know how much moon stuff there is on Earth? Less than 900 pounds. And NASA spent over 125 billion in today's dollars to bring it back. That's almost a million dollars an ounce!"

"Daaaaaaaaaamn!" exclaimed Marcus.

"I'm not saying that's what it would be worth," Tyler explained, "but it would be valuable as hell, so obviously we're going to want to see how much moon stuff we can bring back."

"The ultimate bling!" said Marcus.

"And we're still just getting started," Tyler continued. "Galactic Journeys has a mile long waiting list of people willing to pay a quarter million dollars for a sixty minute rocket ride to the edge of space. What would it be worth for a trip to the moon?"

"I ... really ... have no idea," Tom said thoughtfully. "I know they were paying fifteen or twenty million for a ride to the space station."

"Several wealthy individuals have claimed in the past that they'd pay from 50 to 100 million for a private spaceflight to the moon," Tyler stated. "And that's without landing. I'll bet there are a handful that would easily pay 100 million or more if you could convince them that they'll enjoy the ride and make it back alive, and will be able to get out and walk around a little."

Tom was completely overwhelmed. Instead of this being one of the hardest issues to tackle, it appeared it could be one of the easiest.

"Still just scratching the surface, Mr. Armac. Sales of logo merchandise. Product licensing and royalties. Pay-per-view broadcast rights. On the personal side," he said, looking around the room," whoever goes can probably count on a six figure book deal for a behind-the-scenes tell-all. I'm telling you sir, your very own personal money tree."

"That's ... that's just amazing," said Tom.

"It's still all small stuff compared to the big money maker," said Tyler.

"You've already spelled out how to make hundreds of millions."

"Yes sir, but I saved the best for last. A lottery."

"A lottery? What the hell ... ?"

"You hold a national lottery. Hell, make it worldwide. You do it online, so your overhead is virtually zero. You sell tickets for a shot at a seat on the flight. Twenty-five dollars a ticket, winner gets to walk on the moon. Promote the hell out of it, with the winner to be chosen in a live TV event. How many people in the world would take a twenty-five dollar shot at walking on the moon? Honestly? I think every birthday card and Christmas stocking would have a ticket in it. I think we could easily top 100 million tickets sold. And that, ladies and gentlemen, would be two point five *billion* dollars."

Marcus let out a slow whistle, and then said "Tyler, pull your seat over here. Get out of that damn corner."

Tom sat slowly shaking his head. Everyone waited quietly, watching the range of emotions that played across his face. Finally, he said, "OK, wow, so we're OK with the financials. Guess I won't have to sell the company after all. So what about the shuttle? Does it matter which one we try for?"

"Atlantis has the latest upgrades and was the last to fly," Marcus said. "Looks like she'd need the least amount of work, which means the lowest cost to prepare."

"And since every dollar counts ... " Tom began.

"She'd be the one we'd want," Marcus concluded.

"OK, so we try for Atlantis then," Tom said. "But how do we pull that off? This is all just a fairy tale if we can't obtain the spacecraft, after all."

Nicole smiled, and said, "Well, not to try and top Tyler, but I think you're going to love this. We proposed a 'what if' to our DC lobbyists, asking for their advice on how to go about it, and I think what they came up with is going to blow you away."

***

"And they absolutely assure us it's all legal," concluded Nicole, finishing her brief.

Everyone turned to look at Tom.

"This just keeps getting better and better," he laughed. "I walked in here wondering if we were all wasting our time. Now I think this is going to be the most damn fun any of us has ever had. Good job team, umm, Lost Boys. OK, it's decision time. You five are now basically the board of directors. So what say you? Do we go? Or no?"

Everyone looked around the room, judging the reactions of their peers. They hadn't expected to be given the responsibility for making this decision.

"I say go," said Luke with a shrug.

"Go," said Mike, nodding.

"Absolutely, go," said Nicole.

"Like you said, Mr. Armac, it's too fun to pass up. Go," said Tyler.

Marcus beamed at his team, and then said, "Hell yeah boss, Go with a capital G."

Tom nodded, looking extremely pleased. "All right, let's do it," he directed. "Nicole, call our lobbyist friends and let's see if they can get us that shuttle. It's about time they started earning that retainer we pay them."

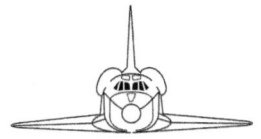

CHAPTER TEN

Tom tapped on Nicole's office door, pushed it open, and stuck his head in. "I just wanted to wish you luck before you leave for Washington," he said cheerfully. "What time is your flight?"

"Thanks, I leave in two hours," Nicole replied.

"Were you able to get a room?"

"Yes, at the Capitol Hilton. Sorry for the expense, but we're meeting early the next morning with the Senator, and I don't want to have to fight DC traffic and risk being late."

"It's OK," Tom chuckled. "I promise to approve your travel claim as long as you bring back the title to a shuttle."

"I'll do my best," Nicole replied.

"Well, I'm looking forward to your report," Tom said, turning to leave. Pausing at the door, he added, "Oh, and no pressure or anything, but we're all counting on you, because the whole project depends on you pulling this off." Smiling, he turned and left.

"Bastard!" she jokingly yelled after him.

***

Richard McConnel, of the aerospace lobbying firm Viter, McConnel and Strong, sat in a leather armchair in the lobby of the Capitol Hilton waiting for Nicole. He had provided Congressional access and advice on pending legislation to Tom Armac's company for five years, but this was by far the most unusual task he'd been given. Fortunately, he had a lot of contacts from his days as NASA's Deputy Administrator, and it hadn't been difficult to arrange today's meeting.

The lobby elevator doors opened and Nicole stepped out, sharply dressed in a blue business suit. Recognizing Dick, she headed toward him.

"Dick, good to see you again!" she said.

"And you as well," he smiled, standing. "Welcome to DC."

"Thanks, wish I had time to stay and sightsee, but Mr. Armac is keeping us all extremely busy. I haven't been to Washington since before law school."

"Well another time maybe." Looking at his watch, Dick asked, "So, it's a beautiful morning outside, would you like to walk or would you prefer to take a cab?"

"How far is it?" she asked.

"Fifteen, maybe twenty minutes on foot. A straight shot up Pennsylvania Avenue."

"Now do these shoes look like they're made for leisurely strolls?" she asked, turning her right foot outward to display her four inch heel.

"No, I suppose not," he said, taking brief note of the shoes while admiring her trim calves. "There should be a cab outside."

Settling into the backseat of the cab for the short ride to the Hart Senate Office Building, Dick quickly briefed Nicole on the protocol for the visit.

"And one more thing," he said as an afterthought. "Make sure you always call her Senator. She can get pretty cranky otherwise."

"I'll try and remember," Nicole replied with a smirk.

***

"Mr. McConnel, Ms. Ferry, the Senator will see you now," said the administrative aide, holding open the door into the adjoining office.

Senator Marsha Battler sat at her desk smiling, framed by the flags of the United States and the state of California.

"Senator, Mr. McConnel of Viter, McConnel and Strong, and Ms. Ferry of Roadrunner Rockets Incorporated," the aide announced.

"Thank you Britney," the Senator said, gesturing for her aide to have a seat while rising to greet her visitors. "Mr. McConnel, Ms. Ferry, a pleasure to meet you," she added. "Please, be seated."

"Thank you for taking the time to see us this morning, Senator," said Dick.

Nicole's gaze wandered about the office while Dick and Marsha Battler continued the welcoming ritual. The garnet red walls were covered with framed pictures of the Senator shaking hands with a range of notable persons in a host of worldwide locations. Representing as she did the state of California, many of the pictures included Hollywood celebrities. She returned her attention to the business before her when she heard Dick say, "And that brings us to the reason for our visit today, Senator."

"Yes, Mr. McConnel, I'm very interested in hearing more about your client's intriguing proposal."

"At this point I'd like to ask Ms. Ferry to outline their project for your consideration," Dick said, passing the baton to Nicole.

"I'd also like to thank you, Senator, for taking the time to meet with us today," began Nicole, playing the part of the proper supplicant.

"My pleasure, Ms. Ferry. I serve the people of California, and the information I've received indicates that your proposal could offer many benefits for my constituents, so naturally I'm delighted to speak with you." Nicole noted that her voice said "welcome," but her demeanor projected "make it quick."

"Senator, in the event that the Shuttle Preservation Act fails to pass Congress, we assume NASA would soon be soliciting bids for static display of the orbiters?"

"Yes, I'm certain they would. The sooner the better as far as I'm concerned," said Marsha.

"Ma'am?" asked Nicole, and then noticed the quick reproving glance Dick gave her.

"I've strongly advised my colleagues in the House to vote against the bill," she explained, ignoring Nicole's failure to use the honorific. "I think we've wasted enough money on those white elephants. We spent over $250 billion going round and round the Earth not doing much of anything. Do you have any idea, Ms. Ferry, how many schools we could have built with that money? How many children we could have provided health coverage to?"

Dick saw the need to intervene in order to regain the initiative and make the most of their time. "They certainly have outlived their usefulness, Senator."

"Yes, well, to all things, a season. Please continue, Ms. Ferry," said Marsha.

"As I was saying, Senator, we believe NASA will be requesting proposals for display of the orbiters," said Nicole.

"Undoubtedly," said Marsha.

"Well, Senator, my company recognizes the long and proud history of the aerospace industry in California. The pioneering work that was done at Edwards Air Force Base. The Jet Propulsion Lab and their remarkable missions of exploration. Your state has been home to virtually every major aerospace manufacturer. The Apollo capsules were built by North American in Downey, and the shuttles were assembled in Palmdale, both just outside of Los Angeles."

"I'm somewhat familiar with this history, Ms. Ferry."

"Yes Senator. My point is this. The working men and women of California built these machines, a job they should be rightly proud of. When a decision is made about where the shuttles should ultimately be displayed, we think special consideration should be given to the role Californians played in their development and construction."

"Go on," said the Senator, waiting to discover Nicole's true agenda.

"Currently there are over a dozen small science and aerospace museums scattered across California that display space program artifacts," Nicole said. "None have the resources to effectively display a shuttle. We think there should be a new facility, dedicated to the display and interpretation of space shuttle hardware, but also showcasing the history of California's aerospace industry. Such a facility, a world class aerospace museum, would benefit the people of California by generating tourism, creating jobs, and paying tribute to the hard working California aerospace worker."

"And where would you propose that such a facility be located?" asked Senator Battler.

"In Long Beach, Senator. On the waterfront."

"Long Beach. I see. Why Long Beach, may I ask?"

"Several reasons, Senator. Long Beach sits at the crossroads of California aerospace history. Rockwell, McDonnell Douglas, Northrop, North American, Lockheed, Hughes Aircraft; all were located within an hour's drive of the Long Beach waterfront. What better place to locate a world class museum that pays tribute to their contributions and history? But more importantly, Long Beach offers the ideal location." Nicole opened her briefcase and withdrew several copies of a satellite image showing the Long Beach waterfront.

"As you can see, Senator, here we have the Aquarium of the Pacific, and right across the bridge is the Queen Mary," she explained, pointing at the aerial view. "Both are successful attractions in their own right that generate millions of dollars in revenue and employ several hundred. Now right here," she said, pointing to a large white dome, "is the Long Beach cruise terminal, formerly known as the 'Spruce Goose' dome. As I'm sure you remember, it was originally built to hold Howard Hughes' aircraft, the Spruce Goose."

"Yes, it's in Oregon now," said the Senator, studying the images.

"Yes, it is," confirmed Nicole, "and the building sat empty for years until it was renovated into the new cruise terminal. That was a good thing for Long Beach, because a half million people a year now pass through that facility to take a cruise. People who often spend an extra day or two in the area visiting some of these other sights, and of course, spending money."

"I know the mayor of Long Beach well," said the Senator, "and he would agree."

"Well, Senator, the cruise terminal occupies less than half of the space in that building," Nicole continued. "We propose to use the remaining space as the initial home of the Aerospace Museum of the Pacific."

"The initial home?"

"Yes, Senator. The dome has sufficient room to hold most of the shuttle artifacts and some space for an archive and small research center. Unfortunately, the amount of space occupied by the cruise lines means we'd have to initially display the orbiter outside under a temporary structure."

"I see," Marsha replied, wondering when the inevitable request for federal funds would be brought up.

"Ultimately, we intend to build a dedicated structure here, if we can get the cooperation of the city," Marsha said, pointing at several acres of waterfront parkland just west of the Queen Mary. Reaching again into her briefcase, she produced a conceptual drawing of a soaring structure of colored glass. "This new facility would be big enough to hold the shuttle, and would be ideally located to draw tourists in an arc from the aquarium to the museum and then to the Queen Mary."

Marsha studied the drawings and images for a moment, and then said, "This all looks wonderful, and I'm sure you'll find the city will be very cooperative regarding permits, licenses, and such. You do realize though that under the present economic circumstances, the ability to obtain federal funding for such projects is severely constrained?"

"Senator, we're not looking for any federal assistance," Nicole stated.

Marsha was momentarily stunned. Every business person who entered her office with an idea and a flashy illustration sought federal dollars. "What exactly is it that you believe I can do for you then?" she asked.

"Senator, we think this would be a terrific thing for the southern California area, but we can't do any of this," Nicole said, gesturing at the illustrations on Marsha's desk, "without gaining possession of one of the shuttles."

"I see," said Marsha.

"We believe NASA intends to go through the motion of soliciting bids, but will ultimately decide to display the orbiters at the Kennedy and Johnson space centers and the National Air and Space Museum. We'd like your assistance in convincing NASA that one orbiter should be displayed on the west coast. Displayed here," Nicole emphasized, pointing at the conceptual illustration of the soaring colored glass building, "in recognition of California's exceptional contribution to the aerospace industry."

Marsha nodded slowly. "Well, I can see the sense in what you propose. Please excuse me for asking, but what is it that your company seeks to gain in this? I thought you were an aerospace company. Is it your intention to enter the travel and entertainment business?"

Nicole smiled. It was time to show the cards. "Senator, for our company to back this enterprise, we need to be certain of its economic viability. Under the terms NASA has previously announced, they would be offering the shuttles under long term loan agreements. Rather than a custodial arrangement, we wish instead to be provided with outright ownership of the orbiter in question."

"Oh? Please explain, Ms. Ferry."

"Senator, you're right, my company builds rockets. We have no interest in running a museum. We will form a 501(c)3 nonprofit corporation, Aerospace Museum of the Pacific LLC, to operate this facility. My company, Roadrunner Rockets, will submit a bid in the amount of one dollar for display of a shuttle. We wish for NASA to select our bid as being in the best interests of the shuttle's enduring legacy. We then wish to be given clear ownership of that shuttle through outright purchase of the vehicle as government surplus material. My company will refurbish and restore this shuttle at our expense, and then donate it to the 501(c)3 corporation. We will then take a tax deduction for the full appraised value of the shuttle at that time for the charitable contribution to the nonprofit corporation."

"But that will give you a potential tax write-off of millions of dollars!" exclaimed the Senator.

"Exactly so, a deduction we will only be able to claim if we actually own the shuttle at the time we donate it to the nonprofit corporation. But that is exactly how we will be able to afford all this," Nicole said, again gesturing at the images on the desk in front of Marsha. *And which will make our $200 million LCL One prize tax free*, thought Nicole, smiling inwardly.

Marsha studied the images on her desk for a moment, and then looked up at Nicole. "And is there anything else that your company seeks, Ms. Ferry?"

"No, Senator," answered Nicole. Then, trying to make it appear to be an afterthought, she added, "Well, actually, there is one thing. Vandenberg Air Force Base has the necessary runway to deliver the shuttle atop its carrier aircraft, and still possesses the buildings and structures for servicing the shuttle from its days when it was being developed as an alternate shuttle launch complex. We'd like your assistance in negotiations with the Air Force for the use of those facilities. This will allow us to do the work in California necessary to make the shuttle ready for public display, from where it would then be easy to transport to our new facility in Long Beach."

"I see," nodded Marsha. "And you'll need to hire local workers to perform that work?"

"Yes, Senator, of course."

"Well, my staff should be able to assist you with the Air Force. Is that all, Ms. Ferry?"

"Yes, Senator, that's the extent of the assistance we seek."

"Well then, I've seen your plan, and I clearly recognize the potential benefits to the citizens of California. I'm curious though if there isn't anything else that you might be able to suggest that may improve this project's likelihood of coming to realization?"

"Senator, in the future we will be seeking a permanent location from which to launch the new heavy lift booster we are developing. We currently intend to utilize facilities at the Kennedy Space Center, but if the Air Force will give us access to the appropriate facilities at Vandenberg, we would be delighted to move our operation to California.

Marsha suddenly frowned. "Ms. Ferry, while my state would welcome the jobs associated with your museum and related work, rockets are nasty, dirty beasts. They do great environmental harm, and I don't believe the people of California would desire to host your launch operations."

Nicole fought to suppress a grin. "Senator, perhaps you are unfamiliar with the work we are doing at Roadrunner Rockets? We have developed a technology that uses fuels that produce no toxins, harmful emissions, or greenhouse gases."

"Really? I wasn't aware."

"Yes, Senator. Our rockets use a paraffin and oxygen fuel that is completely safe, totally non-toxic, and designed to emit only simple water vapor as an exhaust product."

"I see. You could call this a green technology?"

"Why yes, Senator, we are absolutely in the business of producing green, environmentally friendly rockets," said Nicole.

"Well that's simply outstanding. That would certainly increase the likelihood of your proposal being embraced by my colleagues," said Marsha. "I would like to give it some consideration and consult with my staff. Do we have your contact information for follow-up?"

Dick realized his moment had arrived. *Time to bring it home*, he thought. "Senator, may I also add that my client has instructed me to assure you that in consideration for your support of this project, his company wishes to provide whatever assistance you may find useful as you prepare for re-election?"

Nicole could see instantly that Dick had found Marsha's button and had pushed it expertly. "Britney," Marsha said to her aide, "could you please leave us alone for a few minutes? And hold my next appointment. We shouldn't be long."

"Yes, Senator," her aide said, leaving the room and softly shutting the door.

***

"Well, what do you think?" Nicole asked Dick as they exited the building into the bright mid-morning sun.

"What do I think? I think you played her like a violin," Dick answered.

"But do you think we'll get what we want?"

"You really don't have much experience with this, do you?" Dick laughed, gently mocking Nicole's naiveté. "You offered to create jobs and enhance tourism in California in a way that won't require any federal earmark or add a cent to the deficit. The Senator will be able to claim the credit, which will make her a hero to her constituents. In the process she'll get to tweak NASA and strong-arm the Air Force. And then that green technology thing—that was just brilliant."

"So you think we have a shot?"

"My dear, you have this so in the bag that you'd have probably been able to get most of it even without the campaign contribution kicker we threw in. This is the closest thing to a done deal I've ever seen."

"I need to call Mr. Armac and update him," thought Nicole aloud, reaching for her phone.

"And did I hear you tell the Senator she's going to get you a shuttle for a dollar? Where on Earth did that come from?" Dick laughed.

"I made it up on the spur of the moment. It just felt right. I guess it was my 'go big or go home' moment," Nicole replied.

"Honey, let me know if you ever get tired of playing with rockets, I think we might have a position here for you if you're interested."

Nicole dialed Tom's number, and waited for him to answer. "Hi boss, it's Nicole. Guess what? We just bought a space shuttle! You owe me a dollar."

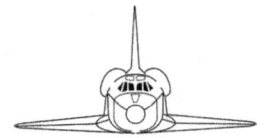

CHAPTER ELEVEN

Mike and Carl stood next to a large work table in Roadrunner Rockets' fuel casting shed at the New Mexico Spaceport studying a detailed drawing of the rocket that Carl had observed exploding two months previously. The term 'shed' didn't do the structure justice, as the polished concrete floor and brilliant white walls gave the cavernous metal building the feel of a large industrial clean room. Around the perimeter sat several previously cast booster segments.

"So this design only requires a single fuel port?" asked Carl, pointing to the circular cavity that ran through the center of the rocket's solid fuel region.

"Yes, that's one of the big advantages of our design," answered Mike with pride. "With our paraffin fuel, we can achieve a high enough regression rate so that only one port through the fuel grain is necessary."

Carl pointed at the top of the diagram. "This control valve and injector assembly is a very elegant solution, Mr. Patrick," he said, paying Mike the highest compliment any engineer can bestow.

"Thank you, Dr. Carl!" beamed Mike. "Luke proposed the basic design, but I modeled it mathematically to get the optimum injector spray pattern."

"So this system is capable of being throttled?" asked Carl.

"Absolutely. We can vary the thrust over a wide range by controlling the liquid oxygen flow. We can even turn this bad boy off completely, and then restart it again later. Show me a solid rocket booster that can say that!"

Carl wished he had done more research on hybrid rockets. The advantages of this design were many and obvious. He continued studying the blueprints on the table before him, slowly nodding his head, his finger tracing various details.

"So the rocket that exploded—you recovered the pieces for analysis, I assume?" asked Carl.

"Of course."

"And what did you discover?"

"Well, there wasn't much left that was bigger than a basketball," answered Mike. "We think there may be some indication that blisters were forming in the body of the fuel, constricting the fuel port."

"Which would lead to pressure oscillations and uneven combustion," observed Carl, nodding.

"Concluding with a big freaking bang," said Mike with dismay.

Carl walked over to one of the previously cast booster segments and examined the surface of the solid fuel. He noticed that the paraffin appeared soft gray in color rather than the pure white he expected.

"Mr. Patrick, you have added some form of material to the paraffin to form a composite matrix, no?" asked Carl.

"Yes, Dr. Carl, we mix 2% carbon black into the paraffin to control optical energy effects."

"Explain please."

"We found we were having a problem with visible light generated by the flame front within the fuel port penetrating into the paraffin, causing it to heat up and slough off. Adding 2% carbon black kept the light from penetrating the fuel, and isolated the resultant heating to the fuel surface where we wanted it. Unfortunately, the solution didn't work when we scaled it up to the 'B' scale rocket. What we call Little Sister now."

"But what about infrared energy?" asked Carl.

"Come again, Dr. Carl?"

"You added carbon black to make the paraffin more opaque to visible light, but what about infrared energy generated by the flame front? What is that doing inside your rocket?"

"Umm, gee Dr. Carl, I'm not sure we paid very much attention to that," answered Mike. "I imagine it would be absorbed by the carbon black?"

Carl turned to look again at the rocket segment and particularly the surface of the wax fuel. Examining the fuel surface closely, he noted subtle variations in the grayness of the color across the surface.

"Mr. Patrick, when did you cast this segment?" Carl asked.

"We did that one as part of a batch about three months ago," replied Mike.

"Was the rocket we watched explode part of the same batch?"

"Yes, it was. We cast segments to do two test firings. This one was for the second test. What are you thinking, Dr. Carl?"

Carl ran his hand across the smooth gray surface of the cast fuel. "Mr. Patrick, how do you blend your carbon black into the paraffin fuel?" he asked, looking up from the booster segment.

"We have an industrial mixer out on the shed floor. We dump 2% carbon black into a batch of wax pellets, and then pass the resulting blend into the liquefier to cast."

"Mr. Patrick, give Mr. Armac a call and tell him I believe we've solved his problem, and that you may very well be on your way to the moon."

***

Mike called Tom's office with the news. "So according to Dr. Carl, we overshot on the carbon black," he explained. "While it was blocking the transmission of visible light into the fuel like we intended, it was also absorbing infrared and getting hot as a bitch."

"I see," said Tom.

"In addition, we're apparently not mixing it thoroughly enough, which is causing hot spots to form. It didn't cause a problem with the smaller rocket, but it bit us in the ass when we built Little Sister."

"So what does he recommend?"

"Some improvements to our mixing process. Probably means mixing it as a liquid instead of a solid to get better dispersion. Oh, and he says to reduce the carbon black loading to 1.5%. He says that will be enough to control the visible light transmission, but exhibit less heating from infrared absorption."

"How long?" asked Tom.

"Say two weeks for the mixer, and another two weeks to do the casting and assembly on the next booster. We should be ready for a test firing in about a month or so."

"Excellent. Tell the Doctor 'good work' for me. Oh, and while you're on the phone, looks like Nicole came through for us. It seems we're gonna have us a shuttle."

"No shit?" exclaimed Mike. "That's outstanding! What did that set us back?"

"Looks like it's going to be about a dollar. We're passing the hat as we speak."

***

The quantity of project charts and diagrams had grown to where Marcus could no longer fit everything on the walls of his office. The Lost Boys had subsequently taken over the main conference room, covering the walls with the same dry erase wall paper. Each team now had its own wall, which was labeled accordingly: technical, political/legal, financial, and personnel. The pace was picking up, and Marcus now provided Tom with weekly updates.

"Why don't you computerize all this?" asked Tom, looking around the room.

"Don't worry boss, I've got gigs of project files on my computer," replied Marcus. "It's just easier to take it all in this way. Plus it makes the collaboration more fun."

"So what's next?"

"Well, we have a bit of down time while Viv and Mike are setting up the new fuel mixing process."

"How's that going?"

"I talked to Viv this morning, and she says we should be casting new Little Sister segments within a week."

"Great. We don't want to lose our momentum now that we're on a roll. So again, what's next?" asked Tom. He found the escalating level of excitement generated by the pace of the project to be intoxicating—much more fun than anything he was doing at Altered State.

"It's too early yet to start the financial ball rolling," said Marcus. "Tyler doesn't think it makes sense to start looking for sponsors until we have a successful Big Brother launch in our pocket."

"Agreed. Not that I wouldn't love some money rolling in, but that will have to wait."

"Nicole wants to give Senator Battler a few more weeks to grease the rails for us before she takes the next step with NASA and the Air Force."

"That's sensible, I guess," Tom nodded. "You can't rush the politics."

"She thinks this would be a good time to take a first look at the personnel issue. And here she is," said Marcus, as the door to the conference room flew open.

Nicole hurried into the room. "Sorry I'm late, Mr. Armac. I was on the phone with Representative Daisy's office."

"You're ready to talk to the Congressman already?" asked Tom.

"Not me, this one's yours. The House just killed the Shuttle Preservation Act, and things are moving pretty fast, so Dick McConnel and you need to get down to see the Congressman a bit earlier than we planned."

"Well I guess that's a good thing," said Tom. "So Marcus tells me you want to start the personnel process?"

"Yes sir, it's time." Nicole moved to the wall devoted to personnel issues and started pointing to blocks on a diagram there. "When we start to move on Vandenberg, we'll need a good consultant to help figure out the shuttle issues. First thing is the pilot though. Then a launch controller. But the pilot's first."

"Have someone in mind?" asked Tom.

"We have several good candidates, but there's one in particular we want to meet with first. He's in New Orleans. Marcus and I thought we'd drive over later this week and meet him."

"What's his name?" asked Tom.

"Eugene Robichaud. But he goes by Robbie," answered Nicole. "He was a backup for the final shuttle flight," she added, turning to Tom. "His training is the most recent."

"Boss, Nicole did discover one thing that she wanted to mention to you," said Marcus.

"As part of normal due diligence," Nicole said, "we've been running background checks on the people we think may be good candidates for our team."

"Is something wrong?" asked Tom, concerned.

"Well, we decided to do a little more research on our Dr. Heinel," said Nicole.

"Oh? And?"

"Remember when he said he had worked at Jacksonville Community College for four years after he was laid off from the Apollo program?"

"Yes, why?"

"Well, apparently he forgot to mention that he was terminated for cause."

"Really. Any indication why?"

"The records say 'failure to maintain good moral character.'"

"Excuse me? What the hell does that even mean?" asked Tom.

"It was the early seventies, that's the way they phrased things back then. It looks like he was fired for persistent drunkenness. Apparently Dr. Heinel has a drinking problem."

Tom looked blankly at Nicole, and then turned toward Marcus, who gave him a shrug that said "Don't ask me boss, I don't know anything about it."

"Well, everyone's got a story," said Tom. "Let's give the Doctor the benefit of the doubt until we get a chance to talk to him about it."

"OK by us," said Marcus.

"So when are you two leaving for New Orleans?" asked Tom.

"We'll give Mr. Robichaud a call and see if he's interested in some consulting work, and if he is, then we'll head over as soon as we can set up a meeting," Nicole answered.

"OK then, move out on that and let me know how it turns out. Next issue: how are you going to swing launch permits for us?"

"That, sir, is why you're meeting with the Congressman," Nicole smiled.

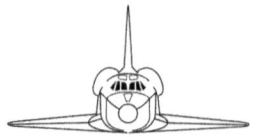

CHAPTER TWELVE

Marcus and Nicole sat with Robbie Robichaud on a balcony overlooking Bourbon Street. Before them sat three Abita Ambers, which they sipped while watching the people below wander up and down the street. The sound of multiple bands spilled from nearby bars, the music colliding in the evening air. The resulting mashup of jazz, zydeco and classic rock enhanced the carnival-like atmosphere of the scene.

"Quite a show," said Marcus, observing the 300 pound belly dancer on the corner below, complete with Scheherazade costume, finger cymbals, and five o'clock shadow. A small group of young men hooted encouragement, dropping dollar bills into her/his velvet turban on the curb while taking deep swigs of a red beverage from large plastic cups.

"The best people-watching on Earth, bar none!" said Robbie, saluting the crowd with his beer and then taking a sip.

A woman wearing little more than a bathing suit bottom paraded down the center of the street, a corrugated metal washboard hanging from her shoulders and covering her breasts. Someone, her boyfriend perhaps, followed closely behind, reaching around her to strum the washboard with two metal spoons, roughly keeping time with the music from the bar below.

"Do these people do this every day?" asked Nicole, amazed at the numerous displays of debauchery.

"Same scene, different people," answered Robbie. "It's pretty early yet, so this is still the tourist crowd. People here for a conference or convention. They fly in from Dayton or Buffalo or wherever, and then head straight down here as soon as the day is over to take a walk on the wild side. Makes for some great stories when they get back home," he added, rocking back in his seat to face Marcus and Nicole.

"They're definitely not in Kansas anymore," chuckled Marcus.

"Wait till it gets dark. Then the beads and boobs come out," said

Robbie, smiling.

"So that's not just a Mardi Gras thing?" asked Nicole.

"No ma'am. Ladies seeking the thrill of anonymous exhibitionism seems to be pretty much a year round impulse. Laissez les bon temps rouler!"

"Well, I don't imagine we'll be here long enough to enjoy the experience," said Nicole.

"I don't know, Robbie might have a lot of questions for us," said Marcus, continuing to observe the crowd below. "We certainly don't want to rush the man into a decision," he added, turning and smiling at Nicole.

"So let's talk about that," said Robbie, anxious to hear more details. "You're offering me a consulting job, and the position of chief pilot?"

"If you want it," said Nicole. "We've looked at a lot of qualified applicants, but we like your experience."

"Chief pilot of what, exactly?" asked Robbie. "You have some sort of spacecraft you're developing? I thought Roadrunner Rockets just did booster development."

Nicole and Marcus exchanged glances. They had talked at length on the drive from Dallas about not revealing too much too soon.

"We are focused on boosters, but we think it's a good idea to start looking beyond that," offered Nicole, hoping to get to "yes" without having to reveal too much. "You have recent shuttle experience, correct?"

"I was backup shuttle commander for Atlantis' last mission," Robbie confirmed. "So yeah, I guess you could say I have recent experience. Why, is that useful somehow?"

"When we finish development of what we call our Big Brother booster, we want to begin regular launches from Kennedy and Vandenberg," explained Nicole. "We need someone on the team with recent NASA experience to help with launch support coordination. You're familiar with Cape management, Alliance Space Systems, all the players we'll have to work with."

"I don't see why you need a pilot for that," said Robbie. "Sounds like you want someone from launch operations."

Nicole thought hard to find the correct approach. "Mr. Robichaud ... "

"It's Robbie, please."

"Robbie, it's like this," said Nicole. "We have some ideas for ways to employ surplus STS hardware. We need someone with relevant experience to help us figure out if what we want to do is even feasible. Who better than a qualified shuttle commander to give us advice?"

"Surplus STS hardware? Like what exactly? Are you planning to recycle shuttle main engines for your launchers?"

"I'm afraid I really can't say any more at this time. We do believe though that your unique experience would be invaluable."

Robbie held Nicole's gaze while casually taking another sip of his beer.

Rolling it around in his mouth for a moment, he swallowed it and set his bottle down. "I'd be lying if I said I wasn't interested," he said. "Working for the city engineer's office lacks the glamour of the space business."

"Tell you what," said Marcus. "We're getting ready to do a major systems test at our New Mexico facility in a week. Why don't you join us and observe the test. You can see our operation and meet more of the team before deciding whether you want to come onboard."

"Yes, that would be an excellent idea," added Nicole. "Any problem traveling on short notice?"

"Things are slow at the office right now, so I should be able to get away for a few days. It's just me, so there aren't any family issues if that's what you're asking."

"No family, Robbie?" asked Marcus.

"I'm recently divorced," Robbie answered. "Turns out the idea of being married to a former astronaut wasn't that appealing to my ex."

"I'm sorry to hear that," Nicole said sympathetically.

"Don't be. Better to find out now and be done with it." Robbie picked up his beer and drained the remainder. "So I guess I'll see you both in New Mexico."

"Hey, I think it's starting," observed Marcus, pointing to the balcony of the hotel across from where they sat. A group of men and women holding purple, green and gold beads were leaning over the railing, attempting to get the attention of young women in the street below.

"Just another night in N'awlins, my friends," said Robbie with a smile. "Good times!"

***

Carl once again stood beside Mike behind the safety barrier observing the distant test stand. The countdown was on hold at T minus 120 while Luke verified that no personnel remained downrange.

The door from the control building opened and Nicole and Marcus stepped out, along with a third individual Carl thought he recognized. Deep in conversation, the three moved to join them.

"And this will be our first test to validate the new Hot Wax fuel mixture," Marcus was explaining to the guest. "Our consultant, Dr. Heinel here, believes he determined the cause of our last failure, and today we'll see if he's right." Turning to Carl, Marcus said, "Hi, Doc, good to see you!"

"And you as well, Mr. Short," said Carl, lifting his hearing protector off one ear.

"Dr. Carl Heinel?" asked Marcus' guest, turning to look more closely at Carl. "Well I'll be damned, Doctor, no one told me you were part of this project."

Carl removed his earmuffs and shook the offered hand. "Have we met?"

he asked, sure he knew the man but still unable to place him.

"I'm Robbie Robichaud, Doctor Heinel, from NASA. Well, formerly from NASA. It's a pleasure to see you again."

"Ah, Mr. Robichaud, yes, so good to see you," said Carl. "To what do we owe the pleasure?"

Luke's voice suddenly boomed over the announcing system. "And we are go for static fire in two minutes. All personnel stand clear."

"This is it, Dr. Carl!" said Mike. "Here's hoping for a better outcome this time."

"We'll talk later, Mr. Robichaud," said Carl, donning his hearing protection again, and then pointing to Robbie's pair. "I suggest you put those on. If you don't, you'll wish you had."

Luke counted down the final thirty seconds. As before, Carl noted the puff of smoke from the distant rocket, and the bright orange flame that steadily grew, reaching a hundred feet or more, parallel to the ground. Then the loud shrieking roar as the flame brightened to yellow and finally to the iridescent white that indicated the rocket had achieved its maximum thrust.

For the next few minutes, the sound rendered all conversation impossible. Carl concentrated on the sights, sounds, and feel of the rocket, sensitive to any sign that something, anything had gone wrong. The instruments would tell the whole story, but from his position behind the safety shield, Little Sister seemed to be performing flawlessly.

Finally, its fuel exhausted, the rocket's exhaust plume turned violet in color, quickly shortening and then sputtering out. The silence that followed was as deafening as the roar that preceded it, until it was pierced by Mike's loud whoop.

"Hot *damn* that was kick-ass!" Mike shouted, bouncing like a pogo stick. "Did you see that? That was freakin' *awesome!*"

Mike high-fived Marcus and then wrapped Nicole with a bear hug, still jumping up and down. Turning next to embrace Carl, he said, "We nailed it, Dr. Carl!"

"Yes, Mr. Patrick, I believe you're right," said Carl, flustered by Mike's exuberance.

Robbie watched the team celebrate, and then turned to study the distant rocket, a wisp of white smoke curling lazily from its exhaust nozzle. *Daaaamn*, he thought respectfully.

***

The team was again assembled in the small conference room where all tests were de-briefed and analyzed. The table was covered with print outs of test results, showing temperatures, pressures, flow rates and thrust readings from the rocket's multiple sensors, while several laptop computers displayed the data as animated graphs.

Robbie stood to one side, invited to the post-test conference but ignored by the team members as they alternated between reviewing data and performing spontaneous acts of celebration.

"How long until we can conduct the next test?" Marcus asked.

"We'll want a day or so to digest the data, but I think we can start pouring the next batch of segments in three, maybe four days," answered Luke. "We should have the next Little Sister ready in about three weeks."

"Outstanding," said Marcus. "Doc, you are man of the hour for sure," he added, turning to Carl. "The boss won't have any reservations about signing your paycheck this week!"

The team began to disperse to take care of their multitude of tasks. As the meeting broke up, Marcus remembered their guest, and turned to Robbie. "Well, what do you think?" he asked. "Want to be part of the team?"

"I'm thinking this would be way more fun than French Quarter sewer maintenance," answered Robbie.

"Well Nicole and I are headed back to base," said Marcus. "Come on along, meet the boss, and we'll fill you in on the rest of the operation. Then you can let us know."

***

Marcus, Nicole, and Carl sat in the conference room at Altered State Software waiting for Tom Armac, who as always was running just a bit late. They had just finished explaining to Robbie the relationship between Altered State and Roadrunner Rockets. Robbie wandered around the room, studying the notes and diagrams on the white-board covered walls, while the rest chatted idly. His eyes widened when he got to the 'technical' section, with its diagrams of a shuttle with a fully filled cargo bay.

"Is this the 'surplus STS hardware' ya'll made reference to?" he asked, pointing to the diagram.

"Just a few more minutes, Robbie, and all will be revealed," chuckled Marcus with a touch of melodrama.

Tom entered the room at a brisk clip, reading an item on his phone and punching out a quick reply. He seemed mildly surprised to realize he had arrived at his next meeting, and quickly shifted his focus to the group.

"Great job everyone! Luke tells me we met or exceeded all test parameters. I can almost smell that prize money now!"

The group laughed and basked in the compliment, and then Marcus introduced Robbie to Tom.

"So, Mr. Robichaud, what do you think of our little operation so far?" Tom asked, shaking Robbie's hand.

"Please, call me Robbie. I have to admit it's more than I was expecting. Ya'll are playing with some serious rockets for such a small outfit."

"Well, Robbie, we have a few things to show you. We're hoping when you see what we're up to, you'll want to help." Turning to Nicole, he asked, "Mr. Robichaud signed a non-disclosure agreement?"

"Yes sir, while we were in New Orleans," she answered.

Turning to Carl, Tom said, "Dr. Heinel, if you would, please."

"Certainly Mr. Armac." Carl dimmed the lights, and began an abbreviated version of his presentation, this time for Robbie's benefit.

"Mr. Robichaud," said Carl, "I'd like to begin by telling you that since I was a very young man, it has always been my dream to go to the moon."

***

The lights came back up in the conference room as Carl said, "And that is it in a nutshell, Mr. Robichaud."

"I always get goose bumps when the astronaut plants that flag," said Marcus. "Wonder which one of us it will be?" he added, looking around the table.

Robbie sat quietly, chewing on the end of a coffee stirrer, and then slowly looked around at the diagram covered walls.

"Well, Robbie, what do you think," asked Tom.

Removing the stirrer stick from his mouth, he said, "I think … have you verified these numbers?"

"Of course," answered Carl.

"And this will work?"

"Without question."

"Well I'll be God-damned … " Robbie said, looking again at the information displayed on the walls of the room.

"Of course this is all just a very elaborate theory," Tom said. "It will take people, the right people, to pull it off."

"No doubt," said Robbie absently, nodding.

"Are you the right person, Mr. Robichaud?" Tom asked.

Robbie continued silently looking around the room, and then took a deep breath and exhaled. "I think you're going to need another pilot."

It felt as if the air had been sucked out of the room.

"This … doesn't … interest you?" Tom asked disappointedly.

Robbie stood and walked slowly to the diagram of the lunar lander. "I think you're going to need another pilot," he repeated, pausing, and then pointing to the lander, "because I'm going to be sitting right *there* and you'll need another qualified pilot to stay with the shuttle."

***

The team worked with Robbie to determine the critical positions they would need to staff, while Tom left to handle another software emergency.

"It's a good plan to sub all this out," said Robbie. "If the shuttle is delivered already prepped for launch, your personnel requirements will go

61

way down. No problem hiring the skills short term, employment at the Cape has been devastated and you could rent boatloads of technicians easy. The key positions you don't want to scrimp on though, you want top notch people."

"Any recommendations?" asked Marcus.

"For pad operations, yeah, I know a guy I'd recommend. I'd get Jean Lutz for launch director. She's a sweet lady, but on launch day she has ice water in her veins, nerves of steel. You'll need her."

"And you think these people are available?" Nicole asked.

"Available? Hell, they took early retirement when shuttle was ended. They'd probably pay you for a chance to make her fly again."

Nicole nodded, writing down names as fast as Robbie called them out.

"And another pilot," added Robbie. "I already said there's no way I'm staying onboard while you folks go walk on the moon.

While Nicole rapidly wrote, she wondered for the first time who from the team would get to make the trip. *That's two seats for pilots, one for Dr. Heinel,* she thought. *Tom will want to go of course. Sell one seat to a space tourist. We're running out of seats.* "As chief pilot, you'll of course want to make these picks?" she asked.

"Yeah, of course," Robbie replied. "I'm curious though what you want me to tell them?"

"What do you mean?"

"I mean when do you want to let the world know what you're planning to do? Because we're going to be talking to a lot of people here, and as soon as one of them says something to the wrong person, your plan is going to be out there for everyone to see. NASA might not be so accommodating if they find out what you want to do with that surplus shuttle."

***

Marcus, Nicole and Vivian joined Tom in his office. "Robbie makes a good point, boss," Marcus explained. "We can't keep something this big a secret forever. And while we're making double damn sure everything we do is legal, the casual observer might feel we're violating the *spirit* of the law."

Tom burst out with a sudden laugh. "Hell, Marcus, this whole project will be one long exercise in misdirection."

"Exactly, and if we're going to pull this off, we have to keep them thinking it's a running play, while we're actually setting up a screen pass."

"So what are you recommending we do? Tom asked.

"We need to work out how we're going to control the story," Nicole said.

"My life would be easier if it wasn't known just yet that we're attempting a moon shot," said Vivian. "I have to negotiate a deal with the ShuttleHab folks, and purchase the Wizard engine from EtherX, and I'd rather get that done before we announce."

"And it would appear extremely self-serving if word got out before you talked with Congressman Daisy," added Nicole.

"But at some point we need to get the word out so Tyler can start on the fund raising," said Marcus.

Tom thought for a moment, frowning with concentration. "All right, here's what I propose," he said. "No one says a word while we work the remaining legal and political issues, we'll make those priority one. Viv, get to work on the hardware. Robbie can start lining up key personnel by telling them that we want them for our heavy lift booster program, and oh by the way wouldn't they love to help us with this old shuttle we're cleaning up as a community service. Once we've successfully tested a Big Brother booster and have secured access to the Vandenberg launch site, we'll use the publicity from the LCL One competition to declare we're going to fly a moon mission using a Hot Wax booster." Smiling, he added, "That's not a lie after all, just a bit of an omission.

"All the work that follows," he continued, "getting the Big Brother Twin's ready to launch the fuel modules out of Kennedy, will keep attention focused on our right hand, while our left hand is prepping the shuttle at Vandenberg. We'll tell everyone the Kennedy launches are to assemble our moon rocket. Again, not a lie, just not the whole story."

"But at some point we're going to have to announce that we're going to fly the shuttle," said Vivian.

"Well, that's why I'm going to talk to the Congressman," Tom said.

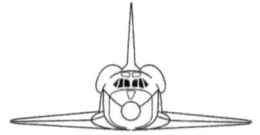

CHAPTER THIRTEEN

"You're sure the Congressman is open to our ideas?" Tom asked, as he looked out the window of the 737.

"Dick McConnel talked to his staff, and they say he's willing to discuss it." Nicole smiled at Tom. "Don't worry, I wouldn't be taking you to talk to him if I thought he was going to be a hard sell," she chided.

"Well you know how I feel about Congressmen. Overpaid public servants who think it's our job to suck up to them," he observed, turning to look out the window again. "So Keith Barton will be there too?"

"When Dick pointed out that we'd be leaning heavily on Alliance Space Systems personnel, the Congressman's staff thought it best for Mr. Barton to participate since he's their site manager for Kennedy."

Over the announcing system, a female voice said, "As we begin our descent into Orlando International Airport, please return your trays and seatbacks to their upright, locked position. Local time in Orlando is 10:45 AM."

"Dick's picking us up at the terminal?" Tom asked.

"Yes, he has a rental car and we'll meet him outside. It should be a 45 minute drive to the Congressman's office in Melbourne."

As the plane began to descend, Tom looked east out the window. The Atlantic coast was clearly visible, the brilliant blue water sparkling in the bright mid-morning sun. Tom could make out the Vehicle Assembly Building at the Kennedy Space Center, so large it was easily visible from 50 miles away.

"Look, there's the VAB," he said, pointing out the window. "Hard to believe we might be working there in just a few months."

"Well let's wait and see how it goes today," replied Nicole.

***

The secretary tapped lightly on the office door. "Congressman, your one o'clock is here," she said.

"Send them in, Mary," came a cheerful reply from within.

Will Daisy swept the Subway wrapper into the trash can, wiped his hands on a napkin, and stood to greet his guests.

"Dick, you old sonofabitch, how are you doing?" he said, grasping Dick McConnel's hand and giving it a vigorous shake. "Glad to see you get out of Washington some."

"It's always nice to visit friends at the Cape, Congressman. May I introduce Tom Armac? He's CEO of Roadrunner Rockets Incorporated."

"Glad to meet you, son," Will said, shaking Tom's hand. "And who is this lovely young lady?"

"Nicole Ferry, Congressman, I'm Mr. Armac's corporate attorney," she said, extending her hand. She smiled when Will took it firmly and shook it without condescension.

"Now Dick, I didn't know we'd have lawyers involved," said Will, with a touch of mock concern.

"I'm really more Mr. Armac's assistant," Nicole chuckled. "I'm here to make sure he remembers his manners." *A charming old gent*, she thought.

"Well have a seat, have a seat. Keith Barton should be here any minute, he just called to say he was five minutes out."

"We're sorry to hear about the failure of the Shuttle Preservation Act," Dick said. "We know you worked hard to try and push that though."

"Well, it's the American public that's the biggest loser," Will said. "There was a lot of life left in those vehicles. It's a damn shame to see them put out to pasture before their time."

After several minutes of casual chit-chat, the conversation was interrupted by the secretary tapping again on the door to announce Keith Barton's arrival.

"Keith, I believe you know Dick McConnel," said Will. "This is Tom Armac with Roadrunner Rockets, and the lovely lady is Nicole Ferry." Pausing, he added, "His lawyer," in a dramatic whisper. "Everyone please sit," he said. "I'm always a bit pressed for time when I'm here in the district, so I'd like to get right to it. First off, tell me about this rocket of yours, Mr. Armac."

"Well, Congressman, we've developed a system we call Hot Wax. It's a hybrid paraffin and liquid oxygen fueled system that we're having great success with."

"This is the system you want to adapt to shuttle solid rocket boosters?" asked Keith.

"Yes, it is." *I see Keith and the Congressman have been talking*, Tom thought. "We've had several successful static tests of a medium lift booster we call Little Sister. Our next step is to adapt Hot Wax to use shuttle SRB segments."

"How would that work, exactly?" asked Keith.

"On a typical four segment SRB, we would convert the upper two segments to contain liquid oxygen tanks, control valves, and the injector. The lower two segments would be cast with our solid paraffin fuel." Tom gestured to Nicole, who pulled several copies of a booster cutaway diagram from her briefcase and passed them out.

"We call this our Big Brother design. It will use the same components as the previous shuttle solids. Everything from the nose cap to the aft skirt is all retained. The only modifications we make are to the fuel segments."

"And what are the advantages of this?" asked Keith.

"More thrust. The booster can be shut off, restarted, or throttled. Non-toxic, non-volatile fuel with clean exhaust. No need to capture and decontaminate pad cooling water. I could go on and on."

The Congressman was slowly nodding. "Very interesting," he said, studying the diagram.

"A great thing about this design is that it doesn't require a hazmat facility to cast the fuel," Tom continued. "After launch, we can recover the booster, clean and inspect everything, and then recast the fuel segments, restack the rocket, refill the O2 tanks, and it's ready to launch again."

"So you're reducing the turnaround time," observed Keith.

"Reducing it significantly," confirmed Tom. "Our goal with Hot Wax is to take a fully reusable rocket, and through the use of innovative technology, reduce the recycle time to a minimum to reduce launch costs by an order of magnitude."

"This is the technology you're bringing to the LCL One competition?" asked Will.

"Which we fully expect to win," confirmed Tom. "Then, we intend to start a space train to continue driving down commercial launch costs."

"A space train? What exactly do you mean by that?" asked Keith.

"Think how much an Amtrak ticket would cost if they waited until they had sold all the tickets, and then manufactured the train to be used for only that trip," explained Tom. "That's how we've historically approached the commercial launch business. Expensive, single use rockets built individually to order. Gentlemen, we're going to turn that paradigm on its head."

"In what way?" asked Will.

"We plan to launch one booster a quarter on a regular schedule. In time, we hope to reduce that to one every four to six weeks. We'll sell 'tickets' in the form of payload space to anyone wanting a ride to orbit. But the launch occurs regardless—the train runs on a set schedule."

"You'd risk having to eat the cost of an unsubscribed launch," observed Keith.

"Yes, but with the significant cost reductions we expect to achieve, we believe there will be more than enough customers to fill every flight.

"A space train. How about that," mused the Congressman. "That's a pretty innovative way of thinking about launch services."

"With regular departures from Kennedy for equatorial orbits, and Vandenberg for polar orbits," said Tom.

"So where do we fit in?" asked Keith, referring to Alliance Space Systems.

"As I said, our plan is to base our heavy lift booster on the existing shuttle SRB. To make the train run on time, we need to be able to stack, test, and launch our boosters, and then quickly recover, recondition, and refuel them. All the facilities needed are already here at the Space Center," explained Tom.

"Next, we need a workforce to do the processing for us. If we contract with Alliance to perform that service, you should be able to bring back hundreds of your workers."

Keith and Will exchanged pleased looks. "That's wonderful," said Will. "How soon?"

"How soon before we start launching?"

"No, how soon before we could start hiring?" asked Keith.

"The area's been hit damn hard," said Will. "It would be terrific news for the local business community to be able to announce a worker recall at the Cape."

"We still have more testing to do before building our Big Brother prototype, but I think we'd be ready to start operations here within six months," Tom said. "You'd probably be able to start hiring in, oh, three, four months I'd guess."

"That's the best damned news I've heard in months!" Will exclaimed. "I can't wait for word to get out that there's light at the end of the tunnel!"

Hook set, time to start reeling, thought Tom. "Of course, this is all contingent on certain, *conditions,* which would be necessary for our operation to be feasible."

Will's smile vanished. "And what would those be, son?"

"First, my company will want to purchase a sufficient quantity of SRB segments and components to have the hardware to maintain a continuous launch schedule. Otherwise the train won't run on time."

"I believe I can talk to my colleagues in Washington and help make sure that happens," said Will. "Heaven knows NASA doesn't have any immediate use for them."

"We'll want an exclusive lease on the solid rocket booster processing and storage facilities at the Cape."

"Again, I'm sure my colleagues and I can impress on NASA the advantages of such an arrangement."

"We'd of course hope for the support of Alliance Space Systems," continued Tom.

Keith looked at Tom incredulously. "Would a hearty 'hell yeah' be enough for you? You had me at the mention of rehiring our workforce!"

"We'd also like some assistance with our test program. Specifically, we'd like to have access to the shuttle SRB test site in Promontory, Utah for testing our Big Brother design. I'm afraid we've outgrown our current facility in New Mexico."

"They've been hit even harder than we have. I think they'll be falling over themselves to have a rocket to test," said Keith. "Let us take that on for you, I'll make sure corporate works out a memorandum of agreement for use of the test site."

Tom smiled pleasantly at the two men, and then said, "Wonderful! That only leaves the regulatory issues."

Will once again looked concerned. "What regulatory issues would you be referring to?"

"We believe the commercial launch industry is crossing a threshold. Today, we have to obtain permits for every launch. Under current regulations, we don't think the space train will be feasible."

"Go on," said Will.

"Look at commercial aviation. Once an aircraft has an airworthiness certificate, a pilot with the appropriate rating can file a flight plan and fly the plane wherever he wants, carrying any approved cargo. We think it's time to adopt that approach for commercial launch services."

"I see. There may be a certain sense to that," said Will.

"If we tried to operate under current regulations, we could turn our rockets around in a matter of weeks, but then sit on hold for months waiting for a bureaucrat to review and approve our paperwork. Obtaining launch permits could actually end up driving our schedule, and the train would never leave the station."

"So how would you propose that this be addressed?"

"I've asked Ms. Ferry to draw up some proposed amendments to the Commercial Space Launch Activities Act," Tom said, accepting the legal folder Nicole pulled from her briefcase and passing it to Will. "In general, we'd like the Act to be amended to increase the amount of flexibility we'd have under the Launch and Reentry Operator's License."

"What kind of flexibility do you have in mind?" Will asked, opening the folder and thumbing through the contents.

"Nothing I think you'll find unreasonable. Overall, we'd like to be able to operate more like a commercial airline. As long as we're flying a licensed vehicle from an FAA approved launch site with an authorized payload, we just submit a launch plan rather than wait to obtain a permit. This will remove most of the delays associated with the current system, and let us maintain our schedule."

"I see," the Congressman nodded, continuing to thumb through the document.

"We'd like to be able to change the configuration of our launcher based on the cargo manifest for that flight, without having to obtain FAA permission. We're proposing some clearer guidelines on when a payload is considered safe and approved for flight, based on additional factors like previous flight history. We'd also prefer to see some changes to how the human-rating certification is handled."

"Oh?" Will said, looking up from the folder. "Are you planning to begin manned flights?"

"Congressman, we're aware of at least five independent efforts to develop manned spacecraft for commercial operation. We naturally want the Space Train to be able to launch any of those vehicles that conform to our payload specs, but the current regulations would require us to validate our launcher for each individual spacecraft. We recommend that a broader set of guidelines be implemented."

"How so?"

"We propose a new approach to human rating, in which our boosters are certified as 'suitable for integration with a human rated spacecraft.' The spacecraft itself will then have to meet the more specific requirements to be human rated. That will allow us to offer launch services to any approved manned vehicle."

The conversation was interrupted by a knock at the door. Will's secretary stuck her head in and said, "Excuse me Congressman, your one thirty is here," and then quickly shut the door.

"Well, Mr. Armac, I'll pass these recommendations on to my staff for analysis. You say though that you believe these changes are necessary to your overall plan?"

"Congressman, I'd go so far as to say that without these changes, we don't believe we could continue with our Space Train program."

Will and Keith exchanged concerned glances, contemplating the impact to the local community of failing to enact what appeared to be a list of reasonable recommendations.

"Well, if nothing in here," Will said, raising the folder Nicole had provided, "results in unreasonable risk, I think there's a good chance we could get this accomplished."

"Thank you, Congressman," Tom said, standing. "Nice to meet you, Mr. Barton. I hope we're able to do business in the future."

"And very nice to meet the two of you," Will said. "I have to admit I've never been a big fan of commercial spaceflight, but this Space Train idea is pretty exciting. Dick, give me a call when I'm back in DC, and we'll have lunch and talk more about this."

"Absolutely, Congressman, I'll check with Mary on the way out and see when you're free."

After shaking hands again, Tom, Nicole and Dick turned to leave. Will continued thumbing through the folder Nicole had provided while Keith studied the illustration of the Big Brother booster.

Pausing, Tom said, "Oh, Congressman, one more thing before we go."

"Yes, Mr. Armac?"

"We can't say enough about how effective we believe NASA's Centennial Challenges have been in moving the industry forward."

"Well, there's nothing like the lure of cold hard cash to foster innovation," Will replied with a chuckle.

"Exactly, sir. When we win the LCL One prize, and we do expect to win it, NASA hasn't outlined any other challenges that have the technical scope to keep pushing this industry forward."

Will smiled and asked, "Any suggestions, Mr. Armac?"

"We think the next logical Centennial Challenge should be a prize for the first commercial moon landing."

Will was startled by the suggestion. "That would be some contest. Do you actually think a private company could even begin to put a person on the moon in the next 10 years?"

"You never know, Congressman. For the right prize, there's no telling what could be accomplished." Tom shrugged and smiled, and then turned and left, followed by Dick and Nicole.

***

"You should have warned me!" Nicole said, as they exited the Federal Building. "I almost choked on my tongue! A prize for landing on the moon. Wait till the guys back home hear that story!"

"Well, I didn't make it this far by not recognizing how to capitalize on an opportunity," Tom replied with a grin. "So Dick, any concerns about the follow-up on this?"

"None at all, Tom. You made it all look so compelling we didn't even have to offer the usual financial support. I'll keep an eye on things when I get back to DC, but I think Congressman Daisy will push hard for the whole package. I wouldn't be surprised if he introduced a bill within the month."

***

The Congressman's secretary knew Bob Brock well—he visited whenever the Congressman was in town. "Go on in, Mr. Brock, he's expecting you," she cheerfully directed.

"Thanks Mary." Bob knocked on the door and then entered Will's office. He was pleasantly surprised to see Keith Barton talking to the Congressman, both holding papers they were closely studying. Sources are important for any reporter, and he tried to stay close to the movers and shakers at the Cape.

Will looked up from the folder he held. "Bob, good to see you, what's new?"

"That's what I'm here to find out," Bob replied. "I thought since you were in town I'd pick your brain about the failure of the Shuttle Preservation Act. By the way, who did I just see leaving with Dick McConnel?" Bob asked, looking for a lead.

"Oh, that was Tom Armac. He's CEO of Roadrunner Rockets."

"Tom Armac. I've heard of him," Bob said. "One of the smaller commercial launch companies. Any idea where he's staying? I'd love to do an interview and see what they're working on."

"I think they were actually heading to the airport, sorry," said Will. "Personally, I'd start paying more attention to Mr. Armac's company. They're talking about some pretty exciting things."

"Such as?"

"Well Bob, I can't talk to you on the record about it just yet. But did you ever hear of a 'space train?'"

"A space train? No idea what that could be. Do you string rockets together like rail cars?"

Will laughed, and then said, "Never mind. Hey, what do you think of the idea of NASA sponsoring a new lunar landing Centennial Challenge?"

"Space trains and trips to the moon. You and Keith must have had one hell of a lunch today," Bob said, bemused.

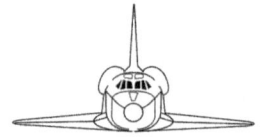

CHAPTER FOURTEEN

Luke was amazed at how large their formerly close-knit group of rocketeers had become. In addition to Mike and the test analysis team, today's observers included Marcus, Dr. Heinel, Nicole, Vivian, several members of Vivian's engineering team, and their new chief pilot, Robbie Robichaud. Robbie had brought along a potential new team member, a woman named Jean Lutz, and Keith Barton from Alliance Space Systems was here as well. It had required a van to shuttle everyone the two hours from the Salt Lake City airport to the test site at Promontory. Everyone was here to observe today's test—the very first of a Big Brother booster.

From the viewing area, the group could see the gleaming white rocket mounted securely to its test stand in the desert valley below. The protective shelter had been rolled clear of the rocket, and the pre-test countdown was in its final minutes.

Luke could hear Robbie explaining some of the engineering details of the rocket below to his guest. Word was that she was a former NASA senior launch controller and the leading candidate to run their launch control team. *Well, if this works*, he thought, *this will become much bigger than me. Time to bring in the professionals, I guess.*

Although today's test was closed to the public, Luke noticed a small crowd gathered further up the hill from where they stood. *Friends and family of test site workers*, he thought. *Hard to keep a good show quiet.*

A siren wailed in the distance, the sound echoing off the surrounding hillsides. "T minus 60 seconds, the motor is committed," announced a voice over the public address system.

A lot of work to get here, thought Luke. *A lot of long hard work.* It had been almost five years since he had first outlined for Tom his ideas for a new, less costly booster design. No one had known whether to take it seriously at first. *Well look at us now*, he thought with satisfaction.

"30 seconds," boomed the voice.

Luke looked at the faces of his companions. Carl with his calm serene smile. Mike's eyes gleaming with excitement. Marcus sporting his same friendly grin, his lips moving slightly as he counted down the remaining seconds ticking off the large timer before them. Vivian and Nicole tense, their jaws tight, as they focused on the rocket below.

The final seconds passed quickly. *I hope I don't let them down*, Luke thought, as the countdown reached zero. It was his project down there, his life's work, about to come to life.

The sudden explosion of light and noise from the valley below was unlike any they had ever experienced. For a brief instant, Luke's heart sank, for he was sure the rocket had instantly consumed itself at the moment of ignition. Then the rocket's exhaust pierced the cloud of smoke and dust that had momentarily obscured the test stand, stabbing at the hillside several hundred yards to its right, and Luke knew everything was all right. The ground telegraphed the energy being released, rumbling under their feet like an earthquake. It was working!

As the rocket burned brightly and powerfully below, Luke's mind journeyed back to the first test, when he had demonstrated the Hot Wax bench top model to Tom so long ago. Tom had been impressed enough to authorize the move to New Mexico. The building of their test center. The early successes with their first designs, and then the difficulties with scaling them up to larger rockets.

Luke looked again at the faces of his companions. He recalled the bad days, when every test was a failure. The wax fuel melting. The oxygen lines fracturing. The nozzle burn throughs. He could still see their grim faces as they poured over the data in their small facility at Spaceport, trying desperately to determine what had gone wrong. So much better to see them like this, their faces reflecting joy and awe as they watched the rocket below blazing steadily.

After two full minutes of continuous, violent, explosive thrust, the long white flame suddenly contracted to a lazy orange fireball and then extinguished, exhaling a final breath of dark gray smoke, which roiled and tumbled as it rose from the rocket's exhaust. Luke heard the test director announce, "Conclusion of burn, activating CO_2 quench system," as the shutdown and safeing procedures began. He stood speechless, still watching the now spent rocket below, his companions joining him in stunned silence. Then, from the hillside behind them, he heard a loud whistle, followed by cheers and applause. Turning toward the distant crowd of spectators, he saw them on their feet, clapping loudly and shouting their approval, the sound drifting down the now silent hillside to where they stood.

It works, Luke thought, slowly turning back to look again at the rocket below. *It's not my baby anymore. It's bigger than me now. Bigger than any of us.*

***

"Boss, you should have been here, it was absolutely amazing!" Marcus reported to Tom, yelling into his phone due to the weak cellular signal.

"How are the numbers?" Tom asked from his office in Texas.

"We topped four million pounds thrust, and cutoff was smack dead on. She burned out less than three seconds over predicted," Marcus answered, reading numbers off one of the laptops inside the monitoring trailer. "This is it boss, this candle's ready to fly!"

"Outstanding," said Tom, delighted. "Make sure you get good data on the turnaround effort. We'll need to know exactly what it takes to recycle and reuse the booster for LCL One." Then, in a sterner tone, Tom asked, "Marcus, is Viv there?"

"Right here boss, you want to talk to her?"

"Yeah, put her on, please."

Marcus passed his phone to Vivian, saying "Speak up, the connection sucks."

"Vivian here," she said.

"You're headed over to EtherX tomorrow?" Tom asked.

"Yes sir, they called this morning to confirm. It'll be a few days before I'm needed again here, so I thought I'd catch a flight out to LA tomorrow morning and try to nail it down."

"Well good luck. Be careful though, don't give away too much. I don't trust the bastard," said Tom.

"I know sir, this isn't your first choice, but we've been through it already. This makes the most sense … "

Tom interrupted Vivian to spare himself another lecture. "I know Viv, you don't have to sell it again, just be careful not to tip our hand. I don't want to give Elton anything that he could use against us."

"Understood, sir."

***

Vivian sat at the polished boardroom table, impatiently drumming her fingers on the glossy surface. She had grown bored with studying the framed photos of spacecraft and rocket launches displayed on the walls, and for the last few minutes had absorbed herself with trying to identify the various exotic woods used to create the inlaid EtherX logo in the center of the table. Standing and moving to the gallery windows, she looked out across the production floor below. From her second floor vantage point she could see examples of the rockets and capsules pictured on the boardroom walls, in various stages of construction. She noted the line of rocket engines sitting neatly in their storage stands along the far wall of the facility.

I wonder if it's already built, just sitting there, waiting to take us to the moon, she thought.

Catching a reflection of movement behind her, she turned toward the front of the boardroom. The entire wall from floor to ceiling was glass, through which she could see the elegantly appointed reception area, presided over by a stylishly dressed woman seated behind a chrome and granite counter. Vivian saw Elton Funk, CEO of Ether Exploration Systems, engaged in an animated conversation with Jonathon Messic, the engineer she had been meeting with for most of the last ninety minutes. She thought their negotiations had been going well, but Jonathon had announced that he couldn't conclude a deal without obtaining Mr. Funk's final approval.

Elton stopped waving his arms at Jonathon and turned, pushed open the glass door, and strode into the room. Jonathon followed closely behind, an embarrassed look on his face.

"Ms. Lee, Mr. Messic tells me you wish to acquire several of our engines," said Elton calmly, in lieu of an introduction. "May I ask for what purpose?"

Vivian extended her hand in greeting, which Elton momentarily ignored, and then shook briefly without breaking eye contact. "Well Mr. Funk, I've already explained our interest to Mr. Messic … "

"Please tell *me*, Ms. Lee," Elton interrupted with a polite smile and narrowed eyes.

"Well sir, we wish to purchase a Wizard engine and a number of Viper thrusters for a project we're working on."

"Yes Ms. Lee, so I've been told. What project?"

"As I explained to Mr. Messic, we're designing a propulsion module for use on orbit that can provide various payloads with an orbital maneuvering and attitude control capability."

"I see," said Elton. "The Vipers I understand, they're attitude control motors. Why do you want a Wizard? That's not what I'd think you'd need for payload maneuvering."

"We want to meet a variety of customer needs, including the ability to boost payloads to geosynchronous orbit or support significant orbital inclination changes. The higher thrust of the Wizard engine matches our target design specs."

"Customer needs," Elton repeated, sarcastically. "I wasn't aware that you *had* any launch customers, Ms. Lee, in light of the fact that unlike EtherX, your company has yet to conduct a single launch."

Vivian paused for a moment, offended by Elton's tone. Taking a breath, she then said, "We're optimistic of success, and we're looking to the future. We want to create a solution for customers that will allow them to simplify their satellite designs. By engineering their payloads to mate to our module, they won't have to develop their own propulsion and attitude control systems."

"So you want me to help you with your Space Train project?" Elton asked with a cold but polite smile.

Now how did he hear about that? Vivian thought with alarm. No one outside the company knew anything about that prior to this week.

"You're not the only ones with friends in Washington, Ms. Lee," Elton said, guessing her thoughts.

Vivian took a deep breath, and met Elton's piercing gaze. "Mr. Funk, I'm just an engineer," she said in her most conciliatory tone. "I'm simply looking for the best solution to a particular design problem. We have a specific set of performance requirements, and you have an engine that meets those specifications. My company believes it's in both our interests for us to strike a deal."

"Do you now?"

"Yes sir, we do. Or," she paused for emphasis, "we could spend the time and money to design and build our own orbital maneuvering engine. That would be an expensive undertaking, Mr. Funk, considerably more expensive than purchasing your Wizard," Viv replied, gesturing toward the distant rocket engines on the production floor below. "Mr. Armac would need to recover that additional cost, so he would bring that engine to market and promote it to other customers. You'd then find us competing with you not only for heavy lift launch services, but also for upper stage engines. A market you'd otherwise own."

Elton quietly studied Vivian. *A lot of tough in a very small package*, he thought.

"We're not interested in that market, Mr. Funk," she continued. "We want to concentrate on our Hot Wax system and become a major provider of launch services. The upper stages quite frankly don't matter as much to us. We're content to purchase that technology."

Elton's eyes locked on Vivian's, as he attempted to discover whatever it was that he sensed she wasn't sharing. Then, slowly nodding, he said, "All right Ms. Lee, I'll have Mr. Messic get started on the contracts. But here are my terms. I don't think your company has the ability to pull this off. You lack the money, the experience, the facilities, and the *leadership* to manage a program of the size you're contemplating. We'll sell you the engines. But when you fail, and I do very much believe you are going to be a failure of epic proportion, I don't want our name associated with it. Tell Tom you can have the engines, but you cannot promote your system by claiming you're using EtherX products. Do you understand, Ms. Lee?"

Vivian had felt a flash of anger at the insult to her company, and particularly its leadership, understanding the implied slap at Tom Armac. It was replaced by a flush of delight when she heard Elton's terms—a feeling she quickly attempted to suppress. Projecting an air of reluctance, she said,

"All right Mr. Funk, I believe my company will find that acceptable."

"Go pick out your rockets, Ms. Lee," Elton said, nodding toward the distant engines on the production floor below.

Elton watched Vivian as Jonathon escorted her to the lobby elevator. *I know there's something else there*, he thought. *They had to have wanted to leverage off our name to add credibility to their project. But that quick smile. She was pleased when I told her they couldn't mention EtherX. Something just isn't right about this.*

Pulling out his phone, Elton quickly scrolled through his contacts and dialed.

"*Orlando Guardian*, how may I direct your call?"

"Bob Brock please."

"Please hold."

"Bob? Elton Funk here. Yes, it's been a while. Listen, I have a favor I'd like to ask. I think you need to take a close look at Roadrunner Rockets. They're up to something. No, I'm not sure what, but whatever it is, they're being low key about it. Yes, I heard about their space train notion. I imagine it's getting everyone there pretty excited, although I don't give it a snowball's chance. What's that? A lunar landing prize? Seriously? Are you sure RRI suggested it? No, I have no idea what that could be about. Ok, thanks, if you don't mind, let me know what you find out. I promise I'll make it worthwhile for you. We have some new hardware being announced soon, I'll make sure you're the first call we make. Yes, good talking to you as well. Thanks."

Elton pocketed his phone, moved to the conference room gallery windows, and watched as Jonathon and Vivian headed toward the distant line of rocket engines. *What are you up to, Tom Armac?* he thought. *What the hell are you up to?*

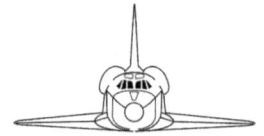

CHAPTER FIFTEEN

Tom noticed the large sign above the conference room door that proclaimed "Now Entering NEVERLAND Where Dreams Take Flight." Stopping to admire the glue stick and glitter artistry, he paused, smiled, and then pushed open the door and entered.

"Big day, boss!" greeted Marcus, looking up from the diagrams Vivian had spread before him on the conference room table. Most of the team was here for the weekly briefing and to watch the show from the Kennedy Space Center.

"I know, I couldn't sleep last night," responded Tom, checking to see that the projection screen was displaying the live feed from NASA TV. Today was announcement day—the day NASA revealed their plans for final disposition of the shuttle orbiters.

"Chill boss, Dick McConnel says it's a lock. This is just making it official," said Marcus encouragingly.

"I'll chill when I have the title in hand, till then there's no telling what politicians might do."

Marcus turned to look at the screen, which was displaying a podium in front of Orbiter Processing Facility One at the Kennedy Space Center. Behind the podium, the facility's open hanger doors revealed the tail of the shuttle Atlantis.

"Well, they're still waiting for the Administrator to speak, so what say we do the update while we're waiting?" Marcus suggested.

"Let's do it," replied Tom, taking his usual seat at the center of the table.

"Vivian was showing the plans for the lander," said Marcus, gesturing for Vivian to continue.

"How did it go at EtherX?" Tom asked. "Marcus says you closed the deal?"

Vivian laughed, and said, "Sir, you're going to love this. They agreed to the sale at the price we negotiated, and oh my God I actually got to see the engine we're going to use on the lander! But that's not the best part," she continued. "Mr. Funk laid one condition on us that we had to agree to first."

"Oh? What was that?" asked Tom, concerned.

"He said we can only have the Wizard engine and the Viper thrusters if we agree not to promote their origin. He apparently thinks so little of our operation that he assumed we'd want to do some kind of "Powered by EtherX" campaign to attract launch clients."

Tom looked at Vivian for a moment, his face blank. He then broke into a big grin. "You mean we're going to do the first private moon landing in history, and we don't have to give the bastard any credit, because we're under contract to not promote the vendor of the engines? Damn this is a good day!"

"I know, right?" Vivian laughed. "So anyway, we're ready to start assembling the propulsion unit in the next couple of weeks," she said, pushing the blueprints in front of Tom. "We got all the critical dimensions and interface data for the engines, so we can start welding the framework and tanks while we're waiting for them to arrive."

"And the crew compartment?" Tom asked.

"The ShuttleHab module should be ready for delivery in about two months."

"I never got a brief on that, how'd that work out?" asked Tom. *I can't keep up with this and Altered State, I'm getting stretched too thin*, he thought.

"I think you were tied up for that week's meeting. They were great. Dr. Heinel was right, the unit is perfect, and RocketTech is very flexible. After the shuttle program ended, they figured with no ride to space, the units were basically worthless, so they were delighted when we proposed modifying one for independent operation."

"So who's handling the engineering details?"

"They are," replied Vivian. "Once we explained our requirement, they were all over how to install an internal fuel cell and improve the life support systems. My guess is that they had already taken a look at the idea before, and just had to dust off some plans."

"So by 'explain our requirement,' I assume you didn't mention using it as a lunar lander?" asked Tom.

"Oh hell no, please, we told them we wanted to be able to provide a free-flying laboratory that customers could lease and launch on a Big Brother booster for short duration orbital missions. They loved it."

Tom briefly studied the blueprints, and frowned. "Viv, how many seats did you ask for?"

"We asked them to put in four," she answered, pointing to the diagram.

Robbie, me, paid passenger, lottery winner, Tom thought. *That would mean no one else from the team could make the landing. And no room for Dr. Heinel.*

"Viv, find room for two more."

"Two more seats? You can't. There's no room, and besides, the environmental systems aren't sized for two more people," she replied.

"Viv, find room for at least two more seats, or else Robbie and I are the only two here who will get to go to the party."

"Damn, I forgot all about that," Vivian said, as she studied the lander diagram. Looking at Tom, she added, "We really need to figure that out soon. Who's going, I mean."

"I know," Tom nodded. "We'll do that. Soon. OK, tell me about the booster tests."

Luke tapped at his tablet, and a video appeared in the lower right corner of the conference room projection screen. It displayed a recording of the last in the series of Big Brother firing tests just concluded in Utah. "Two words for you, Mr. Armac. Unqualified success."

"It was awesome, boss," Marcus beamed. "Luke made the earth shake and tore the sky apart. You should have been there!"

"Sorry I missed it, but someone's got to run the business while you're all out playing rocketman," Tom joked.

"All burns were flawless, and the post burn inspections revealed nothing but normal wear and tear," Luke said proudly, watching the video. Turning to Tom, he added, "With the Little Sisters performing to spec, and now these successful Big Brother tests, we're ready to start building a staged launcher and pick a date for our LCL One attempt."

"How about the inter-stage assemblies and flight control system?" Tom asked, turning to Vivian.

"We've already put in an order for three inertial flight control systems and guidance packages from Launch Control Corporation," explained Vivian. "I'm *sooo* glad these are available off the shelf, it would have been a major distraction to have to build something from scratch."

"How do you find time to run all this down, Viv?" Tom asked.

"Sleep is a highly overrated commodity, sir," she replied. Tom had noticed the faint shadows developing under her eyes.

"I'm finishing the vibration and stress analysis on the interstage assemblies now," said Mike, answering the rest of Tom's question. "Once we're done crunching the data, we'll feed the results into our CNC machine to cut all the components. We're finishing the installation of the friction stir welders in our facility at Spaceport next week."

"So when will we be ready to make the first LCL One launch attempt?" Tom asked. "It sure would be nice to get some money coming *in* the door for a change."

"Three months, boss," replied Marcus. "Maybe ten weeks if we knock off the Sunday afternoon beer runs."

"Agreed," confirmed Luke. "The booster segments will be ready to ship by week after next. If Vivian and Mike can crank out the interstage assembly and guidance package in the next month, we'd have four to six weeks to do integration and checkout prior to launch."

"Seems pretty aggressive," observed Tom.

"Go big or go home," quipped Marcus.

"Go big or go home," echoed Tom. "So what has Dr. Heinel been up to the past few weeks?"

"Dr. Carl is overseeing all the setup at Spaceport," answered Mike. "The guy's a maniac—he's put a cot in the fab building break room, never leaves the site. He was playing with the new welders last I saw, dialing in the calibration. I don't know where the old dude gets the energy from. I hope I have half his enthusiasm when I'm his age."

"I'm surprised he's not here today," said Tom.

"We asked him to come," said Marcus, "but he reminded us that getting the shuttle is our job. Getting it to the moon once we have it is his."

"Well let's hope we don't let the Doctor down," said Tom, noting that the projection screen showed the NASA Administrator taking the podium. "Marcus, un-mute that, would you please?" he added, as the Administrator began to speak.

" ... and each of these shuttles has a story to tell, and a history to share. We hope to let them tell their stories and share their history with as many people as possible over the coming years. Today, I am proud to announce where each of these national treasures will be displayed and enjoyed by millions of Americans, and where their stories will be told for generations to come.

"First, our old friend Discovery, a ship on which I personally traveled into space three times, will have a permanent home right here at the Kennedy Space Center." The crowd of space center workers rose to their feet, clapping and cheering enthusiastically.

Tom leaned back in his chair and crossed his arms over his chest, nodding gently. *Good*, he thought. *Dick pulled it off.*

"Next, shuttle Endeavour will make its final trip to the Intrepid Sea, Air and Space Museum in New York City."

"What the hell!" Tom said, bolting upright. *Endeavour should have been going to Houston ...*

"And shuttle Atlantis, the last shuttle to fly, visible here behind me, will become part of the permanent collection of the Smithsonian Institution's National Air and Space Museum, to be displayed at the Steven F. Udvar-Hazy Center in Chantilly, Virginia."

Everyone sat in shocked silence as the words sank in and a tsunami of confusion and disappointment washed over them.

"Finally, shuttle Enterprise, currently on display at the Smithsonian

Institution, will ultimately become the property of the Aerospace Museum of the Pacific, to be displayed at a new facility to be built in Long Beach, California."

The space center crowd politely applauded, mildly shocked that Houston, the obvious favorite, had been overlooked.

In Neverland, the only sound to be heard was Vivian's muffled sobs.

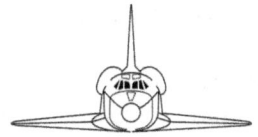

CHAPTER SIXTEEN

"Viter, McConnel and Strong, how may I direct your call?"

"Dick McConnel please," said Tom, fuming. "Dick? What the *crap* Dick! What the hell are we supposed to do with the Enterprise? She can't fly to space, you know that!"

"Tom, calm down, we'll get to the bottom of this," said Dick. "We had a hint there might have been some pressure. The Smithsonian has some pretty strong advocates on the Hill, and they expressed a definite preference for flown hardware rather than a mockup. It's not like we could make the case that you needed a space-worthy shuttle for your museum after all."

"What the hell is that supposed to mean, Dick? You said it was a lock! Do you have any idea how much money I've poured into this?"

"Tom, look, take a breath and cool it. We'll fix this. It's just going to take a little time."

"So what the hell are we supposed to do in the meantime?" Tom asked. "We just had the whole damn thing yanked out from underneath us!"

"Tom, focus," replied Dick. "Your business is building rockets, remember? This whole moon trip was a lark—just a fun diversion. I told you we'll fix this and we will, but in the meantime, build your rockets. That's what's really important here."

Intellectually, Tom knew Dick was right. Emotionally, he felt he was absolutely, completely, monumentally wrong.

"Well keep me in the loop, Dick, I want to know what happened and why, and what we can do about it," demanded Tom, ending the call.

"Well that's that, I suppose," said Vivian sadly, having recovered her composure.

"Like hell," answered Tom. "Dick says it can be fixed, and so we'll give him some time to fix it. In the meantime, what do we know about the Enterprise?"

"Don't even start down that path, boss," said Marcus. "She's not a real shuttle, just an engineering mockup. We'd have to take her completely apart and totally rebuild her to even hope to make her flight worthy."

Nicole said, "And may I remind you that from the legal perspective, Enterprise has never flown to space with humans on board? That means we won't have an angle to exploit with the FAA for our launch permit."

"Crap, you're right," said Tom. "Well that's it then. We give Dick some time.

"Mr. Armac?" said Mike. "Who'd going to tell Dr. Carl?"

"Damn it. I'll call him. And Robbie too," Tom fumed. "Crap, and it started off as such a good day," he muttered to himself.

***

Tom and Marcus sat on the raised dais, looking out at the crowd sitting in folding metal seats before them. Above, the smooth white dome of the Long Beach cruise terminal arched high above their heads, now also home to the Aerospace Museum of the Pacific. Senator Battler was finishing her rambling and self-serving speech, indirectly taking credit for the museum, the shuttle program, manned space flight in general, and pretty much everything else that was good and proper in the world, before finally introducing the mayor of Long Beach. The invited guests fidgeted and politely applauded, stoically enduring the ceremonies while waiting for the bar to open.

"I hate circuses," muttered Tom.

"I hear you, boss," Marcus replied quietly. "At least there aren't any clowns. Clowns are the worst."

"Well there are sure enough plenty of those here," said Tom, gesturing with his head toward the politicians on the opposite side of the dais. "I don't even know why we're here," he added. "We should be up at Vandenberg with Vivian and Luke."

"You're here because Nicole told you to be here, and you know enough to listen to Nicole," Marcus patiently explained. "The Senator wanted her big day, and she wanted Roadrunner Rocket's El Jefe, so you're here. Besides, you need to talk to her anyway, right?"

"Damn right," growled Tom.

"And we want to extend a special thanks to Mr. Tom Armac, CEO of Roadrunner Rockets Incorporated, who's tremendous support and generosity made all of this possible today," said the Mayor from the podium, gesturing toward Tom.

Tom rose slightly, nodded and waved in acknowledgement, and then faced the Mayor and applauded, returning the attention back to him. "OK, I did my part, let's go see where Robbie is," he said quietly to Marcus, as the Mayor continued his speech.

They found him near the northwest edge of the dome, taking measurements and making chalk marks on the floor.

"Done so soon, Tom?" asked Robbie, looking up from his notes. He was one of the few team members who felt comfortable addressing Tom by his first name.

"How's it look?" Tom asked, nodding toward the floor.

"We can excavate here for the pool," Robbie replied. "The shuttle simulators will fit over there," he gestured toward the south, "and we'll put the mission control center over there, with its own entrance," he continued, pointing toward the western edge of the dome. "That way we can do all of our mission training right here in one place. We'll have the pool for the extravehicular activity practice, and we'll be able to run mission simulations by linking the shuttle cockpit simulators to mission control."

"So we're good then?"

"Don't worry Tom, I got this," replied Robbie, and then returned to measuring the floor.

From across the dome, Tom could hear the Mayor inviting the 'honored guests' to join him at the buffet, followed by the scuffle of metal chairs sliding on concrete as the crowd jockeyed for position to be first at the bar.

"Come on, we need to pin down the Senator," Tom said to Marcus, heading into the fray.

Tom waited impatiently while Marsha concluded an interview with a local reporter, and then called out, "Senator? A word please?" before she could begin another.

"Mr. Armac, I'm so glad you were able to attend today," responded Marsha with a glowing smile. "I'm afraid I'm a bit busy at the moment," she said, nodding toward the waiting reporters. "Can it wait until later?"

"Well Senator, I just wanted to let you know that my company will regretfully be withdrawing its financial support for the museum," Tom said, speaking loudly to be overheard. "But if you're busy, we can talk about it another time," he added, turning to leave.

Marsha's face displayed anger as her mask of serene pleasantness slipped for an instant, then, resuming her smile, she said, "Just a moment, Mr. Armac." Turning to the press, she said, "Be right back," and then strode rapidly over to Tom, her heels clicking on the polished concrete floor. "What the hell do you think you're doing?" she asked.

Tom turned away from the crowd and slowly started walking, Marsha following alongside. "Senator, all of our projections were based on obtaining Atlantis. I'm afraid we can't make this work financially now that the decision has been made to give us Enterprise."

"Why are you bringing this up now?"

"Senator, we've been trying to work through your office for several weeks now, with no success."

"We're fighting tooth and nail over the budget right now, I've been too busy to deal with issues like this. A shuttle is a shuttle, what damned difference does it make anyway?"

"Senator, our accountants tell me that the value of the Enterprise, and therefore the amount of the write-off we will be able to take against earnings, is approximately one fifth what that of an actual flown shuttle would be. To be brief, funding this museum is now a losing proposition, and we will therefore have to withdraw our support."

"You can't do that! We've announced the plans! We've … "

"Senator," Tom interrupted, turning to face Marsha, "I do not believe Congress has the authority to compel a private business to make a charitable contribution against its will."

Marsha stared back at Tom, chewing on her lower lip. "All right, what do you want?"

"We want Atlantis. We'll trade Enterprise to the Smithsonian for it."

"They won't make that deal."

"They may, if you assure them that once we refurbish and donate Atlantis to this museum, Aerospace Museum of the Pacific and the National Air and Space Museum can agree to swap vehicles for display purposes after a suitable length of time."

"But you just said you don't want the Enterprise."

"Senator, I don't want to run a museum. What I want is a tax shelter. If you can get the Smithsonian to agree to pass ownership to us, we will guarantee that they will get it back for display. Frankly, I don't really care which vehicle sits here in this building."

Marsha glared at Tom for a moment, and then said, "What makes you think I have any effect on the actions of the Smithsonian? They don't fall under the legislative branch."

"Senator, please. We both know how much of their budget comes from Congress. The Board of Regents will take any suggestions you make strongly under advisement."

Marsha thought for another moment. "You'll tell the press they heard incorrectly, and that you're wholeheartedly supporting this project?"

"If you'll guarantee me that we'll get Atlantis."

Marsha studied Tom, then nodded. "Agreed," she said, turning back toward the reporters. Then pausing, she turned to face Tom again. "Is there anything else, Mr. Armac? There always seems to be something else whenever I deal with your company."

Tom smiled broadly, and then said, "Why yes, Senator, there is something else that you may be able to help us with."

"Of course there is. What may that be, Mr. Armac?"

"My lead engineer is up at Vandenberg as we speak, and she's finding that Rainier Aerospace is being uncooperative regarding access to Complex

Six for our Space Train program. They apparently have a lease on the facility from the Air Force, which they believe gives them exclusive use."

"I see. And you would like assistance clarifying this issue of access?"

"If you could find the time, Senator."

Marsha snorted slightly, paused, and then said, "I'll have a member of my staff contact you. Now let's go talk to the press."

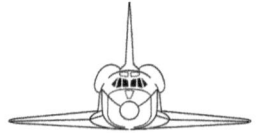

CHAPTER SEVENTEEN

Tom stood with Vivian, Luke and Robbie, shielding his eyes with the palm of his hand from the sun that was just starting to burn through the mists swirling above the surrounding hilltops. Standing in front of the Integrated Processing Facility building, they looked out at the launch platform and mobile structures for Vandenberg Space Launch Complex Six, better known as Slick Six.

"Hard to believe you could build this close to the launch pad," observed Tom, noting the less than 200 yards that separated them from what would be ground zero at launch.

"The exhaust ducts divert everything to the south, but if the acoustic damping system failed, this would be a very bad place to be, for sure," agreed Robbie.

"So how does everything check out?" Tom asked Vivian.

"The launch tower, assembly building, mobile service tower—all the basic infrastructure that was built in the eighties to support shuttle launches—is still there and operational," explained Vivian. "Rainer Aerospace has modified the towers and installed their own launch table for handling their Pyramid IV booster, but I have some ideas on how we can work around that."

"I never doubted for a minute that you'd have a solution," smiled Tom.

"The good news is that the Pyramid IV is liquid fueled," added Luke. "We're looking at a minimal amount of work to accommodate fueling the shuttle external tank."

Nodding with satisfaction, Tom said, "So explain it all to me."

"Well, after Alliance Space Systems at Kennedy finishes servicing the orbiter, it flies here on a shuttle carrier aircraft, landing north of here on the Vandenberg runway," said Vivian.

"Which was lengthened and hardened specifically to support shuttle missions," added Robbie.

"It's lifted off the carrier aircraft and towed to the Maintenance and Checkout Facility," Vivian continued. "Once we have the shuttle safely inside the building, we'll load the lunar lander modules and airlock assembly while the shuttle is getting its final checkout, and then it will be buttoned up and towed here," she continued.

"It's amazing everything is still here," observed Tom.

"Well, they paid something like four billion dollars to build it all, and that was back when a billion was still a lot of money," said Robbie. "So everything found another use after they dropped the idea of launching shuttles from here."

"There's supposed to be a 76 wheel transporter that was designed to carry the shuttle," added Luke, "because it's 17 miles from the MCF to the pad. We've looked everywhere though, and no one seems to know what happened to the damn thing. Not exactly sure how someone could jack a 76 wheel transporter and not be noticed."

"It's California, it could happen," joked Robbie. "It's probably a Rose Bowl parade float now."

"So we'll have to carefully tow it on its own wheels to the pad," said Vivian, ignoring Robbie. "That will be a nerve-wracking trip, because for a lot of it, the wingtips clear the surrounding terrain by less than a foot."

"You're also going to have to figure out a cover story," said Robbie. "To move the orbiter to the museum in Long Beach, we'd be towing it to the south base harbor to load on a barge. There wouldn't be any reason to bring it here to the pad."

Everyone looked anxiously at Tom, who grinned and said, "Tyler Allen is working on that. Don't worry, you're going to love it!"

"OK, well, the Big Brother segments will have already arrived by rail from Kennedy Space Center," said Vivian, "and the external tank will have come in to the south base harbor by barge from Michoud in New Orleans via the Panama Canal."

"We'll use a pair of low-boy trailers to move the external tank from the dock to the pad," added Luke.

"Once the shuttle is at the pad, we'll roll it into the assembly building," said Vivian, "which is parked over the launch tower. With the mobile shelter buttoned up, no one will be able to see what's going on, so we'll have time to lift and rotate the shuttle and attach it to the external tank and boosters."

"Fortunately, we did find the shuttle lifting rig rusting in a scrap yard just north of here," said Luke. "We're getting bids now on getting it inspected and re-painted to make sure it's safe to use."

"Good, the less we have to build ourselves, the better," said Tom. *And it saves some money too,* he thought.

"Once the vehicle is assembled," Vivian continued, "we'll need a week, maybe ten days to do a complete integrated systems test, and then we fuel the external tank and she's ready to go."

"Well, we have this little matter of access to the pad to clear up first," said Tom. "Let's go talk to the Air Force," he added, turning to walk back to the adjacent building.

***

"Mr. Armac? It's a pleasure to meet you, sir. I'm Daniel Brooks, Senator Battler's military affairs coordinator."

Tom shook Daniel's hand, noting that the young man's tailored suit and open collared white shirt did little to dispel the impression that he had arrived at the meeting by surfboard. "Mr. Brooks, this is Vivian Lee, my lead engineer, Luke Rungren, head of propulsion systems, and Eugene Robichaud, chief pilot."

"And this is Lieutenant Colonel Jim Arnold, US Air Force Space Command, and Michael Delany of Rainier Aerospace Vandenberg Operations," said Daniel in reply.

After a few moments of handshakes and the exchange of business cards, the group sat down around the small conference table.

"Mr. Armac, the Senator has asked me to help address your concerns regarding access to certain facilities here at Vandenberg," Daniel began. "She is extremely interested in the progress of your operations here."

"We appreciate the Senator's interest," said Tom. "We're sorry to have to involve you in these discussions, but we've run into a bit of a wall here and we're hoping you can help us break through it."

"Space Command has been very supportive of any requests from Mr. Armac's company," volunteered Colonel Arnold. "Any request for access to facilities they need to refurbish the shuttle, we're happy to accommodate," he added. "We like the project and we feel an affinity for the spacecraft, so we'll help in any way possible."

"Mr. Armac?" asked Daniel, with a "What's your problem, dude?" tone.

"The Air Force has granted access to everything we've asked for to support our shuttle refurbishment project," answered Tom. "That's not the issue here. As we discussed with the Senator some time ago, that project was contingent on certain additional considerations. We want to talk today about our Hot Wax booster program."

"Go on, Mr. Armac," prompted Daniel.

"We want access to Space Launch Complex Six. We're concluding development of our Big Brother heavy lift launch vehicle, and the pad at Slick Six is the only place on the west coast able to handle it."

"Colonel?" asked Daniel.

"As I'm sure the Senator knows, the Air Force selected Rainier

Aerospace and their Pyramid class launch vehicles as our preferred platform for orbital access," replied Colonel Arnold. "The pad at Slick Six was modified to support their Pyramid IV Heavy launcher. I don't see how Mr. Armac's company could be allowed to use the facility."

"We spent almost $100 million in upgrades to support our vehicle," added Michael Delany. "We're not willing to put that investment at risk by allowing others to have open access. Particularly small startups like Mr. Armac's, with no history of conducting safe launch operations.

Tom glared at Michael. Turning to Daniel and Colonel Arnold, he said, "Gentlemen, Pyramid launch vehicles are based on a fifty year old design. They're dinosaurs, and their day has passed. In contrast, our Hot Wax vehicles are modern, fully reusable boosters that will support a launch tempo that blows your 'preferred platform' to hell and back."

"How interesting," Michael said. "If only you actually *had* one of these Hot Wax rockets. But they don't actually exist now, do they sir, except maybe as static test articles?"

"Right, and you have the real live flesh and blood rocket," replied Tom. "Except it's too damned expensive and complicated for anyone to actually want to use."

"Excuse me, Mr. Armac, but our current contract with the Air Force ... " began Michael.

"When is your next scheduled launch?" shouted Tom, jumping from his seat.

"That doesn't factor into this discussion," replied Michael, flustered.

Turning to Daniel, Tom said, "They don't have another launch scheduled for over two years. Their vehicle is so expensive that it's only used for lobbing huge spy satellites into polar orbits, which the Air Force only needs to do every once in a blue moon." Standing and pointing toward the launch pad outside, he added, "Colonel, Mr. Brooks, that launch site is a national asset, which is being completely underutilized because you've let Rainier take de facto ownership of it. Yes, they've fixed it up the way they like. I get that. But I can start launching rockets out of here in less than six months, and one every month after that. And for a hell of a lot less than it costs for Rainier to do it."

"Please sit down, Mr. Armac," Daniel said. "Colonel, he makes a good point. Two years is a long time between uses. Isn't there some way Mr. Armac's company could be given access between Pyramid launches?"

"The pad's configured for our rocket," said Michael. "There's no way we'd allow them to modify our systems."

"We can deal with that," said Tom. "Viv, show them."

Vivian pulled out copies of an illustrated presentation and passed them out. "Gentlemen, the pad modifications Mr. Delany refers to consist primarily of the launch table and servicing tower swing arms. The other structures dedicated to servicing Pyramid IV Heavy's are not associated with the pad. We surveyed the site, and here are the changes we recommend."

Turning to the second page, she said, "Basically, we will modify the rails that service the pad, so that Rainier's Pyramid launch table can be rolled clear when not needed. Our own table can then be rolled into place for our Hot Wax launcher. We've also designed our table with modular elements so that it can be configured to support a variety of Hot Wax vehicles. We can set it for a single, a twin, or even a triple booster configuration by rolling the appropriate modules into place."

"Very cool," nodded Daniel.

"We'll obviously have to add our own servicing arms to the tower to support our vehicles, but we won't have to disturb the ones Rainier needs for their Pyramids. So the launch tower becomes a multi-tool." Looking at Michael, she added, "When you need the pad, our equipment will just fold out of the way like we were never there."

"Colonel, it certainly makes sense to get some use out of these facilities between Pyramid launches," said Daniel. "The taxpayers have invested a great deal of money in them, after all."

"I don't think Space Command would object," replied Tom, "but the Air Force doesn't have the money in the site facilities budget to pay for any of this."

"We'll cover the cost," said Tom. "It actually saves us quite a bit over building our own facility."

"Mr. Delany?" asked Daniel.

"I still don't think my company would support the idea. There's too much risk to our infrastructure in the event one of their launches goes bad."

"OK, Mr. Delany, how about this?" asked Tom, having anticipated this response. "We'll provide appropriate liability insurance to cover any damage to your facilities caused by our launch activities. In addition, we'll sub-let access to the pad from Rainier. Let's say five million per launch plus 5% of any launch fees we receive from customers."

Michael blinked suddenly, caught by surprise. Tom's offer potentially turned the vacant pad into a revenue source. And his bonus was tied to the annual performance of Rainier's launch services division.

"Mr. Armac," Michael said after a moment of silence. "I think we may have a deal."

"Excellent, the Senator will be very happy you were able to work this out," said Daniel, rising. "Now if you'll excuse me, I'll leave you to work out the details. There's a great seafood place down the coast a bit, and I have a date."

***

"That went well," said Tom, as he and his team emerged into the California sunlight and walked toward the launch pad.

"Nicole would be proud of you, sir, you only lost your temper once," observed Vivian.

"Where is Nicole, by the way?" asked Luke. "I would have thought she'd have come with you today."

"She and Marcus are working on another task right now," replied Tom. "I told her not to worry, I could handle it on my own."

The group walked to the edge of one of the launch pad flame diverter trenches and peered down into the concrete canyon. Robbie leaned over the edge and spit into the trench, watching the ball of saliva fall to the bottom. "So now that that's handled, what do you intend to do about the curse?" he asked.

"Curse? What the hell are you talking about?" asked Tom.

"You don't know?" replied Robbie, surprised. "The Chumash Indians call this area the 'Western Gate'. They believe it's where the souls of the deceased pass through to the afterlife."

"You've got to be kidding me," said Tom.

"Nope, God's honest truth. The Chumash didn't want this complex built—claimed it was an affront to their culture. The Air Force broke ground anyway, for the Manned Orbiting Laboratory program in the sixties, and the tribe put a curse on the whole thing. MOL went bust—big cost overruns and construction problems. Then the Air Force decided to update the facility to launch shuttles. Within months of finishing, Challenger blew up, and this site was abandoned again. Then the big aerospace companies started trying to launch out of here, but their rockets kept exploding. The couple that did launch OK, the payloads failed shortly after reaching orbit."

"Sounds like the plot of a movie," observed Luke. "Some *Indiana Jones* thing? No, *Poltergeist*, wasn't that the one with the Indian graveyard? Maybe the whole place will implode into a black hole and suck itself out of existence," he added, looking around.

"Yeah, go ahead, laugh about it," said Robbie. "I'm telling you though, everyone in the program knows the story of the curse." Looking back down into the diverter trench, he added, "And sometimes things like that affect people—it weighs on their minds."

"Christ," muttered Tom. "OK Robbie, you say there's a curse—figure out a way to deal with it. I don't want anyone blaming bad spiritual karma for any issues we may have out here. This job's going to be hard enough as it is."

"Why me, Tom?"

"Because you're the one who brought it up. Hell, you're from New Orleans—see if you can bring some of that Voodoo juju to bear."

"Yeah Tom, I'll get right on it," said Robbie. "How hard could it be to find a Voodoo priestess nowadays?"

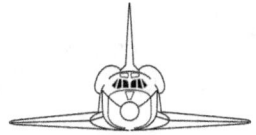

CHAPTER EIGHTEEN

Nichole sat patiently watching Mark Rutherford read the non-disclosure agreement while Marcus answered email on his phone.

"Good news, we got the pad," Marcus whispered to Nicole.

"Yesssssss!" she quietly replied, making a subtle fist clench.

Mark placed the papers on the desk and picked up an engraved silver pen. Clicking it several times, he paused, and then turned to the final page and signed.

"OK, Ms. Ferry, you have my attention," he said, pushing the document toward her. "What's the mission and how can Destination Beyond help?"

"Mr. Rutherford, I'm sure you're aware that our company will be conducting our qualifying launches for the NASA Low Cost Launch Centennial Challenge prize in the next few months."

"Good for you, congratulations," said Mark. "You know we don't broker payloads though—our company markets seats on spacecraft to wealthy space tourists."

"Well, after we win LCL One, my company is going to announce the first private moon mission. We'll have two seats available for space tourists. One we intend to fill by having an international lottery. We'd like Destination Beyond to find a buyer for the other."

Mark looked with dismay at Nicole. "Ms. Ferry, we've been trying to place two passengers on a moon mission for almost five years now. We finally found one customer willing to put up the $25 million down payment, but the Russians won't even start building the necessary hardware until we locate an additional passenger. I'm sorry, but the market isn't there. I don't see any way we can attract the clients to fill another mission when we can't place the one we're already offering."

Marcus smiled at Mark. "You mean that trip around the moon in the Soyuz you've been promoting on your website?"

"Yes," replied Mark. "It's taken us years just to find one passenger, there's no telling if the mission will even fly at this point. I'm sorry, I just don't think we're going to be able to help you."

"Mr. Rutherford," said Marcus, "we're not going around the moon taking pictures out the window in some cramped up stinky Russian piece of crap. We're taking seven people in a first class ride, and we're going to land, get out, and walk around a while."

Mark stared at Marcus, and then snorted and laughed. "Seriously? You're trying to tell me you're going to attempt a moon landing? Sometime this century?"

"We're completely serious, Mr. Rutherford," said Nicole. "In fact, we expect to lift off in less than a year."

Mark looked back and forth at Nicole and Marcus several times. "You know what? I want to believe you. I really, really do. But I think you're completely nuts. I barely believe it can be done at all. But your company? In under a year? Sorry, I'm not seeing it."

"We'll do it, Mr. Rutherford, I assure you. Let me show you how. This is a presentation our Chief Scientist, Dr. Carl Heinel, has put together.

Chief Scientist—the Doc will like that! thought Marcus.

"First, you may not be aware of our company's role in refurbishing a space shuttle for display," said Nicole, opening the presentation package to the first illustration.

***

"Well I'll be God damned," Mark said.

"Funny, we get that a lot," chuckled Marcus. "I wish we'd started a scrapbook of 'first reaction' pictures, 'cause everyone makes that face," he said, assuming a look of exaggerated astonishment.

"Well? Now what do you think, Mr. Rutherford?" Nicole asked.

"If everything you just showed me checks out, then I can see where you would think it could be done," Mark answered. "Whether you're the people to do it or not remains to be seen, but yes, I'll admit it could work."

"So we can do business then, Mr. Rutherford?" Nicole asked.

"It's a very select group of individuals you're marketing to here," Mark replied, leaning forward across his desk. "There aren't more than a few dozen people in the world who can put up 150 to 200 million for a trip like this, and most of them would never take this kind of risk. But yes, I'd almost guarantee that we can find a passenger for you. To be part of the first private moon landing? Absolutely, we can find you someone willing to pay your price."

"Excellent. We'll be interested in identifying that individual as soon as possible."

Mark leaned back in his chair. "Your haste wouldn't be reflective of a cash flow problem, I hope. Your company has the necessary financial resources to see this through, Ms. Ferry? Because any potential clients we contact will want assurances that their investment will not be at risk. It's one thing to be asked by the Russian government to put down a non-refundable deposit. It's quite another thing for you to do it."

"Any deposits will be fully refundable in the event the flight doesn't occur," Nicole replied. *Mr. Armac is not going to be happy with that concession*, she thought.

"All right. So tell me about this lottery you're considering."

"Who hasn't always wanted to go to the moon at least a little bit?" said Marcus. "We think at twenty-five bucks a pop, who could resist taking a shot at fulfilling that dream?"

"Maybe you should let us handle that for you?" suggested Mark. "We have a very thorough process for vetting potential candidates, we'd be happy to take that on."

"Thanks, we got this," said Marcus.

"We will need help arranging the appropriate training for our guests and some of our crew," said Nicole. "The basic space tourism package that you provided for passengers visiting the space station: centrifuge training, zero gee simulation flights, and so forth."

"No problem," Mark said. "We still have our contract with Roscosmos for access to their facilities at Star City."

"We'll also require some assistance obtaining some of the other equipment and materials we'll need," Nicole said.

"Such as?"

"Space suits, for example. We need six Orlan MKs for our flight crew. And several Orlan GNs for training use," Nicole replied, pulling a picture from her briefcase of the Russian Orlan space suit and placing it on Mark's desk.

Mark picked up the picture and studied it. "The Orlan MK is the model for extravehicular activity. You're planning to use the Orlans as lunar excursion suits? They're too heavy."

"Our lead engineer believes she can shave up to fifty pounds off each suit through the use of more composites," Nicole said.

Mark's eyebrow arched. "You're going to *improve* the Russian Orlan MK?"

"You could say that," Nicole shrugged. "She's very good. Can you obtain them for us?"

"Absolutely, that's what we do," replied Mark, looking at the picture again. "Six Orlan MKs, though? It will take our Russian friends a while to fill that order. I don't think they have that many in production at the moment. They don't come cheap. You're probably looking at, oh, I'd say eight to ten million each, if you bought six at once." Looking up, he added,

"Of course, that would include several days of operator training and a full spares package."

"What a deal," smirked Marcus.

"Mr. Rutherford, in addition to your established commission, our company will pay you a ten percent premium on every dollar you can save us below five million per suit," said Nicole.

"Six Orlan MKs for under $30 million?" Mark shook his head slowly, his brow furrowing. Then, with a shrug, he said, "Maybe. With the ISS gone the Chinese are their only customers now, so maybe they'll deal. No promises, but I'll see what I can do."

"That's all we can ask, Mr. Rutherford. There's also an additional task we'd like you to perform for us. If you'd be comfortable with it."

"What might that be, Ms. Ferry?"

"We'd like you to discuss with the Russians the possibility of our purchasing two Soyuz TMA capsules."

Mark was startled by the request. "The Russians won't sell you a Soyuz, Ms. Ferry. They might contract for a piloted launch, but they won't just outright sell them to you."

"Well, the truth is we're not really interested in either purchasing or contracting for Russian capsules. We just want people to think we are."

Mark cocked his head slightly. "So you want me to waste their time?"

"I suppose you could say that," Nicole answered with a smile. "And you can bill us for however many hours you have invested, if you'd be comfortable with that."

"It's your money, Ms. Ferry. I'll negotiate the purchase of Lenin's tomb if I can bill you by the hour. But just for the sake of argument, what would you like me to do if they say yes?"

"Stall. Say your client is having second thoughts or pursuing other alternatives. And don't sign anything that would actually commit us to following through."

"I'm not sure how that will help my credibility with RSC Energia, but the way things have been going, I probably won't be doing much business with the Russians in the future anyway. OK, I'll take that on, Ms. Ferry."

"And please remember, Mr. Rutherford, that we have a signed non-disclosure agreement. Until we announce our plans, you're to make no mention of this project except that necessary to negotiate the services we're seeking," warned Nicole.

"Understood," Mark said, nodding briefly. "But when you announce, I know someone who is going to be extremely unhappy."

"Oh? Who's that?"

"My client who just put down a $25 million non-refundable deposit on the Soyuz circumlunar trip. He will be one pissed off individual."

"Hate it for him," said Marcus with his usual friendly grin. "Hope you already collected your fee."

"Well yes, of course. Oh, one more thing, Ms. Ferry?" asked Mark.

"Yes, Mr. Rutherford?"

"I'd like one of those lottery tickets please," Mark smiled, reaching for his wallet.

***

"I wonder where the boss is gonna get another thirty or forty million for the suits?" observed Marcus with concern, as he and Nicole left Mark's office. "The LCL One prize isn't *that* big."

"I'm sure he'll think of something," Nicole replied. She had enough contacts in accounting to know that the project's accumulating costs had Roadrunner Rockets circling the financial drain. *I hope Tom has a plan*, she thought with concern. *To be this close and go bankrupt ...*

***

Bob Brock's desk phone rang, breaking his concentration. *This article is hard enough without interruptions*, he thought.

"Brock, space desk," he said into the phone absently, while attempting to draft another paragraph about the absolutely nothing that had happened in the aerospace industry that week.

"Bob, this is Marion. Did you see the news?"

"What news is that ma'am?" Bob asked, in response to his editor's question.

"NASA headquarters just announced a new Centennial Challenge. A $250 million lunar landing prize. I thought maybe you should head over to the Space Center and get some local reaction."

"Will Daisy mentioned something about that some time ago. I'll give Keith Barton a call and try to have something by deadline." *Beats the hell out of trying to finish* this *article*, he thought.

"Great, find a good local angle and maybe we'll be able to do a supplement for Sunday's edition," Marion said, and then hung up.

It would be nice to have a feature about something positive for a change, Bob thought, as he picked up his keys and dialed Keith's number on his cell phone.

***

Bob was surprised to see so many cars parked outside the solid rocket booster processing facility complex. The facility's work had come to a halt after the shuttle program ended, but there was definitely something going on there now. Continuing on to the orbiter processing facility, Bob parked close to building two, and then gave Keith a quick call to tell him he had arrived.

A few minutes later, Bob spotted Keith exiting OPF 2, and walked over to meet him. Reaching to shake hands, he said, "Thanks for taking some time out, I appreciate it."

"Not a problem," replied Keith. "I was just checking on my Endeavour crew, it felt like a good day to get out of the office."

Keith escorted Bob into the building and out of the hot Florida sun. Inside, shuttle Endeavor sat like a fish being cleaned, its entrails spilled across the floor. The orbiter had numerous large holes in its body and wings through which workers were in the process of yanking out its guts.

Both men stood for a moment and quietly contemplated the scene. "Sad to see her this way," said Bob, thinking about how much he owed the craft. The stories he had written about its journeys and the men and women who flew her had paid his mortgage and put his kids through college.

"Yeah, it is," agreed Keith, "but all good things and all that ... "

Bob looked at Keith. "You seem to be in a pretty good mood, considering," he said, nodding toward the dead orbiter.

"Well, I guess I'm at the acceptance stage of grief," Keith replied. "For the time being, the orbiter prep work is keeping my team employed, and apparently there's a great big beautiful tomorrow." Keith smiled. He had taken his family to Walt Disney World the weekend before, and the Carousel of Progress theme was still stuck in his head.

Bob shook his head, bemused by Keith's attitude, and then looked back at Endeavour. "So where are you now with the decommissioning?"

"The fluids are drained and the systems purged. Most of the toxic materials and hazardous items are out, and we're down to removing the few things we want to keep in inventory for use on other projects or that the Center wants to display separately from the vehicle. The schedule says we'll be done with rip out by the end of the week. I expect them to start next week on buttoning up and making her presentable."

"And then what?"

"She'll probably just sit here in the OPF until the new building at the visitor's center is finished," Keith answered. "Maybe they'll do tram tours and bring guests out to see her."

"How's Atlantis coming?" Bob asked.

"You want to see her?"

"Sure," Bob replied. *No idea when I might have a chance to get to the DC area to visit with the old girl again once she moves up there*, he thought.

Bob followed Keith as he headed through the low bay structure that connected OPFs 1 and 2. Several Alliance Space Systems personnel nodded respectfully and said, "Mr. Barton," as they passed.

The scene in OPF 1 was remarkably different from the one Bob expected. On multiple occasions he had observed shuttles being prepped for their next flight, and to his untrained eye, that was exactly what appeared to be happening. Rather than looking like a gutted fish, Atlantis looked vibrant and alive.

"What's going on here, Keith?" Bob asked, baffled.

"Funny about Atlantis," Keith replied. "We're being paid to put her in pre-flight status, just as if she were getting ready to fly another mission."

"Why on Earth would the Smithsonian pay for that?" Bob asked, looking back at the vehicle.

"Smithsonian? No, we're under contract to Roadrunner Rockets," Keith replied with a frown.

"Roadrunner Rockets? What the hell do they have to do with any of this? Atlantis is supposed to be going to the National Air and Space Museum."

Keith's frown deepened, and he shook his head. "From what I hear, that's where she's headed. She's just taking a roundabout way of getting there." Turning to the reporter, he added, "That's all I can say about that, Bob. If you want to know anything else, you'll have to talk to the Smithsonian's press office." He turned and headed for the nearest exit, with Bob following along behind.

"Well tell me about this contract then," Bob asked.

"Sorry, that's a private deal between our company and Roadrunner Rockets. Call RRI if you have any questions." Keith pushed open the exit door and held it for Bob. "What did you want to talk to me about again?" he asked, trying to change the subject as they stepped outside.

"Well, I came out here originally to get your opinion on the new Centennial Challenge that NASA has just announced."

"The moon landing?"

"Yes. What are your thoughts on how it might impact the Space Center or the work force? You know I'm always looking for some good news to publish. We've had more than our share of crappy news lately."

"You want good news? Did you happen to notice SRB processing on the way in?

"Yeah, I noticed the parking lot was full. What's going on?"

"Our friends from Roadrunner Rockets again," Keith replied. "They've moved in their fuel mixing and casting equipment and have started stacking booster segments. Looks like they'll be making an attempt at LCL One soon, and they have some pretty big plans beyond that."

"I thought they were at least six months, maybe a year from a launch?" asked Bob.

"Let's just say they're picking up the pace, and it's good news for my people." Keith's phone beeped. Pulling it out and glancing at it, he said, "I'm sorry Bob, it was good seeing you, but I need to go. I have a quality team meeting in 15 minutes."

"Well thanks again, I appreciate the update. Glad to see you're so busy!" Bob shook Keith's hand and started toward his car. Pausing after several steps, he turned and called out, "Hey, do you think the two are related somehow?"

Stopping and turning, Keith shouted back, "What's that Bob?"

"Roadrunner Rockets' booster work and the lunar landing prize. Do you think they could be related somehow?"

"I don't know Bob, you're the reporter, you figure it out," Keith called out, and then waved and reentered the building. His good mood returning, he began whistling happily to himself

CHAPTER NINETEEN

Bob laid it out for his editor. "I can write a puff piece about the bright new day dawning at the Cape, no problem. I'm telling you though, Marion, there's something bigger going on here, and I'd like to have some time to get to the bottom of it."

"Bob, you're a feature writer, not an undercover investigator," Marion replied.

"Marion, the old days are over. The private enterprise folks run the space center now, and they keep secrets."

"So what are you asking for, Bob?"

"I'd like the paper to authorize a trip out to the New Mexico Spaceport. Let me poke around a little and see if I can figure out what Roadrunner Rockets is up to."

"I'm still not sure what you're after," Marion said.

"They've got a goddamn shuttle, Marion! And not only that, but Alliance is prepping it for flight as we speak. Meanwhile RRI is building rockets that look exactly like shuttle SRB's. I'm telling you Marion, I have a hunch something's going on out there. This is a newspaper—hunches used to matter."

"It's a different world, Bob. We don't have the money for field trips anymore. If you can get it locally, fine, if not, give me the puff piece you mentioned."

Bob glowered at Marion for a moment, and then his expression softened. "OK, how about this? I probably have enough airline miles to pay for a ticket, if the paper will pick up my other costs."

"I don't know, Bob. We just don't do much of that anymore."

"I'm talking about one freaking night, Marion. I'll get a compact car and eat at McDonalds. Just let me go and check it out. I'll be back before you know I'm gone."

Marion looked at Bob while tapping a pencil rapidly on the desktop. After a moment, she said, "We'll get more than just the one article?"

"If I find what I think I might, I promise you enough material for a special insert."

"OK, I'll sign off on the request. But I want you back here as soon as you can. Go, look around, and get back. Understand?"

"Bless you Marion!" Bob said, giving her an exaggerated kiss on her forehead. "I'll make sure it's worth it."

***

Bob turned onto the dusty two lane road marked by the large "Welcome to New Mexico Spaceport" sign. Ahead, he could see the gleaming sparkle of Galactic Journeys' new terminal building. He had done a series of articles on their suborbital space tourism program when they first announced their plans several years ago. On the runway in front of the building, he could make out their stark white mothership aircraft, looking like an ungainly stork bending down for a drink of water. Passing the glittering glass building, Bob headed toward the industrial park area, with its utilitarian metal and block structures. Slowing down to read the building numbers, he spotted a flaming roadrunner logo on the side of one of the larger buildings. *Must be it*, he thought. *Hope they don't mind unannounced guests.*

Pulling into the dirt and gravel lot, he parked and opened his door. A blast of hot air caught him by surprise. After almost two hours in air conditioned comfort, he had forgotten exactly how blistering the heat was in the New Mexico desert. Scanning the building, he located what appeared to be the front door.

***

Contentedly observing the friction stir welder as it melted two panels of aluminum sheeting together, Carl was suddenly surprised by a loud and persistent knock coming from one of the facility's doors. *Now that's peculiar*, he thought. *We don't often have visitors.*

Crossing the booster segment storage area, Carl opened the door, allowing a blaze of light and heat to enter the building. A man stood outside, backlit by the sun.

Mike, noticing the sudden brightness, looked up from the framework welds he was examining. "Who's there, Dr. Carl?" he called out.

"That's what I'm attempting to determine, my boy," he shouted back. Turning to Bob, he said, "Good day sir, and who might you be?"

"Bob Brock, I'm a reporter with the *Orlando Guardian*," Bob said, extending his hand.

"I believe you may have the wrong building, sir," Carl replied. "The Galactic Journeys facility is back that way," he pointed.

"This is Roadrunner Rockets?" Bob asked.

"Why yes, it is."

"Then I'm in the right place. I'm writing a series of articles on the commercial launch industry, and I'm here at Spaceport doing some research."

"Ah, I see," said Carl. "Well come in sir, no need to stand there in the heat. I'm Dr. Carl Heinel, pleased to meet you," he added, as he closed the door.

"So who is it, Dr. Carl?" Mike called out again.

"A reporter from the *Orlando Guardian*, a Mr. Bob Brock," Carl replied. "Wait, I know you sir, we've met before at the Kennedy Space Center."

"Yes, and I know your name, Dr. Heinel. You were around NASA a long time," Bob replied.

"Well come and join us, Mr. Brock, we were just about to stop for lunch," Carl said, steering Bob toward the enclosed break room. "Mr. Patrick, let's take a break for lunch," he called out.

"Sure thing, Dr. Carl, be right there."

***

Carl, Mike, and two of their production assistants sat around the small break room table eating sandwiches and chips while Bob sipped on a Coke.

"Like I said, Mr. Brock, our choice to use shuttle solid rocket booster casings was purely a cost saving measure," explained Mike. "It saves us from having to manufacture our own casings, and with the end of the shuttle program, there was a lot of surplus servicing equipment that we could pick up cheap."

"But by doing so, your Big Brother booster would be compatible with the rest of the shuttle system," Bob pointed out.

"In theory, but no way have we ever considered trying to do shuttle launches. Sure, we joked about it once or twice over a few beers, but really, what would be the point?"

"What do you mean?" Bob asked.

"Our whole thing is achieving the lowest possible launch cost," Mike answered. "Once we've flown our booster, we're expecting to corner a lot of the commercial satellite business. Government payloads too. The shuttle is a crazy expensive vehicle to fly. It would run counter to our whole business plan to try and use it to launch payloads. It would drive our costs back up to current levels, when our goal is to lower them by an order of magnitude."

"And yet at this moment your company is paying to have Atlantis prepped for flight," Bob noted, watching Mike's reaction.

Mike glanced quickly at Carl, who was sitting to one side, quietly observing. "You'd have to talk to corporate about that, Mr. Brock. From what we hear, that's some kind of tax thing related to Mr. Armac's pet project."

"Pet project?" Bob asked hopefully.

"His museum. He wants to be a philanthropist I guess, do something to give back to the community and all that. And make a little money in the process. It doesn't really involve us out here. Frankly, we're too busy for stuff like that."

"Well, would you mind showing me what you're currently working on?"

"Sure, be glad to," Mike said. "Come on, I'll give you a quickie tour."

Mike led Bob to the booster segment storage area, while Carl followed. "This is what we're most proud of," Mike said, patting one of the twelve foot diameter casings. "These are the last of the Big Brother segments we poured here. After we cast these, we crated up the equipment and shipped it to Kennedy Space Center."

"I think I saw some of your activity there," said Bob.

"It's mostly the Alliance Space Systems folks. We have a couple of people on site to help, but we're turning all our booster prep work over to them."

"So then these segments here ... " Bob began.

"Will be shipped to the launch site for use." Mike answered.

"Why move your entire booster production to the Cape?"

"Are you kidding?" Mike asked. "Did you notice the expressway and rail line on your drive out?"

"I'm not sure I understand ... " Bob said, confused.

"There aren't any, Mr. Brock. Only a two lane county road. That wasn't a problem when we were building smaller boosters, but these babies right here," Mike patted the segment they stood next to, "are a bitch to get on a truck, and it's 30 miles of bad road from here to the nearest rail line. At Kennedy, we have rail, highway, and water access, so it's way more better for moving these guys around."

"I see. Well, what are you working on here?" Bob asked, heading toward the partially assembled lunar lander propulsion unit.

Again, Mike glanced at Carl, who slowly shook his head sideways one time.

"That's a prototype for an orbital propulsion module we're developing," Mike answered casually.

"Really?" said Bob, as he walked up to the lander and ran his hand around the bell of the rocket motor. "If it's an orbital module, why would it have landing legs?" Bob asked over his shoulder.

"It was easier to weld some legs to it than build a custom assembly cradle," Mike improvised. "This does the job for now, and when we're finished, we can remove them and reuse the materials for another project."

"And these?" Bob asked, walking over to the shuttle OMS fuel modules under construction just past the lander.

"More prototype work," Mike offered. "A design for a liquid fueled propulsion system we're considering."

Bob pulled out his phone, and asked, "Do you mind?"

Mike, believing the reporter felt the sudden need to make a call, shrugged his shoulders and said, "No, go right ahead."

Bob raised his phone and quickly snapped several pictures. Moving to get a different angle, he was interrupted by Carl.

"No pictures please, Mr. Brock," Carl said, moving between Bob and the equipment.

"I don't see an engine, just tanks and valves," noted Bob, peering over Carl's shoulder.

"They're not done yet," Mike stated, aggravated. "Come on, let me show you the interstage assemblies we're building for the rocket we're going to use for the LCL One prize," he added, herding Bob away from the side of the building dedicated to hardware for the moon project.

"Sure," Bob said, allowing himself to be led toward the welding machines on the far side of the building. Looking back at the OMS fuel modules, he thought, *fifteen, maybe sixteen feet in diameter. Interesting.*

***

Nicole tapped lightly on Tom's office door. Entering the room, she found Tom seated at his desk, staring absently out the window.

"Is everything all right?" she asked, as she sat in one of the papasan chairs in front of Tom's desk.

"Yes, everything's fine," Tom answered, turning around to face her. "Everyone should have my problems," he added with a grim smile. "What's up?"

"There's something I thought you'd like to see," she said, picking up the television remote control from Tom's desk and turning on the TV. Switching to C-SPAN, she curled her legs up beneath her in the saucer shaped chair. "It might cheer you up a bit."

The caption at the bottom of the screen read "HR206 Commercial Space Launch Enhanced Access Act." A woman stood behind the elevated podium in the mostly empty chamber, gavel in hand. She said, "The period for voting is now closed. The ayes are 374, the nays are 52, with nine abstentions. The motion is passed." She then struck the gavel on the podium.

"Congressman Daisy came through for us," Nicole observed. "I thought you'd like to see."

Tom nodded slowly. "Yes, that's good. Very good. Still has to clear the Senate though."

"Dick McConnel assures me it'll pass the Senate without debate," Nicole said. Turning to Tom, she added, "And he says that this time, he's absolutely certain, unlike the last time he told us something was a sure thing."

Tom snorted, and then said, "So does it give us what we need?"

"Yes, I'm pretty sure we'll be able to exploit some of the law's new provisions to our advantage."

"Pretty sure?"

"OK, really sure. It's good for the industry, and it helps us. It will still ultimately be up to a judge to decide though."

"I really hate continually finding myself in this situation," Tom growled.

"What situation is that?"

"I do so much, and then everything depends on the whim of someone else to decide if I'll succeed." Turning to look out the window again, Tom added, "Some bureaucrat, or politician, or judge." Pausing a moment, he spat out, "Or board member."

"OK, what's wrong," Nicole asked with concern.

"The board wants to see me," answered Tom. "It couldn't wait until the next scheduled meeting. Had to be today." Turning back toward Nicole, he added, "That can't be good."

"Any idea what it might be about?"

"I know exactly what it's about. We're three months late with the release of our Android game tracking app. Our latest service pack is way behind schedule. And there's the little matter of our negative monthly cash flow."

Nicole nodded in understanding. "Did Marcus mention the approximate cost Destination Beyond quoted for the Orlans?"

"Yes, he said we needed to budget fifty million for the suits, supplies, training, and other miscellaneous hardware and services." Tom turned to look out the window again. "Fifty million we just don't have."

"I know the bills are starting to roll in for the construction work," said Nicole. "I hear we're over budget on the upgrades to the museum site. And Luke tells me the bids for the work at Vandenberg are just crazy."

"I know. We had some contingency funds, but they're gone," Tom replied, leaning back further in his chair. "Plus you should see the estimates I'm getting from Robbie on the personnel we're going to need. The salaries will give you nightmares."

"So what are we going to do?"

"I ... don't know. I'll think of something. We've come too far to give up now."

"Did you explore another round of venture capital financing?" asked Nicole.

Tom sat upright and spun around to face Nicole. "They laughed me out of the room when I told them about shifting our focus to a moon landing," he said with contempt. "Told me we already had everything we needed to get the Space Train rolling, and to just focus on that and forget trips to the moon."

"Some would say there's a lot of sense to that."

"Some would say," Tom agreed wistfully. Looking out the window again, he said, "There's so much money just right there, right beyond our grasp. The LCL One prize, the lunar landing prize. Those two alone would cover our basic operating costs."

"It's not really about making money anymore, is it?" Nicole asked. "You really need to do this. You need it for you."

Tom started nodding slowly. "I know. That's the problem. The emotion is getting in the way of the business considerations. How much I'm willing to risk to achieve it is the question I still have to answer."

Tom's computer chimed an alert. "Thanks for the visit," he said, glancing at the meeting reminder on his screen. "And thanks for that," he added, gesturing at the television. "I needed a shot of good news. Anyway, I'm off to see the board."

"Good luck. You know we're behind you no matter what happens."

Tom paused and gave Nicole a warm look tinged with sadness. His small RRI team had become more than employees. They were his family, for whom he felt deep affection. He was momentarily overcome by emotion, and then managed to squeeze out a quick "Thank you for that" before leaving.

***

"So what do you think, Dr. Carl?" Mike asked, as they watched Bob drive away.

"I wouldn't worry about it, my boy," Carl observed calmly. "He'll undoubtedly be quite upset when he discovers that most of what you told him wasn't exactly true, but by then it shouldn't matter."

"Technically, most of what I said *was* the truth," Mike observed. "Just not entirely accurate," he added with a chuckle.

"True, true, well done," Carl nodded, as they turned to re-enter the building. "As you said, we're not considering using a shuttle for commercial launches after all. And he never did ask if we might take one to the moon."

***

Carl called Marcus with an update. "You were right, Mr. Short," he said. "We have started to generate a bit of interest on the part of the press."

"He actually showed up on your doorstep?" Marcus asked, surprised.

"Indeed he did, actually knocked on the door. Not quite what we expected, but young Mr. Patrick did a fine job at misdirection."

"OK, great, thanks for the report, Doc. I'll let Mr. Armac know when he gets out of his board meeting. How's everything else going?"

"Excellent, Mr. Short. We will have the first interstage assembly ready on time as promised. We're arranging a date for transport now."

"That's terrific, Doc. Let me know if you have any problems that might delay delivery. Talk to you soon."

Son of a bitch, Marcus thought, as he hung up. *We'll have to keep an eye on Brock, it will ruin everything if word gets out too soon.*

Marcus picked up his phone again and dialed. "Nicole? Marcus. Grab Tyler and come see me when you have a chance. We might have a problem."

***

"Tom, don't worry. The board just wants to know your plans for getting development back on track," said Dale Jeffers as the two men waited outside the small room used for board meetings. Dale was vice president of virtual systems, which made him second-in-command. "And when you're done with them, I'd like to be let in on the plan as well," he added with an uncharacteristic edge. "You're squeezing me pretty tightly on resources. I'll need a few of my key people back soon if we're going to fix this."

Before Tom could reply, the door to the room opened. Richard Fennel, a recent addition to the Altered State Software Board of Directors, looked out and said, "We're ready for you, Tom."

Tom followed Richard into the small meeting room, where the half dozen members of the board sat waiting. "Thanks for coming on such short notice, Tom," said Alice Trebone, the current chairman.

"My pleasure, Alice, I'm always available to consult with the board," said Tom, noting that they had left no spare chairs in the room. *Jesus, I guess they expect me to stand here and be scolded like a schoolboy*, he thought.

"Tom, we'll get right to the heart of the matter," Alice began. "The board is very concerned about the company's performance in several key areas for the last three quarters." Shuffling through several papers in front of her, she pulled one to the top. "The systems development team has missed several key milestones on two major projects. Projects essential to meeting our revenue projections for this year," she added, looking up at Tom. Pulling another sheet from her pile, she said, "Technical support response time is trending strongly negative, and the number of unresolved support calls is escalating." Looking calmly but firmly at Tom, she said, "Tom, what the hell is going on here?"

"The truth is, I've been juggling several competing priorities lately, and as a result I probably haven't given the company the attention it requires," Tom began, chastened.

"Let's cut the bull, Tom," Alice bristled. "You're CEO of Altered State. If you've done your job properly, you should be able to go on a year's sabbatical and things here should run just fine. The problem is that you're continually pulling key personnel off task so that they can help you with your rocket hobby."

"Alice, RRI is more than a hobby," Tom explained. "We're poised to revolutionize the commercial launch industry with our designs. It has a hell of a bright future."

Alice read from a list. "Marcus Short, Luke Rungren, Mike Patrick, Tyler Allen; these are all Altered State senior managers, am I right?"

"Yes, they are, but … "

"Nicole Ferry? Several interns and co-ops from coding and production?" Alice continued.

"Yes, well … "

"Tom, look. You're running another whole company with Altered State personnel. And that's negatively affecting our bottom line. Now I understand that Roadrunner Rockets has achieved some level of success, and you have in fact been hiring employees." Alice referred to another list. "Vivian Lee, Eugene Robichaud, Jean Lutz, a Doctor Heinel, and about a dozen others to date." Looking up, she said, "Tom, it's time to quit this. It was one thing when your hobby didn't interfere with our operations or your management of this company. But that's not the case anymore, is it?"

Tom glared at Alice and the rest of the board members, his fists slowly clenching and unclenching.

"We asked for an internal audit, and fortunately there doesn't appear to have been any financial impropriety, beyond the inappropriate utilization of company personnel," Alice continued. "You appear to be financing RRI solely out of your own pocket, thank God, along with the venture capital you've obtained."

Tom's face flushed red in anger. "Do you think for a moment I'd misappropriate company funds for personal reasons? We've tracked every minute of time that Altered State employees have spent working on RRI business, and we've established a reimbursable account that we'll use to reconcile the payroll when we win the LCL One prize." Tom glared at the board members.

"Tom, you know we have a legal and fiduciary obligation to this company. I'm sorry, but what would you have expected us to do? You're the primary shareholder of Altered State. We're actually working to protect you. Protect you from yourself apparently."

Tom unclenching his fists, willing himself to relax, and took a deep breath. "Thank you Alice. I'm aware of your legal obligation and I appreciate your commitment to the company's continued success. What does the board recommend at this point?"

Alice looked at Tom, her expression a balance of friendship and concern. "Get your head out of the clouds, Tom. Get back to doing what you do best, which is making this the best computer gaming company it can be. And get those people back to work so we can catch up with our timelines."

Words of agreement and assent assembled in Tom's mind and started flowing toward his mouth. Somehow, they were intercepted in route and replaced by a single, softly spoken word. "No." Even Tom was surprised by what he had just said.

"Did you just say no?" Alice asked, visibly shocked.

"No. I mean, yes, I did just say no." Tom said, staring into space somewhere beyond the back corner of the room. In his mind, he watched a figure climb slowly down the ladder of the lander, turn, and plant a flag on the surface of the moon. "I can't do that, Alice," he said, returning his focus to the board members. "I won't do it."

"Tom, the board is here to advise you," Alice bristled. "This is a privately held company. You're the majority shareholder. We can't fire you. But if you won't take our advice, then we're wasting our time here. I can't speak for the rest of the board," she said, looking at the other members, "but if you refuse to act on our recommendations, then I'll be resigning." Several of the other members nodded agreement.

"No Alice, that won't be necessary. You're absolutely 100% right. Here's the thing," Tom said, looking warmly at the board members. "I have a small plaque that I keep in my desk drawer. It used to be my father's. It's a quote from Mark Twain. It says, 'Twenty years from now, you will be more disappointed by the things you didn't do than by the ones you did do.'" Again looking off into distant space, he continued. "My father spent his entire life chained to a desk, with that plaque sitting there, daring him every day to take the bold leap." Looking again at the board members, he said, "Well, he died without ever followed his dreams, whatever they may have been. And now that plaque sits in my drawer, challenging me in the same way. I thought this company was my dream. But I have another dream now—a bigger dream—that I intend to follow wherever it may lead me."

Tom paused, unsure if he actually had the courage to say what he was thinking. Then, feeling the warmth of calm assurance wash over him, he said, "Members of the board, I hereby tender my resignation as CEO of Altered State Software. I recommend that effective immediately, Dale Jeffers be appointed acting CEO until the board can make a permanent selection."

Aghast, Alice said, "Tom, don't be hasty. This is your company. Do you think that resigning would be in its best interests?"

"Absolutely, Alice," Tom said with a broad smile. "And I intend to follow up on Axial Infotainment's recent offer to purchase Altered State. Dale will need the board's support with managing the transition. I'm selling the company and following my dream."

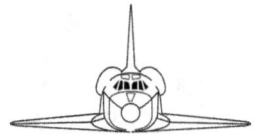

CHAPTER TWENTY

Nicole encountered Tom in the hallway as he left the board of directors meeting. "Mr. Armac, it looks like our concerns about the press may be coming true … "

"Not now, Nicole," Tom interrupted. "Get everyone together at Neverland. I'd like to meet with the entire team in 30 minutes."

"Everyone? Dr. Heinel and Mike are at Spaceport at the moment, Robbie and Jean are … "

"Arrange a web conference, get them netted in. Everyone who's here, please have them meet in Neverland."

"Can I tell them what it's about?"

"Their future."

Nicole's eyes widened, as she said, "Yes sir," and rushed off to track down the team.

***

"This is going to be a big decision for some of you," Tom began. "For others, it won't affect you much at all. As of an hour ago, I am no longer CEO of Altered State Software." Tom heard gasps of surprise. "I've stepped down as CEO, Dale Jeffers is taking over, and I'm selling the company."

"Selling it to who?" Marcus asked, after a stunned delay.

"I'm going to take Axial Infotainment's offer. The good news is that we should be able to use the pending sale proceeds as collateral to arrange a loan to buy the Russian suits and other hardware we need and relieve some of the financial stress."

"But we talked about Axial's offer a few months ago," Marcus said. "They wanted to move the company to New Jersey, and we were all, 'Yeah, that's where we want to live.'"

"I know, but I suspect it's not going to matter," Tom explained. "Viv, you're already full time with RRI. Those of you who are under contract: Doctor Heinel, Robbie, Jean, your respective team members; nothing changes, just keep doing what you're doing. The rest of you: Marcus, Luke, Mike, Nicole, Tyler; you each have a decision to make. You can stay with Altered State and resume your previous duties. The board says they'll be happy to have you back. Or, you can resign your position at Altered State and help me finish this project."

After a moment of silence, Marcus said, "Gee boss, go back to tinkering with game algorithms, or help you make history. Seems like a simple decision. Besides, after the last year, we pretty much already think of ourselves as RRI employees."

"Before you decide, you need to know that I can't guarantee you regular paychecks. Cash flow is going to be a bitch for a while. I can promise you one thing though—it's going to be one hell of a ride."

"Mr. Armac? Where do we operate from now?" Luke asked.

"Good point," replied Tom. "We obviously can't stay here. OK, Luke, you coordinate moving our Big Brother launch operations to the Kennedy Space Center. We'll manage our LCL One launches and Space Train program from there. Talk to Keith Barton, he'll help you find a suitable location.

"Nicole, touch base with the Air Force and tell them we want all the remaining administrative space at the Integrated Processing Facility building at Slick Six. We'll set up our offices there."

Looking up at the video screen, he asked, "Robbie, how much room do you have left there in Long Beach?"

"Not too much, considering someone promised the world a museum and we have to actually make room for some exhibits. How much do you think you need?" Robbie responded.

"We need to move all this," said Tom, waving his arm to indicate the information covering the walls of the conference room.

"Yeah, we can spare enough space for that."

"OK then, Marcus, move Neverland to the dome in Long Beach."

"Roger boss," nodded Marcus. "Oh, and it's the Space Dome now. It's Tyler's idea—generate some marketing buzz for the museum."

"Uh huh, Space Dome, great, I like it. OK, Mike, you and Dr. Heinel are fine where you are, no reason to move our fab facilities from Spaceport for now."

"Glad to hear that, Mr. Armac," Mike replied from New Mexico, Carl visible over his shoulder. "Dr. Carl finally has everything here working the way he wants it."

"Well, that's it then, let's gets busy," Tom said. "Wait, I'm making the assumption that everyone is still onboard. Altered State has been our home for a long time now, and I won't think less of any of you if you choose to remain."

After an awkward silence, Marcus said, "Boss, you know we're not going to let you have this much fun without us."

"I love you guys," Tom said with a smile. He meant it.

***

Robbie took another bite of his sandwich, and then said around a mouthful of food, "I'm telling you Steph, working with civilians is a whole 'nuther world."

Stephanie Peters pushed the remains of her salad away and dabbed at the corner of her mouth with her napkin. "Different in what way?"

"Well, it's almost like working with the Russians, except with a serious work ethic."

"I don't think I understand you," she said.

"At NASA we never did anything unless we had first looked at every possible outcome, developed an appropriate contingency, and then trained on it endlessly until we knew what to do without even thinking," Robbie said. "These guys, they are literally making it up as they go along. They're all 'Oh, that didn't work? Try this then. No? OK, well, how 'bout this other thing.'" Laughing, he added, "it's kind of liberating actually, it keeps you on your toes." Taking a swig of his beer, he said, "And I actually kind of like it."

"I don't know, it sounds a little too seat-of-the-pants to me. It introduces a lot of unnecessary risk."

"I guess. But things get done a lot quicker. Look, remember when the Elektron oxygen generating system went out on the ISS?" Robbie asked.

"Which time?"

"The second time," Robbie bristled defensively. "That first time was just bullshit, you know I didn't do anything wrong, I was following the purge and recycle procedure to the letter!"

"Of course I remember. The system went down hard, but it was Friday afternoon in Moscow, so the Russian flight control team said, 'You'll be fine for a few days, we'll be back on Monday,' and then left for the weekend."

"Right, and NASA went ape shit. If that had been American equipment, they would have worked the entire flight control team through the weekend until the system was back online."

"But everything turned out fine," Stephanie said. "The Russians came in on Monday and helped the crew fix the system before it caused any problems."

"Exactly. These RRI guys are more like the Russians—they take a laid back approach to things. But they're business people, so they react quick to things that drive cost. Anyway," Robbie added, pushing his chair back from the table, "things happen a lot quicker than I'm used to. Someone can throw an idea on the table after breakfast, we're trying it out over lunch, and by dinner it's part of the approved process."

Stephanie nodded knowingly. "You were always pretty impatient with the *process*. The NASA way of doing things. Anyway, you seem happy," she observed, smiling.

"I'm having the time of my life," Robbie confirmed. "You should join me, we can use another pilot," he added, getting to the point of their meeting. "Steph, I want to share a secret with you, but you have to promise me you won't tell anyone."

Stephanie cocked her head slightly. "Oh? What's that Robbie?"

"I'm serious, not a word, this is just between us," he emphasized.

"OK, you have my word," she replied seriously.

"Steph, I'm taking Atlantis up. Soon."

"What are you talking about, Robbie? NASA's not going to fly any more missions, you know that."

"RRI—the company I work for—they bought Atlantis, Steph. Well, they were given Atlantis is probably more accurate. Anyway, we own her outright. And we're flying one more mission."

Stephanie looked at Robbie with confusion. "But how is that even possible? You know what it takes to fly a shuttle mission. How can a group like RRI pull off something of that scale?"

Robbie smiled. "I'm telling you, Steph. They're like the Russians. But with better business sense. When they want to do something, they figure out a way to make it work and then execute, in less time than we used to spend just coming up with a project name. We're flying Atlantis, Steph. But that's not the best part. Want to know where we're flying her to?"

"What do you mean? Space, I'd assume," she replied, still stunned by Robbie's revelation.

"Not just space, Steph. It's not an orbital mission. We're taking Atlantis to the moon."

"Oh, come on, Robbie," she said. "And here I thought you were serious."

"We're taking her to the moon, Steph, no lie. Let me explain the project to you."

***

"Well?" Robbie asked.

"My God," Stephanie mumbled.

Click. Robbie imagined a camera shutter sound. *Another picture for Marcus' scrapbook,* he thought. "Steph, I want you on this mission. I need someone in the right seat to help me fly it."

"But ... I don't even know ... what makes you think it will work?" she stammered.

"It will work, Steph. I believe in these people. I know the ship can do it. But I need the right person to help me fly her."

"But why me, Robbie? I've never piloted an actual mission."

"Look, the truth is, I intend to do all the flying. I just need someone who can take over if something happens. What this mission really needs is a first class arm jockey. And you're one of the best, you have more time on the remote manipulator system than anyone. Plus you're the only person I know who's trained as both a mission specialist and flight engineer, and has pilot training."

"OK, let's say that I agree to go—why don't you let me be your specialist and choose a better qualified pilot to sit in the right seat?"

"Won't work, Steph. This is where it really gets interesting. You and I will be the only real astronauts onboard. Everyone else is just cargo. It's going to be up to us to pull it all off, we can't count on help from anyone else onboard."

"I see," she said distantly. "And you need me to operate the manipulator system ... "

"While I'm out in the cargo bay," Robbie said, finishing her thought. "I figure this mission will require as many as four EVA's to position the lander after launch and capture the fuel modules on orbit. My life will be in the hands of whoever's operating the arm, and you're the only one I trust that much. Fly the mission with me, Steph."

"I don't know, Robbie, this is a lot to digest. Let me think about it a while?"

"Just promise me you'll think about it," he asked. "I know we can do this, Steph. We can pull this off if you'll just agree to fly with me."

***

Robbie called Marcus as he was leaving the restaurant. "We have our pilot," he said when Marcus answered.

"We do? I didn't even know we were looking for one yet," Marcus replied.

"Jean has everything running in the control center now, and I have to have my backup in order to start flight rehearsals," Robbie explained.

"So who is it?" Marcus asked.

"Stephanie Peters. She's a good astronaut, and the best SSRMS operator I know."

"OK, well, it's your call. She said yes?"

"Not exactly, but she will. Trust me—no way would she pass up a mission like this."

"OK then, we'll add her to the roster. Do me a favor though, try not to hire any more crew members without checking with me first, OK?"

"Sure thing brother, see you soon," Robbie said, and hung up.

Marcus looked at the crew list on the Personnel board, sitting on the floor waiting to be packed for its trip to Long Beach. Bending over, he wrote "Stephanie Peters" in the slot next to Mission Pilot. Over half the slots in the table were now filled.

Mission Commander: Eugene Robichaud
Mission Pilot: Stephanie Peters
Passenger One: Tom Armac
Passenger Two: Carl Heinel
Passenger Three: ?
Lottery Selectee: ?
Tourist: ?

Only one spot left for any of us, he thought. *I wonder who will get to go.*

***

Bob leaned back in his desk chair. Staring at his computer screen, he contemplated the pictures of the strange equipment he had seen in New Mexico. *I know these tie together somehow. RRI has a shuttle. And they're working on a booster just like a shuttle SRB. And they have these things*, he thought, considering the equipment in the picture. *That thing with the legs is too big, but those others, they're about the right size to fit ...*

Bob thought a while longer, then decided, *what the hell, might as well.* Opening his contact list, he picked up the phone and dialed.

"Hello? Yes, this is Bob Brock from the *Orlando Guardian*, I'd like to speak to Mr. Funk, please. No, actually, he asked me to call him, it's important. Yes, I'll hold. Mr. Funk? Thanks for taking my call. Yes, I've learned a few things. I thought it was time we got together and talked."

***

Carl and Mike watched the last of the heavily laden trucks slowly pull away. "Well, that's everything, my boy," Carl said.

"I forgot how big the place is when it's empty," Mike observed, looking back through the open loading door. With the lander, the OMS fuel modules and the remaining Big Brother booster segments now on their way to their respective destinations, the fabrication facility was absolutely cavernous.

"You'll fill it again in due time. But first we have a few things to attend to," Carl said with a smile.

"Heard that, Dr. Carl," Mike nodded.

"Are you ready then?" Carl asked. He pushed the button to close the overhead door, checked to ensure it had locked, and then started toward the parking lot. "I'll drive," he said playfully.

"No way, I'm not missing another flight on account of your grandpa driving," Mike said with a chuckle. "I'll drive."

The two sped away into the deepening dusk, chasing the still twirling dust clouds raised by the recently departed trucks.

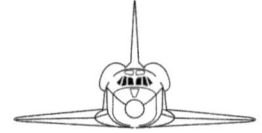

CHAPTER TWENTY–ONE

Tom looked at the boxes scattered about the small cluttered room. He had packed just the items he needed from his spacious office at Altered State to be shipped to the cramped and stuffy space the Air Force had made available at the SLC-6 Integrated Processing Facility. Everything else—the tokens and mementos of a lifetime in the computer industry and his years of rocketry research—was placed in storage back in Dallas. Sighing with resignation, he tore into another box hoping to find his missing coffee maker.

Nicole tapped lightly on his door. "The gang is here, Mr. Armac. Ready when you are."

"OK, be right there. Say, any idea where my coffee pot is?"

With a sigh and a shake of her head, Nicole walked to a pile of boxes in the corner and uncovered one labeled Office Misc. Zipping the tape open with her fingernail, she lifted out Tom's Keurig machine, placed it on the small credenza, and plugged it in. "There. Better?" she said, smiling.

"Yeah, great, thanks," Tom replied, following Nicole as she left his office and headed toward the conference room. Passing her equally small space, he glanced in, and noticed that she was completely unpacked and settled in.

"So, are you going to be ready for the FAA?" he asked.

"Still gaming out the options, but yes, I'm pretty sure we've figured out how to handle them," Nicole replied confidently.

"Good. Hopefully they'll surrender peacefully and not make life difficult for us."

Nicole preceded Tom into the IPF third floor conference room—the same room in which he had negotiated with the Air Force and Rainier Aerospace for access to the SLC-6 facilities several months previously. A freshly signed lease made it theirs now, for use as RRI's headquarters for west coast Space Train operations. Robbie and Jean had driven up from Long Beach for the meeting and were sitting next to Vivian, who shuttled between Space Dome and Vandenberg overseeing the many engineering projects her team was responsible for.

Tom noticed Marcus and Tyler fiddling with the cable on the back of the large TV temporarily parked on a pair of chairs. The screen suddenly came alive, displaying the images of Luke, Mike, and Dr. Heinel at the Kennedy Space Center.

"Can you see me now?" Marcus said, and laughed.

"See you fine, big guy!" Mike replied with a chuckle. "But that wasn't the problem—can you see us?"

"Unfortunately yes, your ugly face is filling the whole screen," Marcus said with mock insult. Turning to Tom, he said, "OK boss, we're ready."

Tom nodded. "Let's do it."

"OK everyone, it's been almost a month since our last status meeting back in Dallas, and I think we all left that one a little shell shocked," Marcus said. "I know you're all very busy, but we're overdue for an update to see if we're still executing to plan."

"As if slave driver Vivian would let us fall behind," moaned Robbie.

Vivian tore the top sheet off her legal pad, balled it up, and threw it at Robbie.

"OK kids, play nice. Who wants to go first?" Marcus asked. Looking at the monitor, he said, "Luke? How are things going at the Cape?"

"The interstage assemblies and OMS modules arrived from Spaceport safe and sound," Luke replied. "Everything is in checkout right now. We should be able to begin stacking booster segments next week."

"Is Keith giving you the help he promised?" Tom asked.

"Absolutely, Mr. Armac. He had space waiting for us. Hell, they even put a fresh coat of paint on it," he added, looking around.

"Nice to be back at the Cape again, Dr. Heinel?" Tom asked.

"Indeed, Mr. Armac," Carl replied. "And under such delightful circumstances. By the way, our friend the Congressman has come by several times. He extends his greetings."

"Tell Congressman Daisy we appreciate his support, and that we'll make sure to save him a seat in the gallery for our first launch," Tom replied. "So we're on track at your end?" he asked.

"Everything's looking good here, Mr. Armac. Barring the unforeseen, we'll be ready for our first launch within the month."

"And how's our girl?" Tom inquired.

"I've actually been pretty busy getting our facilities squared away, but Mike has been over a couple of times to check," Luke answered, glancing at Mike and nodding toward the screen.

"She looks good, Mr. Armac. The crew over there says they're just about done with preps," Mike said. "We should be able to load and transport Atlantis in a few more weeks."

"Good to hear," Tom replied. "I'll sleep easier once she's here and Vivian can start the system modifications."

"The biggest concern right now is lining up the transporter," Mike added. "NASA only has two shuttle transport aircraft, and they loaned one to Rainier Aerospace for carrying an unmanned combat vehicle they're working on. The other one is currently down for some scheduled maintenance. It might be three or four weeks before we have a way to ferry Atlantis to Vandenberg."

"That would mean Vivian can't get started on the mods until after our first launch," Marcus observed with a scowl. "That's not going to help our schedule."

"Well, let's not panic yet," Tom said. "The Congressman was able to get NASA to donate the transport flight to help our museum effort, so we can't push them too hard when we're not paying them anything." Looking back at the screen, he added, "In case anyone's interested, we're all moved in here, and Vivian has a space set up at the Maintenance and Checkout Facility up at north base, where's she's anxiously awaiting the arrival of our girl. Oh, and I found my coffee pot!" Turning to Vivian, he said, "OK, let's have an update on the lander."

"The propulsion unit and crew compartment both made if fine from Spaceport," Vivian explained. "We're working on final assembly and mating now. We need to have it finished prior to Atlantis arriving because we don't have the people to do both at once. Truthfully, a little delay in her arrival might be a good thing right now." Smiling to Tom, she said, "We should have something to show you in a few more weeks. I think you'll be happy!"

"Looking forward to it. Tell everyone about the pad upgrades."

"The grading is done and the rail beds are in place for the tracks that the moveable launch table will ride on, and we accepted NorPac Steel's bid on building the new table components. We decided to pay the higher cost over the Korean supplier we initially selected, because the additional shipping time blew up our schedule."

"OK, well, it's only money," Tom shrugged.

"We just need to finish the diagrams for the new launch tower servicing arms so that we can start the tower mods."

"And how are relations with the resident Rainier Aerospace folks?" Tom asked.

"They were swarming around constantly underfoot until we told them if they'd kindly get out of our way, we'd sub out the tower work to them," Vivian answered. "Mr. Delany has now become very cooperative," she concluded with a smile.

"I'm sure he has," Tom chuckled. "Tyler? You're up."

"The lottery website and ticket sales system is in testing now," Tyler reported. "We're running stress tests to simulate the volume we think we're going to see after we go live."

"Smells like money!" said Marcus with a grin.

"We've finished our marketing plan and have the pro formas and financials ready to send to potential sponsors," Tyler continued. "Really looking forward to the day we can begin selling."

"So do we all," Tom said grimly. "We need to start generating income if we're going to make it across the finish line."

Turning next to Robbie and Jean, he asked, "How is Space Dome shaping up?"

"You'd hardly recognize the place, Tom," Robbie said. "Big changes in the last month. The pool is done, and all our major equipment is in place now. The OMS module mockups are staged so that we can begin rehearsing our on-orbit operations."

"Very good. I need to take a day off and drive down and take a look," Tom said.

"Now that Steph's on board, we can start the launch and flight procedures rehearsals," Robbie added, turning to Jean.

"I have most of my team in place now," Jean began. "A few are still wrapping up their moves and finding a place to live, but we've been doing daily Space Train launch procedures drills for a couple of weeks now. We'll be starting the shuttle drills shortly."

"How are we keeping that quiet?" Marcus asked. "Once they start practicing shuttle launches … "

"The folks on the outside—the ones working the pool and the simulators—we're telling them it's practice for the 'up close space flight experience' show we'll be offering when the museum opens," Robbie said. "The flight control team, well, let's just say they have had it clearly explained to them that their substantial performance bonuses are tied to making sure word doesn't get out until we announce."

"On a related note," Nicole said, "Mr. Rutherford at Destination Beyond has made contact with Roscosmos regarding the Soyuz capsules we discussed. He tells me he's arranged for that information to be 'leaked' to a contact of his. There should be a brief article appearing in *Aviation News* in a month or so."

"That should be just about the time we're ready for our first launch," noted Luke.

"Exactly," Nicole continued. "With the news of our launch and the announcements we'll be making, the Soyuz story will be more noise that will keep people distracted."

"And no one will notice us setting up the screen pass," Marcus said with a smile.

"So what did the Russians say?" Tom asked.

"About the capsules?" Nicole asked. "I don't think they took it seriously. No need to worry, your money is safe."

"While we're on the subject, what's the word on the Orlans?" Tom asked.

"Mark says the Russians have three of the GN training models and an MK ready for immediate delivery as soon as we can write the check," Nicole replied. "The rest will take a few months."

"That's awesome," said Robbie. "The sooner we can get those training suits the sooner we can start doing mission preps in the pool."

"As soon as Axial Infotainment's letter of intent for purchase of Altered State clears legal, we'll close on the bridge loan and finally have some spare cash," Tom observed. "Once those dollars are available, let's get a check cut and get those suits going."

"Yes sir," Nicole nodded. "Oh, and I almost forgot, Mark Rutherford said he believes he may have a lead on a paying passenger."

"Really? That was fast."

"It's just a lead, but he said if the client approves the latest proposal, we may be called soon to see if he passes our screening."

"Well, that's progress I guess," Tom observed. "OK folks, does that about cover it?"

Everyone murmured their assent. "Robbie, will you be able to host the next meeting?" Tom asked.

"With pleasure," Robbie replied with a smile. "We'll have Neverland West fully operational in the next week or so."

"Good to hear," Tom said. "Well everybody, it looks like things are coming along nicely. You all know the schedule, so you know what that means. It's about to get very exciting around here."

***

Sliding the lunch dishes aside to clear a space, Bob Brock dropped a manila folder on the table and pushed it toward Elton Funk.

"What are these?" Elton asked.

"Some pictures I took at RRI's facility in New Mexico. I thought you might be interested. I'd have emailed them, but ... "

"I understand," Elton nodded, reaching for the folder and opening it to examine the contents.

"I guess it can be a fine line between investigative journalism and industrial espionage," Bob said with a smirk.

"You could have overnighted them," Elton said absently, thumbing through the prints. "No one would have known that way."

"Well, I might have if I'd known how long it would take to meet."

"I've been pretty busy," Elton muttered. Looking up at Bob, he added, "we're having some teething pains with the life support system on our Minotaur capsule, and we had a deadline to meet for critical design review."

Bob grunted as Elton returned his attention to the pictures.

"These are obviously interstage assemblies," Elton said, pulling aside several of the pictures. "These concern me, because it means RRI is further along in assembling their rocket for the LCL One launch attempt than I thought."

"My friends at the Cape say they're planning a launch within a month."

"I've heard that also, but I thought it was just bravado. But these tell me otherwise." Looking up at Bob, he said, "Tom Armac knows if he gives me enough time, we'll find a way to lower our Raptor launch costs enough to beat him to LCL One. But if he's built the hardware he needs, he's brash enough to attempt a launch without doing sufficient testing."

"What do you make of the rest of it?"

Studying the photos again, Elton selected one showing an assemblage of framework and fuel tanks standing on four slender legs. "That's our Wizard engine," he said, pointing to the exhaust nozzle under the unit. "We sold that to RRI earlier this year, along with these attitude control thrusters," he added, pointing out the various details. "Their lead engineer told me they were designing an orbital propulsion module. Sharp lady. Very tough. This could be that unit, but I don't understand the purpose of these legs. Normally you'd build something like this in a support stand."

"They told me the legs were temporary and would be removed prior to flight."

"Hmmm. Maybe. But see here?" Elton said, pointing again at details in the photo. "These legs are articulated, like they're meant to retract. That wouldn't make sense for a temporary support rig."

"And these other items?"

"Hmmm. I don't really know. I see some tanks, obviously pressurized, possibly a manifold system of some type. Did they say what they were working on?" Elton asked.

"Just that they were doing some work on a new liquid fueled rocket of some type."

"Liquid fueled?" Elton said with surprise. "They've been fully committed to their hybrid designs. I never imagined they'd have the resources to do parallel development on a completely different system." Looking at the pictures again, he added, "I don't see an engine here, just fuel tanks and associated plumbing. The dimensions also seem wrong. If this were a new booster design, I'd expect it to be taller given its diameter."

"Well they kind of shooed me away at that point, it was pretty obvious they weren't interested in talking about it anymore," Bob said.

"If they're prototyping a liquid fueled upper stage, that means they're planning to take their business in a completely different direction," Elton said. *One that competes directly with our market*, he thought to himself.

"Well, you asked me to let you know what I turned up," Bob said. "I thought I'd be able to make something out of this, but right now I've got nothing."

"I wish I could help you sort it all out, but there's just not enough here to make a coherent whole."

"Yeah, well, I was hoping it might make some sense to you. I promised my editor some good articles, but right now I don't have squat. Needless to say, I'm number one on her shit list at the moment. One more question though."

"Yes?" Elton asked. "What's that?"

"Do you see any way that these items could be somehow related to the shuttle that RRI is refurbishing?"

Elton's forehead briefly furrowed, and then he smiled derisively. "Not that I can discern. What reason could you have for asking?"

"I can't come up with a good explanation for why RRI is paying to put Atlantis in a ready-for-flight status just to turn around and stick it in a museum."

"And where did you hear this?" Elton asked.

"Oh, I have a lot of contacts at the Cape," Bob replied. "And my sources tell me that Atlantis is being prepped like she was getting ready to be launched, not decommissioned like Endeavour and Discovery were."

Elton thought for a moment. "Well, I have no idea why they would do that, but I do know RRI is spending quite a bit of money preparing their museum in Long Beach. As for this," he said, gesturing toward the photos again, "I don't see any connection."

"OK, well, thank you Mr. Funk, and thanks for lunch. I guess I'll go back and try to find something in all this that I can turn into an article or two."

"Thank you for sharing what you've turned up, Mr. Brock. I'll have someone from our press office give you some advance details on our latest Minotaur configuration. You should be able to work that into an article. And here's my card. That's my personal number, please call me if you find out anything else that you believe may interest me."

Bob took the card, gathered up the photos and stood to leave. Then, turning back to the table, he said, "So honestly, Mr. Funk, the thought didn't cross your mind?"

"What thought is that, Mr. Brock?"

Bob pulled the photo of the lander propulsion module from the folder and dropped it back on the table.

"You don't think this could somehow be related to NASA's new lunar landing challenge?"

Elton looked at the picture again. "No, Mr. Brock, I don't." Looking up at Bob, he continued, "I would believe it ridiculous to think that a company that's yet to conduct a single launch would be building hardware for a moon mission." Glancing again at the picture, he added, "I'd say it's most likely just what they claim it to be—an orbital propulsion module." Pointing at the assembly, he said, "There's no place for crew."

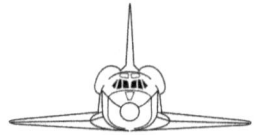

CHAPTER TWENTY–TWO

In dramatic fashion, Vivian had suspended a large fabric curtain between two stands of scaffolding outside of the shuttle maintenance and checkout facility for the unveiling. In front of the curtain sat a small set of aluminum bleachers that one of her engineers had found unused nearby. Most of the seating was occupied by members of Jean's flight control team. She had declared a break from mission rehearsals and had brought the group to Vandenberg to attend the event.

Mike, Carl and Luke had flown in from Kennedy Space Center earlier in the morning on a JetsOnline charter flight to be here for Vivian's big day. The amount of travel now being done between the east and west coasts made a charter membership more flexible and cost effective than flying commercial, and Tom had reluctantly approved the expense.

Tom parked his car after making the 17 mile drive to the north base from his office at SLC-6. Walking toward the grandstand, he anxiously scanned the sky. While the afternoon was still mostly sunny, dark and ominous clouds were starting to roll in from the Pacific Ocean, threatening the arrival of another Pineapple Express and the heavy rains it brought.

"You might want to hurry up and get this over with," he called out to Vivian as he took a seat between Robbie and Marcus. "It looks like it might start pouring any minute."

"Hush!" Nicole said to him from the row behind, while smacking him on the shoulder. "She's worked her butt off for this moment, don't ruin it for her!"

Vivian stepped in front of the suspended curtain and thumped on a portable microphone to verify it was operating. Raising the mic, she said, "Thank you everyone for coming. First of all, I'd like to thank Dr. Heinel for his vision and the guidance and assistance he gave us in bringing that vision to life, and without whom none of us would be here today."

The crowd politely applauded, while Mike, seated in the third row, let out a loud whistle and shouted "Yeah Dr. Carl!"

"Next, I'd like to thank all the members of the fabrication team, who put in long hours to finish this project on schedule."

Mike now stood and gave an exaggerated bow, and then pointed in turn to each member of his team while the others applauded again.

"And finally, I'd like to thank Marcus for his sense of whimsy, which made the selection of an appropriate name extremely easy."

Shrugging his shoulders and looking around innocently, Marcus said, "What, no idea what she's talking about!"

"So now, without further ado, here she is!" Vivian hit 'play' on the docked mp3 player on the chair beside her, and the strains of "Also Sprach Zarathustra" swelled triumphantly, echoing from the metal walls of the nearby building.

"Oh good God," Tom said, his head flopping backward dramatically.

"Stop it!" Nicole scolded, smacking him a second time.

On the third trumpet fanfare, two of Vivian's team pulled lines connected to the suspended curtain, which fell freely to the ground. Behind it stood the completed lunar lander, assembled and configured as it would appear when it touched down on the moon's surface. Emblazoned across one side was the name "Tinkerbell" and a large graphic of the feisty fairy trailing pixie dust.

"Tinkerbell? Seriously?" Tom said with exasperation, while Marcus and Robbie laughed appreciatively, jostling Tom with their shoulders as the crowd loudly applauded.

***

The group walked around the lander inspecting its various parts, while Vivian pointed out features and answered questions.

"So the whole lander returns to orbit? You're not discarding the descent section like Apollo?" asked one of Jean's launch control team.

"We've tried to keep the costs to a minimum," Vivian replied, realizing as she answered that while she recognized the individual, she had no idea who he was. *We've grown so much I've lost track of who's on the team!* she thought to herself. "And that means just one engine for both descent and ascent."

Jean stepped out from under the lander and looked up at the crew compartment. "How is Robbie supposed to be able to see to pilot the vehicle?" she asked. "There aren't any ports or windows that I can make out."

"I told her I could do it blindfolded, and she apparently took me up on it," Robbie said with a chuckle, walking over to join the conversation.

"It was another cost-driven engineering decision," Vivian explained. "When we saw the bid from RocketTech to put viewing ports in the

ShuttleHab module, well, we got pretty depressed."

"And we drank a lot," Robbie added. "But after we slept it off, Viv had another of her great ideas," he added approvingly.

"See this here?" Vivian asked Jean, reaching up to point at a small glass dome on the lander support strut above them. "That's an HD video camera. There are three more, there, there and there," she added, pointing in turn to the other three lander support struts.

"I'll be wearing a pair of 3D goggles that are fed from those cameras," Robbie explained.

"Won't that be a lot to manage, toggling between multiple cameras while trying to maneuver?" Jean asked. "I mean, the human factors issues ... "

"The goggles Robbie will wear contain a motion sensor," Vivian answered. "Whatever direction he looks in, that's the camera that will be active and feeding his display."

"And when I look up or down, software combines the feed from multiple cameras to give me true 3D for judging distance during landing or docking," Robbie added. "Pretty cool technology."

"It was all stuff we had sitting around in our games research department," noted Vivian. "I think some of the guys in programming originally wrote the software so they could fly model airplanes and feel like they were actually sitting in the cockpit."

Tyler and Marcus, on the opposite side of the lander, were examining the docking tunnel adapter the crew would use to enter the vehicle from the shuttle and through which they would exit to walk on the moon.

"Hey Viv, how's this supposed to work?" Marcus called out.

Walking over, Vivian said, "We thought the tunnel was going to be a big headache, but it turned out OK, and even came in under budget."

"Sweet," Tyler observed.

"RocketTech took a surplus tunnel adapter and split it into two parts," Vivian said. "It will connect the shuttle crew compartment to the lander, and it has this external hatch to let you exit to the cargo bay," she explained, pointing to the open access before them. "When the lander undocks, you'll deflate a pressurized collar that holds the two tunnel sections together," she continued. "One part remains attached to Atlantis, but this part goes with the lander to provide access to the surface. The lander will sit upside down in the cargo bay, but once it flips over and lands, the cargo bay access hatch will become your surface egress port."

Reaching up into the opening above her, she yanked on a metal ladder, which ratcheted down like a fire escape.

"And you'll use this to climb down to the moon," she added with pride.

"She looks great, Viv," Tom said, approaching the group. "So now that, ah, Tinkerbell is done, you'll be able to jump right on Atlantis when we bring her out in a couple of weeks?"

Before Vivian could answer, Tyler felt splashes of water on the back of his neck. Looking up at the darkening sky, he said, "Guys, looks like it's starting to rain."

Heavy drops from the rapidly approaching front began spattering about them, promising an intense shower. The entire group sought shelter beneath the lander, but gusts of wind began to blow the rain sideways, soaking them. Everyone dashed the thirty yards to the shuttle checkout and maintenance facility and stood in the open high bay door watching the rainstorm.

"Is she alright out there?" Tom asked Vivian, nodding toward Tinkerbell sitting in the weather.

"She can take high temperatures, hard vacuum, and micrometeorite strikes," Vivian replied confidently. "A little rain isn't going to hurt her."

The intensity of the shower increased, and streams of water cascaded off the lander's sides. A small trickle ran along the bottom of one of the craft's landing support struts, where it encountered a weld relief hole in the strut latch assembly. The break in the smooth metal surface caused the stream of water to detach from the strut and fall free to the ground. A few milliliters wicked into the hole, however, where it accumulated unseen inside the body of the latch assembly.

***

The sound of a Star Trek communicator informed Bob that he had new mail. Checking his inbox, he found a press release from RocketTech Corporation. *Hmmm. Haven't heard from* them *in a while*, he thought, opening the message.

RocketTech Delivers First ShuttleHab ADCAP Module.
RocketTech has delivered the first ShuttleHab Advanced Capabilities Module to Roadrunner Rockets Incorporated of Dallas, Texas. Among the improvements incorporated into the module were enhancements to the onboard life support systems, the addition of an internal fuel cell for generation of power and water, and alteration of the entry tunnel to incorporate a modular docking assembly. These module modifications enable the upgraded ShuttleHab to support independent orbital operations by a crew of two for a period of ten days. Crews of up to six can be accommodated for shorter duration missions.

It went on, but Bob had stopped reading. *RRI again*, he thought. *Christ, those guys are everywhere lately*. Scanning to the bottom of the press release, Bob found the contact information and dialed the number. "RocketTech, this is Martin," answered a bored voice.

"Martin, yes, hello, this is Bob Brock from the *Orlando Guardian*."

The media mention notably improved Martin's demeanor. "Yes, Mr. Brock, how are you today?" he asked cheerily.

"Great, thanks. Listen, I just received your press release. The one about the upgraded ShuttleHab module. I was wondering if I could ask you a few questions."

"Of course, Mr. Brock, what can I answer for you?"

"The improvements you've made to the unit. They basically make the module a full blown spacecraft?"

"Yes, isn't it exciting?" Martin replied. "It now incorporates every capability needed for completely independent operation on orbit except for propulsion and attitude control."

"Yes, really exciting," Bob replied blandly. "So, what, you'll just kick it out the hatch and let it drift around?"

"We believe the customer intends to attach their own external platform to add propulsion and maneuvering."

"I see. So this module was originally designed for shuttle operations, right?"

"Yes, it was originally designed to be flown within the cargo bay of a space shuttle."

"And did your customer change that?"

"I'm not sure that I understand your question," Martin replied.

"Did RRI request that you change anything on the module that would make it incapable of being flown on a shuttle in the future?"

"Well, no, in fact they were very concerned that none of the structural modifications would affect the external envelope and mount points. But why would you ask, Mr. Brock? There won't be any more shuttle flights after all."

"No, of course not," Bob replied. "Thanks Martin, I think I have what I need. Is it all right if I call you again if I have any more questions?"

"Absolutely, Mr. Brock, anytime at all."

***

Luke stood in Tom's office reading the press release. "Crap! Why in the hell did they do that?" he asked of no one in particular.

"It's publicity, it's just what you do," Tyler replied, sitting on Tom's credenza. "You always want to keep your name in the trade press. If your CEO's dog has puppies, you issue a press release."

"They're undoubtedly trying to reassure their shareholders and give their stock price a bump," observed Tom. "I imagine it's been pretty grim for them lately since the majority of their business was tied to shuttle operations."

"Unfortunately, we didn't think to forbid all release of news related to the project," said Nicole. "I'll take the blame, that was my oversight."

"It probably would have seemed pretty odd to them if you had," Tom reassured her. "Don't worry about it. No one is going to make anything of it, and tomorrow it will be totally forgotten."

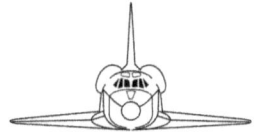

CHAPTER TWENTY–THREE

"Lower. Lower. A bit lower, Steph," Robbie directed, as he struggled to reach the OMS fuel module interconnects, his pressure suit making it difficult to reach through the module framework. "OK, just a little push now, down a half, more, a bit more, OK, *latch!*"

The capture light lit on the indicator panel to Stephanie's right. The panel had been added to the flight deck aft control station by Vivian's crew to show the manipulator operator when each OMS fuel module was firmly seated in the shuttle cargo bay. Breathing a sigh of relief, she released her clenched fist from the SSRMS arm controller and flexed her hand repeatedly. *Didn't realize I was gripping it so tight*, she thought. *Gawd this is nerve-wracking.*

"OK Steph, we're going to have to bring that in a little quicker next time," Robbie radioed from inside the training pool as he strained to reach deeper into the framework of the module. "I don't want to be out here all day." Mentally, he was already on orbit, rather than in the Space Dome's EVA training pool surrounded by scuba divers.

"Damn it, Robbie, I'm not used to having someone standing under a payload when I'm bringing it in," Stephanie complained. "I could do this a lot easier if you'd get out of the way while I'm seating the module."

"Can't do it, sweetheart," Robbie replied. "These damn interconnects get tangled up with the aft bulkhead fittings if I'm not in here holding them out of the way." Stephanie could hear Robbie's labored breathing as he struggled with the fittings. "I just can't … hold on to the suckers … they keep drifting," he added. "*Damn it!* OK, I'm done, get me outta here," he said with disgust.

The divers helped him onto the suspended platform, and he was winched clear of the water. As the platform landed on the pool's edge, a technician unlocked and opened the suit's rear hatch and he quickly climbed out. Turning to Vivian, who had been observing the session from a poolside monitor, he said, "We need to redesign those connections, Viv. There's no way I'm going to be able to hook those up in zero gee. The damn hoses dance around like snakes."

Vivian frowned deeply. "Robbie, it will take a month or more to build a new interconnect system, and the modules have already been shipped to the Cape. We can't afford to push the launch back, we need to figure out how to make this work."

"I'm telling you, Viv, I can't do this by myself." He paused to think for a moment. "Only way I see this working is if I have someone else in the bay with me, on the other side of the module. They could reach through from their side and help push the interconnects back toward me when they drift."

"But you need Stephanie at the RMS controls," Vivian protested. "And there's no way you'll be able to train one of us to operate the arm well enough in the remaining time."

"I know, I wasn't thinking of Steph. I'll need one of you out there with me."

"Go EVA in the cargo bay?" she asked incredulously.

"It won't be that tough to teach one of you to stand there and stay out of the way," he replied.

"Well, I guess that means ... " Vivian began.

"We're going to have to determine exactly who's going on this little adventure," Robbie said.

***

"Mr. Armac, we can't put this off any longer," Vivian explained to Tom. "We need to assign mission tasks, so we have to know exactly who's going to be onboard."

Tom nodded. "I know. I haven't been avoiding the decision. I've just been, well, putting it off."

"We've been looking forward to the day with a bit of dread ourselves, because that's the day a lot of people's dreams end," Vivian said, knowingly. "But it's a mission imperative now. Robbie has to have someone go EVA with him in the cargo bay for the fuel module captures, and we need to know who we have to work with. It's time to stop procrastinating."

"OK, you're right. Get everyone together at Neverland and we'll decide."

"*Everyone* everyone, or just the core team everyone?"

"The core team. You, Robbie, Marcus, Luke, Mike, and Tyler. Ask Dr. Heinel to come, he'll want to be there. And Nicole too."

"OK sir, it will take a couple of days, we'll have to arrange a jet for the Kennedy crew."

"That's fine," Tom replied. "A couple of days will be great, there's something I need to do first." Tom thought for a minute. "Viv, before the meeting, I'd like to get together separately with you and Marcus."

"Oh? Why is that, sir?" Vivian asked.

"It will make things a little easier, I think," Tom replied.

"OK, I'll set it up."

***

Vivian met Marcus in the Space Dome parking lot. "Any idea what this is about?" she asked.

"None at all," he replied. "Too early for Christmas bonuses," he added with his usual grin.

Entering the dome through the employee's entrance, they passed through the viewer's gallery for the small mission control center. Inside, Vivian and Marcus could see Jean running her team though another mission simulation. Watching them for several minutes as they worked through a lengthy checklist, Vivian finally turned to Marcus and said, "Let's go or we'll be late."

"Sure," he replied. "It's just so cool to watch them practicing. I want them good and trained when they launch us!"

The two exited the gallery and headed for the equipment staging room where Tom had asked them to meet him. Entering the room, Vivian and Marcus saw Robbie and Tom engaged in conversation. Behind them in its storage frame was suspended one of the Russian Orlan training suits, its rear hatch open.

"Ah, Marcus, Viv, glad you're here," Tom said. "Robbie and I have something to talk to you about."

"What's up, boss?" Marcus asked.

Tom looked at both of them grimly. "You know everyone's here today so we can talk about who's flying the mission."

"Sure boss, of course," replied Marcus, cautiously.

"I wanted to meet with you two first, before we sit down with the rest of the team." Tom looked at them each in turn. "Look. None of this would have been possible without either of you. You've thrown everything into this project and for that I'm more grateful than you can ever imagine."

Marcus had been on the receiving end of enough let-down talks during his football days to sense where Tom was heading. "I don't understand, boss … " he began.

Tom silenced him by holding up his hand. "Robbie, tell them."

"This is a Russian Orlan GN," Robbie said. "It's the training version of the Orlan MKs we'll be using on the trip. It has the same interior and exterior dimensions as the MK. Marcus, climb in."

"Me?"

"Yes, hop on in."

Marcus approached the suspended suit and eyed the access hatch. His shoulders were half again as wide as the opening, and he stood several inches taller than the suit. "How exactly would I … " he began.

"Grab it here with both hands," Robbie explained, pointing at the top of the access hatch, "and swing your legs in, followed by your upper body."

"Uh huh, sure," Marcus said doubtfully. Grabbing the suit as indicated, he turned sideways and inserted his right leg. When he turned to bring his left leg through the access, his hips wedged in the opening. "I think I'm stuck," he said, wiggling strenuously.

"OK, let me help you out," Robbie said, grabbing Marcus around the waist and yanking him free.

Marcus stood dejectedly before the suit. "So I'm too damn big," he said.

"That's what I wanted you to see, Marcus," said Tom. "What's the suit designed for, Robbie?"

As if reading from a sales brochure, Robbie rattled off, "The improved Orlan MK will accommodate individuals from 165 to 190 centimeters in height." Turning to Marcus, he added, "That's five foot four to six foot three, my friend."

"And you're, what, six five?" Tom asked. "And close to 300 pounds?"

"Two hundred eighty," Marcus confirmed glumly.

"So you see, brother, you just don't fit," Robbie said sadly.

"And so I don't go," Marcus concluded.

"You don't go," confirmed Tom. "Viv, you're next."

"That's OK, sir, it won't be necessary." *Five foot four—I'm not that tall in heels*, she thought.

"Try it, Viv. There's always a chance," said Tom encouragingly.

Robbie was yanking the straps on the suit to shorten it to its smallest possible size. When he finished, Vivian approached the suit, kicked off her shoes, and grabbed the top of the access hatch. In one smooth movement, she lifted her legs and gracefully swung through the access and into the suit. And disappeared.

Robbie and Tom approached the suit and peered through the visor. They could just make out the top third of Vivian's head inside the helmet.

With a snort, Robbie doubled over in laughter. Holding his middle with one arm and attempting to catch his breath, he said, "I'm sorry Viv, but that's the funniest thing I've ever seen," and started laughing again.

"Ha ha ha, very funny," they heard echo from inside the suit. Vivian climbed out the rear access and recovered her shoes. "I'm five foot one on a good day," she said.

"Viv, step outside a moment," asked Tom. "I want to talk to Marcus for a second. Don't go anywhere though."

Vivian looked at Tom quizzically, and then turned and left the room. As the door closed, Tom put his hand on Marcus' shoulder. "I never thought we'd make this trip without you, my friend."

"I get it boss, it's OK. Damn my big bones anyway."

"Marcus, listen. We can't take you, but Robbie and I have figured out a way to take Vivian. I wanted to talk to you about it first though. This isn't the way I thought it would go. I really planned for you both to come with us. But she's designed a lot of the stuff we're going to use on this trip, and we need her onboard in case there's a problem."

Marcus looked momentarily confused, but then broke into a bright grin. "You can take her? Really? She deserves to go. That's great news, she'll be so happy!"

A lump formed in Tom's throat as he was briefly overcome by emotion. "You're a good man, Mr. Short," he finally said, clasping Marcus' hand. Pausing for a moment, he added, "OK, send Viv in, and then go tell the team we're on our way."

"You got it, boss," replied Marcus. Opening the door, he motioned for Vivian. As she entered, he gave her a big hug, physically lifting her off the floor, and then put her down and left.

"What was that?" she asked, startled.

"Just Marcus being Marcus," Tom said with a laugh. Picking up a package from a nearby chair, he tossed it to Vivian. "Here, put that on. Join us in Neverland when you're ready."

***

Tom was happy to see that the glue stick and sparkle Neverland sign had been brought from Dallas and hung with pride over the door to the room at Space Dome that was their new operations center. The white boards from the old conference room at Altered State had been carefully packed and then re-hung in their new location without so much as a smudge. A superstition had arisen during the move that having to re-create any part of their original notes, plans, or diagrams would bring bad luck to that part of the mission.

Everyone looked up as Tom and Robbie entered the room. "I'm glad everyone could make it on such short notice," Tom observed. "Good to see everyone's smiling faces again."

"Where's Vivian?" asked Nicole.

"She'll be here shortly," Tom answered. "OK, so this is the day we all knew was coming," he began. "Crew selection." There was a murmur of nervous acknowledgement from everyone. "Robbie and I have talked at length about who would be the best addition to the crew. No point in dragging it out, here's what we've decided.

"First, as those of you who were at our first meeting may remember, we promised Dr. Heinel that in exchange for helping us, he'd get to go with us.

So welcome aboard, Dr. Heinel," Tom said, nodding to the doctor.

"Thank you, Mr. Armac. I am very much looking forward to the trip," Carl replied with a smile.

"Next, as you all know, I've paid for all this," Tom said, looking around the room, "so of course, I'm going."

A chuckle spread quickly through the room.

"Robbie's commanding the mission, and he's picked Stephanie Peters to fly as pilot, so that makes two more."

Everyone nodded assent.

"We're taking two passengers, who have yet to be identified, but their seats are reserved. One is being brokered by Destination Beyond, and the other will be for whoever wins Tyler's lottery," Tom said.

Six, everyone thought to themselves. *There's only one more spot.*

"Speaking of Tyler," Tom continued, turning to face him directly. "Managing the mission sponsors and riding herd on the press will really kick into high gear once we're off. So I'm sorry, but you're needed here to oversee that," Tom stated.

"I know, I never expected to make the flight, but I appreciate being considered," Tyler replied gratefully.

"You earned that consideration, enough said," Tom confirmed. "Nicole? You and I both know we're going to need you here protecting our backs from the FAA and NASA. I don't even think you'll get to watch the launch, you'll be so tied up in court," Tom added with a smile.

"You're most likely right, unfortunately," Nicole said sadly.

Everyone turned to look at Marcus. "Don't look at me!" he said. "Couldn't pay me enough to strap myself to some crazy-ass rocket."

Tom smiled warmly at Marcus. "Marcus and I have already discussed it, and we both agree that we need him here overseeing the ground operation. So, that leaves you two," he said, looking at Luke and Mike. "Luke, Hot Wax was your idea. Next to Dr. Heinel, we probably owe you more than anyone else for getting us this far. Welcome aboard, we'd like you to join us."

Everyone applauded, approving the selection. If it couldn't be them, then Luke was everyone's second choice.

"Mr. Armac?" Luke said hesitantly. "I, well, the truth is, I don't really want to go."

Everyone was stunned to silence. A seat on the mission was the golden ticket that they had each hoped for since the very beginning.

"Luke? Are you sure?" Tom asked. He hadn't anticipated anyone turning down a chance to make the trip.

"Mr. Armac, my wife and I talked about it. We talked about it a lot. There's the baby, and we just found out she's pregnant with our second ... "

Tom held up his hand. "It's OK Luke, I understand."

"It's just that, you know, if something happened to me … "

"It's OK Luke, really. You have your priorities and your family comes first." Everyone then looked at Mike, watching as his face reflected his dawning realization of what Luke's refusal meant. "I'm going," he muttered. "I'm going!" he said loudly. "I'M GOING!!!" he shouted, jumping up from his seat and dancing.

"Dude, tell us how you really feel," chuckled Marcus, as Mike continued dancing around the room.

Just then, the door to the conference room opened. Framed in the doorway stood Vivian. She was wearing a skintight nylon and spandex suit that covered her from neck to calves, white with blue accents, along with tight black leather boots. Cradled under her left arm was a blue space helmet with a polished gold visor.

Mike stopped dancing as everyone's jaws dropped.

"Daaaaaaaaaaaammnn," Marcus quietly exclaimed.

"Oh, I almost forgot," said Tom, smiling at Vivian. "Robbie and I were talking about the shuttle recently." Turning back to the team, he said, "Did you know you can mount an additional seat on the middeck? Turns out the shuttle can carry eight, and not just the seven we thought." Looking again at Vivian, he said, "Welcome aboard, Viv. We're taking you with us."

***

"It's called a space activity suit," Tom explained, as Vivian examined the material of the outfit she had recently removed. "Robbie did some consulting with the company that provides pressure suits for Galactic Journeys' passengers on their suborbital flights. We'll be using those same ones ourselves for launch and re-entry. Unfortunately for you, they fit pretty much the same size range as the Orlan. But he knew they were doing some developmental work on this new type of suit, and they can be made a lot quicker and in a larger range of sizes."

"How does it work?" she asked, examining the interior of the collar.

"It's basically a body condom," Robbie said with a chuckle. "Instead of providing full pressurization like a normal space suit, it uses spandex to compress the body, simulating the effect of gas pressure. The only part that's really pressurized is the helmet. It has to fit like a second skin to work properly though."

"So I'll be the only one wearing one of these?"

"Yep, like Tom said, the rest of us will be using standard pressure suits for the launch," replied Robbie. "We talked about letting you go without a suit, we actually used to launch shuttles that way for a while, but we decided it was just too risky."

"Also, Viv, it's not an Orlan," said Tom. "You can't wear that outside the ship, it's not really designed for it."

"Actually, you'd probably be fine for a short duration excursion," said Robbie. "As long as you stayed out of the direct sun. It doesn't have the facilities to maintain body temperature that a pressurized suit does."

"My point is, you can't take it out on the surface of the moon," Tom said.

"Oh, definitely not," confirmed Robbie. "The sun would cook you."

"So that means when we take the lander down, I'm afraid you'll be staying onboard the shuttle with Stephanie."

"That's all right, sir, at least I get to go. I just wish it wasn't so, well, tight."

"Truth is, Viv, that one there is a demo," Robbie said. "The real one will be much tighter, a custom fit."

"But it already looks like body paint."

"Well, we can probably get some kind of coverall for you to wear over it if you don't feel like sharing the goods with the whole world," Robbie joked.

***

"OK Steph, down one, again, hold it, *latch!* Much better!" Robbie said. "Mike? *Mike!* Hellooo! Stop breathing so hard, you'll wipe out your air in no time."

"Sorry Robbie, it just freaks me out a little. I'm not used to being underwater like this," Mike said, the strain evident in his voice.

"That's OK. Tell you what, next day off we get, I'm taking you to get started on your scuba certification. There's a good dive shop here in town I can hook you up with. Now push that connector back this way."

"OK, sounds good, here you go," Mike replied, leaning into the module framework and pushing the fuel connector towards Robbie.

"OK, great, got it, *got it!*" With a snap, the fuel interconnect engaged with the cargo bay aft bulkhead fitting. "Now the other one. Good, good, *got it!*" Both connections were fully engaged.

"That's it, Steph, we're done. Coming out!" exclaimed Robbie. "Tell Viv we're good to go, the extra set of hands makes all the difference."

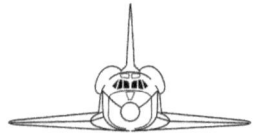

CHAPTER TWENTY–FOUR

The day dawned bright and clear, the sun slowly rising from the ocean and illuminating the sky with a rosy golden glow. The brilliant white lights that had shone on the towering rocket through the dark night switched off as the dawn reached out for the booster with luminous orange fingers. At the base of the rocket, the launch pad crew completed their final tasks and departed, the flashing lights of their vehicles fading into the pre-dawn shadow. Finally, the rocket stood alone, silhouetted against the glowing sky, wisps of white vapor swirling from multiple points along its body.

Against the backdrop of what was now stillness and quiet, a thousand things were occurring silently, unseen. Multiple systems checks were electronically performed, the results carefully measured and tabulated. At each critical threshold, computers would acknowledge and record the data and then evaluate the next in turn, until finally, they reached agreement that all was ready.

"We are go for launch, the vehicle is now on internal power," declared Jean Lutz, the launch director, from her remote location in Long Beach. The electrical service arm rapidly swung clear. Deep inside the rocket, the flight control system computer now managed every remaining step of the process. Cycling a bank of relays, it applied battery power to a set of heater strips, warming the liquid oxygen tanks. Measuring the temperature rise, satisfied with the result, it then opened a valve allowing high pressure helium to enter the tanks.

Sensors confirmed that proper tank pressure had been achieved. "We have O_2 pressurization, we have a commit," Jean announced. The remaining tower swing arms quickly retracted, leaving the rocket bound to Earth by only the launch pad hold-down clamps.

Noting that all servicing arms were clear and satisfied that systems were at nominal pressure and temperature, the computer checked the navigation and guidance system one last time for a final positional fix. The system then commanded the oxidizer pintle valve to open. Instantly, pressurized liquid oxygen was forced through the injector nozzle, which imparted a turbulent swirl to the unbelievably cold liquid as it rushed down the length of the central fuel port.

Sensing that the fuel grain was now completely bathed with a wave of semi-gaseous oxidizer, the computer performed the final act necessary to bring the rocket to life. Energizing a ring of pyrotechnic initiators mounted just below the injector nozzle, the burst of intensely hot particles ignited the oxygen paraffin fuel. In milliseconds, the flame front rushed down the length of the fuel port. Like an awakening fire breathing dragon, the rocket began to exhale.

"We have ignition," announced Jean.

While waiting for thrust to build, the computer rapidly swiveled the vehicle's exhaust nozzle 360 degrees to verify proper operation through its full range of motion. Inside the rocket engine's fuel port, temperature continued to increase until fuel surface vaporization began. Combustion now detached from the fuel grain's surface and moved to the entrained fuel mist in the turbulent boundary layer generated by the oxidizer injector assembly. Thrust instantly leaped to maximum.

The computer noted the jump in thrust, now exceeding four million pounds furiously pulling against the pad hold-down clamps. One, two, three seconds slowly ticked by as it verified that pressures and temperatures remained within carefully calculated limits. Finally, satisfied that all the data readings were exactly as they should be, the computer commanded the frangible nut detonators to fire, releasing the hold-down clamps and freeing the rocket from the restraints that held it to Earth.

"And *liftoff* of the first Big Brother Single for its initial LCL One qualification launch!"

The flight control computer sensed the earth fall away, continually measuring the distance that separated the rocket from the pad below. When that distance exceeded the height of the support tower, it began pitching the vehicle eastward onto the proper course to achieve orbit.

Data poured in from multiple sensors, which the computer observed and compared to nominal values while simultaneously transmitting them to the ground as a stream of telemetry. Forty-five seconds into the flight, the guidance system noted a deviation from the programmed flight path, which the flight control computer acknowledged. Stronger winds than the system has been programmed to expect were generating a shear force, nudging the vehicle off course. Evaluating several options, the computer elected to increase the rate of climb in order to punch through the wind shear as rapidly as possible. Quickly clearing the layer of high altitude winds, the computer then gently guided the rocket back onto its intended upward arc.

For slightly over two minutes, the Big Brother booster burned hundreds of thousands of pounds of fuel and liquid oxygen, generating millions of pounds of thrust. The rocket's flight control computer closely monitored the rate of fuel consumption while continuing to fly the vehicle along the center of the prescribed launch track. It sensed the brief oscillation in exhaust pressure that indicated pending fuel exhaustion, followed by the total loss of thrust as the motor burned out. "First stage burn concluded within expected parameters" the system radioed in the appropriate computer language to its brother systems on the ground. The rocket continued on its parabolic arc.

***

Tom and Marcus craned their necks to follow the ascent of the rocket as it rose higher and higher in the early morning sky. The rest of the team had gathered in small groups around them. No one spoke. There was nothing to say. The team had exchanged more words than could be counted getting to this point, but now there was nothing left but to bear witness, wordlessly, as the tangible results of their years of effort rose toward the heavens on a pillar of flame.

"We have conclusion of first stage burn, standing by for confirmation of staging, all systems nominal," Jean announced from mission control.

Tom and Marcus continued to follow the vehicle, which was reaching the limits of their visual perception. Without taking his eyes off the sky, Tom quietly asked, "Do you believe in God, Marcus?"

Marcus looked briefly at Tom, and then returned to watching the sky. "Sure boss, doesn't everybody?"

"No, not really. Many don't," Tom said.

"Well boss, I played a lot of ball," Marcus replied. "I saw some good friends go down with bad injuries. The worst kind, the kind that leave you wishing you'd died. And when the coach came into the locker room and said, 'Men, let's pray he'll be all right,' I never once saw anyone who refused." Looking at Tom, he added, "People who say they don't believe in God are just people who haven't yet suffered a serious enough blow."

Looking back at the sky, he said, "Why do you ask?"

"I keep thinking about how what we're doing right now—this path we're on—is something that was set in motion almost fifty years ago." Tom glanced at Carl, who was standing nearby beside Mike. "All the people, all the things that led to this ... it just seems like it's something that's supposed to be." Tom looked back at the sky. "And it has me thinking ... "

"Well, I believe they call that taking stock of your life," Marcus observed. "You wouldn't be the first person to get closer to God as a result."

"I used to believe we each made our own destinies," Tom continued musing. "But I had nothing to do with Luke's ideas. Or Vivian's parents moving to this country so their daughter could have a better life. Or Carl's tragedies and all he's been through. But they happened, and here we all are as a result. We're each as affected by those and a hundred other things as if they'd happened to us personally." Tom continued studying the sky. "So I know we're going to do this thing."

"This thing? Go to the moon?"

"Yes. I used to have doubt. A lot of doubt. But not anymore. This is something that's meant to be."

"Because God wants it?" Marcus asked, amused.

"God. The universal spirit. Whoever or whatever decided 50 years ago to start the dominos falling."

Marcus smiled. "God's a good person to have in your corner. We could do worse."

***

The flight control computer calculated that the rocket had coasted sufficiently, and issued commands to the second stage to prepare it for firing. Once readings indicated all was in readiness, it detonated the fasteners holding the interstage assembly between the two boosters, freeing the second stage for flight. Powerful springs, now released from compression, pushed the stages forcefully apart, while a small thruster fired on the now expended first stage, causing it to tumble. Even in the extremely thin air at this great altitude, the tumble would increase drag to more rapidly decelerate the booster, allowing it to fall clear without interference and begin its inevitable drop back to Earth. Miles below, people were already rushing into position to recover it.

Sensing that the second stage was safely clear, the computer now ignited the Little Sister rocket that comprised the upper half of the vehicle. Throttling quickly and smoothly to 100% thrust, the now lighter vehicle accelerated rapidly to orbital velocity. The flight control system relayed the good news to the ground below.

***

"Staging complete, second stage ignition confirmed," Jean announced with excitement tinged with pride. While she always took figurative ownership of every rocket she launched, this was the first that she literally owned a piece of. Her future was tied to its success in a way that had never before been true.

She looked up briefly from her console to quickly observe her launch control team as they intently focused on the displays before them, their faces illuminated by the streams of data rapidly scrolling across their monitors. She was pleased by their professionalism and how quickly this amalgam of former NASA engineers and young computer geeks had

145

coalesced into a cohesive team. They had learned their jobs well—an observer would have thought that this was their twentieth launch, rather than their first.

Glancing over her shoulder, she noted the dozen or more people behind her in the viewer's gallery, their faces pressed against the glass, displaying expressions of anticipation, awe and delight. She debated whether it would be professional to give them a quick wave, but before she could decide, an electronic whoop jerked her attention back to the control room. One of the engineer's faces was now illuminated by a red glow emanating from his display.

***

An aberrant reading onboard the Little Sister rocket generated an interrupt that momentarily demanded the flight control computer's primary focus. An unusually high temperature reading was detected in the lower fuel segment. Isolating the pressure sensor data in the immediate vicinity, the computer compared the readings. Calculations indicated an anomaly—pressures didn't match the temperature indicated. The system diagnosed a failed temperature sensor and isolated its data stream from the digital data flow. Establishing a separate processor thread to maintain an eye on the errant sensor, it deactivated the alarm and returned its primary focus to piloting the vehicle.

***

"Flight, systems, the board is green again, all readings nominal."

"The board is back to green, acknowledged," Jean replied with relief, while scrutinizing her master display.

***

Aiming for a 20 meter circle in space, the computer compared internal inertial data with external GPS readings and determined that it had hit the bulls eye. Meeting its programmed objectives, it shut off the flow of liquid oxygen and snuffed out the engine. The rocket coasted into orbit.

***

"Second stage burn concluded. Little Sister has achieved stable orbit." The pride and satisfaction was evident in Jean's voice. Everyone had been waiting to hear those words: achieved stable orbit. An incredible amount of blood, sweat, tears, love, anxiety and effort had gone into accomplishing what could be stated with just three simple words.

A beaming Congressman Daisy approached Tom, slapped him on the shoulder, and then grasped his hand and began pumping it vigorously. "One hell of a show, young man! One hell of a show!" he said. "When's the next one going up?"

"Thank you Congressman. Let's get through the rest of this flight before we start planning the next one," Tom cautioned.

"Well I'm looking forward to seeing you accept that nice fat check!" Will said, as he turned to leave.

Tom thanked each team member individually. "Everyone deserves a good rest," he said. "As soon as the party is over!"

Carl approached Tom as the group began to leave the viewer's gallery and head toward the telemetry center. "You appear to have done it, Mr. Armac," he said with a gentle smile.

"Yes, Dr. Heinel, it appears so," Tom replied. "Now the fun really begins."

***

The expended Big Brother first stage tumbled rapidly toward the ocean below. In a carefully timed sequence, its recovery logic controller preformed its programmed duties, releasing a drogue parachute to stabilize the falling rocket, followed by the main parachutes to slow its descent.

Suspended now by an acre of fabric, the booster floated rapidly downward until it impacted the water at 50 miles per hour, throwing an enormous column of spray into the air. The booster's body trapped air inside, causing it to bob back to the surface and float vertically, the top 30 feet standing clear of the water like a lighthouse.

Approximately 10 miles away, the captain of the M/V Freedom Star had been following the descent of the booster. He now ordered the throttles forward on the ship's diesel engines and accelerated toward the expended rocket. Pulling cautiously up to the gently bobbing booster, divers entered the water and installed the nozzle plug to seal the end of the rocket so that it could be pumped free of water, while lines were prepared to grapple and tow the booster back to shore.

"Sure looks just like an SRB," a deck hand observed, as he attempted to get a line on the casing floating beside the ship.

"It is, just with a different fuel I guess," replied a second. "I heard it uses candle wax."

"No shit?" said the first. "Now how the hell do you think they got a candle to fly like that?"

"Don't know, it's a new type of rocket, they call it … wax something, can't remember, ah, *bikini* wax, that's it." Both men laughed as they hauled on lines.

***

"So we have several important announcements to make today," Tom said to the reporters and space center workers interested enough to attend the post-launch press conference. "First, let me give you an update on today's flight." Reading from a sheet of paper, he said, "At 7:23 AM, the first Big Brother Single lifted off on its maiden flight. This is the first of two launches through which we expect to claim the NASA Low Cost Launch Centennial Challenge prize. The only issues noted were some minor sensor discrepancies, which were diagnosed and corrected by the onboard systems."

"Why do you call it Big Brother Single?" asked a voice from the crowd.

"Because it uses a single Big Brother Hot Wax booster as the first stage."

"And what is hot wax?" the same voice called out.

"It's the internal name we gave to our paraffin fueled hybrid rocket designs," Tom said, glancing at Luke and smiling. "It sort of stuck."

"Will there be other configurations?" asked another voice.

"Yes, we intend on our next flight to launch a Big Brother Twin, which will be a super heavy lift vehicle based on two Big Brother boosters, but more on that later. Please hold the questions and let's finish talking about this flight."

Resuming reading from the page in his hand, Tom continued, "After a successful separation, the second stage," looking up at the audience, he said, "we call that a Little Sister, for obvious reasons," then, returning to the prepared comments, "the second stage successfully achieved planned orbit at approximately 7:31 AM. Remaining mission objectives are the recovery of the expended Big Brother for return to Kennedy Space Center for refueling, and an on-orbit restart of the Little Sister to raise its orbit. We expect that to occur in two days. We want to let the rocket acclimate before we test the on-orbit restart capability." Looking up from the prepared comments, he said, "Are there any questions?"

"Does this launch mean you've claimed the two hundred million LCL One prize?"

"No, not at this time," Tom answered. "Winning LCL One requires demonstrating the ability to orbit a payload for under $250 a pound. In order to determine our total launch cost, we will need to recover, refuel, and re-launch the Big Brother booster that flew this morning. Then we'll claim the prize."

"So you're sure you'll beat the cost necessary to win?"

"Absolutely. With the superior characteristics of our design, we're sure we'll beat it comfortably."

Bob Brock stood up. "Mr. Armac, why do you believe your design is better than that being developed by other commercial launch companies? The EtherX Raptor, for instance."

Tom bristled. "Sir, the Raptor core unit uses nine liquid fueled engines. Their super heavy lift version uses three Raptor cores. That's twenty-seven individual rocket engines with high speed turbine pumps, bearings, valves, plumbing, and so on that all have to work perfectly on every launch. Then they have to tear down and inspect the whole assemblage before they can certify it for re-launch. Our Big Brother booster has one hybrid rocket motor, with only one major moving part, the oxidizer pintle valve. To re-launch the booster, we merely pressure wash out the expended fuel segments, fill them full of wax, reassemble the stack and refill the liquid oxygen tank. Now you tell me which sounds like the cheaper, more reliable option."

Bob sat down as the audience chuckled. Another member called out, "When do you think you'll be ready to conduct your next launch and claim the prize?"

"The Big Brother we launched this morning is already on its way back to be refueled," Tom replied. "We're estimating we'll be ready in less than a month."

"What can you tell us about the Big Brother Twin?"

"The vehicle will be very similar to what we launched this morning, with the exception that it will have two Big Brother boosters as the first stage. This will give the launcher the ability to place one hundred metric tons in low earth orbit."

The members of the aerospace press were momentarily stunned. The holy grail of launch capacity—one hundred metric tons to orbit. For less than $250 a pound!

Everyone started talking at once. Tom held up his hand and began speaking again. "This brings us to the next item we wanted to discuss this morning." Looking over his shoulder at the other team members on the podium, he smiled broadly, nodded, and mouthed "Here we go," and then turned back to the audience.

Tom took a deep breath. "Ladies and gentlemen, I'd like to announce that with the launch of our next rocket, we will be embarking on a bold new journey. Having met the challenge of achieving a dramatic reduction in the cost of access to space, we wish to employ that capability to expand man's reach beyond Earth orbit. Our next launch will be carrying a payload into space. That payload will be the first component of a spacecraft we will assemble in orbit. A spacecraft that will become our planned lunar voyager, with which we intend to embark on the first commercial manned expedition to the moon."

What followed could best be described as pandemonium.

***

"Tonight on *Evening Line*, we examine today's announcement by Roadrunner Rockets Incorporated of their intention to undertake the world's first commercial moon voyage. Here's our chief science editor Marshall Wheeler with more on the story. Marshall?" The network news anchor swiveled in his chair to face the monitor behind him.

"That's right, John. They call it the Lunar Voyager. Details are currently sketchy, but based on a diagram that was briefly observed at this morning's press conference at the Kennedy Space Center, Roadrunner Rockets apparently intends to build a spacecraft composed of a pair of Russian Soyuz capsules attached to a central truss that will contain the fuel, oxygen, and other items necessary to undertake the long voyage."

"After over forty years since man last walked on the moon, what revolution in space flight technology now makes a trip like this possible?" John asked Marshall's projected image, expertly following the prepared script.

"Two things, John. First, there is today's announcement by Roadrunner Rockets of a stunning new launch vehicle. Belonging to a class known as 'super-heavies,' their Big Brother Twin booster will be capable of lofting one hundred metric tons into low earth orbit." The screen momentarily switched to a computer animation of a Big Brother Twin lifting off. "That's one hundred thousand kilograms, or roughly a quarter of a million pounds," Marshall said for the benefit of the American viewing audience, who were not as familiar with metric measurements. "This will allow them to orbit the necessary components, which can then be assembled into the Lunar Voyager."

"And what's the other advance you noted?" John asked, exactly on cue.

"Simply this, John. After over fifty years of manned space flight, there now exists a huge stockpile of surplus space hardware, much of which has a lot of life still remaining in it." The view now switched to a scene from within the warehouse of Kramden Sales of North Hollywood, where a local Los Angeles reporter had walked the aisles earlier in the day gathering footage for the segment. "As you can see, John, here at this aerospace industry salvage store you can purchase anything from a pressure modulator to a complete rocket engine for pennies on the dollar, making it possible for someone without the resources of, say, the US Government, to be able to afford to build a functional spacecraft."

"That's amazing, Marshall. But where will Roadrunner Rockets find the people to fly their Lunar Voyager to the moon and back?"

"Well John, as you know, with the end of the shuttle program, a lot of experienced astronauts have left NASA and entered the private sector. Speculation is that Roadrunner Rockets has hired several of these highly trained experts to pilot their proposed lunar mission."

"I see. But will only highly trained astronauts be able to embark on this voyage?" John asked, already aware of the answer.

"Not at all, John. In a stunning departure from past practice, Roadrunner Rockets is proposing to bring along a member of the general public. Yes, you heard me right," Marshall said, turning to look directly into the camera. "One of *you* will have the opportunity to join the crew of the Lunar Voyager and walk on the surface of the moon."

"That's amazing, Marshall. How exactly would that person be chosen? I'm sure there are millions of viewers who would love to have the opportunity to go."

"Well, John, Roadrunner Rockets has created an international online lottery to select one lucky individual to accompany the crew of the Lunar Voyager on their historic mission. Simply go to www dot my moon voyage dot com where you can purchase a chance to participate in this amazing adventure."

"Are there any restrictions on who can be selected?" John asked.

"The company declared this morning that anyone who can pass a qualifying physical and complete the required pre-flight training is eligible. Oh, and they will also have to be fluent in English, in order to ensure good communication during the flight. See their crew selection lottery website for additional details.

"And what was that website again?"

"John, it's www dot my moon voyage dot com," Marshall replied, while on the screen viewers could see the URL being typed into a browser, which then jumped to the lottery home page.

"Got it, Marshall, thank you. I'll certainly be checking it out after tonight's broadcast," John said with a false laugh, and then turned back to the camera. "Up next on *Evening Line*, new research shows that bananas may improve your sex life ..."

***

"Son of a bitch," Elton Funk muttered, angrily switching off his television.

"Son of a bitch," Tyler Allen exclaimed, as the lottery servers crashed from the load of tens of thousands of simultaneous hits.

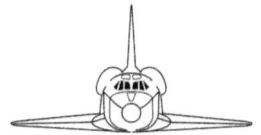

CHAPTER TWENTY–FIVE

Tom stood with Keith Barton and Congressman Daisy at the bottom of the boarding stairway that climbed to the 747 parked before them, while Marcus and Nicole conferred briefly with one of the flight crew. Atlantis sat securely fastened to the aircraft's back, ready to leave the Kennedy Space Center on its journey to California. Behind a barrier tape boundary, a large group of Alliance Space Systems employees and NASA personnel had assembled to bid a final farewell to their old friend of almost 30 years as it departed on what they believed would be its last flight. A smaller group standing to the side carrying an assortment of duffels and overnight bags waited to board the plane.

"This must be what if feels like to be President," Tom chuckled, looking up at the huge aircraft, and then stepping to the podium to address the crowd and the small group of reporters that were waiting.

"I don't really have much to say in the way of prepared remarks," Tom began, reciting the remarks Nicole had prepared for him, "except this: thank you. Thank you for entrusting us with the task of preserving and protecting this wonderful piece of history, this incredible machine, Atlantis."

Spontaneous applause and a few appreciative whistles rose from the assembled crowd.

"Thank you for the opportunity to prepare Atlantis for its next and final mission—her most noble mission of all. Like other great ships before her: the Constitution, the battleship Missouri; Atlantis will become a memorial dedicated to preserving the memory of the wonderful feats it performed and commemorating the courageous acts of the men and women that operated and maintained her."

A longer and louder wave of cheers and applause erupted from the crowd, which persisted for several moments.

Tom held up his hand to quiet the crowd. "And finally, but most importantly, to continually challenge and inspire future generations to achieve even greater things by following her example and the trail she blazed."

Tom stepped back from the microphone, rejoining Keith and the Congressman, who added their own enthusiastic clapping to the crowd's thunderous applause. As the clapping finally subsided, Tom stepped forward again and said, "Are there any questions before we're off?"

"Mr. Armac! How long will it be before Atlantis is put on display?" a local TV reporter shouted.

"We expect that we will have Atlantis ready for her big debut within three or four months."

"Why are you taking Atlantis to Vandenberg Air Force Base rather than directly to Los Angeles?" another reporter asked.

"Vandenberg has the runway and equipment necessary to handle the shuttle carrier aircraft, and it will be easier to transport Atlantis from there to the Aerospace Museum of the Pacific by barge. If we flew into Los Angeles or even directly into Long Beach, there's no easy way to get Atlantis from the airport to the museum."

"Why will it take three or four months to get Atlantis ready for display?" shouted a voice. "Endeavour and Discovery were ready in much less time."

"Well, it's primarily due to some delays we've had with the Long Beach facility," Tom answered, having anticipated the question. "We do of course have some additional work to do on Atlantis, and that's another advantage of taking her to Vandenberg, where there are excellent facilities available where we can finish her preparations."

Bob Brock waited for his opportunity. "Mr. Armac, can you tell us why you had Atlantis prepared for flight, rather than decommissioned as the other shuttles were?"

Nicole's head snapped around, and she left her conversation and started easing toward the podium. Tom and Keith exchanged a few words, and then Tom said, "Mr., Brock is it?"

"Yes sir, Bob Brock, *Orlando Guardian.*"

"Well, Mr. Brock, it's no different than when an aviation museum does a complete restoration on an old aircraft."

"How do you mean, sir?"

"An old plane only needs to *look* good for display, the public doesn't care if things are missing inside. But a curator wants every part fully restored as if the craft were just manufactured. We haven't had Atlantis prepared for flight, we've had her restored to flyable condition. There's a difference."

Nicole slid quietly behind Tom.

"It doesn't seem like much of a difference to me, sir," Bob continued.

"It certainly wasn't necessary with the other two."

"Yes, well, let's just say that the facilities where Endeavour and Discovery will be displayed weren't as concerned about the financial aspects as we are with Atlantis. Feel free to contact our office if you'd like more information."

"But sir, I'd like to know … " Bob began, before being cut off by Nicole as she stepped around Tom and spoke into the microphone.

"I think that's all we have time for today, ladies and gentlemen," she said. "The carrier crew needs to leave immediately to beat a weather front that's approaching." Turning to Tom, she quietly said, "Let's go, now."

Tom nodded to Keith, who in turn made a gesture toward the small group waiting with suitcases. The dozen or so men and women began climbing the stairway to board the plane.

Tom shook Keith's hand, and said, "Thank you Mr. Barton, it has been a pleasure working with you."

"Take good care of Atlantis for us, Mr. Armac. Do her proud!" Keith said with emotion. "She's been a terrific lady. We'll miss her."

"Don't worry, we have some great plans for her," Tom replied with a wry grin. "I think you'll be really pleased at the outcome when we're done," he added.

"We'll see you back here in a few weeks for the next launch?" Keith asked.

"Absolutely, we've been working on the LCL One prize for five long years, there's no way I'd miss being here when we cross the finish line."

Will Daisy then stepped up and shook Tom's hand. "I can't tell you how glad I am that you came to my office that day," he said. "It's meant the world to these people to have a real program to work on again."

"None of it would be possible without the work you did on the amendments to the Commercial Space Launch Act that you pushed through," Tom replied. "If there's anyone here that deserves thanks, it's you."

He's actually starting to get pretty good at this, Nicole thought warmly.

Tom turned and followed Nicole up the stairway to the aircraft's door, looking up with a thrill at Atlantis perched on the 747's back. *Oh, the things we're going to do together!* he thought.

Marcus, having boarded during Tom's speech, stepped out of the aircraft and met Tom on the top landing of the stairway.

"OK, boss, everything is looking good for the flight," Marcus said.

"Aren't you coming back to Vandenberg with us?" Tom asked.

"Not right now. I decided to stay here with Luke a little while and see if I can help," Marcus answered. "For the next couple of weeks this is where the action is going to be, getting ready for the next launch. Jean and Robbie have things running so smoothly at Space Dome it's kind of boring there right now. I mean how many mission simulations can a man sit through? I'll be back out in a week or so."

"All right, we'll see you in a bit." Shaking Marcus' hand, Tom watched as he started down the stairway. He then looked out over the crowd, and couldn't resist the urge to raise his arm above his head and wave. *Yep*, he thought, smiling, *just like the President!* He then turned and entered the aircraft.

Any notion that he was an important person was instantly dispelled upon boarding. The truly important passenger was mounted to the top of the huge plane. The people on board were of secondary concern. Looking to his right, he could see the interior of the aft three quarters of the aircraft. It had been completely stripped to the bare aluminum, with frames and plumbing plainly exposed to view.

"This way, Mr. Armac," Tom heard. Nicole was standing in what remained of the former first class compartment, summoning him. Several rows of worn gray leather seats sat forward of the spiral staircase that ascended to the upper level, surrounded by stained and wrinkled blue carpeting loosely held down with Velcro. The group that had previously boarded were still getting settled, attempting to shove their bags into the few remaining overhead luggage bins.

"Come, sit," Nicole said, patting the back of a window seat in the last row.

Tom slid into the indicated seat and raising the window screen to look out.

"Quite a week," Nicole observed with a sigh, sitting in the seat next to him and buckling her seatbelt.

"Yep, quite a week," Tom nodded. "It has been that."

***

As the 747 began to taxi toward the runway, Bob worked his way through the crowd towards Keith and the Congressman.

"Sad to see her go," Bob observed, as he reached Keith's side.

"Yes, it is," Keith replied. "But she's going to be well looked after."

"I still don't understand this whole shuttle swap thing going on between Roadrunner Rockets, the Smithsonian, and that museum in Long Beach," Bob observed.

"You still don't get it?" Keith asked with a touch of contempt.

Bob was startled by Keith's tone. "No, not really. For instance, I don't understand why they'd put so much money into making Atlantis flight ready, nor why it will take another four months to roll her out for display. I thought their facility in Long Beach was getting ready to open soon."

"Well, let me explain the money issue," Will said. "Completely off the record," he added.

"OK, sure, off the record."

"You know RRI's Space Train is going to mean the world to the workers here at the Space Center?"

"Yeah, sure, I get that," Bob replied.

"And you know that they're on the verge of winning LCL One?"

"So I hear."

"Well, Mr. Brock, for doing so they will win a considerable sum of money. Two hundred million dollars."

"OK," Bob said, waiting for Will to make his point.

"Mr. Armac apparently feels that that money will go a long way toward funding the next phase of Space Train development. And creating jobs here in Florida. Provided he doesn't have to pay a third of it in taxes."

"Wait, you're saying ... " Bob began.

"Boy, we have to draw you a picture today," Keith noted. "What's an operational space shuttle worth, Bob?"

"Hell, I have no idea."

"A lot," Keith said. "A lot more than RRI has in it to make it flight ready."

Realization finally began to dawn on Bob. "So the difference between what they've invested and what it's worth ... "

"Will result in a significant deduction they can apply against their earnings once they donate Atlantis to the charitable foundation they've established to run the Aerospace Museum of the Pacific," the Congressman said. "Nicely done actually, it should just about result in their LCL One prize money being tax free."

"So the whole thing is just a huge corporate tax write-off," Bob said.

"You say that as if it's a bad thing," observed Will. "Look at everyone who's being helped here. Los Angeles gets a new aerospace museum, the folks here have jobs, the country, hell, the *world* gets cheaper access to space, and eventually the Smithsonian will end up with a fully restored orbiter to display on permanent loan. All for the cost of a few million in lost taxes that we probably wouldn't use half as well."

"Christ, that explains a lot," Bob said. *You can certainly tell I'm no business major*, he thought. "With some of the things I've come across, I was beginning to think that they were actually planning to try and fly Atlantis."

Keith laughed, while Will slowly shook his head in disbelief.

"That's absolutely crazy," Keith said, wiping laughter induced tears from his eyes. "You've been around long enough to know what it takes to launch a shuttle, Bob. How the hell do you think they'd be able to do something like that?"

Bob's response was drowned out by the roar of the heavily laden 747's engines spooling up to full power as it began its take off run. Slowly the aircraft gained speed as it advanced down the runway and then ponderously lifted into the air. Banking one time around the Kennedy Space Center in a final salute, the craft then pointed north and disappeared into the distance.

"So were those your people boarding the flight before it left?" Bob asked Keith as they turned toward the parking lot. "I thought I recognized some of them."

"Yes, they were some of my orbiter servicing team leads," Keith replied. "RRI asked us to provide some senior technicians to help with the final preparations out at Vandenberg."

"Wait, what?" Bob asked, stopping. "Why on earth would they need more support after everything you've already done to prep the orbiter?"

"Bob, for Christ's sake, let it go," Keith said impatiently. "It's a tax thing, nothing more."

Bob scowled, lost in thought, as they started walking again. Then he remembered something he'd made a mental note to bring up. "Where's the Pegasus, by the way?" he asked.

"Pegasus?" Keith said.

"The external tank transport barge. I noticed it wasn't in the vehicle assembly building basin when I came in. Where'd it go?"

"It left this morning, heading to Michoud in New Orleans," Keith replied, referring to the facility where shuttle external tanks were manufactured.

"Michoud? What the hell for?" Bob asked.

"RRI wants the tank that was built for the cancelled STS-136 flight."

"Wants it for what?"

"To display at their museum in Long Beach."

Bob stopped again, turned, and looked directly at Keith. "I've seen the drawings for the Aerospace Museum of the Pacific," Bob said.

"Yeah, we all have," Keith replied, matter-of-factly.

"There is no place in that entire facility with the room to display an external tank."

***

"Please tell me there won't be a ceremony when we get to Vandenberg," Tom said, looking out the window at the passing clouds. "I want Viv to get Atlantis into the maintenance and checkout facility as quickly as she can."

"Well, the Air Force does love ceremonies," Nicole said with a wry grin. "But with the refueling stops, it will be late afternoon by the time we make it in, so I can't imagine there will be much planned."

"Any word on our launch site operator's license?" Tom asked, leaning back in his seat.

"I expect to hear final word from Dick McConnel soon," Nicole replied. "Stop worrying so much!"

"It's just all coming together so nicely now," Tom replied. "And experience tells me that that's when something usually bites you in the ass."

***

Bob sat slowly rocking in his office chair, looking again at the artists conceptions of the Aerospace Museum of the Pacific. *There's still something here that just isn't adding up*, he thought. *There is NO place here with the room to display an external tank.*

Opening his inbox, he dug back through his recent mail. *Where is it where is it there it is*, he thought, opening a press release he had received the previous week.

The Aerospace Museum of the Pacific announces the planned opening of Space Dome, the interactive space flight exhibit featuring actual space shuttle hardware. Experience the thrill of a simulated shuttle launch. Watch former NASA astronauts conduct simulated mission training. Don a spacesuit and take the controls of an orbiter flight simulator. Tour the operations center and watch members of mission control as they manage commercial satellite launches. Get up close and see behind the scenes of space flight today. Space Dome—the world's premier interactive spaceflight experience.

The notice was an invitation for members of the press to tour the facility prior to the grand opening to be held later the following month.

Three to four month delay my ass, Bob thought. *I need to get out there and see this. But there's no way Marion is going to approve another trip. Not for a damn museum opening.*

Bob debated his options, and then made his choice. *Oh well, technically, freelancing isn't unethical as long as I tell the paper.* Reaching for his phone, he dialed Elton Funk's number.

***

The 747 banked gracefully over the Pacific Ocean and then lined up with the long concrete runway for its final approach. The sun, low in the western sky, illuminated the coastline with a golden light, enhancing the colors and contrasts of the California hills and headlands.

The plane flared and floated down the length of the runway, touching down lightly and then shuddering as the pilot applied brakes and reverse thrust to slow the heavily laden craft. Rolling smoothly to a stop at the runway's southeastern end, the pilot then slowly eased the plane toward the taxiway where Atlantis would be de-mated from the carrier aircraft and towed to the shuttle checkout and maintenance facility.

As the plane rolled to a stop for a second time, Tom looked out the window and swore. Outside, he could see Vivian smiling broadly and waving her arm over her head. Behind her on an elevated platform sat dozens of uniformed personnel sparkling with gold braid and surrounded by flags. He could just make out the sound of the band starting to play.

"It's not funny, damn it!" he said, as Nicole sat beside him laughing deeply.

***

Like the other Alliance Space Systems personnel onboard, Juan Meneurez unbuckled his seatbelt once the plane had stopped, and stood up to recover his overnight bag from the overhead bin. Peering out the window, he took in the view of the central California hills while waiting for the arrival festivities to end. He'd never been to the west coast before, but he'd jumped at the chance to earn some serious overtime pay doing the final inspection and closeout work on Atlantis. When contacted by his former employer about the job, he thought the work should be easy, because who really cared since Atlantis would never fly again. More importantly, it allowed him to put three thousand miles between himself and his soon to be ex-wife Theresa, or "the skanky bitch" as he referred to her, with whom he was currently embroiled in a bitter divorce battle.

Maybe I'll even stay out here and see if I can get on permanent, he thought, enjoying the view outside. *I'm sure they can use a top notch tech once this Atlantis BS is over. You just never know what can happen* …

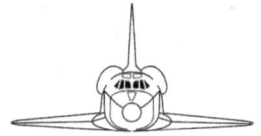

CHAPTER TWENTY–SIX

Tyler tossed restlessly, alternately pulling up and kicking off the thin sheet that covered him. Though asleep, his mind worked furiously, inventing numerous elaborate scenarios and playing them through, denying him the rest he needed.

"Honey, what's wrong?" Tyler's girlfriend Eva asked sleepily, reaching out to touch his shoulder, noticing he was damp with perspiration.

"Uh, guh, wha," Tyler muttered, awakened by her touch. "Uh, nothing baby, it's OK." One particular scenario played out in his mind, and he lay there, half awake, watching it as if it were a television show. A television show. *A television show!*

I need … need to write … write this down, he thought, desperately wanting to capture the image in his mind, realizing if he fell back asleep, it may be days, months, never before he dreamed of it again.

Willing himself awake, he began fumbling with the light, knocking the clock onto the floor in the process. "Honey, what's going on?" Eva asked, sitting partially upright and rubbing her eyes.

"Nothing, baby, it's OK, I just need a drink of water, and I want to write something down before I forget it."

"OK," Eva said, rolling onto her side and pulling one of her pillows against her stomach.

Tyler rummaged briefly though the nightstand drawer. "Babe, do you know where I can find a sticky pad?"

"There're in the kitchen desk drawer, where they've always been," she sleepily replied into her pillow.

Tyler walked slowly into the kitchen, shaking his head lightly to clear the cobwebs from his mind. Flicking on the light above the stove, he rummaged through the desk area drawer until he found a notepad and pen. Slowly but deliberately he wrote a few brief words describing the vision stuck in his head. Peeling off the note and sticking it to the refrigerator, he filled a glass with water and drank it, while staring at the note. Finally, finishing his water, he turned off the light and went back to bed. His mind now at rest, he lay down, patted Eva's behind, and then fell immediately asleep as she pushed back to spoon up against him.

***

Nigel hoisted the bottle of gin to his lips again, taking another deep swig, killing the bottle. Throwing it aside, it smashed to pieces, producing a shower of glass shards that skittered across the polished concrete of the studio floor. Leaning unsteadily against the wall, he wiped his mouth and bloodshot eyes with his right sleeve. Pushing himself back upright, he then staggered to the double glass doors that opened into the now dark kitchen set.

Nigel stopped and stared at the doors, rocking unsteadily on his feet, and contemplated the large *Menu Wars* logo etched in the glass. Leaning his head back, he laughed drunkenly.

"*Menu Wars*? Bloody *Menu Wars*? My bloody arse!" he slurred. "A big sodding farce is what it is!"

Nigel pushed the doors to enter the kitchen, but found them locked. Looking around, he spotted a fire extinguisher hanging from a nearby support. Removing it, he hurled the heavy metal cylinder at the doors, shattering the glass in an explosion of diamond-like crystals. Picking up the extinguisher again, he then proceeded to beat on the door frame about the lock area. Finally realizing the futility of his attack on the lock, Nigel switched the extinguisher to his left hand and reached through the shattered glass of the door frame to unlatch the bolt from the inside, in the process opening up his forearm from wrist to elbow on a sharp glass shard.

Pushing open the now unlocked doors, Nigel roared in pain and anger as he charged into the kitchen set, where he began systematically battering everything to pieces with the heavy extinguisher.

"Nigel, stop it! Stop it right now!" he heard from behind him. Twirling unsteadily, he turned to find Melissa, his publicist, standing in the shattered glass doorway.

"Bugger off, you!" he yelled, raising the extinguisher threateningly.

"Nigel, I know you're upset, but we need to get out of here right now. Studio security has called the police," Melissa said urgently.

"What the bloody hell are you doing here?" he yelled, again wiping his eyes with his sleeve, this time covering his face with blood from his forearm, stinging his eyes.

"I was worried that you'd do something stupid. Everyone at the party could see how drunk you were. Now come on, let's *go*!"

"You don't give a bloody whit about me or my cooking! It's all just a

161

sodding show to you. Just *entertainment*," he spat, as he turned and started smashing the glass doors of the row of ovens behind him. "You know I won today, I beat those other bloody bastards!"

"Nigel, I know, but the producers think it's better television if you lose occasionally. It keeps the viewers engaged."

"Bollocks on the bloody viewers! It's bloody *Menu Wars*, and my food bested theirs! You know it did!"

"Nigel! We can talk about this outside. Now stop that right now and come with me!" Melissa stepped forward and grabbed Nigel's arm as he drew back to swing the extinguisher at another oven front. Howling in pain as Melissa's fingers tore at his wounded forearm, he swung around suddenly. The fire extinguisher crashed hard into the side of Melissa's face with a sickening thunk, and she dropped to her hands and knees, moaned deeply, and then fell onto her stomach amid the blood and broken glass.

Nigel stood unsteadily, contemplating Melissa's prone form for a moment. "Good bloody riddance," he exclaimed, and then, pulling the pin on the extinguisher, began spraying thick white powder over her and the remainder of the kitchen.

***

"A game show?" Tom asked skeptically. He had learned to trust Tyler's instincts—his best ideas had initially seemed the strangest.

"Not a game show, Mr. Armac, a reality show," Tyler replied.

"But the lottery has already started. We're up to," turning to Marcus, he asked, "how many tickets sold?"

"Two million, four hundred thousand and change as of nine o'clock this morning," Marcus replied.

"Two million. Do we really want to do anything at this point that messes with that?" Tom looked at Marcus, who simply smiled and shrugged his shoulders.

"Absolutely. We absolutely do, and here's why," Tyler explained. "The lottery is generating a lot of interest, for sure. But it's also about the sponsors. We're hoping to raise one to two hundred million from sponsorships. Right now, the only thing we have to offer them is a chance to attach their name to a historic event. So far we're off to an OK start, but a lot of them are having trouble seeing the benefit. So think about this. Instead of selecting our final passenger with the lottery, we use it instead to pick ten or twelve semi-finalists. Now we've got these people, and we have them actually compete for the chance to go with us on the flight."

"You mean a *Survivor* in space kinda thing?" Marcus asked.

"Yes, sort of. We run them through all the training we know they're going to need for the flight, and in the process present them with a bunch of different mission-related challenges. Then each week, the crew votes off a member."

Marcus intoned in a deep voice, "I'm sorry, but the crew has spoken. They do not wish to fly with you."

"Yes, exactly!" Tyler exclaimed. "So for, I dunno, ten, maybe twelve weeks, we have this show to choose the last passenger. And the sponsors will love it. They'll love it because they'll understand it! Instead of just offering them an opportunity to slap their logo on our rocket, they'll be able to have product placements for an entire television series, leading up to the actual mission. The flight then becomes the "stunning series finale." I'm telling you, it will work. It'll drive sponsor interest through the roof."

Tom had been sitting impassively, his face blank. Now, the corners of his mouth curved slightly and then steadily grew into a huge grin. Shaking his head slowly, he said, "Tyler, I don't know how you do it, but you've definitely found your calling in life."

"And you want to know the best part?" Tyler asked. "We drop this all in the lap of a production company, and they actually end up doing all the work and paying for training our crew member. It's not much I know, but it helps."

"Hey, a million here, a million there, and before long we'll be able to buy enough fuel to come home," Marcus said.

"So how would we actually pull something like this off?" Tom asked. "We can run the lottery, it's almost entirely online, and we have a lot of good computer talent. But I don't have a clue how you'd go about producing a television series. And is there even enough time?"

"You're right, obviously this requires outside help. Plus we'll have to move pretty quickly, because it will take a while to pitch it, and then get it produced and aired. I took some marketing classes with a guy who's an assistant producer now for a production company in Hollywood. If you're OK with the idea I'll give him a call and see what he says."

"Nicole? Would it be legal to change the terms of the lottery?" Tom asked.

"We stated in the rules that the terms and conditions for selection are subject to change at our sole discretion, so yes, we can do pretty much whatever we like. Just to be fair though, we may want to provide everyone who has already purchased a ticket the option to opt out and get a full refund."

"I'll be surprised if anyone objects," Tyler observed. "We promised to pick a winner, and we will. But this way, a dozen people get to become minor celebrities in the process."

"So what would we call it?" Tom asked.

"Seems obvious," replied Tyler. "We'd call it *The Last Passenger.*"

***

Len Goldman glowered at the group seated in his office at New Millennium Multimedia. "Is she pressing charges?" he asked sourly.

"Yes, she is," answered Ron Nement, NMM's lead attorney. "She's looking at partial facial reconstruction and potential long term medical issues, undoubtedly a lawsuit, so pressing charges would be the logical thing for her to do."

"Great. That's just freaking great," Len observed. "So where does that leave us with the network?"

"The doctors say she'll be fine eventually, in case you were concerned," said Lanetta Rawls, executive producer for *Menu Wars*, with a trace of sarcasm. Reaching into her bag, she pulled out a photo of Melissa Martez that had been taken in the hospital emergency room and threw it on Len's desk.

Len glanced dismissively at the battered and bloody face and then looked back at Lanetta. "Uh huh, glad to hear it. So what about Nigel?"

"He's been charged with aggravated assault and attempted murder, so even if the studio was willing to drop the destruction of property charges, it wouldn't help much," said Ron.

"That's just freaking great."

"This is, what, the third time Nigel's been drunk and gone out on a bender this year?" Lanetta said. "The judge told him the last time that if he didn't get into rehab and an anger management program, he'd be looking at some serious jail time. They'll drop the attempted murder charge I'm sure, but he's still facing a physical assault charge. I'm afraid they'll have his balls."

"There's nothing we can offer this Melissa girl to make this go away?" Len asked.

"Len, did you look at that picture?" Lanetta asked. "That's a piece of her *skull* there, above that big gaping wound."

"But Nigel Carneel IS *Menu Wars*. We can't just drop in another celebrity chef in the middle of the season and expect that no one will care. The network will scream. It's his volatility that the viewers love." Len turned to Bruce Trunly, Lanetta's lead production assistant. "Bruce, how many episodes are in the can?"

"Three. We have the 'Ultimate Pig Roast' and the 'Ostrich Surprise' episodes wrapped, and 'King Carnivore' is in final edit," Bruce replied.

"Three. OK, let me think," Len said, sitting back in his chair and making a steeple with his fingers. "How hard would it be to get some of the past challengers back for additional episodes?"

Lanetta and Bruce exchanged puzzled glances. "To do what?" Lanetta asked.

"We have three episodes in the can," Len explained. "If we can get some of the chefs Nigel previously beat to come back and do, hell, I dunno, maybe a bitch-fest episode with highlights of some of Nigel's rants, or maybe even some head-to-head cook offs, we could probably milk our outtakes for another couple of episodes."

"And then what?" Lanetta asked. "Without Nigel, we can't finish the season, and the network will sue us for breach of contract."

"Look, that will buy us at least four, maybe as many as six weeks if we sneak in a rerun. Don't you think Nigel will be clear of this by then?" Len asked.

Lanetta glanced with exasperation at Ron. "He's still not getting it," she said.

"Leonard, Nigel is going to jail," Ron explained. "Jay A Eye El *jail*. He's not coming back. Not for twelve to eighteen months anyway."

Len's face started to display panic. *Menu Wars* was NMM's top grossing show. To sell it, he had given the network an ironclad guarantee that they would be able to control their volatile chef and deliver a complete season of what had become the highest rated cooking reality series in the country. "Well I guess we're totally screwed then," he said with resignation. "The network will sue the living crap out of us."

After a moment of silence, Bruce quietly said, "What if we offered them something else?"

"There isn't anyone else of Nigel's caliber available," Lanetta said dismissively.

"No, I mean something else to fill in while we're waiting for Nigel to clear the legal system. Another show. Something the network can use to plug the hole in their schedule until *Menu Wars* can resume production."

"Another show?" Len asked. "What other show? We don't have anything else in the pipeline, and the only concept even under discussion is that damn pet tricks show for the Tiny Tykes network."

"A friend of mine just called me last week pitching an idea," Bruce said. "I was going to bring it up at the next production meeting. Get this. It's a space exploration concept. Part reality adventure, part docudrama. They called it *The Last Passenger*."

"Go on," Len said, skeptically.

"It's those people with the lottery, the one to go to the moon. The idea is to assemble a pool of candidates, and then run them through a series of challenges every week, with the weakest performer being eliminated each episode. The last person standing goes on their moon trip with them."

"You're serious?" Len asked.

"They are, yes. They've already announced the trip, and they're doing that lottery thing now," Bruce said.

"Lanetta?" Len asked hopefully.

"Well," she replied, thoughtfully. "If it were done on location, no sets or props, we just needed to run a video crew with some steadicams, we could be in production in less than a month," she replied. Turning to Bruce, she asked, "They're talking pure reality, with a *Colossal Race* format? Each week is a competition and then someone gets the axe?"

"That's what they're saying," Bruce replied. "No special effects, no stunts, no scripts, just real people going through real astronaut training."

"So say a week of post-production on each episode. We could be on air in six, maybe eight weeks," Lanetta concluded.

"I dunno. Sounds like it could be boring as crap," Len said. "People love *Menu Wars* because of Nigel's antics. You never know what to expect. What's the hook with this?" Len asked.

"Did you miss the part about going to the moon?" Bruce answered. "This isn't *Celebrity Dancing*, where at the end they hand out a trophy and everybody goes home. The final episode of *The Last Passenger* is a two week live trip to the moon."

"So we're talking adventure *and* danger," Len said, visibly warming to the idea. I'm liking this. I'm liking this a lot. And you know what I like the best?"

"What's that?" Lanetta asked.

"If this doesn't totally suck and we're able to get ten, maybe twelve weeks of programming out of it and keep the network happy, it gives us time to work a deal to get Nigel paroled. He'll be a *convicted felon* celebrity chef—he'll be freaking *huge*. Who else has one of those, baby? Who else has one of those! We just doubled our ad rates!" Turning to Bruce, he said, "These space guys. Who's their rep?"

"They're not working with an agent that I'm aware of," Bruce replied. "Like I said, it was just a call from an old friend. I really don't think they know much about the business."

Len smiled his predatory shark grin. "Get them in here, fast," he said to Bruce. "Let's see what they've got."

***

Tyler was sitting with Marcus and Nicole in her office when his phone buzzed. They had been reading the details of the counterproposal that AT&T had submitted for the right to be the sole telecommunications sponsor for the flight.

"Tyler Allen here," he said. "Oh, hey Bruce, how are things? Really? That's great! Sure, we can do that. Let me check with my boss and I'll get back to you. Yes, soon. OK, bye."

"Good news?" Nicole asked inquisitively.

"Yeah, really good news," Tyler replied. "That was the guy I know at New Millennium. He ran *The Last Passenger* by his team, and they think they might like to produce it. They want to know if we can come by tomorrow and give them the details."

166

"Come by where?"

"They're over in Van Nuys. Just a couple of hours from here."

"Awesome, let's tell the boss," Marcus said, excitedly.

"Well, I guess the terms of this deal just changed," Nicole said, closing the folder on the AT&T proposal.

Walking next door to Tom's office, Nicole tapped on his door. Marcus impatiently pushed it open.

"Hey boss," Marcus called out, "Tyler's got something to tell you. We're gunna be TV stars!"

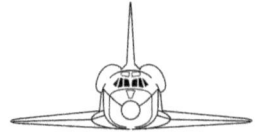

CHAPTER TWENTY–SEVEN

Robbie was getting very tired of the drive from Long Beach to Vandenberg. But Vivian needed his expertise in evaluating the work being done to prepare Atlantis. So on Mondays, Wednesdays and Fridays he performed mission rehearsals at Space Dome, but on Tuesdays, Thursdays and Saturdays he made the three hour drive north, leaving Long Beach at five o'clock in the morning to be another set of eyes at the maintenance and checkout facility.

I'm glad this should only last another month, he thought, as he made the turn into the facility parking lot just in time to see the sun start to clear the hills to the east. *Today should be an interesting day though.*

Tinkerbell had been split into her two components: the former ShuttleHab module that would be the lander's crew compartment, and the propulsion unit that had been fabricated by RRI. The crew compartment was being loaded into Atlantis' payload bay today, while the propulsion unit, its articulated legs now folded compactly into their stowed position, sat waiting on a nearby support stand. The crew compartment would be installed in the forward part of the bay, connected to Atlantis' mid-deck airlock by the docking tunnel. For balance reasons, Atlantis would launch with the lander propulsion unit mounted in the aft section of the bay. Before it could be loaded, the work to install the new fuel interconnects through the payload bay aft bulkhead had to be completed.

The small team Vivian was managing, assisted by the technicians from Alliance Space Systems, was working twelve hour shifts to complete the necessary modifications to prepare the shuttle for flight. While the schedule was ambitious, it was achievable, if just barely, because most of the work had been completed before Atlantis left the Kennedy Space Center. They had begun work that day, as they did every day, at seven o'clock in the morning. Nobody was getting much sleep.

Nodding to the guard at the door, Robbie noted as he entered the building that they were making good progress. The crew compartment was already suspended over the forward part of the payload bay. *Now it feels like we're getting somewhere*, he thought.

Spotting Vivian on an elevated catwalk near Atlantis' tail, Robbie donned his hardhat and headed for the stairway to join her.

***

Juan dropped heavily into the commander's seat on Atlantis' flight deck, plopping the large test procedures manual he carried onto the console beside him. Leaning back against the headrest, he wearily rubbed his eyes to clear his vision. He'd been given a tip that the Flight Line Sports Bar in Lompoc was a great place to meet lonely Air Force wives from Vandenberg Village looking for some company while their husbands were deployed.

I'm getting too old for this shit, he thought, as he pressed on his forehead with his fingertips to try and relieve the headache that was building. *I didn't think that bitch was ever going to give it up.*

Since yesterday was Friday, he had headed to the bar immediately after his shift, and had found it to be what the Air Force called a "target rich environment." After testing the waters with several different ladies, he finally settled on a raven haired beauty with great tits named Melissa. Or maybe it was Alyssa. He wasn't really sure. In any event, while friendly and flirty, she'd been a real challenge. It had taken most of the night and a half dozen top shelf Margaritas before he'd convinced her to leave. After more drinks at her place, it had been almost 4AM before he'd finally slid between her thighs and collected his prize for the effort he'd invested. Now here he was, with virtually no sleep and too nauseous to eat breakfast, caught in that painful stage between the night before and the morning after.

It's going to be a screamer, he thought of his developing headache as he pressed his knuckles to his temples. Then smiling despite the ache, he thought, *just like she was while I was banging her.*

OK, gotta get some work done. Don't know why we're bothering with this shit when this bird's never flying again though. Sitting upright in the seat, Juan opened the reaction control system maintenance manual and turned to the test procedure checklist. This morning's plan was to run through RCS electrical systems checks one last time before signing it off as flight ready.

Juan read aloud from the checklist to help himself concentrate. "Aft RCS fuel system breaker to off." Killing the power to the fuel system control valves would allow him to test the system's pressurization, logic and alarm circuits without actually firing the rockets.

Climbing from the seat, Juan moved to the flight deck circuit breaker panel indicated by the procedure. As he stood, a hammer hit him deep in his skull, bringing tears to his eyes, and then started a softer pounding in time with his pulse.

Christ I need to quit drinking tequila, he thought, as he reached for the panel and fumbled for the appropriate breaker.

Juan almost got it right. He flipped off the aft RCS heater control breaker instead.

***

Robbie stood with Vivian on the catwalk platform alongside the port Orbital Maneuvering System pod, observing the work being done on the new fuel system interconnects in the payload bay below. "It's coming along quickly," he noted with approval.

"We're just teeing into the existing systems, it's not much more than your standard aerospace grade plumbing," Vivian replied. "We do that pretty well," she added, smiling.

***

"RCS mode switch to manual, test switch to test," Juan read aloud. Putting the system in manual test mode allowed the control circuits for each reaction control system rocket to be individually tested and overrode the fuel tank level sensors that would normally prevent tank pressurization from occurring when the fuel tanks were empty.

"Rotate aft RCS helium isolation valves to open," Juan continued reading, performing each step in turn. He noted that the amber caution lights switched to green on the status panel, indicating the appropriate fuel tanks had pressurized properly.

***

What the hell is that? Robbie thought. He heard a whirrrrr-click from within the OMS pod beside him, followed immediately by the whoooosh of pressurized gas. He glanced at Vivian, who was deep in discussion with her shift leader. He unconsciously noted she stood directly in front of the port RCS thrusters.

***

"Aft port RCS tank isolation valve to open." The indicator panel showed that the cluster of rockets in the aft reaction control system now had pressure to their individual isolation valves. Juan hiccupped convulsively and then fought to swallow a mouthful of acidy bile that erupted from his empty stomach as he checked off the next step.

***

Robbie heard another click, followed this time by a quick, higher pitched pssssst. Looking at the cowling that housed the reaction control system rockets, he mentally peeled away the skin of the pod and visualized the plumbing and hardware within. In fractions of a second, he reconciled the sounds he heard with his knowledge of the systems within.

Someone's firing the freaking reaction control system! he realized, and then dove for Vivian.

***

"Aft port RCS 1 isolation switch to open," Juan read, as he reached for the designated switch. With the RCS fuel system breaker open, nothing should happen, but because the system was in test mode, the indicator panel should show a good burn.

***

Robbie hit Vivian squarely in the back, knocking her over and landing on top of her as they were enveloped in a cloud of venting gas. For an instant he thought they were going to die, incinerated by the exhaust plume of the rocket motor pointed directly at them. As the realization dawned on him that they weren't being burned alive, his mind raced.

Just venting gas, he thought. *Like someone hit us with a fire extinguisher. What is this, some kind of freaking practical joke?*

Quickly scanning the faces of the other workers, Robbie noted that no one looked amused. Most were startled, some actually afraid. *Not a joke then. So what the hell just happened?*

"Jesus, Robbie, what the hell was that?" Vivian asked, as she extricated herself from underneath him.

"Someone fired the RCS. I thought you were dead," he replied, standing.

"But the system isn't fueled, there's no way it could fire," Vivian replied, confused. Then, sorting it out, she stood on her tiptoes and gave Robbie a kiss on the cheek. "Thanks for saving my life though," she said, smiling. "Or at least thinking you were."

"Yeah well, I'm not here every day, so I'm not up on every little detail," he said. Then, his anger building, "Who the *hell* is on the flight deck?"

***

"We don't have the people to provide a test supervisor for every evolution," Juan's foreman explained to Robbie. "It was a simple test that he's done dozens of times. It shouldn't have been a problem."

"But he's drunk," Robbie replied, still fuming. "And he could have killed someone."

Juan stood uneasily, his head bent, as both men glared at him. "Look, I fucked up, I know it," he offered, attempting to mitigate the damage. "I'm in the middle of a shitty divorce, and sometimes I can't sleep, and a few drinks help—you know how it is?" he asked, hopefully.

"What do you want me to do?" the foreman asked Robbie.

"If he were my man, I'd can his ass on the spot," Robbie replied.

The foreman frowned. Alliance was a big company with strong labor rules, and he couldn't fire an employee for a first infraction. Turning to Juan, he said, "You have a week's unpaid leave, and I'm making a disciplinary entry in your personnel folder. After your week is up, and *after* you complete four hours of safety training, report back to me so I can decide if I'm going to let your sorry ass go back to work."

It hurt Juan more than they knew. *Docked a week's pay with overtime, but I still have to support the skank back in Florida and cover my expenses here*, he thought bitterly.

"Now get your ass out of my sight," the foreman concluded. "And if you show up again with even a whiff of booze on your breath, you're outta here," he warned.

***

Nicole and Marcus sat on one side of the chrome and glass conference table at New Millennium Multimedia's offices, facing Len Goldman, Lanetta Rawls and Ron Nement. At the end of the table, Tyler sat next to his college friend Bruce Trunly.

"We like the concept, and if we can work out the production details, we want to pitch it to the network and move out on this right away," Len said.

"When is 'right away'?" Nicole asked.

"Like immediately, as in why the hell haven't you started yet," Len replied intensely

"Do things normally happen this quickly in Hollywood?"

"Let's just say that some very particular circumstances have created a unique opportunity," Ron explained to Nicole. "A unique opportunity with a limited window that you may be very well positioned to take advantage of, if you're willing."

"We're willing. I'm not sure if our timeframes coincide though," Nicole replied.

"We planned to run the crew member selection lottery for a minimum of three months," Tyler explained. "We thought that that would be the minimum time necessary to reach the numbers we need."

"That won't work for us," Lanetta said. "We need to have the debut episode ready to air no later than six weeks from now. Eight weeks tops."

Nicole and Marcus exchanged concerned looks. "We could move up the end date, do the selection early?" Marcus offered.

"But we won't get the numbers we need," Tyler objected. "You know we're counting on the ticket revenue, we can't do anything that undercuts those projections."

Everyone sat silently for a moment, contemplating the situation.

"OK, how about this," Len said. "What's your current marketing strategy for this lottery?"

"Targeted web ads, banners on related sites, and some limited print ads in industry publications," Tyler replied.

"That's it? No broadcast media?"

"No radio or television," Tyler explained. "We're almost totally web based to keep the costs as low as possible."

"You really do need a media consultant," Lanetta said with disdain. "You're leaving a hell of a lot of money on the table."

Tyler was stung by the criticism. He realized he was out of his league though.

"OK, well, we need to do promos and teasers for the show," Len continued. "I'm thinking 15 second spots on normal rotation to all demographics." He looked at Lanetta, who nodded agreement. "So here's the thing. Instead of just teasing the show, we use the promos to also push the lottery thing."

"I'm not sure exactly what you mean," Nicole said.

Len held his hands up, his fingers framing an imaginary screen. "I'm seeing a scene," he said. "The black of space, the Earth in the distance. The camera pans down to show the moon's surface scrolling past. The narrator says:

'One of man's greatest dreams will be realized.

Many will try.

Few will be chosen.

But only one will be ...

The Last Passenger.

Will it be you?'

Swell dramatic music. Then plug the lottery by throwing the web site address on the screen while the narrator gives the date and time for the premier. Run that on everything from SyFy to Oxygen."

"That should kick your sales to a higher plane," Lanetta added. "Properly done, a good broadcast media campaign will get you to your goal in a tenth the time."

Nicole and Marcus again exchanged glances. "Who will be responsible for developing and coordinating all that?" Nicole asked. "And what would it cost?" she added with concern.

"Not to worry, we'll handle all that for you," Len said. "That's what a production company does. And it's not going to cost you a cent, the network will pay for it all, as soon as we can get them to green-light the concept."

"OK, well ... " Nicole said hesitantly, "I guess we should talk business then?"

"OK sweetheart, Ron will go over the standard royalties and residuals package with you, and of course there's the overseas distribution rights, merchandising, yada yada yada to work out. First, talk to Lanetta to nail down the format so we can take it to the network. Love the idea! Gotta go, see you later." With that, Len got up to leave.

"OK," Lanetta began, "so I'm seeing a weekly one hour format here. We'll start off with a two hour premier … "

I can't believe these rubes didn't bring an agent, Len thought as he left the room. *Ka-ching!*

***

So what do you think, boss? Marcus asked Tom.

"We get one hundred percent of the income from flight sponsors, plus an additional ten percent of the gross on broadcast and streaming ads?" Tom asked.

"Yes, in exchange for five percent of the lottery income, overseas marketing rights and waiving future residuals," Tyler replied.

"What do you think?" Tom asked, turning to Nicole.

"Well," she said, hesitantly. "I honestly have no experience with putting entertainment deals together."

"I only had an hour to punch numbers," Tyler said, "but I really think we're making out, Mr. Armac. We turn the entire process over to them, they manage it all, and we have no out-of-pocket expenses for crew training."

"Well, tell me how this would work," Tom said.

"The commercials will start running in ten days," Marcus explained. "After four weeks, we run the lottery and select a pool of two dozen semi-finalists. Then we do a preliminary screening and come up with a list of ten finalists to be contestants."

"They want to have input on that, to make sure the ten we choose are big enough personalities to make for good television," added Tyler.

"Once we have the ten, the series goes into production," Marcus continued. "They want to do a two hour premier where we do the whole *Publishers Sweepstakes* thing and show up at each candidate's home, make the announcement, get their scripted reaction, and do some biographical stuff on each one."

"OK," Tom said.

"Then we do about seven weeks of screening them through various training activities, cutting one each week," Marcus said.

"Wait, we can't have our people tied up for that long," Tom said, alarmed. "There's no way any of our key personnel can be away from the project for two months!"

"They won't be," Tyler explained. "It will take two months to broadcast the episodes, but the selection process will occur during the week we already have blocked out in the schedule for our crew training. We'll be screening out about one person a day, and that's when all the footage will be shot. When it's edited for television, each day will become a weekly episode."

"OK then," said Tom, nodding.

"So now we have three candidates left," Marcus said.

"We agreed that at that point, they'd probably all be equally qualified," said Tyler. "So then they want to get public involvement through social media."

"How so?"

"The plan is that after some final challenge, we do a board where we critique them and assign them a grade, but then they also solicit votes via social media, and the person with the best combined total becomes our passenger. Sort of like how *Celebrity Dancing* does it."

"They have the data to show that adding public involvement increases ratings and thus advertising rates, and therefore income," Nicole said.

"So what do we have to do if we agree?" Tom asked.

"They said if we can give them a tentative verbal agreement by tomorrow, they'll have the contract here by the end of the week, meanwhile they'll start on the promos," Nicole replied.

"Damn, they work fast, don't they?" Tom observed.

"Oh, I almost forgot," added Nicole. "They said they'd have no problem providing the film crew you asked for. I couldn't tell them very much about what you wanted them for though, since you haven't been very forthcoming."

"You'll see," Tom said, as he and Tyler exchanged smiles.

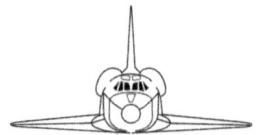

CHAPTER TWENTY–EIGHT

The group of journalists stood under a large fabric shelter supported by stout steel pillars. "If you'll all please gather around, I have your passes and nametags for you," said the attractive young pony-tailed woman wearing a tailored blue jumpsuit. "And here are your press packets, which include your information sheets and a copy of today's agenda."

Bob accepted his package, undid the closure, and briefly examined the enclosed publicity brochures promoting the Aerospace Museum of the Pacific and its interactive space flight experience, Space Dome. Grunting in mild contempt, he returned the contents to the folder, and then said, "Excuse me, Miss?"

"Yes sir, you have a question?" she asked.

"Is it all right if we take pictures during the tour?"

"Only in authorized areas, please," she perkily replied. "I or another of our hosts will let you know when photography is allowed."

Bob scowled. "But isn't this supposed to be a public museum?"

"Yes sir, but as you'll see once we're inside, some of our personnel may be performing actual mission support tasks, particularly in the Mission Control area, which may require concentration. We'd hate to impact operations or even heaven forbid have an injury as a result of inappropriate flash photography."

"How about I turn off my flash ... " Bob started to say, before being cut off.

"OK, I see our shuttle is here," the guide noted cheerfully, as a large van pulled up. It had been painted a two tone white over black paint scheme reminiscent of a space shuttle, and the rear sported a short fiberglass tail and set of mock rocket engines. "Let's please get on board for a brief tour of the facilities that are currently under construction, and then we'll return here to the museum dome." Heading toward the open door of the shuttle, the guide added, "I'm sorry we won't be able to stop at these locations, but since they are active construction sites, well, insurance regulations, don't you know."

Don't you know, Bob thought mockingly. *I'm not in the mood for freaking astronaut Barbie today.* Although the hotel suite that EtherX had provided was infinitely nicer than anything his paper would have authorized, he had been jolted awake in the middle of the night by a mild earthquake, and had slept poorly after that, convinced that the roof was going to fall in.

"The locations you will see on today's driving tour are all part of the phase two expansion we are just beginning," the woman Bob now thought of as Barbie explained. "These locations should be completed in the next six to ten months."

The van drove slowly past the first construction site. "The first area we'll be passing will be the location of our Space Explorer's Memorial," Barbie said. "During daylight hours, sunlight will be captured by a polished reflector dome and channeled through iridescent light guides to illuminate a series of crystal and aluminum pylons engraved with the names and missions of astronauts, cosmonauts, and taikonauts who died while bravely exploring the universe. At night, lasers will take the place of the sun to illuminate the memorial. If you'll look in your information package, you'll see an artist's conception of the completed memorial."

Bob looked out the window as the van slowed. He saw only a jumble of unfinished concrete, some exposed rebar and a pile of cement stained plywood.

"Next we come to our Pioneers Sculpture Garden," Barbie continued in her singsong voice. "Here bronze statues will immortalize the leading figures of early California aviation history such as Glenn Martin, Jack Northrop and the Lockheed brothers, set amid playfully located splash fountains."

Bob saw more unfinished concrete, this time with stubs of plumbing accenting the rusting rebar.

"As we approach the waterfront, the construction you see before you will be the museum's main dining and gift shop complex, where visitors will be able to experience an elegant sit-down meal and then browse through an extensive selection of space themed merchandise for sale."

I can see it now—teddy bears in space suits and packages of freeze dried ice cream, Bob thought.

"Something we're very proud of is our restaurant's collaboration with the University of Southern California's School Of Culinary Science. Our chef and her staff will work with USC nutritionists to develop new and tastier cuisine for NASA's Space Food Systems Laboratory for use on future space missions. Many of these dishes will appear on the restaurant's menu for sampling by our guests."

"What future NASA space missions?" Bob asked loudly. "NASA is grounded for the next decade. The commercial spaceflight folks, that's who you should be working with."

The guide scowled as if she had bitten a lemon and became momentarily less perky. "Sir, we're not officially open yet, and we're still making adjustments to our tour script."

Oh, OK, Bob thought, nodding. *Astronaut Barbie has no freaking clue, she's just reading a script someone wrote. Well, the restaurant deal is still something I can check into for a puff piece.*

Resuming her perky demeanor, the guide now said, "The site we are now passing will eventually become the highlight and centerpiece of the museum. At this location, we are building a soaring chromatic glass hanger to house and display the museum's most prized artifact, the space shuttle Atlantis."

This time Bob raised his hand. Biting another lemon, the guide asked, "Sir?"

Bob lowered his hand. "I thought I understood that you were getting Enterprise, and Atlantis is going to the Smithsonian?"

"I really wouldn't know about that sir," Barbie said. "I've been told that Atlantis will be on display here at the museum for at least a year."

Another thing to check on, he thought. *This is really getting confusing.* "But the museum is supposed to open next month?"

"Yes sir, we are hopeful that we will be able to meet our proposed grand opening date at the end of next month."

"Where will Atlantis go then? That building obviously won't be ready," Bob said, gesturing toward the construction site behind her.

"Until the hanger is ready, Atlantis will be displayed in front of the main museum entrance, under the fabric awning from which the tour departed."

"And that's ready now?" Bob asked.

"Yes sir."

"And you could put Atlantis there as soon as it arrives … "

"Yes sir," Barbie answered, annoyed with the repeated interruptions to her carefully rehearsed script.

Three or four months, my ass, Bob thought.

Making the final turn and arriving back at the main entrance to the dome, the guide said, "Now if you would please exit the shuttle, we can enter the museum as a group."

Again, Bob raised his hand. "Yes? Another question?" she said with a forced smile.

"I didn't notice where you will be displaying the shuttle external tank. It looks like every available inch of space already has construction going on."

"A shuttle external tank?" Barbie asked, confused.

"The big fuel tank the shuttle is mounted to? You know, the enormous orange thing?"

Bob saw comprehension dawn on her face. "Oh, no sir, there are no plans to display one of those here. As you can see, we've already planned our site utilization."

Now isn't that interesting, Bob thought.

***

Stephanie exited the cockpit simulator, having successfully completed another abort-on-launch drill. Arching her shoulders and rolling her head in a circle to work out the kinks in her muscles, she headed toward the break room to grab something cold to drink. Crossing between the simulators and the mission control area, she noticed a large group of people entering the building being shepherded by Melinda, one of the new hosts the museum had recently hired. Curious about the visitors and anxious for a break, she wandered over.

"In addition, the museum houses a comprehensive archive of shuttle program documentation," she was explaining to her group, "including flight logs and maintenance records, available to scholars for historical research and review."

"Hi Melinda, what's going on," Stephanie said.

Melinda, Bob thought. *Humph. Barbie suits her better.*

"Oh, good morning Ms. Peters. These are members of the press. They're here for a pre-opening tour of the museum facilities."

"Mind if I tag along for a while?" Stephanie asked.

"Oh, not at all," Melinda/Barbie said cheerfully. Turning to the group, she explained, "Ms. Peters is one of several actual former NASA astronauts we have on staff here at the Aerospace Museum of the Pacific!"

Bob recognized Stephanie, but elected not to mention it.

"If you'll please follow me, our first stop will be Space Dome Mission Control," said Melinda, leading the group toward a set of double doors. "From here, flight controllers will monitor launches and on-orbit operations for the recently announced Space Train program, which will begin later this year."

Bob thought the facility was nowhere as impressive as its name would imply. Passing through the double doors, they stood in a small hallway, one wall of which was glass. On the other side of the glass was a small, dimly lit space filled with inexpensive office furniture arranged in two short rows. On each desk sat a pair of computer monitors. The large projection screen on the far wall and the elevated desk labeled 'Flight Director' were the only indications that he wasn't looking at just some random wage slave office area. Inside the mission control space, Bob could see a small group of men and women wearing headsets who appeared to be finishing whatever task they were working on, shutting manuals and stacking paperwork. One man's computer screen suddenly switched to Solitaire, as he leaned back in his seat and began playing.

"During periods in which no actual flight operations are occurring," Melinda continued, "our controllers will conduct space shuttle mission simulations for the benefit of museum guests so that they may see how a modern flight control facility is operated. Let's listen for a moment to what they're doing right now." Melinda toggled a switch on the wall which activated a speaker allowing them to hear the discussions taking place inside.

"OK folks, that was a good run, no one got killed this time. Let's take 30 minutes, and then we'll reset and try an abort with crew escape."

I know that voice, Bob thought. Looking to identify who it belonged to, he spotted a woman standing with her hand to her right ear. Her back was to him, and he couldn't make out who she was.

"Also, I need to hear from each section by lunchtime whether you're go for tomorrow's launch simulation," she said, speaking again.

That sounds like ... Jean Lutz! Bob thought. *She retired out of shuttle operations last year. She swore she was never going back to work once the shuttle quit flying.*

Flipping the switch to kill the audio to the viewer's gallery, Melinda said, "Well darn, I guess we caught them on a break. OK then, please follow me to the neutral buoyancy pool," as she led them back toward the doors they had entered through.

As Bob was leaving the viewer's gallery, he glanced over his shoulder for one more look at the woman inside the control center. Noticing the motion of the crowd in the viewer's gallery behind her, she turned around. For an instant, her eyes met Bob's. He thought he caught a flicker of recognition. He quickly looked away and hurried to catch the group.

***

Bob lagged behind the crowd as they entered the pool area. He really wanted to ask Stephanie Peters some questions about exactly what the role of a former shuttle astronaut was at an "interactive space flight experience," but he was worried that she would recognize him. It might not matter, but his paranoia over the fact that he was there as a spy rather than a reporter made him cautious.

Bob noted that the pool they were now standing beside resembled a smaller version of the neutral buoyancy training pool at the Johnson Space Flight Center in Houston. Suspended above it was a bridge crane for placing large items in the water, and a smaller lift platform to raise and lower personnel into the pool. At one end, a currently unmanned control console with multiple monitors displayed various underwater views. Next to it stood a rack containing scuba tanks and diving equipment.

"Behind me is our neutral buoyancy training pool here at Space Dome,"

Melinda said, resuming her practiced narrative. "It is a fully equipped training and research facility, one of only a handful of such facilities worldwide. When not being used for training or research, the pool can be outfitted with a mockup of the space shuttle payload bay, and our guests can observe former NASA astronauts performing simulated mission operations." Melinda moved to the edge of the pool and motioned for the group to join her.

"Guests who choose to upgrade to our Commander level premium spaceflight experience are given the opportunity to don a spacesuit similar to those used by NASA and actually enter the pool and participate in simulated zero gee activities."

"How much does that cost?" someone asked.

"Ticket prices for our Specialist, Pilot, and Commander level experience packages are detailed in your information packets," Melinda replied. "Any other questions?"

"Is the water heated?" asked someone else.

Everyone chuckled. "Oh yes, we keep the pool at 85 degrees year round for the comfort of our staff," Melinda answered. "Are there any more questions? Good. Now please follow me this way as we head to our space shuttle flight simulators."

Bob stepped to the edge of the pool and looked into the depths of the still, clear water. He could easily see the familiar outlines of a shuttle cargo bay below the surface. *She's got a full load*, Bob thought, noting that the payload bay mockup was completely filled with modules. *Wait, I've seen those before!* Bob recognized the two OMS fuel modules that filled most of the cargo bay. *I saw those at RRI's facility in New Mexico. Took pictures of them.*

Turning to follow the tour group, he thought, *Wonder why they didn't just fess up instead of giving me that crap about a new rocket design. What's the big secret about a museum display?*

Bob caught up with the group next to the shuttle simulators just as Melinda was about to begin her next presentation. He suddenly realized that the three cups of coffee he'd had with breakfast were making their presence urgently known—he really needed to pee, badly. *Must have been from looking at that damn pool*, he thought.

"Excuse me Miss, could you point me to the nearest restroom?" he asked.

Scowling slightly, Melinda pointed over his head. "The closest is just through that door, then down the hall on the right. Or you can use the public facilities just off the main entrance lobby."

"Thanks, this is closer," Bob said, heading toward the indicated door. Noting the 'Authorized Personnel Only' sign, he pushed it open and found himself in a long hallway, where he spotted the men's room ahead on the right as promised.

After relieving himself and washing his hands, he started to head back to the tour group. Exiting the men's room, he glanced to his right. Something sparkled above the door at the end of the hall, catching his eye. Being a reporter, Bob suffered from an overabundance of curiosity, and was drawn to the sparkle. As he approached, he saw that it was a crude, handmade sign made of poster board and glitter that read "Neverland."

An employee break room? Bob thought, trying the door and finding it unlocked. He pushed it open and entered. He found himself standing in a medium sized conference room containing a non-descript table and a dozen or so standard office chairs. A large flat screen monitor hung at one end. The walls were covered by dry erase white boards, most of which displayed lists, equations, and diagrams. A large drawing in the corner of the room caught his eye. It showed a figure in a space suit standing on what appeared to be a cartoon moon, holding a flag emblazoned with 'RRI'. Behind the figure was some kind of gangly spacecraft sitting on the moon's surface.

Holy crap, Bob thought, slowly turning in place, studying the walls. Different sections had different titles and themes, he noted. He headed to the one labeled "Technical" to get a closer look.

***

Stephanie had enjoyed the brief break from training, but she needed to grab a quick bite before the afternoon's mission simulation. Slipping away from the group, she decided to take the direct route to the refrigerator where she kept her lunch rather than circle around through the pool area. Entering the staff passageway, she noticed the door to Neverland at the end of the hall was ajar.

Walking toward the door and pushing it open, she was surprised to see a man standing before one of the white boards studying the notes and diagrams there. She was pretty sure she recognized him as the person who had left the tour ten minutes earlier.

"Excuse me, sir? You're not supposed to be in this area," she said firmly. "This is a staff space only. It's not open to the public."

Bob had been so engrossed in the details before him that he hadn't heard Stephanie enter the room. He jumped when she spoke, startled. His shoulder brushed against the board, smudging part of the lunar lander diagram he had been examining.

"I'm sorry," he said contritely. "I went to the restroom, and I got turned around ... "

"Well you need to hurry up and catch your group, sir," Stephanie scolded. "You'll find them in the Challenger gallery," she added, holding the door open to emphasize that Bob should linger no longer.

"The Challenger gallery?" he asked, exiting the room.

"Down the hallway, through the door, and then turn left toward the main entrance."

"Oh, OK, great, thanks," he mumbled, and left.

Stephanie shut the door and locked it, and then examined the area of the board that Bob had been studying. She noticed the smudged area with dismay, and then stepped back to look at the walls of the room, trying to see them as an outsider might.

Damn it, there's a lot of information here, she thought. *A high school kid could figure this out.*

***

Jesus Christ, Bob thought, his mind whirling, as he headed back to the tour group. *Not just* flying *a shuttle. Taking it to the goddamn* moon!

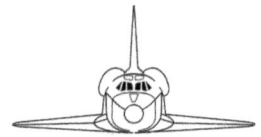

CHAPTER TWENTY–NINE

"So who was that group I saw you with today?" Jean asked, pulling her bowl of soup from the microwave.

"They were reporters, here for their pre-opening tour," Stephanie replied, setting down her sandwich and magazine. "Mostly local newspaper folks. I think the TV people are coming next week," she added, picking up her magazine and turning the page. "I'm totally losing track of time, we've been so busy."

"Me too," Jean concurred, taking a sip of her soup. "Things are just happening so fast now." After a moment, she said, "I thought I recognized one of them."

"Oh really? Who?"

"Pretty sure one of them was Bob Brock from the *Orlando Guardian*. I met him a few times at the Cape, he covers the news from the space center."

"Oh my God!" Stephanie said, suddenly sitting upright. "You're right, that *was* Bob Brock."

"Wonder what he's doing all the way out here?" Jean mused, not noticing Stephanie's reaction.

"Jean, I found him in Neverland!" Stephanie said.

"What? When? What was he doing there?"

"He said he got lost coming back from the restroom. I found him looking at the lander diagrams."

"How long was he there unsupervised?" Jean asked with alarm.

"When I found him, it had been about ten, maybe fifteen minutes since he'd left the group."

"If news gets out before we're ready, it could ruin everything!" Jean said with despair. "We need to tell someone, right away!"

***

"So what do we know about this guy?" Tom asked, as he exited the Capitol Beltway at Tyson's Corner and made the turn into the office complex parking lot.

"He's a 36 year old Croatian named Goran Jadranko," Nicole replied. "Mark Rutherford said that Mr. Jadranko had initially contacted him about the Russian circumlunar trip, but he didn't feel that the Russians were offering good value. When Mark called him back to brief him on our mission, he was extremely interested."

"He's supposed to be a software gazillionaire, runs a company in Zagreb," Marcus added, leaning forward from the back seat.

"Software?" Tom said. "OK, at least we have something in common then. Does he do game development by any chance?"

"Haven't been able to find out too much about him," Marcus said.

"Mark wouldn't have asked us to come do an interview if he thought Mr. Jadranko wasn't physically or fiscally qualified," Nicole observed.

Tom parked the car and the three entered the lobby of the office building, boarded the elevator, and rode to the tenth floor. Entering the Destination Beyond suite, the receptionist immediately ushered them into Mark Rutherford's office.

Mark stood up from behind his desk. "Ms. Ferry, Mr. Short, good to see you both again. And you must be Mr. Armac?" he asked, reaching for Tom's hand.

"Yes, please call me Tom."

"Well, Tom, I'd like you to meet Mr. Goran Jadranko and his associate Tihana," Mark said, indicating the couple seated on his office sofa.

Tom turned to see a man, a bit younger than himself, seated next to a stunningly attractive and well-endowed blonde. He had closely trimmed light brown hair and was wearing a well-tailored pale gold suit with a white shirt and white silk tie. Each hand sported several large rings studded with diamonds and on his wrist he wore a gold Rolex.

Studying Tom for a moment with his cold blue eyes, Goran finally stood and said, "A pleasure to meet you, Mr. Armac," in slightly accented English, giving Tom a brief but firm handshake. He made no move to introduce his companion.

"Please, everyone sit," Mark said, sliding several office chairs toward the couch. "Tom, as I told Ms. Ferry, Mr. Jadranko wished to meet in person to discuss certain terms he is requesting before signing the commitment letter and making his deposit."

"Terms?" Tom said quizzically, turning to Nicole.

"Yes, I believe you'll find them to be quite reasonable, but they're beyond the scope of what I have been authorized to negotiate," Mark said.

Goran made a dismissive wave with his hand. "These things we can discuss in a moment," he said. "First, tell me. Will you three all be going on this adventure," he asked with a charming smile.

"No, I'm the only one here who will be making the flight," Tom replied. "Ms. Ferry is our corporate attorney, and Mr. Short is our ground operations coordinator. They will both be needed here during the mission."

"Ah, a shame," Goran said, smiling at Nicole. "To have traveled with such a lovely companion would have made the trip seem all too brief."

Holy Christ, he's flirting with me, she thought, astonished.

"So why are you interested in flying with us, Mr. Jadranko?" Tom asked, changing the subject.

"Yes, I see, we take each other's measure," Goran said, nodding. "Good. I wish to make this trip, Tom, because while I am a wealthy man, I believe that material things do not truly matter." Pointing to himself and then gesturing to his companion, he said, "Clothes, jewelry, even the company of a beautiful woman, all these things can be easily lost or taken. But experiences, Tom, these can never be taken once lived. Memories of a life well lived provide comfort long after things lose importance."

She's just a piece of jewelry to him, Nicole thought with amazement, looking at Tihana, who smiled back blankly.

"Yes, well, I can understand that perspective," Tom said.

"I am a fortunate man," Goran continued. "I have the ability to do many things. But to go to the moon. That would be the greatest experience of all. I could not live knowing it was within my reach and I did not grasp it."

"I see. Well, what are these conditions Mr. Rutherford mentioned?"

Goran's expression changed. His smile left, and his eyes became icy. "Very well. If I am to make this trip, then you should know that I will travel with you to the moon's surface."

"Yes, of course, that's already a given," Tom nodded.

"And once we are there, I will be the first one to step upon the surface."

Tom's head snapped back in surprise. He looked at Marcus and then Nicole, who both looked equally shocked.

"We haven't really discussed that yet, Mr. Goran," Tom finally said.

"There is no discussion," Goran replied. "If I am to go on this journey, then the first step on the moon will be mine. Only the name of the first one will be remembered."

Tom's eyes narrowed as he stared at the Croatian. "For now, let's say I agree. What else, Mr. Jadranko?"

"During the launch and the reentry, I will assist with piloting the craft."

You're totally freaking crazy, Tom thought. Looking at his companions, he noted that Nicole's mouth hung open slightly, and Marcus looked as if his head was ready to explode.

"Tom, just so you know, Mr. Jadranko is an experienced pilot who has flown in MIGs and has been through most of the spaceflight training program at Star City," Mark said.

"Mr. Jadranko, we already have both a mission commander and a pilot, who are intensively training for the flight," Tom said. "I don't believe what you're asking will be possible."

"Oh, they will both go, but I will sit in the assistant pilot's seat during the launch and the reentry," Goran said calmly. "If you do not agree to this thing, then I will not pay what you ask."

How the hell will I get Robbie to agree to that? Tom thought incredulously. "Well, our mission commander has the final say on all safety issues, so we'll have to discuss this with him before we can give you an answer," Tom said. Looking to ease the tension and buy some time to think, he changed the subject again. "So I understand that you are in the software business, Mr. Jadranko?"

Goran smiled. "Yes, in a fashion. I own a software services business in Zagreb. It is Nemisis Systems. Perhaps you have heard of it?"

Revulsion swept over Tom's face.

"Nemisis Systems is the world's biggest spam generator," Marcus said angrily.

"That's their *best* feature," Tom added with disgust. "They also make most of the tools used to hack ATMs, support identity theft, and build phishing sites."

"You say these things as if we are to blame," Goran said calmly, examining his fingernails. "We merely make services available for the use of others. We are not responsible for what they may do with them." He looked up from his fingernails and smiled.

"Mr. Rutherford, we are done here," Tom said, standing suddenly. "Good day, Mr. Jadranko." Nodding toward Goran's companion, he added, "Miss, whoever you are." Nicole and Marcus followed as he turned towards the door.

"But Mr. Armac," Mark said, rushing to intercept Tom. "What's wrong? I know his demands are a bit extreme, but … "

"Mr. Rutherford, this *gentleman* is the antithesis of everything we work for and believe in," Tom replied. "In the software industry, we spend half of every waking moment trying to contain the damage caused by Mr. Jadranko's clients and their use of his services. If that bastard flew with us, I'd never get a chance to kill him, because someone else on my team would beat me to it."

Mark looked at Tom forlornly. "I'm not sure if it will be possible to find another candidate … "

"Find one," Tom said firmly. "Because *this* one is unsuitable. I wouldn't let that son of a bitch within ten miles of our facility, much less fly with him. I'm not completely sure how he even got into the country."

"All right, well, we have a few more leads we can still pursue. Mr. Jadranko was your best option, however."

"Lower the price if you have to, but find us another candidate," Tom replied angrily. He stormed out of the office, Nicole and Marcus following close behind.

***

Marcus thought enough time had passed for Tom to have a rational discussion. "That's going to leave a big hole in our budget, boss," he observed, as Tom took the Beltway exit toward Dulles airport.

"We'll figure something out," Tom replied. "We always do."

After another few moments of tense silence, Nicole asked, "Would you have done it? Would you have met his conditions?"

Tom clenched his jaw, and then said, "Being the first one out? Sure, why not. If that had been the only thing standing between us and the mission, then damn right I'd had agreed." After a pause, he added, "But risking everyone's safety by letting him sit in the pilot's seat? Not a chance in hell would I let some son of a bitch with an inflated sense of self-importance put any of my people at risk."

"We sure could have used the money though," noted Marcus sadly.

"Well, let's hope Mr. Rutherford can pull another rabbit out of his hat. We might still be able to pull this off without that money, but it sure makes things a hell of a lot harder."

They continued toward the airport in silence, each lost in their own thoughts.

***

The drive north through afternoon Los Angeles traffic took Bob longer than he had expected. By the time he arrived in Lompoc, it was too late to contact the Vandenberg public affairs office to see if he could get a tour of the base. He was hoping to catch a glimpse of the facilities at Space Launch Complex Six, but it would have to wait until tomorrow.

Checking into the Embassy Suites, Bob charged the room to EtherX's corporate account. *I could get used to this*, he thought for the umpteenth time, considering again whether a job in a corporate press office might indeed be superior to being a journalist in a mid-sized market like Orlando.

Having settled in, Bob decided he had a craving for wings and beer. Following the recommendation of the clerk at the front desk, he headed north on H street. *There it is*, he thought, pulling into the parking lot of the Flight Line Sports Bar.

It was still too early in the afternoon for the happy hour crowd. Bob looked around the dimly lit interior and noted a handful of patrons scattered along the bar sipping beers and watching a replay of USC's last game. One person in particular caught his eye. He was sitting by himself at the end of the bar, head hung slightly, slowly nursing a beer. He wore a jacket emblazoned with the Alliance Space Systems logo showing a grinning jackass kicking a satellite into orbit.

Bob made his way toward the bar, stepping on peanut shells strewn across the floor in route. The seated man turned at the sound and watched Bob climb onto a barstool several spots to his left. He took a small sip of beer and then looked back at the television.

Bob ordered a draught beer and picked up the bar menu, then turned to the person and said, "I couldn't help noticing you're with Alliance."

"Yep," the man replied, glancing at Bob and then taking another small swig.

"Are you out from the Cape or are you local?" Bob asked.

The man glanced at Bob again. "The Cape. Been here two weeks now."

"Me too," Bob said. "Out from Orlando for a site visit."

"That's nice." He continued watching the television.

Bob noticed the man's beer was almost empty, but he seemed reluctant to finish the last sip. Motioning to the bartender, he said, "How about an order of hot wings, and let's have a refill for my friend here."

The man looked at Bob a little longer. "That's not necessary," he said.

"That's OK. Some of you Alliance guys have done me a few favors in the past. Besides, I'm on per diem, so the company's paying for it."

"Cheers to that," the man said, finishing his last sip and then toasting Bob with the refill the bartender set down in front of him.

Bob slid over to the empty seat next to the man. "I'm Bob Brock, I do the space column for the *Guardian*."

"Juan Meneurez," the man replied, reaching to shake Bob's offered hand. "I've read your stuff." Turning back to the game, he added, "Sometimes you talk shit but sometimes you know what you're talking about."

"You out here working on Atlantis?" Bob probed.

"Yep. Sort of."

"You on the late shift? Seems a bit early to be off already," Bob said, looking dramatically at his watch while watching Juan's reaction.

"There ain't no late shift, we're all doin' twelve on twelve off," Juan replied, turning to face Bob. "Not really on any shift at the moment. My fuckin' boss put me on the beach for a week, so I guess I'm on vacation for now."

"That sucks," Bob said sympathetically. "What'd you do to deserve that?"

"Made a minor mistake on a silly-ass systems check," Juan replied bitterly. "Total bullshit, 'cause it doesn't even matter."

Bob noticed Juan was taking bigger swallows now that someone else was picking up the tab. "What do you mean?"

"I mean the bird's goin' in a freakin' museum, but they got us running checks like she's gettin' ready to fly next week."

Juan tilted his mug back and finished it, then slapped the mug on the table. Bob motioned to the bartender to set him up again.

"That doesn't make any sense," Bob said.

"No fuckin' sense at all," Juan replied. "They even have inspectors following behind us bustin' our balls if they find any violations."

"What kind of violations?"

"Procedural violations. I saw a guy get shitcanned last week because he dropped a tool in a void on a closeout inspection and he didn't bother to retrieve it, he just signed it off. They put him on the next plane home. I mean, what freakin' difference does it make if there's a tool rattling around in a void when the bird is sitting on blocks in a museum?"

The bartender set Juan's next mug down. He picked it up, but before it reached his mouth, he stopped and said, "And you know what's really weird?"

"What's that?"

"They got some people working, not our people, some of their own people, up there making system mods and changin' shit."

"Changing things on Atlantis?" Bob asked. "What kind of things?"

"Like fuel systems and shit," Juan answered, attacking his next beer. "They think we don't see what they're doing, but we're all 'what the fuck man, why are they doin' that?' Makes no sense."

"Who are you talking about? What people?"

"Those Roadrunner Rockets guys. The ones running the show." Juan took another deep swallow of beer and then wiped his mouth on the sleeve of his jacket. "Word is now they're getting ready to roll the bird down to the pad at Slick Six. I tell you man, it makes no freakin' sense."

"When are they supposed to be doing that?" Bob asked.

"I dunno, next couple of weeks maybe. Soon."

Bob's wings hadn't arrived yet, but he'd lost his appetite. Plunking two twenty dollar bills on the counter, he motioned for the bartender, and then stood to leave. Turning to Juan, he said, "Keep the change and have another round on me."

"Thanks, man," Juan said to Bob's back as Bob headed for the door.

***

The wheels of the charter jet had just hit the runway at John Wayne airport when Marcus pulled out his phone and flipped it on. Within seconds, it chimed to notify him that he had multiple voice mails. With a sigh, he dialed in to retrieve them. Most of the calls were inconsequential. The last was from Jean Lutz. As he listened, Marcus' eyes grew large. Hanging up, he turned to Tom seated directly across the narrow cabin. "We got trouble, boss," he said urgently.

"What now?" Tom asked. It hadn't been the best of days, and he had been hoping for an uneventful return.

"Jean called. Steph caught someone from today's press tour wandering around unattended."

"So?"

"When she found him, he was studying the walls in Neverland."

Tom sat bolt upright. "Crap! How the hell did he get in there? Who was it?"

"Jean says she knows him. It was that Bob Brock guy, the one from the fly away asking the questions about what we're doing to Atlantis."

"Damn it. It's too soon." Tom thought for a moment. "OK, we need to get ahead of this immediately." Pulling out his phone, Tom powered it on and dialed.

"Tyler? This is Tom. Yes, we just touched down. Meet us at the dome in an hour. We need to kick off that plan we discussed. Yes, immediately."

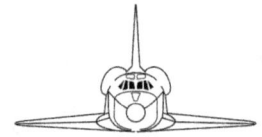

CHAPTER THIRTY

"You can go in, sir," the young airman said. "The Colonel is expecting you."

Tom smiled and nodded, and then walked over to the slightly ajar door and knocked.

"Come in," came a voice from inside.

Pushing open the door, Tom entered the office. "Jim, good to see you!" he said. "Appreciate you getting back to me so quickly."

Jim Arnold stood and shook Tom's hand. "I always have time for my best tenant," he said warmly.

"Congratulations on making Colonel," Tom added. "Think there's a star in your future?"

Jim scowled slightly, and then said, "Well, I think not. That would mean another tour in DC, and Marie likes it here too much to leave and go back to that rat race. I'll probably just retire at the end of this tour."

"Well I can't tell you how much we've enjoyed working with you. Things here have gone much better than we anticipated, and you're mostly to blame."

"I'm not going away anytime soon," Jim observed. "I'm in the zone for retirement, but I'll probably stay in this billet for at least another year. So what was it that you wanted to see me about?"

Tom dropped a two inch thick manuscript on the Colonel's desk with a light thud. "This," he said.

Looking at the pile of paper with puzzlement, Jim picked it up and started thumbing through it. "What is this?" he asked.

"A script."

"I see that."

"For a movie we want to make."

"Really? What type of movie?"

"It's basically a remake of an old science fiction film called *Destination Moon*," Tom explained. "Except this one goes to Mars."

"Oh?" Jim said, cocking an eyebrow. Continuing to thumb through the script, he added, "Rich industrialist builds a rocket to fly to the moon? That *Destination Moon*?"

"That's the one. Rich industrialists aren't as popular as they once were though, in this case it will be an idealistic internet entrepreneur saving mankind from climate change."

"Can't imagine why the story appeals to you," Jim observed with a chuckle, closing the script. "So I assume you want the Air Force's support?"

"We do," Tom confirmed. "We want to use Atlantis and the facilities at Slick Six."

"Use them how?"

"Well, we have Atlantis about finished, and we had planned to move the barge in soon to transport her down to Long Beach. We're a bit behind schedule finishing our museum facilities though, so we'll have to park Atlantis here for a month or two. When this idea hit our inbox a while back, we thought it sounded pretty cool, but it wouldn't fit with our schedule," Tom said, gesturing at the script on Jim's desk. "We took another look though in light of the delays, and now we're thinking it could be a perfect way to showcase Atlantis. We'll end up with a shuttle that's also a movie star. Bound to help get more people through the museum door, don't you think?"

"So how are we involved?" Jim asked.

"Well, we want to transport Atlantis down to Slick Six for a couple of weeks and sit her on the pad for filming."

"Really? I would have thought you could do all that with special effects."

"You can. Effects aren't as expensive as they used to be, but the accountants say it would still be cheaper to shoot on a live set."

"Won't you need an external tank and a pair of solids if you want to stand her up on the pad?"

"Already covered," Tom said. "As you know, we're getting ready to start stacking our first Big Brother boosters for the west coast Space Train tests, and they're good stand-ins for shuttle SRBs. We'd like to get your approval to bring in an external tank."

"Where did you score one of those?" Jim asked.

"Michoud in New Orleans had several left over when the shuttle program ended. Believe it or not, it's cheaper to pick one up surplus and barge it around than it would be to build a fiberglass mockup."

"Well I know the prevailing wages for the film trades in this state are sky high," Jim said. "So do you have the equipment to move everything?"

"We're going to roll the external tank from the barge pier to the pad on a pair of low-boy trailers," Tom explained. "We're just going to hook a tractor to Atlantis and tow her from the maintenance and checkout facility at north base down to the launch complex."

"That's over seventeen miles," Jim said.

"It will take a whole day, but if we can get your cooperation in closing the road, there shouldn't be a problem. I promise we'll be careful."

Jim opened the script again. "Well, you know how this works. I'll need to submit this for the Air Force public affairs folks to review. As long as it doesn't portray the service or any of its personnel negatively, they should give you the green light. You've convinced me that you know what you're doing down there, I don't think you'd do anything that would put your investment or our infrastructure at risk."

"Appreciate the vote of confidence," Tom said, smiling.

Turning again to the title page, Jim read, "Written by Tyler Allen. Never heard of him."

"He's new. But I hear he has a bright future."

"Humph. OK, well, let me submit this through the chain, and I'll let you know what the decision is. Sooner is better I suppose?"

"Yes, because we'd like to take advantage of the downtime while we're finishing up our museum. Once it's ready, we need to get Atlantis transported down there as soon as we can."

"I'll see what I can do," Jim said.

"Thanks, we appreciate it."

"Before you go, mind if I ask a question?" Jim asked.

"What's that?"

"Any chance you might need some extras for filming? Joining the Screen Actors Guild might look pretty good on my resume when I retire," Jim said, smiling.

"I'll see what I can do," Tom chuckled.

***

Marcus swiped his ID in the newly installed badge scanner. The light turned green and the latch clicked. Pushing the door open, he entered Neverland.

"So are we ready to do this?" he said to the small group sitting at the table, waiting.

"Is Tom coming?" Robbie asked.

"No, he and Viv are doing a walk through with the pad contractors this afternoon, he said we should do it without them."

"OK, well, we're ready when you are," Tyler said, a laptop computer open before him. He tapped a key, and the projection screen on the wall switched to show the computer's display. The words "Passenger Lottery Management System" appeared at the top.

"That's the current count?" Marcus asked, studying the data on the screen.

"Yes, we've sold just over twenty seven million tickets total," Tyler answered.

"The number is still increasing," Marcus observed, noting that the count was incrementing every four or five seconds.

"Half the world probably hasn't gotten the word yet about the cut-off date being moved up," Tyler explained. "People are still buying about twenty thousand tickets a day. Once I push 'go' on the selection routine, it will shut off new registrations and kick out anyone who's in the middle of filling out their application."

"So every minute we stand here talking … "

"We make another three hundred dollars or so," Tyler said.

"Just like you said, a license to print money," Marcus chuckled.

"Well, ready to see whose lucky day it is?" Tyler asked.

Marcus nodded. "Let's do it."

Tyler typed his password into the system and accessed the main menu. Choosing "Final Candidate Selection" from the drop down box, he hesitated for a moment over the "Execute" button. "Here we go," he said, and clicked.

The algorithm created by Tyler's team analyzed the demographics of everyone who had completed the online registration process and produced a list that was balanced by age, gender, and geographic location. Two dozen names scrolled up the screen, while the printer began spooling up to print each candidate's personal information.

"Seems a bit anticlimactic," Nicole observed, picking up the pages and scanning them as they began ejecting from the printer. "There should be balloons or something."

"You're right," Marcus agreed with a laugh. "Well, let's see if Jean and Steph are free later so we can take a first pass at this list."

"I'll call Bruce at New Millennium Multimedia," Tyler said. "They'll want to be in on the review."

***

"You're quite sure about this?" Elton asked Bob.

"Hell, I'm not sure about anything anymore," Bob replied. "Every time I think I have it figured out, something else pops up that makes me feel like an idiot. But based on what I saw, yeah, I'm pretty sure."

"And there's no other explanation … " Elton thought aloud.

"Look, here's what I know," Bob explained. "Roadrunner Rockets has declared that they're heading to the moon. Soon. They're supposed to start launching components for this 'Lunar Voyager' of theirs any day now. But there's nothing I'm hearing that confirms that they've worked out any kind of deal with the Russians to help with the flight. Support equipment and training, sure, but no flight hardware."

"I've heard that also," Elton agreed. He had access to many of the same sources as Bob, and others besides.

"So suddenly all this effort to make Atlantis flight ready makes sense. And then when I heard they're planning to move it down to the old shuttle launch facilities at Vandenberg, well, what the hell else could they be doing?"

"I see your point. Still, I didn't think a shuttle was capable of making a flight like that." *This changes everything*, Elton thought. *Taking a shuttle to the moon...*

"I think maybe I read something once that talked about the possibility," Bob said. "They could be planning to just do an orbital flight. But it's like one of their guys said out in New Mexico—what would be the point? Bob leaned back in his seat. "No, it's got to be the moon. All the drawings they had on the boards pointed that way."

"So what are you going to do now?" Elton asked.

"I'm not exactly sure. I have to confront them with this somehow, try and get confirmation before I publish, but I get the feeling that they're not going to be open to an interview."

"I suppose not. Maybe you should just let it be and see what happens next."

"Maybe. Well listen, thanks again for covering my expenses. Is there anything else I can do for you?"

"No, this is what I wanted, thank you," Elton replied absently, lost in thought.

"I hope what I've turned up is useful in some way."

"It could be," Elton said quietly. "It very well could be."

***

Bruce had brought Lanetta to Long Beach to help with the initial screening. She was now thumbing rapidly through the selectee's applications.

"White male, white male, white male, white male—what, did you guys only sell tickets at Tea Party rallies?" she asked, looking up from the files.

"Apparently the lottery was really popular in the aviation community," Marcus replied. "Commercial airline pilots, fighter pilots and aircrew, guys like that."

Lanetta scowled. "OK, well, we want two of those on the show, because the testosterone makes for good television when they fight it out to see who's top dog. Only two though!" Setting those files aside, she started flipping through the remainder.

"Too old, too old," she said, discarding two more files. Pausing over a third to study it in more detail, she then threw it aside also. "Too young."

196

"We didn't put a specific age limit on applicants," Marcus protested. "We only wanted to ensure that they were capable of making the flight."

Lanetta gave Marcus a look that said "you poor dumb bastard." "Advertisers want shows with cast members who are between the ages of 18 and 49. Why? Because that's who buys their stuff. Who are you going to sell ad spots to on a show where grandma wears a spacesuit?" she said, holding up the file of one Helen Matheny, age 67, from Patterson, New Jersey. "Space bladder control garments?"

"I don't really think this is what we had in mind when we agreed to include you in the selection process," Nicole observed, mildly distressed.

"Look, sweetie, under the terms of our contract, we get to control the ad space for the series," Lanetta responded curtly. "And we want cars, beer, and consumer electronics, not electric scooters and Medicare supplement policies and erectile dysfunction drugs. Or acne meds, either."

Lanetta sorted through several more files. "OK, we want this one," she continued, pushing a file across the table. "She's Canadian, and we have a big market there. And this one from South Africa. And this one from Australia. That builds a nice international flavor," she added, pushing several more files to the center of the table. "These will be our two alpha males," she said, pulling two files from the previously stacked white male pile. "And *damn* it I can't believe we have no idea what anyone's sexual orientation is. How are we going to get at least one gay and one lesbian if we have no *freaking* idea which way they swing? Could you have not asked that one simple question?"

"I'm pretty sure that would have been illegal," Nicole observed. "Quite sure, in fact."

"This has got to be the stupidest way to select a cast I've ever seen," Lanetta railed. "There aren't even any head shots. These people could all be ugly as sin for all we know."

"I'm pretty sure the moon won't care," Robbie observed with a smirk.

"Yes, but the viewers will," Lanetta snapped back. "By the way, I keep meaning to ask—please tell me they'll be in the water for some of this?"

"Well yes, they have to pass their swimming and water survival tests, why?" Robbie answered.

"Because we want them all in swimsuits and wet. Wet swimsuit shots make the best publicity stills, it brings the most repeat views to the website."

Everyone but Lanetta and Bruce rolled their eyes.

"OK," Lanetta continued again. "Those people, and these here; this one, this one, and this one," she said, adding more files to the pile. "That gives us both a black and a Latina woman, and someone from middle America," she said, lingering on the last file for a moment. "This one lists his occupation as cattle rancher, so he'll play big with the rednecks and hillbillies in flyover land." Picking up another file and studying it, she said, "This guy says he's an interior designer, so I'm pretty sure this may be our gay guy," and added it to the pile as well. "So where are we now?"

"That makes nine," Marcus replied.

"Nine. OK, one more." Lanetta reached for a file that she had pushed aside earlier, opened it, and leaned back in her chair. Rubbing her chin, she then closed the file and threw it on the top of the pile.

"OK, her. We definitely want her," she said.

"What's special about her?" Marcus asked.

Lanetta smiled. "She only has one leg."

"Excuse me?" Marcus asked, startled.

"She's only has one leg," Lanetta repeated. "Her bio says she was a soccer player in college. She got cancer and lost her leg. That works on so many levels. Young woman beats cancer, defies the odds, and flies to the moon. The viewers will eat it up."

"I don't think that's such a good idea," Marcus said with concern. "Robbie?" he asked, wanting the mission commander's opinion.

Robbie and Stephanie conferred for a moment, and then Robbie said, "Actually, big guy, if she's young and in good physical shape, we don't see where it would be a problem."

"But how is she going to get through the training, or get around if she makes the flight?"

"Missing a leg won't hinder her a bit in zero gee," Robbie replied. "She might even handle it better than most. And as for getting around, the moon's only one-sixth gee and we'll most likely be hopping everywhere we go. She's probably better at it than we are."

"Great, then it's settled," Lanetta said. "Handicapped female student athlete cancer survivor—let's just hope to God she's a lesbian as well."

***

It had only taken Elton a few minutes of searching online to locate what he suspected he would find. On his desk was a printout of a NASA Technical Memorandum entitled "Feasibility Analysis of Cislunar Flight Using the Shuttle Orbiter." It was dated June 1991. Dr. Carl Heinel was a co-author, who Elton knew now worked for Tom Armac's company. Inside, it explained exactly what RRI was doing.

Those are additional fuel tanks, he thought, looking again at the pictures Bob had snapped on his first trip to RRI's facility. *They have everything they need to go to the moon.*

Looking out his office window at the production floor below, he saw dozens of workers methodically assembling a Raptor booster. Further across the shop floor, a team of technicians were making modifications to the life support system of a Minotaur capsule. The capsule that Elton had hoped would make EtherX NASA's principle ride to and from space in the post-shuttle era. They were both just stepping stones, though, on what he'd privately considered the beginning of a twenty year journey. A journey that would ultimately take him to the moon and beyond.

We'll get there eventually, he thought. *And we'll get their on our own, with hardware that we've built ourselves. But they'll get there first.*

Looking for a few more moments at the rockets being assembled below, Elton reached for his phone and dialed.

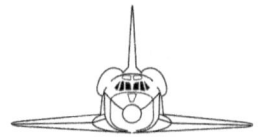

CHAPTER THIRTY–ONE

The second launch was as flawless as the first. This time, two Big Brother boosters producing a combined eight million pounds of thrust erupted into life and climbed aggressively into the eastern sky. The payload shroud separated cleanly, allowing the first of the two fuel modules that would feed Atlantis' engines on its journey to the moon to enter orbit. A subsequent firing of the Little Sister second stage lofted the module into a higher parking orbit where it would patiently wait for the arrival of its companion. The two Big Brother first stages floated gently back to Earth to be recovered, refueled, and reused.

Several of the observers at the launch noted the unusual inclination of the departure track, the rocket climbing southeast rather than due east as the previous launch had done. No one thought to ask why.

***

The celebration had been underway for over an hour. The large poster board check that the NASA Administrator had presented to Tom during the formal ceremony for winning the Low Cost Launch Centennial Challenge was sitting on an easel in the corner of the room. Members of the team who had contributed to today's successful launch were lining up to have their pictures taken holding it. Drinks flowed freely and the buffet had suffered a fatal blow.

"Well young man, how does it feel to be two hundred million dollars richer?" Will Daisy asked Tom with a slight slur.

"You'd think it would feel wonderful, Congressman, but actually, I'm just relieved," Tom replied. "We've already spent the money getting here, that and more. At least now we can pay a few of the bills. Oh, and maybe provide some back pay and a bonus for the team!" he added, raising his voice and his glass. A cheer erupted from the assembled celebrants in response.

"So how long will it be until the next party?" Will asked, pronouncing "next" as "nesht".

"How's that, Congressman?" Tom said.

"When are you going to do this moon trip of yours? I like giving away money and I want to do more of it!"

"It will be quite a while yet, Congressman," Tom explained. "We have to get our human rating for our Big Brother booster, and we're still trying to get our operator's permit for our Vandenberg site. And there's still quite a lot of work to do to get our Space Train system running."

Will waved his hand dismissively. "You call, call me, call my office next week and we'll fix it for you. Have someone call me." Will looped his arm around Tom's neck and smiled.

Tom glanced at Nicole, his eyes saying, "Are you getting this?" She nodded and then put her arm around Will's waist.

"I'll call your office first thing on Monday, Congressman," she said. "Now let's go see if we can find a lady a drink somewhere."

"That would be de, delightful, young lady," Will said with a hiccup. "I know just the place," he added, allowing Nicole to steer him toward the bar.

"Someone's having a fun time," Marcus chuckled, approaching Tom and watching Nicole escort the tipsy Congressman away.

"Well, he is having a pretty good day," Tom noted. "He has a lot of happy constituents here." Looking around, he asked, "Have you seen Luke and Dr. Heinel by the way? I haven't seen them since the presentation."

"They grabbed a quick bite and then headed over to the booster recovery dock," Marcus said. "The Big Brothers were expected to arrive soon, and they wanted to be there to take an initial look."

"The hardest working people I know," Tom said with pride. "They're missing a hell of a party though."

***

Bob could hear the noise and laughter coming from the ballroom ahead. As he approached the door, a young staffer stationed there stopped him and asked, "Your invitation please?"

Flashing his press credentials, he failed to impress the door guard. "I'm sorry sir," she said, "but this is a closed event, by invitation only."

"OK, wait a minute," he said, and then made a show of fishing around in his pockets. Pulling out a creased and stained post card, he handed it to her. "I sort of spilled some coffee on it," he added sheepishly.

"Thank you, sir," she smiled, glancing quickly at the card and then opening the door for Bob.

Well that worked well, he thought. It had been a simple matter to borrow an invitation from a friend who worked for Alliance Space Systems and make a quick color copy on card stock. He thought adding some grime would make it less likely that it would be scrutinized too closely.

Entering the room, Bob surveyed the crowd. Deciding it was essential to his cover, he headed to the bar to get a drink. "Any single malts?" he asked the bartender.

"No sir, only Johnnie Walker and Chivas."

"OK, I'll take a Chivas on the rocks, make it a double," he said, throwing a dollar in the fish bowl on the counter. Picking up his drink and turning around, he found himself face to face with Nicole and Will.

"Bob, you old bastard, how're you doing?" Will said a little too loudly. "Where you been? The party started hours ago!"

"Congressman," Bob nodded politely, while eyeing Nicole warily. "I had some things to do first before I could make the drive over."

"I didn't think this event was open to the press," Nicole said icily.

"Don't be silly, Bob's a friend!" Will said sloppily. "Of course he's welcome!"

"If you'll both excuse me, I see someone I need to talk to for a moment," Bob said, turning to lose himself in the crowd.

"Come by later and I'll buy you a drink!" Will called after him. Nicole attempted to follow Bob with her eyes, but in a moment he was lost in the crush of loud celebrants.

That was close, Bob thought, as he headed toward where he believed he had seen Tom Armac when he first entered the room. Spotting Marcus' bald head above the crowd, he navigated in that direction.

Tom, Marcus and Tyler were laughing loudly at a story about Carl that Mike had just finished telling when Bob found them. "Mr. Armac, congratulations!" he said as he pushed through the ring of people that surrounded them.

"Mr. Brock. Welcome to our party," Tom said curtly, while giving Marcus a sidelong glance. "Thank you."

"Mr. Brock, this party is for employees and invited guests only," Marcus began, taking a step forward. Tom held up his hand and cut him off.

"It's OK, Marcus, no harm done. Please have a drink, Mr. Brock, and help yourself to some food if there's any left."

"Thank you sir, I already have," Bob said, holding up his scotch. "Can I ask you a couple of questions, Mr. Armac?"

"We're not doing a press availability this evening, Mr. Brock. It's been a long day and a very long journey and we just want to celebrate our accomplishment if you don't mind."

"I understand, sir, and it's well deserved. It's just that I'm getting ready to release a series of articles, and I thought you might like the chance to comment first."

"Articles on what, Mr. Brock?" Tom asked.

"On how you used your museum in California as a front to obtain Atlantis."

"That's not much of a story, Mr. Brock," Tom said coolly.

"And how you plan to use Atlantis as the 'Lunar Voyager' you've supposedly been developing for your moon mission."

Tom gazed calmly at Bob, but said nothing. Those close enough to hear grew very quiet.

"Mr. Armac, is RRI planning to fly Atlantis to the moon?"

"I'm sorry, what was that question?" Tom asked, looking over the crowd.

"Is RRI planning to fly Atlantis to the moon?" Bob repeated, more loudly this time.

Tom looked at Marcus, who looked at Tyler, who looked at Mike, who looked back at Tom. Suddenly, they all burst out laughing.

"Are you serious, Mr. Brock? Because that's amusing as hell," Tom said.

This wasn't the response Bob had expected. "Mr. Armac, I have information that you do intend to use Atlantis to fly your moon mission, and that your museum was just a ruse to make it possible. If you'd care to comment on that, I'll consider revising my article, but if not, then I'll go with what I have."

"You do that, Mr. Brock. Go right ahead and publish whatever you want," Tom said with a smile. "Flying Atlantis to the moon. Why the hell didn't we think of that, Marcus? Think of all the money we could have saved!"

"I know, boss, right? Stupid us!" Marcus said with a grin as he smacked himself in the forehead with the palm of his hand.

"Well thanks for the laugh, Mr. Brock. It was good seeing you again," Tom said, and then turned back to his companions.

Bob stood awkwardly for a moment and then turned and headed for the door. Finishing his drink, he set it down on an empty tray. *We'll see how damn funny it is,* he thought angrily as he left.

Tom leaned over and spoke quietly to Marcus. "Pry Nicole loose from the Congressman for a moment and ask her to come see me."

"You got it, boss."

***

Bob was startled by the 'bleep bleep' sound of his office phone announcing he had an internal call. He'd come in on the weekend specifically to work without distractions. Glancing at the phone display, he was surprised to see that his editor was paging him.

What's Marion doing in on a Saturday? he thought as he answered the phone. "Good morning Marion. Yes, just came in to finish the next article for the series I showed you. What brings you in on a weekend? Sure, be right there," he said, hanging up the phone. *Wonder what she needs to see me about that couldn't wait until Monday?*

Grabbing his coffee and taking the stairs to the third floor, Bob headed to his editor's office. "Come in," he heard in response to his tap on the door. Pushing it open, he almost dropped his coffee cup in surprise.

Inside, Nicole was sitting in one of Marion's' guest chairs holding a copy of the draft article Bob had submitted. He stood in the doorway, his mouth silently opening and closing like a gasping goldfish.

"Come in, Bob, close the door and have a seat," Marion said. Bob complied.

"Bob, I believe you have met Ms. Ferry?" Marion asked.

"Um, yes, yes I have," he replied cautiously.

"Ms. Ferry called me at home this morning and asked if she could come in and speak to me about the series you've been working on."

"I'm sorry to have to inconvenience you both by asking for a weekend meeting," Nicole said pleasantly, "but I have to be in DC tomorrow and I thought we should discuss my company's concerns as soon as possible."

Bob looked back and forth from Nicole to Marion. "They're trying to kill my series, aren't they?" he asked indignantly.

Marion smiled confidently. "Now Bob, you should know me better than that. I don't fold up when someone applies a little pressure over printing something. No one is trying to kill your story."

"My company is just concerned that if you intend to publish an article about our moon program, that it be accurate," Nicole observed. She held up the article Marion had given her. The headline said "Atlantis As Lunar Voyager?" "We're engaged at the moment in final negotiations with dozens of potential sponsors, and we're concerned that the release of false or misleading information that could potentially cast doubt on our ability to successfully complete this project will have a negative impact on those negotiations."

"And this is my concern why?" Bob asked defiantly.

"Well, if you publish information that damages my company's position in ongoing financial negotiations, and that information turns out to be inaccurate or meritless, your paper could incur legal liability for damages."

"Is there an implied threat there?" Bob asked.

"Now Bob, I just want to give you an opportunity to defend your research and explain your conclusions," Marion said. "The paper doesn't want to incur unnecessary legal liability, after all."

Bob looked angrily at the two women. "You've been spending a fortune getting Atlantis ready for flight," he declared to Nicole.

"To maximize the value of the vehicle in order to obtain the largest possible tax benefit when it is donated to the charitable foundation that runs the Aerospace Museum of the Pacific," Nicole replied. "Trust me when I say the enhanced value more than compensates us for the additional expense."

"You're claiming that a delay in completing your museum requires you to keep Atlantis at Vandenberg for months, but I saw your facilities myself, and they look ready now."

"And you have the background in engineering and architecture to visually evaluate the site and determine its readiness? Or are you basing this on something a newly hired social host casually mentioned to you?"

"I talked to one of the ASS techs who's been working on Atlantis," Bob said, less confidently. "He told me that there are unusual modifications being secretly made to the vehicle."

"You spoke to a disgruntled employee who has subsequently been terminated by Alliance Space Systems," Nicole said, pulling a page from her briefcase and reading from it. "One Juan Meneurez, whose last words to his supervisor were 'I'll make you bastards pay for this.' And if I may, wasn't he in fact intoxicated the day you spoke to him?"

Bob felt a wave of panic. "You're moving Atlantis to the launch pad at Slick Six, which you've been preparing to handle a shuttle launch for almost a year."

"We're moving Atlantis to the launch pad to support development of a feature film we intend to produce while waiting for our museum facilities to be completed," Nicole said firmly. "A launch pad that we have upgraded to support Space Train launches expected to begin early next year."

"A film? What film?" Bob asked desperately.

"Ms. Ferry outlined to me her company's plans to assist with production of a motion picture featuring the space shuttle," Marion said. "The pad you mentioned will be one of the sites used as a set for filming."

"But I saw your plans on the walls in that conference room in your museum. It was all there, the whole thing!" Bob cried.

"You saw a movie set that was being prepared for filming in support of the planned production," Nicole said calmly. Reaching again into her briefcase, she pulled out a business card and handed it to Marion. "This gentleman is our creative director at New Millennium Multimedia in Hollywood, California. You can call him if you wish to confirm what I'm telling you."

"But, but," Bob sputtered.

"Mr. Brock, we can go back and forth like this all day if you'd like, but the bottom line is that you looked at two and two and came up with five. We have an alternate explanation for every deduction or conclusion you have reached in this article. The *correct* explanation," she added dismissively.

"Marion, I'm telling you, I've been there, I've talked to people. What she's saying sounds good but it's not the truth. The truth is right there in that article," he said, pointing at the pages in Nicole's hand.

Nicole sighed deeply. Returning Bob's article to Marion, she said, "Thank you for the opportunity to review this. You of course are perfectly within your rights to publish whatever you wish. But we will immediately offer our explanation for what is actually occurring with Atlantis. Your reporter will undoubtedly end up looking extremely foolish and in the process tarnish your paper's reputation. And then there is the liability issue if your reporting undermines our ongoing financial negotiations. Now if you'll excuse me, I have a lot to do before leaving town." Standing to leave, she offered Bob a business card.

"My card, Mr. Brock, in case you need further explanation. Please note my additional contact information on the back. Thank you both for your time." Shaking hands briefly with Marion, she left.

Bob glanced at Nicole's card, and then briefly flipped it over. On the back, he spotted a small handwritten note that said "Parking lot, 10 minutes, be there."

"Well, Bob?" Marion asked. "What are we to do about you and this story?"

"Marion, can you hold that thought for a few minutes? I really need to run to the restroom, I'll be back in fifteen minutes or so. Bad breakfast burrito, I think," he said, holding his stomach.

***

Nicole stood beside her rental car impatiently tapping her foot as she talked on the phone.

"Yes, I think it went very well. Here he comes now, I'll call you back shortly." Hanging up, she waved to attract Bob's attention.

"You really worked me over good in there," he said as he approached. "Bravo on making me out to be a complete fool."

"Get over it, I'm about to make your day. Your life, possibly."

"What the hell do you mean by that?" Bob asked, startled.

"Look, I'm short on time, so I'll get right to the point. If you were right about Atlantis, and we were intending to fly her to the moon, that would be a pretty amazing story, wouldn't it?" she asked.

"Damn right it would, why do you think I've been like a dog after a bone for so long on this?"

"Well, someone would have to write that story, wouldn't they? And then afterwards, there would be books. Lots of books. Official histories and narratives; biographies of the crew. A lot of juicy opportunities for a well-connected writer."

"OK, I'm listening."

"Drop the story, Mr. Brock. Tell me right now that you're dropping it. You can say whatever you'd like about the museum or our Space Train program, but no more about Atlantis and the moon."

"And if I do?"

"How does exclusive rights sound? Sole access to project principals? How about 'official historian' and 'authorized biographer?' The principal documenter for one of this century's most historic events of exploration. Would you like that, Mr. Brock?"

It only took seconds for Bob to realize the potential in the implied offer. Freedom forever from petty deadlines on minor articles that no one read or remembered. Real financial security with the ability to someday retire.

"How do I know this is legit?" he asked.

"Tell me you're dropping it and I'll give you proof."

"OK, it's dropped. Pretty sure my editor is going to kill it anyway after today."

"Not good enough," Nicole said firmly, looking Bob squarely in the eyes. "Tell me you're dropping it completely and not just letting your editor kill an article. I don't want to have this same conversation again with you a month from now."

"OK, I'll totally and completely drop the story if you can back up your offer. You have my word."

"Good enough," Nicole said, and then reached for her phone and dialed. "Hello? Yes, he's ready. OK, I'll put him on." Nicole passed the phone to Bob.

"Hello?" Bob said.

"Hello, Mr. Brock. Tom Armac here. Welcome aboard. Let me tell you about a project we're working on that I believe you might find interesting ... "

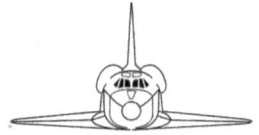

CHAPTER THIRTY–TWO

Mark Rutherford couldn't wait to share the good news. After the Jadranko debacle, he'd thought that finding a more suitable candidate would require a long and arduous effort, but the perfect person had simply appeared as if pre-ordained. The financial transaction was already in process, and Mark had a big decision to make—was his new Porsche 911 going to be silver, or black? Smiling, he picked up his phone and dialed.

***

Marcus hit "end" and hung up, still stunned by the news. *The boss is going to freak*, he thought. He dialed Nicole, who was still in Washington working with Congressman Daisy's staff on the final details of their permits.

"Nicole? Marcus. You're not going to believe this. Mark Rutherford called. He has our passenger for us. Yep, paid in full. But get this ... "

***

Nicole hung up, anxious and drained. *Mr. Armac is going to completely flip out*, she thought. *What to do. Think.* She pursed her lips in concentration. *OK, I know ...*

She called Tom, hoping to catch him before his plane left for the west coast. "Mr. Armac? Hi, listen, have you left Florida yet? Great, could I get you to stop off here in Washington for a day? Check with JetsOnline and see if they can reroute you. We're having a little issue with the FAA's Commercial Space Transportation office regarding our human rating certification, and I'd like you to go talk to them with me. Sure, tomorrow morning will be fine. I'll meet you at Dulles airport. OK, see you then."

Hanging up, she let out a deep breath. *I sure hope I still have a job after tomorrow*, she thought.

***

Nicole waited for Tom in the main lounge of the civil aviation terminal. She had been practicing what to say most of the morning. She waved to catch his attention as he entered the building.

"How are you this morning?" she asked pleasantly, leading him toward her waiting car.

"Fine, thanks. The flight was pleasantly uneventful. I'm sure you've heard that both Big Brothers checked out fine in their post-flights?" Tom said as they walked.

"Yes, Marcus sent me a message. That's great news."

"So tell me more about this certification problem," Tom said. "I thought the Congressman had promised us clear sailing?"

Here goes, she thought. "Oh, that. That's taken care of. I convinced the FAA to agree that if our next launch is successful, they'll go ahead and issue our human rating, since that will make five boosters flown and three more fired in static tests. That gives us a good baseline for safety projections."

Tom stopped and looked at Nicole with puzzled irritation. "Then why didn't you tell me so that I could head straight back to Vandenberg?"

"Well, after I spoke with you yesterday, Mark Rutherford called and asked to meet with us," Nicole said, starting to walk again, Tom following. "Since you were already heading this way, I told him we'd stop in before lunch."

"Meet with us about what?" Tom said. "I still have a bitter taste in my mouth from the last time we met."

"You told him to find someone else, and I think he has, but he wants to talk to you about it."

"OK, well, this shouldn't take too long then, right?" Tom asked.

"An hour, ninety minutes tops," Nicole replied.

"Let me see then if I can get them to hold the plane for me. I can still make it back to Vandenberg this evening."

Nicole drove as Tom called the JetsOnline scheduler. Fortunately for her, the drive from Dulles to the Destination Beyond offices took less than 20 minutes, and Tom spent the entire time rescheduling his flight.

"OK, good," Tom said, finally hanging up. "They can hold the plane here for two hours, so I can still make it back to the west coast tonight."

"Well let's just see what Mark has to say, and then I'll get you right back to the airport," Nicole said, parking the car.

"So what do we know about this candidate," Tom said, as they waited for the elevator.

"Not much," Nicole replied, "but apparently he paid in full."

"You're not holding out on me again are you?" Tom asked. "No *conditions* this time that you aren't telling me about?"

"None that I'm aware of," Nicole said with a smile.

As the elevator doors opened, Nicole turned to Tom and said, "Now remember, we really need this money to finish the work at Vandenberg and keep to our schedule."

"OK … " Tom said hesitantly.

"I'm just saying. Remember that."

Reaching the Destination Beyond suite, Tom pushed open the frosted glass door and held it for Nicole. Entering the office lobby after her, he saw Mark Rutherford talking to another man—a man Tom didn't immediately recognize because he stood with his back to the door. As Nicole and Tom entered, they heard Mark say, "Here they are now."

The man turned around, smiled, and said, "Hello, Tom."

Tom stood face to face with Elton Funk. "Oh hell no!" he said. Then, turning to Nicole, he added, "You're fired!"

***

"Look, Tom, I know we've had our issues," Elton said. "But it's clear that I underestimated you and your team."

"Underestimated? How about denigrated, disparaged, and belittled. What was it you said to that *Aviation Monthly* reporter? We were children playing in a grownup world? That we should give up before we hurt ourselves?"

"Yes, well … " Elton said, rubbing the back of his neck with his hand.

"Or the industry panel at the commercial launch symposium, where you said only fools would think a candle could fly?" Tom continued angrily.

"It's business, Tom, not kindergarten. Sometimes you let a few elbows fly."

"It's business? Right. And part of being in business is strangling your competition in their crib before they can become a threat. That's how the grownups do it, right? I know it was you who was leaning on all the venture capital firms to not return my calls back when we needed seed money to get off the ground. And now you come to me and say you want to fly with us? Grab a piece of our glory? No way, not going to happen."

The two men glared uneasily at each other.

"So is Mr. Funk also an unacceptable candidate?" Mark asked glumly.

"Hell yes he is," Tom said firmly.

"Well maybe you should give me a list of everybody you find unacceptable, so I can work backward from that," Mark said with exasperation, watching his Porsche dreams evaporate. "It would result in a lot less frustration for everyone."

"Well maybe we need to conclude this relationship, and we'll go find someone else to broker our passenger seat … " Tom began.

"Listen, you two!" Nicole said forcefully. "Knock it off!" Turning to Tom, she said, "Mr. Armac, you need this seat sold, because you need the revenue to finish this project. You know how over budget we are. If you say no to this deal, we're done."

"We can find the money."

"No we can't. You don't have the luxury of time any more. Right now, we can't pay the transport costs on the external tank when it arrives next week, or the performance bonus we've promised the pad contractor for finishing construction ahead of schedule. You've got people who believe in what you're doing so much that they're working at half salary, but you won't do what's necessary to pay the bills because your feelings have been hurt!"

"Mr. Rutherford?" Tom asked, turning to Mark. "Tell me this isn't all you've got."

Mark shrugged his shoulders. "I told you at the beginning that this was going to be difficult. I said I could find you a candidate, and I can, but I'll need at least another six months, possibly a year."

"I'd rather fly with the Croatian hacker," Tom said bitterly.

Everyone stood in uneasy silence for a moment.

"Look Tom, I was wrong," Elton said. "I thought your booster ideas were unworkable, and yes, even dangerous. But you proved you know what you're doing. Congratulations to you. And that Space Train, that's just brilliant. But you and I share a common dream, you know."

"What dream would that be?" Tom asked angrily.

"To go to the moon, of course. To break out of low Earth orbit and actually get out there. EtherX was never just about launching rockets. My plan from the beginning has been to develop the systems capable of making trips to the moon and beyond. But my development plan spans decades. You've figured out a way to go now. It's not the way I'd do it, it's more a onetime stunt, but it will work. And I want in."

"How much do you actually know about our plan?" Tom asked.

"I read Dr. Heinel's paper, so pretty much everything. And I had Bob Brock do some checking to help me figure out how far along you were."

"Bob Brock," Tom sniffed. "He works for us now."

"So I hear."

After another moment of awkward silence, Tom asked, "And what would your conditions be?"

"No conditions. It's your mission, I'm just a paying passenger."

Turning to Nicole, Tom said, "And you knew about this?"

"Yes sir, since yesterday. What Mr. Funk is failing to mention is that in addition to paying the entire fee up front, he's also offered to provide technical support for the mission hardware we purchased from his company."

"The Wizard engine on Tinkerbell?" Tom asked.

"Tinkerbell?" Elton said, confused by the reference.

"Tinkerbell is our lunar lander," Nicole explained. "Yes, the Wizard, and the Viper attitude thrusters. A full technical team for mission support."

"Viv would like that," Tom observed, nodding.

"Yes, she would, very much," Nicole affirmed.

Tom thought furiously for several moments. He wanted to say no with every fiber of his being. But he knew they faced an imminent financial crisis, and he finally admitted to himself that Elton Funk was indeed the perfect candidate. Not only would their immediate cash shortage be solved, but he would provide Vivian with additional technical resources, increasing their odds of success. And in this case, success was defined as everyone making it home alive. It made too much sense to reject.

"So we declare a truce," Tom offered.

"A truce?" asked Elton.

"I hate your guts, and I don't see that changing in the immediate future. But apparently we need each other right now. So we both agree to put what's past behind us and work on accomplishing this mission. Afterwards, we'll just have to see."

"A truce," Elton declared, extending his hand.

"All right, it's a deal," Tom said, shaking Elton's hand. "Pack your bags, we leave in eight weeks."

"Wait, what?" Elton said, his eyes large with surprise.

Tom smiled. "I guess there may be a few things you might not have heard."

***

Marcus added Elton Funk's name to the crew list on the personnel board at Neverland. Standing back, he shook his head. "Did not see that coming. Nope, sure didn't."

"He'll be flying out next week for his initial orientation," Nicole said, sitting down at the conference table in the empty seat between Robbie and Vivian.

Tom entered the room and sat down in his usual spot. Turning to Nicole, he said, "I thought I fired you."

Everyone's head suddenly jerked around. Nicole laughed lightly.

"Yeah, as if you could run this operation without me," she said. "Are you planning on staying behind to fight with the FAA in my absence?"

"OK, well, since I can't get rid of you, why don't you go first," Tom said, looking up at the display to ensure that Luke, Mike and Dr. Heinel were linked in from the Cape.

"You'll have to bring Congressman Daisy back a nice moon rock," Nicole began. "I had to remind him of our conversation at the post-award party, but he made sure we received our site operator's permit as he'd promised. And the FAA will issue a human rating certification for our Big Brother when they see a bit more flight data to validate our safety

212

calculations."

"You hear that Luke? No mistakes," Tom said to Luke's broadcast image.

"Boss, please," Luke said, feigning insult.

"Don't worry, I know you guys are giving it one hundred ten percent," Tom said. "How's the schedule looking?"

"Both Big Brothers handled the flight extremely well," Luke said. "We're on track to start fuel casting next week."

"OK, great. Jean? How's Wendy?" Tom asked, using the nickname the team had adopted for the first OMS fuel module now orbiting the planet.

"Wendy's a good girl," Jean replied. "Orbit is stable, patiently awaiting arrival of her companion."

"Excellent. Viv?" Tom said, working around the room.

"The external tank should be arriving in three more days," Vivian said. "They ran into some weather and put in to San Diego to wait it out, but the tug captain reports Pegasus should be underway again tomorrow morning."

"Any problems securing the pier at Vandenberg?"

"No, the Air Force says we can leave the barge tied up for as long as we need, there's no rush to offload the tank. I've made arrangements to move it to the pad once we all get back from Star City."

"Glad you brought that up," Tom said, looking up at the screen. "Mike, Dr. Heinel, do you two have your bags packed? We'll be leaving for Moscow at the end of next week for mission orientation training."

"Indeed, Mr. Armac, although I'm afraid I recently realized that my passport has expired," Carl replied, standing behind Mike and peering over his shoulder. "I've requested expedited renewal, so with luck I should have it back any day now."

"It's always the little things that trip you up," Tom chuckled. "OK, Tyler, how did the filming go?"

"That was the most fun I've ever had with my clothes on," Tyler replied. "It took four days to hit all ten candidates, but you've never seen so much excitement. New Millennium is editing the footage for the premier now."

"OK, well that's about the quickest status brief ever," Tom noted. Looking at the screen, he said, "Dr. Heinel, I believe you had an issue you wanted to discuss?"

"Yes, Mr. Armac, thank you," Carl said, shifting to take Mike's seat in front of the web cam. "Ladies and gentlemen, one outstanding issue still to be resolved is the matter of where exactly we intend to land upon achieving the moon's surface."

"We've worked out a selection of possible primary and alternate sites," Robbie said, looking briefly at Stephanie.

"I've looked at the list Mr. Robichaud has proposed," Carl said, "and while they each have merit, I would submit that we consider visiting a different location than the ones identified."

"And what site would you recommend, Doctor?" Tom asked, glancing at Robbie.

"Palus Putredinus," Carl said simply.

"How's that Doctor?"

"The Marsh of Decay. Mons Hadley, specifically."

Robbie and Stephanie exchanged a quick glance. "You mean Hadley Rille, Doctor? The Apollo 15 landing site?" Robbie asked.

"Precisely, Mr. Robichaud. I think there is merit is re-visiting one of the Apollo mission landing sites. This one specifically."

"OK, Doctor, why, and why this one?" Tom asked.

"Well, Mr. Armac, first of all, I believe it would be more interesting to *make* history while *revisiting* history. Better *buzz*, as young Mr. Allen might say. And it would give us the opportunity to gather more than lunar regolith as samples. We could potentially recover artifacts from the previous mission, which I'm sure you realize would make very attractive additions to our museum. It would also provide opportunities for scientific research to determine the effects of long term exposure to the lunar environment on hardware and materials."

"Backpacks, tools, surface experiments, even the flag they planted," Robbie said, nodding. "He's right, it would be nice to be able to bring some of that back, see how they held up."

"Not to mention the first lunar rover," Carl continued. "Quite a prize that would be, though I regret that as attractive an exhibit as it would make, we may find it a difficult object to recover due to its size. Regardless, I believe there is much merit in re-visiting a previous landing site."

"I see what you mean, Doctor," Tom said, nodding.

"The Apollo 11 site should remain sacrosanct in recognition of its historical significance, as I believe the Apollo 17 site should as well," Carl said. "Apollo 15 was squarely in the middle, with no unique historical significance. As the first of the extended 'J' missions, it carried additional experiments and equipment, which increases the likelihood of finding recoverable artifacts. Moreover, the unusual geology of the area offers ample opportunity to perform useful science. And of all the Apollo missions, it was the only one that generated some small degree of controversy."

"Controversy? What type of controversy?" Marcus asked.

"Contraband," Robbie said. "The crew took unauthorized postal covers with them on the flight. They'd made a secret deal with a stamp dealer to fly them to the moon and then sell them when they returned. They got in a world of shit for it when word got out. It ended their careers, none of them ever flew again."

"Indeed," Carl said. "And as we are also bringing along postal covers, well, the parallel history is somewhat amusing to contemplate, don't you think?"

"If NASA were to make a stink about any of these sites, this would probably be the one they'd be least interested in protecting," Robbie said.

"What do you think, Robbie? You're the mission commander," Tom asked.

"If I remember my lunar geography, we'll have to drop in over the Apennine Mountains to hit the valley where they landed. Could raise the pucker factor quite a bit. But if they could do it with late-sixties technology, I'm sure we'd be just fine."

"There is one more reason why I would prefer this specific location," Carl interjected.

"Go ahead, Doctor," Tom said.

"I realize this may be considered a matter of personal interest, but as you know, this trip is in fulfillment of a promise I made many years ago."

The mood in the room turned somber. "We remember, Doctor," Tom nodded.

"Well, in addition to my personal loss, I also experienced the loss of many fine colleagues over the years. I was acquainted with many of the brave young men and women who were on Challenger, Columbia and the ISS when each suffered catastrophe. As a personal tribute to their memories, I would like to add their names to the Fallen Astronaut memorial."

"I'm sorry, the what?" Tom asked.

"Another Apollo 15 controversy," Robbie answered. "But one that NASA eventually embraced. The crew paid an artist to make a small aluminum sculpture that represented a space suited astronaut. It's a tiny thing, only like three or four inches tall. They left it on the moon along with a small plaque that listed the names of all the astronauts and cosmonauts that had lost their lives prior to their flight. They turned off the surface broadcast for a few moments and had a little ceremony. They didn't tell anyone about it until after they got back."

"I ... didn't know that," Tom said earnestly.

"It's well known in the community," Robbie said. "Doc, you've convinced me. I'd definitely like to help you with that."

"Absolutely," Stephanie confirmed.

"That's very admirable, Doctor," Tom said. "OK, it's settled them. Palus Putredinus is our spot. I just wish it had a more upbeat name."

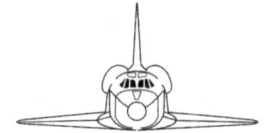

CHAPTER THIRTY–THREE

On a Thursday night in mid-October, millions of people sat in front of their televisions, tickets in hand, to watch the premier episode of *The Last Passenger*. Most realized that because no one was waiting on their doorstep with a television camera, they weren't among the lucky few. Some still believed that they were watching a live broadcast, and held on to hope. As is typical of Hollywood, a few liberties had been taken with the details of the event.

"Hush, it's starting!" Vivian said, un-muting the sound on Neverland's projection screen as the opening credits appeared.

"Popcorn?" Marcus asked, pushing the freshly popped bag to the center of the table.

"Shhhhhhhh!"

"So who's this guy?" Tom asked, shoving a handful of popcorn into his mouth while indicating the person on the screen who was describing what was about to happen.

"That's Bryant Hastings," Nicole answered, opening a can of soda and reaching for the popcorn. "He's big on reality TV, he hosts a bunch of shows."

"Never heard of him," Tom observed, munching.

"That's because you never watch television."

"Shhhhhhhh!"

Bryant walked down a darkened hallway, paused before a closed door and turned to look at the viewers over his shoulder. "And now, the time has come," he said dramatically. Opening the door, he stepped into a brightly lit computer center in which numerous lab coated scientists were performing a variety of indecipherable tasks. Visible on the walls between the racks of blinking servers were photos of rockets lifting off.

"Man, their Neverland is *so* much cooler than ours," Marcus observed.

"Are you ready, Dr. Williams?" Bryant asked an attractive brunette wearing red framed glasses and matching red lipstick, her hair in a tight bun. Her lab coat sported a large Roadrunner Rockets logo.

"Who's she?" Marcus asked. "I don't remember hiring her!"

"That's Tyler, can't you tell?" Robbie replied. "Well, the hot female Hollywood version of Tyler, anyway."

"Would you be *quiet!*" Vivian said, throwing a handful of popcorn at Marcus and Robbie.

"Ready, Mr. Hastings," the hot doctor said, adjusting her glasses. She turned to the console before her and started typing. "Beginning selection process now."

Bryant addressed the audience again. "As each candidate is identified, a collection team will spring into action to locate and intercept the selectee wherever they may be and return them here so that they can begin their training and start the final selection process."

"They had one team of three people do all the notifications," Tyler explained, "but they changed clothes and hats each time so you'd think they were different teams."

"Oh man, stop it, you're ruining the magic!" Marcus laughed.

"Localizing our first candidate now, Mr. Hastings," the hot doctor said, as the lights on her console blinked and emitted various electronic sounds. She looked to the large display screens on the wall above her. The one on the left had been cycling through a blur of images, but now stopped and displayed the standing figure of an adult male, his vital statistics printing out alongside. One corner of the display showed a close-up of his face.

"John C. Sullivan, of Palo Alto, California," she announced. The image on the right hand display above her showed the Earth from space, and it now placed electronic crosshairs above Palo Alto and then flew rapidly in to show the continent, the state, the town, the neighborhood, and finally an aerial view of John's house.

"Collection team one deploying now," another lab-coated person said, pushing several buttons. The screen on his console showed a small group of people running to a parked van, jumping in and speeding away, a yellow light flashing on its roof as a siren wailed.

"Yeah, we totally filmed that shot in the studio parking lot," Tyler said. "One of them is my girlfriend Eva."

"Well I can't hear a damn thing with you all babbling on the way you are," Vivian said, annoyed.

The scene now showed the van pulling rapidly up to John Sullivan's house. The team got out, knocked on the door, confirmed John's identity when he answered, and then escorted him to the van.

"Took us almost a day of phone tag to meet up with him, and then we needed three takes to get the abduction scene right," Tyler noted.

"Localizing candidate number two," the hot doctor said.

The screens now displayed Melissa Lowell of Perth, Australia.

"Deploying international collection team zone three," the technician said. The entire scene played out again, this time with the van making the 'NEE nee NEE nee' sound of a foreign siren. They 'found' Melissa shopping for groceries in her local market and spirited her away, leaving her half full cart behind.

"Man, this is just too funny," Marcus laughed. "I'm never going to believe anything I see on television again."

***

"Are the overnights in?" Len asked anxiously the moment he entered his office.

"Not yet, I'm checking again now," Lanetta said, entering her password on the rating system's website for the eighteenth time that morning. "Wait, here they are … oh my God."

"What? Bad? Are they bad? If they're bad we still have the overseas numbers, they aren't in yet," Len said, panicking.

"Look," Lanetta said in disbelief, turning the screen slowly toward Len.

"That, wait, that can't be right. Can it?" Len asked in amazement. Slowly, he read aloud, "a forty-two rating, and an eighty-three share?"

"My God," Lanetta said again, slumping in her seat.

Len shook his head, and then let out a big whoop. "That's it baby! Who's got the highest rated cable show ever? We do, that's who! Uh huh!"

Len's desk phone rang, and Lanetta absently reached out and picked it up. "Hello?" she said distantly. Holding the phone out to Len, she said, "It's for you. It's the network."

"I'll bet it is, baby! Tell them I'm busy, I'll get back to them!" Then, dancing around the office, he began chanting, "Who's got the highest rated cable show ever? We do, that's who!" over and over.

***

Marcus had moved to a quieter spot in the airport lounge to take the call. "So that's good news, right?" he asked. "OK, I'll let him know, thanks man," and then hung up and headed back to where Tom and Vivian were sitting.

"Hey boss, that was Tyler. He says he just spoke with Lanetta at New Millennium. Apparently we set some sort of ratings record with the premier."

"OK," Tom shrugged.

"Get this. Because the numbers were so good, they're going back to renegotiate the ad rates. He says we'll be five million dollars richer as a result. Thought you might like to know."

"Well hell, if I'd known that earlier, we'd have taken a charter to

Moscow instead of flying commercial," Tom said with a smile.

Across the lounge, the group of *The Last Passenger* candidates milled about, along with Bruce Trunly and his small three person video crew. Fortunately, the airport had been able to provide them with a private lounge, as the candidate's status as celebrities-of-the-moment had meant constant attention from the other passengers at the public departure gate.

"So what are they doing?" Tom asked, gesturing with his chin toward the group.

"Shooting pre-departure interviews for the show," Marcus replied. "Most of the video crew's gear is checked, but they brought some pocket HD camcorders to do spontaneous pickup stuff. They'll probably be at it the entire flight."

Studying the group, Tom noticed one of the candidates, a woman, fortyish, sitting alone off to one side, her hands firmly gripping the armrests of her seat.

"What's up with her?" Tom asked.

"Umm, that's Barbara something...Barbara Mackie I think?" Marcus replied. "She flew in from Montreal."

"She looks tense," Tom observed.

"She does, doesn't she," Vivian concurred, looking up from her book to observe the woman.

As they watched, one of the video crew approached Barbara and spoke to her. They saw her firmly shake her head "no," and the videographer shrugged and returned to the group.

"Interesting. Doesn't look like she wants to play," Tom observed. "On the other hand, Nikki looks like she's having the time of her life."

Nicole Biccari stood comfortably, one leg real, one not. She was wearing a Florida State hoodie, and her aluminum forearm crutch leaned against the seat behind her. She had an infectious smile and was grinning broadly as she conversed with Bruce and one of the videographers. She had asked to be called Nikki, which suited everyone on the team. It minimized confusion between her and their lead attorney.

"She's certainly caught Bruce's eye," Vivian noted, and then returned to her reading.

Over the public address system, they heard an automated voice announce "Aeroflot Russian Airlines flight 322 nonstop to Moscow will begin boarding momentarily through gate twenty-seven. Please gather your belongings and prepare to board Aeroflot Russian Airlines flight 322."

"OK, let's get this show on the road," Tom said, standing and grabbing his carry-on bag. "What time are Mike and Dr. Heinel arriving?" he asked Marcus.

"They should be in about an hour before us, they're flying through New York," Marcus answered.

A loud commotion caught their attention. Barbara Mackie now had a death grip on the arms of her seat and was deeply hyperventilating. Then, shaking violently, she began to cry.

"What the hell ... " Marcus began, as an airline attendant and several members of the group gathered around her.

"What's wrong, honey?" they heard the attendant ask, kneeling down and placing her hand on Barbara's arm.

In between rapid deep breaths, Barbara said, "I ... can't ... can't ... do it."

"Do what honey? You can't do what?"

"I ... can't ... can't ... get ... on." Her face now turned a bright red.

Bruce motioned to his video team. "Roll on this," he directed. They pulled out their cameras and began recording.

***

"So what was it?" Tom asked, leaning back in his seat as the plane leveled off.

"They said it was an acute anxiety attack," Marcus replied. "Apparently today was the first time she'd ever flown, and her flight in from Montreal hit some pretty rough turbulence over the Rockies. Scared the ever loving crap out of her."

"She'd never been on a plane, but she wanted to fly to the moon?" Tom asked incredulously. "How did she make it through the screening?"

"Well, it's not something that ever occurred to us to ask about," Marcus replied with a shrug. "And I guess even she didn't know how she'd react, since she'd never flown before. I mean, come on, who's never been on an airplane!"

"And then there were nine," Tom said, settling back in his seat.

***

Moscow in October is a gray and dreary place. Actually, Moscow is gray and dreary most of the year, but particularly so in October when the mild but too brief summer is only a fading memory and endless months of brutally frigid weather loom ahead. The long cold winters may be a major reason why Russians drink so heavily.

The motor coach stopped at a gated entrance in front of a nondescript glass and brick building, and the driver opened the boarding door so a uniformed guard could climb aboard. The guard quickly scanned the passengers, most of whom were in a mild stupor from the long flight followed by the hour-long bus trip. The driver handed him a clipboard that had been sitting on the dash. Giving it a quick review, the guard handed it back and spoke a few words. The driver then engaged the guard in what sounded like an argument, gesturing first to the clipboard, then to them, and then back to the clipboard again. He finally smacked his forehead with his palm and forcefully rapped on the clipboard with his knuckles. This apparently convinced the guard to let them pass. He climbed off the bus and nodded to a waiting associate, who opened the gate. As they drove through, Tom glanced out the window at the sign on the building. He couldn't read the Russian text, but below it the smaller English translation said "Yuri A Gagarin State Scientific Research and Testing Cosmonaut Training Center."

Rolling along a narrow highway through dense pine forest, the trees fell away and they emerged into a small gray town of featureless concrete buildings arranged along a long central thoroughfare. Stopping in front of one of the buildings, the driver opened the door, shut off the engine, and shouted, "You are here, everyone off," in accented English as he climbed off the bus.

Amid much groaning, everyone roused themselves, gathered their personal belongings, and shuffled off the bus. The driver had opened the baggage compartments underneath and was tossing their luggage into a large pile on the sidewalk.

"Hey, that's video equipment, be careful!" one of the film crew shouted.

Tom spotted Mark Rutherford standing to one side next to a man in a Russian military uniform.

"Greetings," the Russian called out. "Welcome to Star City. I hope you have had a pleasant journey."

Mark stepped forward. "Everyone please grab your bags and gather around, I have your room assignments. This is going to be home for the next week while you're receiving your orientation and training."

Tom shook Mark's hand. "Did Dr. Heinel and Mike Patrick make it in OK?" he asked.

"Yes, I gave them their room. You might find them in the lounge if they haven't already gone to bed," Mark replied.

"Welcome to Star City. I hope you have had a pleasant journey," the Russian said again.

"Yes, thank you, very pleasant," Tom said, with an exaggerated head nod.

"Don't mind the Colonel, that's the only English he knows," Mark explained.

"Well, he speaks more English than I do Russian," Tom said. Turning to shake the Colonel's hand, he said *"Thank you!"* very loudly.

"OK everyone, it's now a little after 10 PM local time, and your first briefing is at 6:30 tomorrow morning," Mark called out. "I'd recommend that you all get a good night's sleep, because you're going to have to hit the ground running tomorrow."

The Colonel said several sentences in Russian. It sounded friendly, and Mark smiled.

"The Colonel says there is a celebration tonight in your honor, to which you are all invited," Mark said to the group. "It would be polite to accept, but I'd recommend that you not stay too long. Particularly if you have no experience with Russian vodka."

"You speak Russian?" Tom asked Mark.

"A little, it helps with business."

"Then thank the Colonel for the hospitality if you would," Tom requested.

"It's not necessary. They find a reason to get drunk every night of the week," Mark replied. "Your arrival is just the excuse of the day."

***

Most of the group made a brief social visit to the party and then headed to their rooms, exhausted by the day of travel. A few tried to keep up with the Russians for a while, but quickly realized that they were dealing with professional drinkers and were sorely outclassed, and finally gave up around midnight. Willard Rogers, the cattle rancher from Nebraska who naturally preferred to be called Will, was certain that his years of knocking back Jack Daniels straight had toughened him for the challenge. He was determined to match his hosts drink for drink. He passed out shortly after one o'clock, and the Russians toasted his unconscious form.

***

"Where's Mr. Rogers?" Bruce asked, looking around the room. "The crew's ready to start filming."

"Are you missing someone?" Mark asked Tom, concerned. "The group needs to be at their orientation and safety brief in less than ten minutes so that they can make it to their physicals on time."

"He was still snoring as I left," said Drew Hibbert, the airline pilot and former Naval aviator from Virginia Beach. Drew was Will's assigned roommate.

"Did you try and wake him?" Mark asked.

"I kicked his bed, but he was a mess and told me to leave him alone, so I left him alone."

"Jesus Christ," Bruce said, as he and Mark headed to Will's room.

They found Will laying on his stomach amid a pile of vomit, one leg dangling off the bed. Bruce shook him vigorously, but his only response was a loud moan.

"Jesus Christ," Bruce said again. "OK, roll on it, but try not to get the puke in the frame," he said to his crew.

"Another one bites the dust," Marcus said, peering over the cameraman's shoulder. "Not quite the way we thought this was going to go."

***

Latonya Williams of Atlanta, Georgia didn't quite drown, but she did have a near-death experience. Apparently she'd grossly overstated her swimming ability when she had completed her submission form. Everyone before her had done relatively well at the water survival skills class. Nikki in particular swam with exceptional grace, removing her artificial limb and mimicking a dolphin's fluid motion with her single leg. She revealed afterwards that she'd been a competitive diver in high school.

When Latonya's turn came, she folded her arms and entered the water feet first as directed, and then sank like a stone. The moment her head went under, her mind apparently cleared of all the instruction she'd just received, and rather than inflating her survival vest as taught, she thrashed and flailed on the bottom of the pool, giant bubbles streaming from her mouth as she silently screamed. Both divers went in to rescue her, and once laid out beside the pool, she started breathing again on her own without needing artificial respiration.

***

"Here, put these on," Bruce said to Tom, Marcus and Vivian later that evening, handing each a crisply pressed white pilot's shirt with shoulder boards.

"What are these?" Vivian asked.

"Your uniforms for the elimination panel," Bruce replied. "We want you to look official, like real spacemen. Pin this over your left pocket," he added, handing each a small pair of gold wings.

The three sat side by side behind a table that displayed the *Last Passenger* logo. Marcus sat in the center, as the producers had chosen him to represent the flight crew due to his commanding presence and deep resonant voice. Before them stood Latonya Williams, shifting uncomfortably from one foot to the other.

"I'm sorry Latonya, but we have reviewed your performance today, and you have been removed from the mission," Marcus intoned somberly.

Seven candidates remained.

***

"Nice of you to join us," Tom said dismissively.

"I had several commitments I couldn't reschedule," Elton replied. "I received my orientation at your place in Long Beach, by the way. It's coming together very nicely. Mr. Robichaud said to say hello. I'm surprised that he and Ms. Peters aren't here."

"Robbie felt he and Stephanie have forgotten more astronaut stuff than we're going to learn in a week here, so he didn't see the need," Tom replied. "Did you catch the direct Aeroflot flight out of Los Angeles?"

"No, I caught my Gulfstream G650," Elton said with a smile.

"Of course you did," Tom scowled.

"So what have I missed?" Elton asked, watching with interest as the next candidate, James Nicholson from Cape Town, was fitted with his headgear and oxygen mask.

"We're down three already," Vivian said. "One never made it out of LAX, and another passed out in a drunken stupor the first night here." Turning to the viewing window of the hypobaric chamber, they watched as the chamber safety observer seated James inside and belted him in. "Nothing too dramatic yet today," she added. "It's been amusing though to see how silly everyone gets once hypoxia sets in."

They watched as the chamber was slowly depressurized to simulate an altitude of ten thousand feet. The safety observer removed James' oxygen mask and had him perform a series of simple tasks such as drawing geometric figures and counting how many fingers he was holding up. After five minutes he nodded to the chamber operator, who then rapidly reduced the pressure in the chamber to the equivalent of thirty thousand feet in order to simulate a sudden decompression.

James let out a loud shriek as blood suddenly spurted from both his ears. Everyone grimaced in sympathetic pain while Marcus rapidly sucked in his breathe and said, "Oh man, that's gotta hurt. Glad I'm not going in there."

James apparently had particularly delicate eardrums. "I'm sorry James, but you've been removed from the mission," Marcus said to him at that evening's panel.

"What's that?" James asked, holding a hand to his ear.

Only six were left.

***

By the third day, everyone had learned that when they were told to eat lightly and get a good night's sleep, it was good advice to follow. Tom, Elton, Vivian, Mike, Dr. Heinel, and the remaining six candidates had been suited up in flight gear and were now lying prone on the padded floor of the huge Ilyushin Il-76 cargo plane, mothered by several safety monitors and a flight surgeon. Bruce and his video team were securely belted to the bulkheads to keep them safely out of the way.

Nicknamed the Vomit Comet, the enormous plane began flying a repeating series of parabolic arcs to produce thirty second periods of weightlessness. The stated purpose was to test their performance in zero gee, but it actually seemed intended to induce the worst possible case of motion sickness in the least amount of time.

Drew Hibbert, the airline pilot, enjoyed himself immensely. During each period of weightlessness, he curled up into a ball and let several of the observers pass him back and forth.

As Robbie predicted, Nikki did very well. As the gravity came off, so did her handicap, and she moved even more effortlessly through the air than she had through the water.

Melissa Lowell, the candidate from Down Under, earned the nickname "The Fountain" for her awe-inspiring display of continuous projectile vomiting.

"Melissa, I'm sorry, but you've been removed from the mission," Marcus said that evening. Then turning to the cameraman behind him filming the elimination panel ceremony, he added, "Man, go take another shower, you still smell like puke."

Half of the original candidates had now washed out.

***

The fourth day began with another trip to the airfield. The training schedule was taking a lot out of everyone. On the bus ride out, Tom made it a point to sit next to Carl. "How are you holding up, Dr. Heinel?" he asked. "We could probably give you a pass on today's jump if you'd rather skip it."

Carl smiled his usual serene smile. "No, Mr. Armac, I need to prove that I'm not going to be a burden to anyone on the flight. I'm fine, please don't worry about me."

"You're on the flight regardless, Dr. Heinel. You don't need to prove anything to us."

"Oh, I'm not proving it to *you*, Mr. Armac. I'm proving it to myself," Carl said. "I would rather remain behind than be a burden and risk jeopardizing the success of the mission."

"Don't worry, boss, I'm keeping a close eye on Dr. Carl," Mike said, leaning forward from the next row. "I've promised him that I'll kick him in the ass if he freezes at the door."

"I believe I said *push*, Mr. Patrick, not *kick*," Carl said humorously.

Yeah, I guess he's doing just fine, Tom thought.

Once at the flight line, everyone was paired with an instructor for a tandem skydive. Watching as Tom and Vivian were fitted with their harnesses, Marcus said, "Now this one I wish I could do. I always thought it would be way cool to try."

"Do they make a super-double-extra-large parachute?" Mike asked.

"Oh man, don't be hatin' on big people like that," Marcus laughed.

Everyone sat quietly in their assigned spots on the benches as the plane climbed skyward. They really had no choice, as the noise from the twin turboprops drowned out any attempt at conversation. Once at altitude, the jumpmaster stood and grabbed the handle on the bottom of the fuselage door and lifted, rolling it up and out of the way, opening a six foot hole in the side of the plane.

"Everyone up!" he shouted, gesturing upwards with both open palms.

Everyone released their lap belts and stood.

"*Link up!*" he shouted next, interlocking his fingers. The instructors clipped their harnesses to the backs of their assigned partners to form tandem teams.

"*Number one ready!*"

As in each of the preceding tests, the *Last Passenger* candidates went first, followed by the rest of the flight crew. Drew Hibbert was number one. He and his instructor shuffled to the door together and paused. The jumpmaster tugged on their harnesses to ensure they were properly belted together, and then shouted "*Go!*" Drew and his partner leaped immediately out the door and were gone.

"*Number two ready!*"

Brian O'Connel, the interior designer from Huntington, New York, was second in line. He and his instructor now shuffled to the doorway. Brian was shocked by the force of the airstream that suddenly tore at him, and he rocked unsteadily on his feet as he stared uncertainly into the sky beyond.

The jumpmaster checked their harness, and then shouted "*Go!*" Brian instantly lashed out with his arms and grabbed hold of both sides of the doorway.

"*Go!*" the jumpmaster shouted again, rapping Brian sharply on the helmet with the palm of his hand. Brian rapidly slid his feet sideways so that he now formed a large human "X" in the doorway. As everyone watched, a wet spot appeared in the crotch of his polyester jumpsuit and quickly grew.

***

"Oh man, he actually peed his pants?" Marcus asked, shaking his head.

"The jumpmaster dude actually chucked him out the door when it started spraying on him," Mike said, laughing.

"Man, that is just so wrong. Everyone else was OK though?"

"Yeah, Nikki was cool with it. John hesitated for a moment, but then he was OK. You know Drew loved it, he's like bailed out of flaming fighter jets or something. I didn't even notice Mariana because I was getting ready to go, so I'm guessing she was fine too."

"So it's definitely Brian then," Marcus asked.

"Yeah, definitely. He's the only one who choked. Well, whizzed."

At that night's panel, Marcus said "I'm sorry Brian, but you've been removed from the mission."

He was the first candidate to actually start crying upon elimination.

There were only four candidates left.

***

"To the final four!" The remaining four candidates raised their glasses of sparkling cider and toasted. The producers had requested some celebration shots in case they needed extra footage for a "behind the scenes" episode.

The final four candidates were going through the motions as the film crew hovered around. No one drank alcohol, because they had an appointment the next day with the centrifuge.

"Well, there are more of us now then there are of them," Tom said as his group stood to one side observing the mock celebration.

"How do you think they stack up?" Mark asked.

"Well, I think Drew is the obvious lead contender," Tom said.

"Yeah, he has that whole fighter jock airline pilot thing going for him," Marcus agreed. "You can tell he'd be a real asset on the flight."

"John seems competent enough. A solid middle of the pack performance," Tom noted. "Nikki's doing very well. We all had our doubts at first, but her athletic background has put her near the top in each round."

"That and the fact that she just really wants to be here," Mike noted. "The girl is loving life."

"Mariana is still a bit of a mystery to me," Tom concluded. "She does everything well enough, but something about her rubs me the wrong way. I get the feeling the woman has a temper. I'm concerned about how well she'd integrate into the crew."

"That's the Latin blood in her," Bruce chuckled. "She has that whole Sao Paulo South American vibe going on."

"How do you see them from your perspective?" Tom asked Bruce.

"Well, for the best ratings, I'd say John Sullivan should get cut next. He's about as exciting as a beige Camry. I actually wish he'd gone today instead of Brain. Brian was a hell of a lot more colorful."

Everyone laughed. No one thought John would make the crew.

"I agree with you on Drew. He'll probably sail through the last two challenges. Interesting that the tension we expected between him and John never developed."

"John doesn't want it badly enough," Marcus said. "I think this all turned out to be a little bit more than he expected."

"As for the girls, we'll, we'd go with Mariana," Bruce said.

"Really? Why's that?" Tom asked.

"What you said. She's potentially volatile, and that makes for tension, which is always interesting to viewers. She's also a Latino, which speaks to an entire demographic. So speaking for the producers, we'd like Drew and Mariana as the final two," Bruce said.

"So we're going with two, and not three like we originally planned?" Tom asked.

"The woman freaking out at the airport robbed us of an episode," Bruce replied. "Lanetta says we'll go with a final two. It will still work with the viewers calling in to vote for their favorite."

Carl had stood quietly, listening to the group dissect the candidates' performances and personalities. "Ms. Biccari should make it to the end," he said quietly.

"Nikki?" Tom asked.

"Yes. She has an indomitable spirit and a beautiful soul." Carl looked calmly at everyone. "She's endured great hardship in her life, that has scarred her deeply. She deserves this chance to restore her confidence and reclaim her feeling of self-worth. This trip is her personal redemption."

Carl turned and walked quietly away.

"Was he talking about Nikki? Or himself?" Marcus quietly asked.

***

The group sat in stunned silence as the staff physiologist delivered their safety briefing in accented English.

"We take you to three gee," she said loudly. "Three gee not a problem. You hold *this* in left hand," she said, holding aloft a small object shaped like a pistol grip. "This is called dead man switch. How many left handed?"

Only Nikki raised her hand.

"You hold in *right* hand," she said, pointing at Nikki. "Hold red button with thumb." She turned the device so that they could see the red button at the top, and then showed how to grasp the device in the palm of the hand and hold down the button.

"If you let go, centrifuge stop. If you need to stop, let go red button. Do you understand?"

Everyone nodded.

"At three gee, we give you task. You push lighted buttons on panel. *Only* push buttons that are lighted. After one minute, we rotate capsule to create negative three gee, and you push more lighted buttons. Then fun starts. We rotate capsule to positive gee again, and we give you *ten* gee."

Several people gasped.

"We do ten gee for ninety seconds. If your vision stops, let go red button," she said, holding the handheld device aloft again and demonstrating. "Centrifuge stop."

"Jesus, does she mean if we go blind?" John muttered.

"If you feel or hear like bones break, let go red button!"

Everyone started shifting uncomfortably in their seats.

"If you feel like you vomit, let go red button, or you could breathe vomit and die.

Some nervous coughs spread through the group.

"If you pass out or die, you not worry, because red button will be let go and you will stop," she said with a smile. "Now, who is go first?"

No one raised their hand.

***

Mariana sat in the cushioned seat, her eyes darting anxiously from side to side as the technicians fitted the monitoring cap to her head and plugged in

228

her EKG lead.

"You ready?" the physiologist asked.

Biting her bottom lip, Mariana gave a quick nervous nod.

"Good, you go now. Remember, let go red button, centrifuge stop."

The chair in which Mariana sat was mounted on rollers. The technicians pushed it forward into the round metal capsule before her, loading her into the arm of the centrifuge like a turkey being shoved into the oven. She felt the mechanical snap of the latches engaging the chair frame. The door behind her closed and for a moment everything was still and quiet, the only sound the faint whirr of a ventilation fan and her own beating heart. Then she heard a small, distant voice from the earphones in her tightly fitting cap.

"You go now?" It sounded like a question.

"Yes, I'm ready to go," Mariana answered timidly.

"You push red button so you can go."

Mariana realized she hadn't held down the thumb switch on the safety control. Squeezing it to depress the switch, her thumb almost immediately slipped off. The sweat from her palm had made the smooth plastic object slippery. Trying again, she held it down.

"Good, you go now." It was a statement this time, not a question.

Marina felt the capsule begin to move. Her thumb immediately slipped off the switch again, and the movement stopped.

"What is wrong? You not go now?" she heard the distant voice ask.

"I'm sorry, my thumb slipped, no, I'm ready, let's try again."

Not wanting to preemptively abort her test again, Mariana pressed the thumb switch firmly and then jammed the unit between her thigh and the edge of the seat to keep her thumb on the switch.

"Ok good, we go again now," she heard.

The capsule again began to move, slowly at first, then rapidly gaining speed.

Halfway through the test, the centrifuge operator motioned for the physiologist. "I don't understand," he said to her in Russian, pointing at the indicators.

"Is there something wrong?" Mark Rutherford asked, observing the test from the control booth.

"She does not let go button," the physiologist answered. "But heart rate is very high, and there is this … "

She reached up and flipped a toggle switch, which activated a speaker. The room was suddenly filled with Mariana's shrill screaming.

***

"I guess she got her arm wedged in, and when the gees piled on, she couldn't get her hand free to release the safety switch," Marcus explained to Tom. "She was pretty hysterical by the time they shut it down and freed her."

"OK, well, is she the one then?" Tom asked.

"Look, I don't care what Bruce wants, she's the only one who had a problem today, and she refused to try again. How could we cut one of the others?"

Later that afternoon, Mariana stood glumly before the panel.

"I'm sorry Mariana, but you've been removed from the mission," Marcus announced.

Only three candidates remained.

***

The group gathered around the neutral buoyancy pool for what was to be their final day of training.

"Where's Mr. Funk this morning?" Vivian asked.

"Important matters to attend to," Tom replied. "He called in his private air force to come collect him."

"Well isn't that special. He's missing the best part though."

"We'll provide a few suit training sessions for him at Space Dome after we get back. The customer is always right after all," Tom said with a smile.

Deep within the pool, Nikki worked to unbolt an instrument canister from a simulated space station truss.

"How are you doing?" the monitor asked her.

"This is awesome!" she said, her bright grin clearly visible through her spacesuit faceplate. "I can't wait to do this for real!"

When John's turn came to enter the suit, Tom noticed his forehead was beaded with perspiration. Turning to Marcus, he asked, "Is it hot in here to you?"

"No boss, it's actually a bit on the chilly side," Marcus replied. "Why? You feeling OK?"

"I'm fine. Not sure about him though," Tom said, nodding toward John. They watched as he received his final instructions for entering the Orlan, and then quickly climbed inside.

"Huh. Seems OK to me," Marcus noted.

The crane operator hoisted the platform John stood on into the air, and then swung it over the pool. It felt as though the suit was contracting around him like a python, and his skin began to itch. He closed his eyes and breathed deeply.

"Is everything OK?" he heard over the helmet headphones.

"Yes, everything's fine, everything's OK," he said with as much confidence as he could muster.

The man operating the crane looked quizzically at the safety monitor, who nodded and pointed downward with his index finger, giving the signal to lower John into the pool.

John felt a slight bump as the platform on which he stood hit the water's surface and began to sink. He imagined he could feel the water level rising through the pressurized suit. His breathing became rapid and shallow.

The technician monitoring John's biotelemetry noted his rapid respiration rate. A cosmonaut in training would not be allowed to continue until he had calmed down, but he had learned that these rich space tourists got very upset if you interfered with their "experience." He said nothing.

John's eyes grew large as the water lapped at the bottom of his visor and then rose until it covered his entire head. He knew the spacesuit would protect him, but he was sure he could feel the cold water hitting the back of his throat, choking him. He gasped and gurgled, shaking his head violently within the helmet.

Approaching John and peering through his visor, the safety diver saw the fear and panic in his face. "Stop! This one is panicking. Take him up now!"

***

"So what was it?" Tom asked Marcus, who had just finished speaking to the facility physician.

"Claustrophobia mostly. He insists he's able to deal with it, but when the water closed over his head, it made it a whole lot worse."

"Huh. So what do we do then? Can we risk having this guy onboard?"

"Not a lot of water on the moon, they tell me," Marcus replied.

"Still. We're down to the last three, and I'm not sure I want to make the call on this one. Let's see if we can get Robbie on the phone and ask his opinion."

"OK, so, it's eleven hours difference I think? It's three o'clock here, I guess that makes it, what, four o'clock this morning there? Looks like we're going to be waking him up."

They were surprised when he answered on the second ring.

"Dude, not sleeping much?" Marcus asked.

"It's Thursday, brother, I've got that long-ass drive to Vandenberg," Robbie replied. "But you guys wouldn't know about that, being as you're all on vacation at space camp."

"Well listen, we have a situation, and we need your opinion." Marcus briefly described the day's events.

"It's not the water thing that worries me," Robbie finally answered. "It's the claustrophobia. If you have even a little bit of it, it can just reach out and grab you when you least expect it. This guy's supposed to be going to the surface with us, and Tinkerbell is too damn small to be cooped up in for a day with someone who needs room to breathe."

"All right, thanks, man," Marcus said.

"You got it, brother," Robbie said, and hung up.

"He's done," Marcus said to Tom, nodding toward where John sat, still talking to the doctor.

***

After Marcus informed John that he had been eliminated from the mission, they set up to film one last scene. As Drew and Nikki took their places on their marks in front of the table, Bruce ran Marcus through the script he had quickly written.

"And ... action," Bruce said, pointing to Marcus.

"Drew Hibbert, Nikki Biccari, you are our final two candidates to fill the one remaining spot on our crew. You have passed every test, and have outperformed all other candidates to earn your chance to be chosen. We deem you both worthy and qualified to join us on our mission. The final decision now rests with the viewers. Will they choose you, Drew, the experienced airline pilot and former Naval aviator, or you, Nikki, the young cancer survivor and former student athlete. The decision is in their hands to see who will be ... "

Looking directly into the camera, Marcus dramatically concluded, *"The Last Passenger!"*

"And ... *cut!* " Bruce shouted. "That's a wrap. You nailed it first time, nicely done. Maybe we should talk about this when we get back, there may be a future for you in this business."

That's the moment Marcus earned his nickname, "Hollywood."

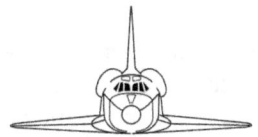

CHAPTER THIRTY–FOUR

Tom, Marcus and Vivian thought it would be amusing to wear their uniforms to the status meeting.

"Hi, guys! Welcome back!" Nicole said, giving Tom a hug. Then, stepping back and looking at him, she added, "Whoa, what are you guys supposed to be?"

"I thought Halloween was next week," Robbie said, as he entered Neverland and took a seat. Then, noticing the shoulder boards, he turned to Tom. "Does this mean I have to call you Captain now?" Counting stripes, he then added, "Actually, Marcus is the captain, you're just a first officer."

"Yeah, I outranked the boss all week," Marcus noted with a grin.

"So when did you get in?"

Glancing at his watch, Tom said, "About four hours ago."

"I thought you all looked a little ragged, even with the pretty shirts. Seriously, are those astronaut wings?" he asked, leaning forward to look closer.

"Brian insisted we wear them for the elimination panels," Vivian said.

"Good morning Luke," Tom said, looking up at the video screen and changing the subject. "Did Mike and Dr. Heinel make it in this morning?"

"Yeah, they're both here someplace," he said, looking over his shoulder. "I'm glad to have them back, we'll be running systems integration tests on the next Big Brother Twin soon."

"So the booster stacking went OK?"

"Yes, and we're getting ready to load Tiger Lilly later today," Luke said, referring to the second OMS module payload.

"So what did we miss?" Tom asked.

"Episode two of *The Last Passenger*, for one thing," Nicole said. "That poor woman, was she OK?"

"You mean the one who freaked out in the airport before we left? God, that seems like a month ago," Tom said.

"We haven't heard anything about her since that day," Marcus observed. "But don't worry, that's nothing compared to what's coming up."

"So who's our final two?" Nicole asked.

"The airline pilot, and the girl who had cancer," Marcus answered.

"I promise we'll go over everything about our trip in a bit, let's just first finish with the status update if you please," Tom groused.

"Sounds like someone has a bit of jetlag," Nicole teased.

"That's where we are here, Mr. Armac," Luke said from the Cape. "We're still on track for our next launch at the end of the month."

"And when will our segments for Atlantis be shipped?" Tom asked.

"Oh, sorry, they're cast and inspected, we'll be putting them on the train as soon as we're done with the payload integration for our launch here. It takes about twelve days to make the trip coast to coast, you should be receiving them at Vandenberg the week after we launch Tiger Lilly."

"Vivian?" Tom asked.

"Provided everything else is on track, that should be perfect," she said. "I obviously haven't had time to check in with my crew yet, but the reports I've been getting have all been good."

"Atlantis is buttoned up and ready to move down to the pad," Robbie said. "We sent the bulk of the Alliance Space Systems folks home and have just kept the ones that we'll need for doing the final prelaunch checks. They're the ones that are in on the plan, obviously."

"I'm really pleased that we've been able to keep a lid on this for so long," Tom observed. "Speaking of which, what's our pet reporter up to?"

"This," Nicole said, dropping a newspaper on the conference table. "A very nice article about the work our museum restaurant chef is doing with the School of Culinary Science at USC."

"Humph," Tom acknowledged, glancing at the article.

"Oh, and the Air Force gave two thumbs up to the script," Nicole said. "By the way, did you promise Colonel Arnold a part in this movie of yours? Because he seemed very disappointed when I told him I had no idea what he was talking about."

Tom laughed for the first time that morning. "It's OK, I'll give him a call and take care of it. So it looks like everything is ready for us to execute once the next launch is completed?"

"I need to file the launch plan with the FAA for the shuttle launch at Vandenberg," Nicole said. "I'm sorry, I mean for our first west coast Space Train validation flight."

"And I still have one thing I need to do," Robbie added.

***

"I appreciate your assistance with this," Robbie said, as he and James Leon slowly climbed the hillside trail to the south of Slick Six. James was a medicine man of the 'antap, a spiritual society of the Chumash tribe.

"And we appreciate your donation to our cultural center," James replied. "Although this isn't really necessary. There is no curse on this place."

"Well, it couldn't hurt, right? I mean, we're not going to introduce a problem or anything?"

James laughed. "No, this will not anger the spirits."

Reaching the top of the hill, they turned to look down on the launch facilities below, the sea clearly visible a mile to the west. James stood surveying the scene, his chin slightly elevated. Turning to the south, he pointed toward Point Conception. "That way is homqaq," he said.

"The western gate," Robbie said. "We've heard the legend."

"It is not a legend," James said calmly. "It is one of our cultural myths, and part of our heritage." Sweeping his arm across the horizon, he said, "Through this place the souls of the dead pass on their way to Shimilaqsha."

"So long as they don't stop off and engage in a little mischief first, we have no problem with that," Robbie said.

James scowled at Robbie. "In all seriousness, Mr. Robichaud, spirits seeking the way to the afterlife do not stop first to meddle in earthly affairs."

"I didn't mean any disrespect. Just, if you could do something to make everyone feel a little better about this, it would be great."

Laying the deerskin parcel he carried on the ground, James untied the cord that bound it and unrolled the bundle, spreading out the several objects it contained. Turning to Robbie, he said, "I'm going to have to ask you to wait for me at the beginning of the trail. We do not allow others to observe our rituals."

"Of course, absolutely. I'll just wait for you down there then," Robbie said, turning to head back down the hill.

Shortly after beginning his descent, he heard a song-like chanting begin from the hilltop behind him. Looking back over his shoulder, he saw James holding a spoon shaped object over his head, which made a loud rattling sound as he shook it. Then, bending over to place it on the ground, he picked up what appeared to be a board attached to a length of cord, which he began to swing through the air in a large circle. It produced an eerie low moaning sound reminiscent of Robbie's notion of what spirits might sound like. Stumbling over a rock, he returned his eyes to the trail and hurried downward.

About fifteen minutes later, James rejoined Robbie at the bottom of the hill. "It is done," he said.

"Great, thank you very much for your help. This is going to make everyone feel a lot better, I promise you."

"Yes, well, I'm not sure if I should commend you for your sensitivity to our cultural traditions or condemn you for your belief in this non-existent curse, but regardless, my tribe thanks you for your generosity. Now if you'll excuse me, my shift begins in an hour."

"Your shift?" Robbie asked, as they turned to walk toward their parked vehicles.

"Yes, I'm a floor manager at our casino in Santa Ynez. I need to go help my people relieve your brothers and sisters of more of their money. Maybe in time, we'll have enough to be able to repurchase our ancestral lands."

Robbie stopped and turned to James. "Look, I'm from New Orleans, and we have a strong history of the Voodoo. I respect the power of the spirits, and I'm really sorry for what might have occurred in the past."

"You had no role in what is past, my friend," James replied somberly.

"Well, no, but you see, some associates of mine, no, that's not right, some *friends* of mine and I are getting ready to depart from this place on our own journey. And if it's all right with you, I'd be honored if you'd allow us to take something along. Something that symbolizes your people and the importance of this place in your culture."

James gazed at Robbie impassively for a moment, and then the corners of his mouth curved into a subtle smile. Setting down the deerskin bundle, he opened it and took out the spoon-like object Robbie had seen him shaking. On closer examination, Robbie saw that it was composed of a clam shell lashed to a stick and filled with rocks to impart a rattle when shaken.

"We are the Chumash, which means the sea shell people," James said solemnly. "We use this in both our rituals and in our music. It represents who we are, our reverence, and our joy. Take this." Placing the shell rattle in Robbie's hands, James then clasped both of Robbie's hands with his own. "You honor my people. Thank you."

As they turned to continue walking to their vehicles, Robbie said, "So, a floor manager. Any chance I could get some comped show tickets?"

"Not going to happen my friend," James said with a smile.

***

Arriving at the viewer's gallery to observe the launch, Tom burst out in laughter when he got his first glimpse at the rocket. The bulbous nose of the payload fairing had been painted as a giant jack-o'-lantern, its orange and black face grinning eerily down at the crowd below.

"Now you see, this is why I like working with civilians," Robbie laughed. "No way would NASA have let us paint a pumpkin on a ship. They're just too damn uptight."

"So whose idea was that?" Marcus asked anxiously.

"Oh, it was Mr. Rungren's," Carl said. "It is Halloween after all, and he wanted you to know that he does in fact have a sense of humor."

"Huh, who would have guessed Luke had a funny bone," Marcus snorted. "Still, I dunno. It gives me a bad feeling ... "

"When did you get so superstitious?" Tom asked.

"Good morning, Mr. Armac," Bob Brock interrupted, approaching the group.

"Good morning, Mr. Brock," Tom replied. Turning to look again at the rocket, he said, "I read your recent article, the one about our chef and her work with USC. Very nice."

"Thank you. Of course, it wasn't the story I *wanted* to write, but my editor is happy for now."

"You'll have more interesting news to report soon, I imagine," Tom observed casually.

The voice of Jean Lutz from mission control in Long Beach boomed across the viewer's gallery. "We are at our final systems safety hold at T minus three minutes. The rocket will be switching to internal power momentarily."

"How much latitude do I have with today's launch?" Bob asked.

"Just say it's the next step in validating our Space Train program, and that we've launched another component for our Lunar Voyager," Tom said. "And please mention that our next launch will be from our new west coast Space Train facility."

"And the countdown is resuming," Jean's voice announced. "The vehicle is now on internal power and all systems are go for launch. T minus two minutes thirty seconds."

"I get a thrill every time I hear that," Nicole said, moving between Tom and Bob.

"So I understand Mr. Funk has joined your team," Bob said.

"You'll have to speak to Mr. Funk about that, we aren't going to comment on our crew composition prior to the flight."

"I would, but he's not returning my calls anymore."

"A pity," Tom said curtly.

Bob turned and went to find someone warmer to talk to.

"You ought to be nicer to him," Nicole said to Tom. "He's on our team now, after all."

Tom looked over at Bob. "I know, you're right. But he hasn't earned my respect yet. Not like the rest of the team. And he *was* spying on us."

Nicole shook her head. "For such intelligent creatures, you men can be such children at times. He was just doing his job. Nothing to get your feelings hurt over."

Marcus joined Tom and Nicole. "The last piece of the puzzle," he said. "It's been a long time coming."

"Yes, it has," Tom agreed.

"Still feeling God's hand?"

"More and more each day, my friend."

"Still hard to believe that next time, you all will be *in* the rocket."

"I don't think I'll really grasp it until they actually strap us in the seats," Tom replied.

After a moment of silence, Marcus said, "Sure wish they hadn't painted a pumpkin on it."

Jean counted down the last ten seconds. "We have ignition. And *liftoff* of the first Space Train validation flight."

As the wave of concussive sound washed over them, Nicole reached out to take Tom's hand and squeezed. They stood that way for a full two minutes, holding hands as they watched the mighty Big Brother Twin rocket climb aggressively away. Finally, as it disappeared from sight to the southeast, she gave his hand an additional squeeze and then let go.

"Staging complete, second stage ignition confirmed," Jean announced. A small cheer went up among the viewers in the gallery. A few minutes later, a larger one erupted when they heard her say, "Tiger Lilly has achieved stable orbit."

"So whose turn is it to buy the drinks this time?" Marcus asked with a big grin.

"I think it should be Dr. Heinel, since the booster he helped us with just obtained its human rating," Tom noted.

Tom's cell phone chimed, followed immediately by Marcus' and Robbie's. They each pulled out their phones.

"Damn it," Tom muttered, reading the message from Jean. "Payload fairing failed to separate, call me," it said.

Robbie and Marcus, receiving the same message, joined Tom as he read Jean's text to Nicole.

"I told you that pumpkin was a bad idea," Marcus said.

***

"OK, so what do we know?" Tom asked the group gathered in Luke's office. Jean and Vivian were teleconferenced in from Space Dome, their grim faces displayed on the monitor on Luke's desk.

"Telemetry indicates that the payload fairing failed to separate," Jean replied. "We don't know if that means it's still engaged and the payload is inside, or it's partially released like a blossoming flower, or maybe it's even a sensor failure and everything's just fine.

"Worst case, what does it mean to the mission?" Tom asked.

"If the fairing failed to release and the fuel module is trapped inside, we should probably scrub the moon mission," Robbie said. "We can't risk launching Atlantis only to find that we can't free the fuel module. We'd have no choice at that point but to deorbit the shuttle since we wouldn't have the fuel to make the moon."

"But we could make it to orbit and find out that everything is fine," Tom said, "or that whatever is wrong can be fixed and we can free the fuel module and load it onboard."

"Look," Robbie said, "I know I've said I'm really loving this free and easy approach to space travel we have going on here, but even I would draw the line at launching into an unknown situation. If there's a problem with the shroud, we don't know if it would even be possible to do an EVA and free it, and it's certainly not something we've practiced. We've been doing drills on our planned orbital operations for six months now, and this ain't one of them."

"Plus it would be a half billion dollar gamble," Vivian noted. "If we couldn't make the moon trip, then there's no lunar landing prize, no sponsor money, no anything coming in as a result of the flight. It would just burn through all of our remaining resources and probably mean we'd have to shut down the Space Train program before it even begins because we'd be bankrupt."

"Could we orbit a replacement?" Tom asked hopefully.

"It would take us a couple of months to get another one built, tested, and shipped here for launch," Mike said. "By that time, Wendy will have exceeded her on orbit shelf life. We'd have no way of knowing if she was still ready to go."

"How about the mockups in the pool at Space Dome? Could one of those be made flight ready?"

"They're just that—mockups," Mike replied. "They were just frames built for practicing with, they aren't aerospace grade. Sorry, but no."

"There's got to be something," Tom muttered. "We're too close now." He once again faced the horrible possibility of having the entire project, so tantalizingly close to fulfillment, completely slip away.

Everyone sat in sullen silence for several moments wracking their brains for possible solutions. Then Carl, sitting on a corner of a desk off to one side, cleared he throat and said, "If I may make a suggestion, why don't we see what happens when we give Tiger Lilly a kick."

"Give it a kick?" Marcus said quizzically, followed by an "Ohhh ... " as understanding dawned.

"Yes, a kick," Carl reiterated. "A shroud separation problem has always been one of our more common flight anomalies," he explained, sounding like the experienced NASA engineer that he was. "Often times, a good swift kick in the pants corrects the underlying fault."

"We'll restart the Little Sister second stage, and hope the jolt knocks loose whatever is holding up release of the shroud," Jean said from mission control at Space Dome.

"Exactly right," Carl confirmed. "You must fire the booster to elevate Tiger Lilly's orbit to match that of Wendy's, so let's proceed, and hope that in the process the shroud has had time to reflect upon its transgression and relinquishes its hold on our dear Tiger Lilly."

***

Jean counted off the remaining seconds. "And the burn is in five, four, three, two, one, ignition—we have second stage restart."

All eyes were glued to the payload telemetry display. The shroud separation indicator remained a solid red square.

After a full minute of thrust, Jean said, "coming up on termination of burn, in three, two, one, cutoff."

Everyone lifted slightly off their seats and leaned into the display panel. "Come ON, let's GO," Luke commanded.

The shroud separation indicator remained stubbornly, infuriatingly red.

"Approaching auto sequence separation," Jean announced, as the onboard system on the Little Sister counted down the required number of seconds. Reaching zero, the flight control computer fired the pyrotechnic fasteners holding the rocket to the payload module, and the separation springs shoved the two quickly apart.

And the indicator suddenly turned green.

"*Yes!*" Mike shouted, as everyone exhaled deeply in relief.

"Seriously, boss, I don't know how much more of this my heart can take," Marcus said, wiping his forehead with a tissue.

Tiger Lilly slid smoothly into orbit twenty-five miles behind Wendy, as the two halves of the enormous grinning jack-o'-lantern tumbled slowly away into space, their mischief completed.

***

"All secure, Captain," the deck foreman reported. "Ready to get underway in all respects." Looking out the pilot house windows of the recovery vessel M/V Freedom Star, Captain Myers could see the dock crew maneuvering the giant travel lift over the second of the two Big Brother boosters that they had just recovered and returned. Behind them at the pier sat the Liberty Star, the twin of Freedom Star and the other of NASA's two booster recovery ships that were now on long term lease to Roadrunner Rockets for the Space Train program. The program had been a godsend for the Captain, because he was only a few years from retirement and a full pension, but he'd been anticipating a layoff after the end of the shuttle program.

Picking up the bridge microphone, he keyed the mike. "Liberty Star, Freedom Star, six eight."

"Roger that, Liberty Star going to six eight," he heard in reply.

Changing quickly to channel sixty-eight, he said, "Liberty Star, Freedom Star. Ready to get this show on the road?"

"Everyone's aboard here, Captain, ready when you are."

"Well let's get going then. Last one to Sloppy Joe's buys the first round."

"Roger that, Captain, Liberty Star going back to one six."

The two ships eased away from the pier and headed south toward Port Canaveral and the Atlantic Ocean beyond. It would take a full day to reach Key West, their first stop on the three week trip to California.

Should be an interesting trip, the Captain thought, as he watched the VAB disappear from view to the north.

He had no way of knowing how interesting it would ultimately become.

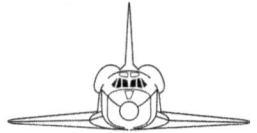

CHAPTER THIRTY–FIVE

A cool ocean breeze blew gently from the Pacific in the predawn darkness, reaching into the sheltered hollows of the rolling landscape and dissipating the tendrils of mist settled there. The only sound heard in the quiet stillness was that of surf crashing on the distant beach. To the east, bands of purple and orange began to appear above the hills as dawn's first light crept over the landscape. Nothing moved along the stretch of black pavement that wound its way northward, disappearing over a nearby rise, only a star filled sky visible beyond.

Suddenly a vehicle appeared, heading rapidly southward. Its rooftop light bar emitted bright flashes of blue light while its headlights stabbed at the darkness with alternating strobes of brilliant white. Its engine roared as it quickly accelerated down the deserted stretch of road.

Silence returned. Minutes passed. Then, the sky above the rise in the road began to pulse with a throbbing pale yellow light, barely perceptible at first, then increasing in intensity. The yellow pulses continued to brighten until finally a truck slowly cleared the rise, moving at the pace of a slow walk, its flashing emergency lights illuminating the surrounding landscape. A bank of brilliant white flood lights mounted to its rear bathed the shoulders of the road behind the truck in a daytime-like brightness. It stopped for a moment at the crown of the rise, as if waiting for something, before resuming its slow crawl south.

As the truck began its creeping descent down the gently sloping hill, a large white object gradually ascended from behind the rise. As the sun began to appear over the eastern hills, its morning rays painted space shuttle Atlantis with warmthless orange color as it slowly rose into view. A tow tractor attached to the shuttle's nose wheel drew it steadily southward. Dozens of people sat along the leading edge of both wings, their feet dangling, intently watching the ground below, while dozens more walked beneath the spacecraft, each carrying a shovel.

The sudden blast of a horn pierced the air, and all movement halted. One of the wing sitters had noticed that Atlantis' starboard wingtip had come within inches of striking a high spot along the road's shoulder. Immediately, people with shovels attacked the ground below the wing, lowering it to give adequate clearance. Satisfied with the effort, the wing sitter nodded and then blew two short blasts with his horn, giving the all clear to proceed. The ponderous procession resumed.

Tom, Marcus, and Vivian stood on the crest of a nearby hill, accompanied by Bruce Trunly's video crew, their cameras capturing the action below.

"Was that Colonel Arnold?" Marcus asked Tom.

"Which one?" Tom asked.

"The dude on the wing with the air horn."

Tom smiled. "As a matter of fact, it was. I promised him a part as an extra." Pointing to the truck that preceded Atlantis, he said, "See that woman with the lighted batons?"

"Yeah."

"Base commander's wife," Tom said with a smile.

"No way!" Marcus laughed.

"We've got enough people down there who know what they're doing to keep it safe, but most of them are just locals who wanted a part in a movie."

"There's gonna be some pretty pissed off people when they find out there isn't really a movie being made," Marcus said.

"Well, I think that ten years from now, they'll get a lot more mileage out of saying 'I helped make history' than they will from having been an extra in some movie."

***

Ray Mainard was busily surfing the web researching hotels for his family's upcoming Veteran's Day weekend getaway. As he switched idly between several sites, his email chimed. Opening his inbox, he scanned the subject line on the latest message to see if it needed immediate attention or could be put off until after the long weekend. It read "Notification of Launch Operations 18 December." He worked in AST 200, the FAA's Commercial Space Transportation Office licensing and evaluation division, and his office had to bless all commercial launch operations.

Damn it, he thought, *who submits a launch notification form on a Friday afternoon before a three day weekend?*

Opening the attached form, he quickly scanned it. *OK, Roadrunner Rockets, launching from Vandenberg SLC-6. Yep, that's cool, they have their site operator's permit now. Booster type is a Big Brother Twin. Nice, I'd love to see one of those big mothers launch. Payload is an experimental package; purpose is systems validation for development of their Space Train program. Nope, nothing here that throws a red flag. A little short notice, but this can wait till next week.*

Ray dragged the file to his "pending" folder for further review and approval and returned to goofing off.

***

The mobile service tower and the assembly building had been rolled into place over the launch table like two halves of a vertical shoebox, forming a towering enclosure over the pad. The overhead cranes had carefully lifted the Big Brother segments one by one, stacking them vertically until both boosters were completely assembled. Then, the enormous external tank had been pushed into position through the large rollup door and lifted into place, nestled securely between the two boosters. It had been an amazing aerial ballet, as massive objects weighing hundreds of tons were maneuvered within fractions of an inch. After a week of nail biting anxiety, the stack was ready to receive Atlantis. Vivian gave the crew Sunday off.

The most nerve-wracking task still remained. The crew reported to work bright and early Monday morning to lift Atlantis and attach her to the external tank. In a carefully choreographed series of simultaneous operations they attached the enormous lifting rig to the orbiter, raised her clear of the ground, retracted the vehicle's landing gear, and then rotated the shuttle into a vertical position. Once vertical, she was lifted and aligned with the three mounting points on the external tank and then securely bolted into launch position.

Within Atlantis' cargo bay, Tinkerbell's propulsion unit sat nestled tightly against the aft bay bulkhead. As the orbiter was rotated to vertical, a small volume of rain water trapped within one of the lander's strut latch assemblies started to seep past a retaining washer and deeper into the latch mechanism.

***

Early the following week, the call Tom had been expecting finally arrived. He and Vivian were observing booster preparations from one of the catwalks inside the mobile service tower when his phone rang.

"Mr. Armac? This is Airman Rodriguez in Colonel Arnold's office. The Colonel would like to know if you would have time to stop by his office later this afternoon."

Crap, here we go, Tom thought. "What time would the Colonel like me to be there?"

"He has an opening at three o'clock if that would be convenient, sir."

"That will be fine, please tell the Colonel I'll be there," Tom said, and then hung up. "Damn it."

"What's wrong?" Vivian asked.

"That was the Colonel's office. He wants to see me at three."

Vivian frowned. "Well, how do you know it's not just a social call? Or maybe he wants another part in the movie?"

"Because he wants me to come to his office. If he was in a mood to socialize or ask a favor, he'd be showing up here."

Vivian nodded. "Well, good luck. Let me know if there's anything I can do."

Tom gamed out several possible conversations in his head during the twenty minute drive to north base. Arriving at the Colonel's office fifteen minutes early, he was kept waiting until exactly three, when the phone on the Airman's desk buzzed. Picking it up briefly, he set it back down and said, "Mr. Armac, the Colonel will see you now."

"Tom, thanks for coming," Jim Arnold said as Tom entered his office. "Please sit."

"What can I do for you today, Colonel?"

"Oh, I just had a few things I wanted to discuss with you. I've been enjoying your show, by the way. It definitely brings back memories from my flight training days."

"I wish I could say it was fun to make, but I needed three days to recover when it was finally over."

"So you're actually going to make this moon trip?" Jim asked.

"That's the plan. We certainly think we have the rocket to do it, and there's an awful lot of money to be made."

"So where and when will that launch take place?"

Bingo, Tom thought. "Well, there's still some preparation to do before we'd be able to fly a mission like that," Tom said. "We're focusing on getting the Space Train up and running first."

"Uh huh. So how's it going down at the complex?" Jim asked. "With the movie."

Wow, I guess he really wants to dance a bit, Tom thought. "Good. We're getting some great establishing shots right now, we'll start shooting action scenes in another week or so. I'm really trying to just stay out of the way and let the pros do their job."

The Colonel nodded his head. "So base operations tells me you've started having cryogens delivered," he said, picking up a pen from his desk and turning it end over end. "Quite a few tanker trucks, apparently."

"Well, the fuel transfer systems at the pad haven't been exercised since Rainier Aerospace launched their last Pyramid," Tom answered warily. "That was quite a while ago, as you know. We'd like to verify that everything is up to speed for our first Big Brother launch."

"Uh huh. I thought I understood that your Hot Wax boosters used paraffin and liquid oxygen?" Jim asked.

"Yes, that's right."

"Interesting. So if you don't mind my asking, why are you also taking delivery of liquid hydrogen? A *lot* of liquid hydrogen. Some sudden need that you might have neglected to mention? Or maybe it's for your movie?"

Tom thought the Colonel had put too much emphasis on the word "movie."

Jim decided he'd had enough cat and mouse. He leaned forward across his desk. "Tom, I got a call this morning from Space Command asking about the launch plan you filed last week. Imagine my surprise when I realized I had no idea what they were talking about."

"I'm sorry, Colonel, I'll have to go raise hell with my crew, we certainly didn't intend to leave you out … "

"Did you think you could file a launch plan and not have me find out about it? Do you not know how the system works?"

"Colonel, I … "

"We fly ICBM's from here, Tom. That means that nothing leaves the ground without our first notifying the Russians and the Chinese of what's being launched and when. You see, we don't want them surprised by something showing up on their radars unannounced. It makes them very nervous, and that's bad for us. Very bad. So when you file a launch plan with the FAA, they tell Space Command, and Space Command tells the Russians and the Chinese, and yes, eventually I find out. But you know what? I don't like finding out last. Because that's *my* pad down there."

"Colonel, it wasn't our intention to keep you in the dark about our plans," Tom said.

"Then why the hell didn't you let me know first that you were planning a launch for next month? And another thing. Just what the hell are you intending to launch, Tom? Because right now, there's a goddamn space shuttle sitting on that pad. Or are you going to tell me that you're going to clear the pad and get your real rocket ready to launch in just a few weeks?"

"We're launching a Big Brother Twin, Colonel, just like our launch plan states."

"Seriously? You're going with that story? OK, Tom, you're going to launch a Big Brother Twin. So what are you going to do with Atlantis?"

"It's the payload."

Colonel Arnold's head snapped back in astonishment. "You're joking, right?"

Tom had decided on the drive up that if the Colonel had figured it out, there was no point in continuing the deception. He had to be informed at some point prior to launch, and it looked like today was the day.

"Look, Colonel, you want to know what we're doing? Well here's what we're doing." He then briefly outlined the entire mission.

I haven't seen that look for a while, Tom thought, as Colonel Arnold adopted what they called "that face, you know the one people get when they find out."

"But … you can't do that," the Colonel said.

"Sure we can."

"You can't fly a space shuttle."

"Why not? We own it. We have the paperwork that says so."

"But … your launch permit won't allow it. It's not the approved payload."

"We plan to file an amended manifest prior to launch."

"You can't do that—you can't completely change the payload without filing a new launch plan."

"Sure we can. The changes made under the Commercial Space Launch Enhanced Access Act specifically allow us to fly any approved payload on a licensed booster, no permission required. And our Big Brother Twin is licensed."

"But … a shuttle wouldn't be considered an approved payload."

"Really? A system that's flown into space 135 times is now not safe to fly?" Tom asked. "You want to see our paperwork from Alliance Space Systems certifying the vehicle is flight ready?"

"But … I'll have to notify Space Command, tell them about your plans."

"Of course you will, we'd insist that you do that. But it doesn't really have to be done immediately, does it?"

"What?" the Colonel asked, confused.

"It's just that we'd prefer to wait a little longer before submitting our official manifest change to the FAA. When word gets out that we're getting ready to launch our moon mission, the resulting publicity could make it a challenge to complete the flight preparations on schedule. I mean, as long you tell them before we actually submit the paperwork, you'd have fulfilled your obligation, right?"

"I … but why would I wait?" Jim said. "It would make me look like I don't know what's going on at my own command."

"Yes, well, I guess I see your point. We wouldn't want your superiors thinking you weren't paying adequate attention. Especially since you're getting ready to retire. Obviously you want to do your utmost to protect your professional reputation. Oh, that reminds me Colonel, I've been meaning to ask you a question."

"Yes?" Jim said distractedly, still trying to process what he had just heard.

"After this mission, we're going to be starting regular Space Train flights. We already have a good site operations manager for our east coast location, but we need someone to manage our west coast operations here at Vandenberg."

"What?"

"It would have to be someone with extensive experience in launch facilities management. Previous NASA or Air Force experience, obviously.

Someone familiar with both the military and civilian sides since they'll have to liaison with the base here. Know anyone who may be available in the near future with those qualifications? They'd have to be willing to live here close to Vandenberg. It's a solid six figure salary, by the way."

Jim slowly smiled. *You sly son of a bitch*, he thought. "Why yes, I think I know someone who may be available soon. And as for that other thing, well, I don't see the harm in giving you a little more time to get things tidied up here before I tell Space Command about my concerns."

"Well thank you, Colonel, it's been a pleasure talking with you today."

"Likewise, Mr. Armac. Likewise."

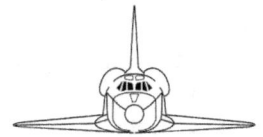

CHAPTER THIRTY–SIX

"How many days do the requirements give us?" Tom asked.

"Fifteen working days," Nicole answered.

"Fifteen working days," Tom repeated, glancing at the calendar on his office wall and counting backward. "So that would be … "

"Today," Nicole said. "Today's the day."

"Today's the day," Tom nodded, and took a deep breath. "OK, well, give it an hour. I promised the Colonel he'd have time first."

"All right," Nicole said, turning to leave Tom's office. "But I want to have this done by lunch."

"I'll make the call right now," Tom replied. "And I guess you might as well let Bob Brock know the restraints are off."

"I'm sure he'll be delighted to hear that," Nicole said. Pausing before leaving the office, she turned and asked, "You're coming tomorrow, right?"

"For Thanksgiving? Of course, I wouldn't miss it."

As Nicole left his office, Tom picked up his phone and dialed. "This is Tom Armac for Colonel Arnold, please. Yes, I'll hold." Then after a brief pause, "Jim? This is Tom. Listen, I think it's time you tell your superiors about your concerns over what's going on down here. Yes, we're submitting the revised launch manifest in one hour."

***

Ray Mainard was working intently, trying to clear his desk of anything that he could act on quickly, or better yet unload on someone else. His office had been granted four hours of administrative leave on this last work day before Thanksgiving, provided they had no unfinished business. Unfortunately, everyone in the department had the same strategy. In the time it took to review and forward an item to another branch for action, three more items would land in his inbox.

Taking a break to refill his coffee and grab another doughnut from the lunch room, he returned to his desk to find six more items requiring his attention. Sighing deeply, he elected to open the only one that wasn't marked "urgent."

"December 18 Launch Manifest Change Notification" read the subject line. *Really cutting that one close*, Ray thought, glancing at the calendar. The new guidelines in the recently passed Enhanced Access Act really played hell with their processes. They only had weeks now to review things that they used to have months to act upon.

Let's see what this is about, Ray thought. Opening the attached form, he quickly scanned it, looking for the red highlighted changes. *Let's see, looks like payload and mission changes. Former payload identified as experimental instrument package, new payload ... no way, this has to be a joke. Space Transportation System orbiter OV-104—the Atlantis? What the hell?"*

Glancing at the clock, Ray picked up the phone and began frantically attempting to reach anyone in Operations who hadn't already left early for the four day weekend.

***

Bob Brock smiled with satisfaction as he hit "send," forwarding the article he had written weeks before to his editor. Leaning back in his chair and putting his feet on his desk, he opened the latest copy of *Smithsonian Air & Space* magazine and waited. It took less than 20 minutes for his phone to ring. Glancing at the display, he was pleased to see it was his editor calling. Picking up the phone, he said, "Yes, Marion?"

"Roadrunner Rockets Flying Atlantis To Moon?" she asked, reading Bob's headline. "Are you starting that again, Bob? I thought we had an understanding."

"Things have changed, Marion," Bob said. "Now that they've actually notified the government, I think it's safe to run it."

"I'm not sure that's a good idea," she replied.

"Marion, it's official. Do you want to wake up tomorrow and be the only paper in the country that isn't running a story on it?"

"You're sure about this?"

"Absolutely, Marion," he replied. "Matter-of-fact, I'm uploading that to the wire services as soon as we're done."

"If you can support this, then we'll run it."

"OK then," Bob said, and hung up. *Man it feels good to be right*, he thought smugly.

***

"Tonight on *Nightly News of the World*, we have a report that Roadrunner Rockets, who previously announced the first commercial flight to the moon, plans to use the retired space shuttle Atlantis to make their historic

250

voyage. Here with more is our chief science editor Marshall Wheeler."

"That's right, Denise," Marshall began. "After almost a year of speculation as to the nature of Roadrunner Rocket's Lunar Voyager, we now know that they apparently intend to use one of NASA's recently retired space shuttles to make the first commercial flight to the moon. Details are still emerging, but what we know so far ... "

***

"Yes, I have it on right now," Tom said to Nicole. "We knew word would spread fast. I know, all we can do now is wait and see what they do in response. OK, I'll see you tomorrow."

Tom ended the call and then leaned back in his chair. So, FAA, what's your next move?

***

The caterers had delivered a holiday banquet, which was spread across the table in the Integrated Processing Facility's conference room. Most everyone with family had gone home for Thanksgiving, but a large number of the team assisting with the final launch preparations were single, separated, divorced, or unable to spare the time or money to travel home, and faced Thanksgiving alone. Nicole has suggested a feast, and Tom had immediately agreed.

He was pleased to see that Dr. Heinel had come. "Doctor, happy Thanksgiving to you!" he called out as Carl entered the room.

"A happy Thanksgiving to you as well, Mr. Armac," Carl replied. "This is delightful that you've done this."

"It was Nicole's idea, but how could we say no?" Tom replied. "Everyone has been working night and day, and we thought it was the least we could do for them. Thank you for choosing to spend the day with us."

"I felt it appropriate that I be here," Carl said, looking about the room and smiling. "This is my family now, after all."

"Doc!" Marcus shouted, crossing the room while balancing a huge plate of food. "I thought you were going to Mike's house for dinner?"

"While I very much appreciated Mr. Patrick's fine offer, he does in fact have family to celebrate with, while most of the people I feel closest to are here in this room."

"Well come on, let's get you some turkey!" Marcus said, leading Carl toward the food.

Alone for the moment, Tom's thoughts turned inward, and he didn't notice Nicole's approach. She surprised him by asking, "So what are you thankful for today?"

"This. All of it. Them," he nodded toward the group crowding around the food. "You. How well everything seems to be going. Just ... everything."

Nicole's phone chimed and she pulled it out to read the message she had just received. "Well, the FAA just issued an emergency order suspending our launch."

Tom nodded. "Good," he said. "That's good." Then smiling, he said, "Hungry? Let's go load up a couple of plates."

***

First thing in the morning on the Monday after Thanksgiving, Dick McConnel called his old friend David Wheeler and explained the situation. David was an administrative law judge who worked with several Federal agencies, including the FAA.

"So we'd like to request a hearing on the suspension order," Dick asked. "The sooner the better."

"Yes, I see," Judge Wheeler replied. "Well, with the Christmas holiday coming up, and then New Year's of course, I think it would most likely be late January at the earliest," he said, checking his calendar. "Or I do have some time available the first week of February."

"Well that's the thing, David. I'm afraid we can't afford to wait until next year to resolve this. We're requesting an expedited oral presentation and a determination for the record under 5 USC 554."

"I see, well, what's the urgency behind your request?"

"My client's scheduled launch date is the 18th of December, and failure to obtain a determination by that date is a de facto finding for the complainant."

"Well there's just not a lot of time between now and then," the judge protested.

"I understand, but my client has a significant financial investment at stake, on the order of a half a billion dollars, and failure to address this in a timely manner could result in significant financial harm."

Frowning as he perused his schedule again, the judge said, "The only day I have available is Wednesday, December 16th, but it's just one day, which won't allow me any time for travel."

"My client will be happy to make the trip to DC to obtain an expedited hearing, and I imagine that it would be very convenient for the FAA as well."

"All right, I'll hold the day for you, pending notice from the FAA. This is highly unusual, you know, contacting me directly."

"Believe me, I wouldn't have done it under normal circumstances, it's strictly due to the urgency of the matter. I'll let the FAA know that you've made time available for an expedited hearing when we notify them of our intent to seek a review and determination."

"All right, Dick, I'll see you and your clients in two weeks. Merry Christmas to you."

"And Merry Christmas to you, Judge. I owe you one."

Ending his call, Dick then dialed Nicole. "Hello? Yes, I've set it up. Go ahead and notify the FAA that we're requesting an expedited oral hearing and determination. If they give you any lip about not being able to line up an administrative law judge before the 18th, have them contact Judge Wheeler directly."

***

Tom arrived at Neverland thirty minutes early. Taking his usual seat at the center of one side of the conference table, he slowly turned in his chair contemplating the information captured on the white boards covering all four walls. Two years of plans, programs, diagrams, schedules, and milestones covered virtually every square inch. Most were crossed out in red marker, indicating that they were already accomplished. Only a few pending items remained. For two years he had run the show, made the decisions, and had the final say. Today he was turning it all over to Jean. With the launch now less than two weeks away, the launch director would now make the decisions and Tom would become merely a VIP passenger.

He noticed with a smile that someone had drawn a Santa hat on the stick figure astronaut planting the RRI flag on the moon. *I'm going to miss this when it's over*, he thought. *What are we ever going to do to top this?*

Vivian entered the room, interrupting his melancholy reflection. "Did you get the time wrong?" she asked as she sat across from him, curious why he had arrived so early. "Or was the traffic really light?"

"No, I just wanted a little time to myself to take it all in, I guess," Tom said.

"So who do you think will be picked?" Vivian asked, addressing the week's number one topic. The final episode of *The Last Passenger* was scheduled to air that weekend.

"I would have bet money that it would be Drew," Tom replied, "but personally I'm really starting to favor Nikki. She's a hard worker."

"I know, right? She's been here every day practicing and observing, and I think she has more pool time than any of us. Meanwhile we haven't seen much of Drew."

"He returned to work at the airline as soon as we got back from Russia," Tom explained. "Anyway, it's all up to the viewers, there's no way to predict who they'll favor."

"Is Mr. Funk coming to today's status review? It should be the last one before our final preflight meeting."

"I don't think so. He has a lot to attend to prior to our departure. Just in case something happens … " By unspoken agreement, the possibility of anyone failing to return from the mission was never addressed. But Elton was the CEO and majority shareholder in both EtherX and the internet payment company PayBuddy, and that required that he complete a great deal of estate and succession planning before departure, just in case.

The remaining team members slowly drifted into the room, exchanging greetings and holding short sidebar discussions. When Jean finally arrived, she started to pull up a chair next to Vivian, but Tom stood up and said, "Here, take my seat," and then moved to another chair. It startled everyone for a moment, but it was now the launch director's show to run.

"All right everyone, let's go around the circle," Jean said. "Pad operations."

"Launcher fueling systems certifications have been completed," the head of their pad operations team began.

Tom's mind drifted away, and he slowly tuned out the discussion. His eyes found the cartoon astronaut once again, and he smiled. *Less than two weeks*, he thought.

***

Too busy to attend the viewing party at Space Dome, Vivian sat in Tom's office at Vandenberg watching the final episode of *The Last Passenger* unfold. After a forty-five minute recap of the events from the previous episodes, Bryant Hastings' personal interviews with the two remaining candidates were now playing.

"They did these right after you all got back?" Vivian asked.

"Yes, they didn't fly Bryant to Russia, he did all his work here in LA between tapings of some other show he's doing."

"This really did turn out a lot better than I expected," Vivian noted.

"Yes, Tyler did good," Tom nodded. "We'll have to find room for him *next* time we go to the moon." They both chuckled. Turning to Vivian, he asked, "So tell me, do you worry at all?"

"Worry? About our safety?"

"Yes."

"Of course I do. But I try not to dwell on it. I trust my team. I know they built good hardware. And the shuttle is generally pretty safe."

"It sounds somewhat unconvincing when you say it that way," Tom chuckled.

"Is there something wrong, Mr. Armac?" Vivian asked, concerned.

"No, not really. Just … a feeling I have. It's nothing. I'm sure it's perfectly normal given the magnitude of what we're about to do. Astronaut cold feet, maybe."

Tom watched as Bryant did his set up for the big ending. "And now, it is time. The polling is complete, and all votes have been tabulated. The world has decided that *The Last Passenger* will be … Nikki Biccari!"

Although his disappointment was visible, Drew was gracious and applauded enthusiastically. He now slid into the backup passenger slot, as

Nikki had just been awarded the final seat on the mission.

"This is the greatest thing that's ever happened to me!" she effused, smiling brightly while wiping a tear from the corner of her eye. "Thank you! Thank you so much!"

I hope you're right and we don't all end up regretting this trip, Tom thought, haunted by a vague apprehension.

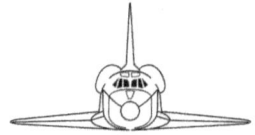

CHAPTER THIRTY–SEVEN

Dick McConnel once again sat in the lobby of the Capitol Hilton waiting for Nicole. Feeling a touch on his shoulder, he looked up from his newspaper to find her standing beside him. "Good morning," he said, folding his paper. "Ready to do this?"

"Absolutely, I've been looking forward to this for months," Nicole replied with a smile.

"They don't stand a chance, do they?"

"Fish, meet barrel," she chuckled. "Still, you can never be completely sure with these things."

It was only a ten minute cab ride from there to the headquarters of the Federal Aviation Administration. Presenting their identification and signing into the building, they were given temporary visitors passes and escorted to the conference room reserved for the hearing.

Ray Mainard had brought his boss Stewart Thompson to the meeting. Stewart was the head of the licensing and evaluation division. They both knew Judge Wheeler very well, having worked with him to arbitrate other licensing disputes.

"Judge Wheeler, how are you!" Dick said, shaking his old friend's hand. "I'd like you to meet my client, Ms. Nicole Ferry, lead attorney for Roadrunner Rockets Incorporated."

After introductions and pleasantries, the judge got down to business. "I'd like to remind everyone that this is not a trial, but it is a legal proceeding," he began. "After listening to both your testimonies, I will render a determination on the record. The Deputy Administrator will have 60 days to appeal that decision if he so desires. OK, Mr. Thompson, why don't you go ahead and give your opening statement."

"Thank you, Your Honor," Stewart began. "In my capacity as manager of the Federal Aviation Administration Office of Commercial Space

Transportation Licensing and Evaluation Division, it is my responsibility to determine whether proposed launch operations represent a threat to public health and safety or threaten public or private property. We believe that the launch plan filed by Roadrunner Rockets Incorporated, under which said corporation intends to utilize a pair of commercially developed hybrid boosters to launch space shuttle Atlantis into Earth orbit on 18 December of this year, represents a significant threat to both property and public safety. We have therefore utilized our authority under 14 CFR part 405 to issue an emergency order immediately suspending said corporation's launch site operators permit."

"Very well," the judge nodded. "So noted. Ms. Ferry, your opening statement?"

"Your Honor, we request that you grant a motion to dismiss, as the complaint is without merit. Under 14 CFR Part 405.3, authority to suspend or revoke a license or permit is limited to a clearly defined set of conditions, none of which we believe are applicable in this case. Specifically, our planned launch operation as outlined represents no undue threat to public health or safety, or the safety of property."

"Well I guess that's what we're here to determine," Judge Wheeler said, smiling. "I'll take your motion to dismiss under consideration and will issue a determination after I've had an opportunity to learn a little more about the particulars, if that's all right with you?"

"Certainly, Your Honor," Nicole nodded.

"Your ball, gentlemen," the judge said, looking at Stewart and Ray.

"Your Honor, we believe there is in fact great potential risk in allowing this launch to proceed."

"Specifically, gentlemen?"

"First, we consider the space shuttle to be an inherently dangerous vehicle to operate, and it would be particularly so in the hands of an organization not deeply familiar with the operation of this complex system."

"As to the matter of the vehicle's inherent dangerousness," Nicole replied, "may I point out to Your Honor that there have been 135 shuttle missions flown to date?"

"It does seem a little shaky, gentlemen, to argue that the shuttle is not a safe vehicle to operate," the judge commented.

"Your Honor does realize that there were two catastrophic failures resulting in loss of life during the conduct of those 135 flights?" Steward commented. "This would not conform to our current definition of acceptable risk for commercial launch activities."

"Your Honor, if I may," Nicole replied. Looking at the men from the FAA, she held up her hand and ticked off each item on her fingers as she spoke. "First, there was the Challenger accident in 1986, the cause of which was clearly identified and an appropriate engineering fix applied. In over twenty-five years of subsequent flights, there have been no recurrences of that problem. Second, the loss of Columbia was not due to any specific fault with the vehicle, but rather with the insulating system on the external fuel tank. This is also a well understood phenomenon for which a satisfactory solution has been developed and applied."

Turning back to the judge, she said, "Two clearly understood and corrected faults in 135 flights with no subsequent recurrences allows us to project a greater than ninety-nine percent probability of safe mission completion, which falls within the guidelines for acceptable risk. In addition, may I point out that in none of these failures was a member of the general public adversely affected, nor did damage to public or private property occur. The only loss of life was that of the crew. While tragic, each crewmember was aware of the risks and undertook them willingly, as indeed our crewmembers are also.

"As to the matter of our inexperience with operation of the shuttle system, I'd like to enter into the record the background and qualifications of the individuals whom we have employed to prepare the vehicle for flight and conduct and manage the launch and flight operations." Nicole handed a thick stack of paperwork to the judge. "You will note the extensive background and experience each has in shuttle operations."

Thumbing briefly through the document, the judge said, "At first glance, it looks like you moved most of the NASA shuttle operations team to Vandenberg."

"Exactly, Your Honor."

"Gentlemen?" he asked. "Anything else?"

"Your Honor, we believe the proposed launch site, located as close as it is to major population centers, represents an unacceptable risk for public injury in the event of a launch anomaly."

"Your Honor," Nicole responded, "Vandenberg Space Launch Complex Six was specifically developed by the United States Government as an alternate shuttle launch facility. What specific change may have occurred that would now render this location unsuitable as a safe and appropriate launch site?" Turning to the men across from her, she added, "Or do the gentlemen claim that the US Government willfully and knowingly located said facility in a location that offered unacceptable risk for loss of life or damage to public or private property?"

Stewart sat stonily silent for a moment, and then turned to glare at Ray. "I thought this was supposed to be a slam dunk," he muttered to his subordinate.

"You'll be launching over downtown Los Angeles," Ray blurted out. "That's just not safe."

Looking at the judge, Nicole said, "Your Honor, as you can see in the site operations permit application we submitted, and the FAA approved, our intended launch track of fifty-one degrees south places our vehicle well offshore from any dense population centers. We have no intention of launching over downtown Los Angeles. Our launch might pose some small threat to sea lions on the Channel Islands, but not to anyone on the west coast. And again, I'd like to remind everyone that this site was selected and approved by the US Government specifically for shuttle operations.

"Is that all you have, gentlemen?" Judge Wheeler asked.

Stewart decided to change his approach. "Your Honor, we have specific concerns about the fact that this is supposed to be a manned launch. We're worried about crew safety."

"Your Honor," Nicole replied, "the boosters to be used for our launch—two examples of what we call our Big Brother booster—have recently been certified as human rated. The FAA has determined that they are indeed safe for use in manned operations."

"But they've never launched a shuttle!" Stewart said.

"No, but under the amendments implemented by the Commercial Space Launch Enhanced Access Act, any vehicle certified safe for manned operations can be launched utilizing our man-rated booster."

"But shuttle was never issued a human rating," Stewart said with satisfaction, thinking he'd finally found a weak spot in Nicole's arguments. "As a Government-owned vehicle, the shuttle was waived from the requirements. So it technically doesn't have a human rating."

"Seriously?" the judge said with mild contempt. "You're saying that the FAA doesn't consider the shuttle to be safe for manned flight, even though it was our sole vehicle for manned flight for over thirty years?"

"It's not a matter of what we think, Your Honor, it's what the regulations state," Stewart responded with a smug smile.

Nicole smiled back. "I'm pleased to see the level of respect you hold for the regulations." Turning to Judge Wheeler, she said, "Your Honor, again, under the Commercial Space Launch Enhanced Access Act section three, paragraph six, an exception to the human rating criteria is specifically identified for any spacecraft that, and I quote, has an existing and established history of successfully conducting manned suborbital or orbital flight operations, unquote."

Steward glared again at Ray. "Did you know that was in the new regulations?" he asked.

"We flagged it when it was proposed, but everyone assumed that the provision was intended to cover a launch permit holder who may want to launch a Soyuz capsule. We thought it would be diplomatically awkward to require the Russians to submit to our human rating requirements when we'd already put dozens of our own astronauts in them." Looking back at Nicole, he said, "No one ever considered that the provision would also cover a shuttle, since they were retired."

"So you see, Your Honor," Nicole continued, "as the FAA admits, the stated provision defines the shuttle as possessing a human rating, as it is grandfathered in under the section three criteria. This makes it legal and safe for us to integrate it with our Big Brother booster."

Dick McConnel leaned back in his chair and held his hand over his mouth to hide his enormous grin. *She's damned good at this*, he thought. *I wish I'd brought popcorn.*

"Your Honor, Roadrunner Rockets has abused the permit process and has acted in bad faith," Stewart said, trying yet another approach. "Clearly they knew that the launch plan they originally filed did not represent their true intentions."

Nicole's subtle smile broadened slightly. "Your Honor, if the complainants accept our position regarding the safety of personnel and property, then we again request an immediate motion for dismissal. 14 CFR Part 406 clearly states that a complaint may be dismissed for failure to state a claim for which a civil penalty may be imposed. As amending a filed launch plan is clearly allowed under the law, we have broken no regulation or violated any term or condition of our license." Turning to Stewart, she added, "If you yield on the issue of safety, you can't use an emergency order to prohibit the launch merely because you're not happy with how we applied the rules."

"Gentlemen, it appears that the nature of your complaint may be, shall we say, evolving," Judge Wheeler said. "If that is the case, then I would agree that your use of an emergency order is probably not appropriate, and that you should re-file your complaint." Leaning back in his chair, he made a steeple with his fingers. "Applying a bit of common sense though, I don't want to have to go through this entire process again in a few weeks, so for the moment let's hear what your thoughts are regarding abuse of process. Although I will say that it seems unlikely that the appropriate remedy for such a complaint would be to prohibit the launch."

"Your Honor," Stewart said, "we acknowledge that Roadrunner Rocket's Big Brother boosters are human rated, but we contend that by using them to launch a space shuttle, it is not appropriate to consider the shuttle as payload. This in fact represents a significant reconfiguration of the launcher, a configuration that has not been reviewed and approved by this office. Therefore using the provisions within the Enhanced Access Act to redefine the payload for an approved launch does not apply, and this would be an abuse of that provision."

"Your Honor," Nicole replied, "under the provisions of the Enhanced Access Act, a payload is defined as a component of the launch vehicle that provides less than twenty percent of the total thrust at liftoff. That provision was specifically incorporated to reduce the administrative burden imposed by the FAA when dealing with payloads that also provide some small additional contribution to overall vehicle thrust. In the case of our pending launch, eighty-three percent of the thrust at liftoff will be provided by our Big Brother boosters, and only seventeen percent will be provided by the shuttle and its components. This clearly classifies the shuttle as payload under the terms of the Act, and allows us to use the launch plan payload modification provisions to incorporate it into our launch vehicle in substitution for the one originally proposed.

"Your Honor," Stewart pleaded, "it's clear that Roadrunner Rockets has made shrewd use of specific provisions within the Enhanced Access Act to enable and justify their actions in this matter, but it was never the intent of the Government to support this type of action on the part of commercial launch providers."

"Your Honor, may I speak to the issue of intent?" Nicole asked.

"Certainly, Ms. Ferry," Judge Wheeler replied.

"Your Honor, it is not for us to speculate as to the intent of Congress in this matter, especially when they have made these intentions abundantly clear." Pulling a paper from her briefcase, she read, "51 USC Section 50901 subparagraph (b) clearly defines the purpose of the Commercial Space Launch Activities Act as follows: to encourage the United States private sector to provide launch vehicles, reentry vehicles, and associated services by, and I quote, facilitating and encouraging the use of Government developed space technology, unquote." Looking up at the Judge, she said, "Now I ask you, how could they have made their intentions more clear?"

Dick McConnel made a sudden snorting sound as he tried to suppress a burst of laughter. Stewart and Ray both clenched their jaws tightly, the muscles in their cheeks flexing.

Everyone sat silently for a moment. Then Judge Wheeler sat upright and said, "All right, I'd like to think about this for just a moment before I issue a determination, so if you will all excuse me briefly, I'd like to go get a cup of coffee. Don't go far, I won't be long."

Nicole began sorting her paperwork and putting it back in her briefcase as the two men from the FAA alternately glared at her and spoke quietly to each other. Finally, Ray said, "You know, there's another issue that we intend to bring up on appeal. The Smithsonian isn't happy with what you're doing. They feel they have a security interest in Atlantis by virtue of the contract you signed stating that the orbiter would be placed on permanent display at the National Air and Space Museum, and they feel you're risking that agreement and their implied property rights through this flight."

"Yes, well," Nicole said, continuing to fill her briefcase, "first, their contract is with the Aerospace Museum of the Pacific LLC, and not with Roadrunner Rockets. Although they could certainly bring that issue up with them, until my company donates Atlantis to the museum, they have no ownership. And second, even when they take ownership, a review of the basic contract will show that several of the provisions specified therein state that in the period before said transfer to the Smithsonian takes place, the museum may use the shuttle in ways that advance scientific knowledge, contribute to a greater understanding of space flight and space exploration, and/or demonstrate or highlight characteristics and capabilities of the space transportation system." Smiling and looking up, she said, "I think you'll find a big enough loophole there to drive a truck through, or a space shuttle, even. It would be very easy to argue that flying Atlantis to the moon is allowed under any of those provisions."

Re-entering the room, Judge Wheeler returned to his seat and sipped his coffee for a moment, and then set his cup down. "All right, here's my determination on this matter." Turning to Dick and Nicole, he said, "First, it is apparent that as the Government contends, Roadrunner Rockets did in fact act in bad faith, in as much as they knowingly submitted false or misleading information in their initial launch plan for the purpose of deceiving the FAA as to the true nature of their operations."

Nicole's face fell a little, while those of the two FAA men brightened.

"In fact, it appears that your manipulation of the process extends back several years at least, as you undoubtedly had some hand in crafting the relevant provisions within the Commercial Space Launch Enhanced Access Act cited today that seem tailor made to enable just such behavior as your company has exhibited." Looking at Stewart and Ray, he added, "That is something the Government may wish to address in a future action.

"However," he continued, "the matter before us today is that of Roadrunner Rocket's request for dismissal of the complaint filed by the FAA and the abrogation of the emergency order rescinding their launch permit. In this matter, I find that the Government has failed to make its case. There does not in fact appear to be sufficient risk to public health and safety or the safety of personal or public property to justify issuance of said emergency order. I therefore grant Roadrunner Rocket's request for dismissal, and the emergency order is lifted effective immediately."

***

While they were inside, a light snow had begun to fall over Washington. Waving his arm at a passing cab, Dick turned to Nicole and said, "You really should come work with me. I think you have what it takes to do very well in this city. I'm sure you'd find the salary very attractive compared to what Tom Armac may be paying you."

Climbing into the cab, Nicole said, "But I don't think you could match the benefits. Do you have any idea how many airline miles a trip the moon earns?" Pulling out her phone, she dialed Marcus. "Marcus? It's Nicole. Tell Jean to continue the countdown. The order's been lifted, and with the

Christmas holiday I doubt they're going to be able to get an appeal together until sometime next year. OK, see you soon."

Ending the call, Nicole settled back in the seat and looked out the window at the snow starting to accumulate on the Capitol steps. Turning to Dick, she said, "Before you take me to the airport, do you think we could swing by the National Christmas Tree? I've always wanted to see it, and it's probably beautiful now with the snow."

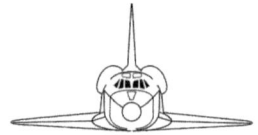

CHAPTER THIRTY–EIGHT

Initially there had been only a handful of requests from the press for access. While the launch of a Big Brother Twin might interest the surrounding communities, no major media was concerned enough to send a crew all the way to Vandenberg to cover a routine commercial launch. Everything changed after the news broke. The first manned mission to the moon in almost forty-five years! Interest intensified as word leaked about the way it had come about—the enormous but unseen back-story involving secret deals and front companies and political machinations. It read like a suspense novel! The media couldn't get enough, and their requests for access multiplied, first to provide live coverage of the launch, followed quickly by requests for crew interviews. Fortunately, Tyler had a plan ready.

Vandenberg Space Launch Complex Four sat a little over three miles north of the pad on which Atlantis sat. Conveniently, it was currently under lease to Ether Exploration Systems. Elton Funk had been in the beginning stages of updating its antiquated facilities to support future launches of EtherX's Raptor Heavy rocket. Its large parking area, adequate supply of electrical power, and position outside the launch safety perimeter made it the perfect location to park the small city of television vans and mobile news trailers that had descended upon the site. Its only drawback was that a range of intervening hills blocked a direct view of the pad at Slick Six where Atlantis sat undergoing final preparations for liftoff.

Some of the press realized that a better place to watch the launch and general mission operations would be from the viewer's gallery at the Space Dome mission control center, where Jean had already announced the call to stations for the launch control team. Their trucks departed for the Aerospace Museum of the Pacific's parking lot to observe the controllers as the launch countdown ticked away.

A few reporters determined that the best view of the launch could be had from offshore, and the local fishing boats were doing a brisk business auctioning spots on launch viewing charters to members of the media.

Like the game clock at a football game, the remaining time of a launch countdown bore little resemblance to actual, real world time. Numerous built-in holds in the count created huge discrepancies between the displayed count and the actual time remaining until liftoff. It was now late Wednesday morning, just a little over two days before Atlantis and its crew were scheduled to depart the planet. The countdown clock read T minus twenty-seven hours and holding.

Tyler was enjoying himself immensely. The monitors mounted around the perimeter of the room in which this morning's press conference was being held displayed the image that was being beamed around the world of Atlantis sitting on the pad awaiting launch. He couldn't remember whose idea it had been to paint the segments of the two Big Brother boosters straddling Atlantis to resemble a stack of soft drink cans, but he knew that the sponsors were delighted by the prominent placement of their products.

Tom was not enjoying himself at all. Fortunately, this was the last interview the crew was scheduled to provide before being sequestered to make their final preparations for the mission. Sitting between Elton and Vivian, Tom had been able to avoid most of the questions, which had been directed primarily at Robbie and Nikki, sitting at opposite ends of the dais. As the mission commander, Robbie was asked the bulk of the questions about the details of the flight, and Nikki, well, the press just couldn't get enough of her. After the numerous personal interviews, Tom wasn't sure if he could answer one more question about how it felt to be preparing to travel to the moon without completely losing his patience.

Dr. Heinel was explaining once again that no, he was not the oldest person to ever travel into space, that would be Senator John Glenn, who had been seventy-seven at the time of his mission onboard shuttle Discovery, but that yes, he would undoubtedly be the oldest person to ever walk on the moon, and how sincerely he appreciated it that everyone thought he looked younger than his actual age of seventy-five.

"Doctor Heinel, Doctor Heinel," another reporter cried, trying to attract Carl's attention to ask the next question.

"Yes, the gentlemen in the yellow shirt," Carl said, pointing.

"Thank you, Doctor Heinel. Phil Harmon, with *Aviation News*. Can you tell me, sir, what prompted you to want to make this trip? After all, a journey of this nature wouldn't normally be something a man your age would attempt."

Carl's face slowly assumed a serene look, as his gaze drifted to a distant place and time. Everyone on the crew, knowing the story, turned toward him.

Softly, Carl said, "I am here in fulfillment of a promise I made a very long time ago. An important promise that I very much intend to keep."

The reporter tried to ask a follow-up question, but Carl cut him off by saying, "I'm afraid that's all I have to say on that issue, Mr. Harmon."

"Mr. Funk," another reporter shouted out, "will there be future joint missions involving your company and Mr. Armac's? Are we seeing the emergence of a new commercial space heavyweight created by the alliance of EtherX and RRI?"

"We haven't discussed the possibility of conducting future joint operations." Elton said. "Let's see how this mission goes before we begin speculating about what the future may have in store."

Tom leaned toward his microphone. "I think it's also important to note that this isn't a joint operation of our two companies. This is strictly a Roadrunner Rockets mission, and Mr. Funk is merely a paying passenger on our flight." Putting his hand over his microphone, Tom turned to Elton and added, "That way you're off the hook if anything goes wrong." Unfortunately, Elton's microphone picked up the comment and broadcasted it.

"On that issue," an unknown reporter called out, "are any of you at all concerned about the safety of this mission?"

The room became silent. Tom looked left, then right, glancing at each of the members of the crew. Then, seeking out the reporter in the crowd who had shouted the question, he said, "Anything truly worth doing has risk. I think I speak for everyone here when I say we're all aware of the risk involved. I'm sure we each have our own reasons for believing that the risk is worth it. Of course we're concerned. But we're going anyway. Because it's not lack of fear that makes a person brave, it's the ability to act in spite of fear. And these people, this crew of ours, are the bravest people I've ever met." Then, pushing back from the table, he stood up and turned around. "I'm done," he said to Tyler, as he left the stage.

"All right everyone, that's all for today," Tyler said, as the other members of the crew stood and followed Tom. "Next we'll have a presentation on mission milestones, followed by an update on the progress with the countdown."

Marcus met Tom as he left the stage. "Good news, Boss. Nicole just called."

"And?"

"She kicked some serious Government butt. The mission is a go."

"That's my girl," Tom said, smiling.

***

What began as a light snowfall had turned into a significant winter storm. Washington was usually a quiet place during the Christmas season, as most Federal workers generally had unused vacation time remaining that had to be taken before year's end. In addition, the city was always paralyzed by any snowfall, as the municipal government was generally inept at snow removal. Put the two together and the city became a ghost town.

Living in an apartment right across the river in Crystal City, Stewart Thompson usually rode the Metro rail to his office on Independence Avenue. Due to the weather, he was one of the few who had been able to make it in today, which meant that there was no one available to help him prepare a request for an appeal of Judge Wheeler's determination. As a department manager, he was much better at directing others to perform such a task than he was at doing it himself. But the Associate Director had asked for more time to review the FAA's position on RRI's pending launch, and he needed to find a way to delay it. Once the appeal was filed the emergency order could be immediately reinstated, but it looked increasingly as if there just wasn't enough time. *I wonder if that was another part of their plan, pushing this into the holidays*, he thought. Realizing he needed to explore other options, he began working the phone. *I'd better start with the Pentagon. I'll have the best chance there.*

***

Nicole was greeted as a conquering hero upon her return. Tom had been in a dour mood since the previous day's press conference, but he cheered up dramatically as she recounted each blow in the verbal sparring match that had occurred the day before in Washington.

"And then they brought up the Smithsonian and their implied property rights," she gleefully described. "I wish you could have seen their faces when I paraphrased the relevant passages in the museum contract. Priceless!"

"So they absolutely followed the script to the letter?" Tom asked.

"Just as we'd predicted," Nicole beamed. "They have no idea how unintentionally cooperative they were. And then oh my God it started to snow! I knew immediately that if they had had any chance at all of getting an appeal together in time, the snow put an end to it."

Tom glanced at Marcus, who smiled and nodded knowingly. "I guess it's just meant to be," he said.

Tom's phone rang, interrupting the celebration. Seeing that it was Colonel Arnold calling, he momentarily left the room.

"Colonel Arnold, how are you? Yes, everything is on track, we're at the T minus eleven hour hold now and we're proceeding nicely. You don't say. I see. Well, we did expect that, didn't we? OK then, see you tomorrow. So long now."

Stepping back into the room, Tom motioned to Nicole.

"Have they started?" she asked.

"Yes. That was Jim Arnold. It seems someone from the FAA has been calling the Air Force asking about our launch. They're trying to find some way to put a hold on it. Space Command wanted to know if Jim saw any reason why we shouldn't be allowed to go ahead."

"And he said … ?"

"That everything we were doing was in accordance with the terms of our lease and covered by an approved launch plan, so he saw little recourse, much less reason to interfere."

"A nice moon rock for the Colonel then, also," Nicole smiled.

"Plus he said that just a few minutes later, they called back and told him that Congressman Daisy's office had contacted them to express how important the members of his committee felt this launch was to the development of the Space Train program. He's now been directed to provide all possible assistance."

"I think the Air Force actually admires us for what we're doing," Nicole observed. "They've wanted to see a shuttle fly from Vandenberg for thirty years."

"Yes, and having Dick McConnel call the Congressman again put us over the top."

"Sounds like moon rocks all around," Nicole said with a laugh.

"Now we just need to see if the state is going to make a move," Tom said.

***

Stewart hung up, frustrated. The Air Force had decided that they had neither the grounds nor the inclination to interfere with the next day's launch. He'd run out of options at the federal level. The Department of Homeland Security hadn't even returned his call, and the lone individual he'd managed to contact at the Environmental Protection Agency had laughed at his request to issue a cease and desist order on environmental grounds. Anxiously looking at the clock, he picked up the phone again. *Only one more shot*, he thought.

"Yes, this is Stewart Thompson with the Federal Aviation Administration in Washington, DC. I'd like the Governor's office, please. Yes, I'll hold."

***

Tom awoke slowly, drifting gently toward consciousness. The series of fragmentary dreams through which he floated created a feeling of disconnectedness, his mind unsure of his location in time and space and unable to define the boundary between imagination and reality. Gradually, a specific sense of here and now took hold, and the dreamlets receded to the edge of perception and then beyond. Lying quietly in the darkness, he became aware first of his heartbeat, and then the coolness of air moving gently across his face. He next sensed a rising wave of mild anxiety. There

268

was no fear to it, it was more a feeling of anticipation. Analyzing it to understand its origin, he took the last step to wakefulness as a single thought formed in his mind: *today is the day!*

Pulling on his jeans and a polo shirt, Tom opened the door of the small room in which he had spent the night and peered into the hallway. An area within the Integrated Processing Facility had been configured for crew preparation and each member of the flight crew had spent the night sleeping here. Seeing no movement in the hallway, he headed toward the conference room, from where final launch preparations were being locally monitored and coordinated.

Marcus looked up as Tom entered the room. "Morning boss. You're up kinda early. We weren't planning to wake anyone for another hour."

"I couldn't sleep anymore," Tom replied absently, as he moved to the monitor showing Atlantis sitting on the launch pad illuminated in the predawn darkness. "Have you been here all night?"

"Just got here thirty minutes ago," Marcus replied, as he thumbed through a stack of documents on a clipboard.

"How's the count going?" Tom asked.

"No problems overnight. Jean just called the T minus six hour hold. We're getting ready to clear everyone from the pad and begin fueling the external tank."

"How long is the hold?"

"Should be about two hours."

"OK, good. I'm going to go get a shower then. I guess I'll beat the rush for the hot water."

"I'd recommend you take a nice long one, 'cause it's strictly sponge baths for you for the next two weeks," Marcus said, looking up from the clipboard.

"Somehow I think it will be worth the sacrifice," Tom said with a smile, as he turned to leave the room.

"No doubt," Marcus chuckled, returning his attention to his paperwork and the actions of the small team of people in the room.

Tom stood in the shower a long time, the temperature turned as hot as he could stand it, letting the water run over his shoulders and back, trying to wash away the anxiety he felt. His mind replayed the key events of the previous two years that had led to his being here today. He smiled as he considered how dramatically different his life was from what he would have predicted on the day he had first heard of Dr. Heinel and his proposal. He distinctly recalled his initial reaction. He thought the man was crazy. And yet less than two years later, here he was, showering before breakfast on launch day.

Turning off the water and toweling dry, Tom quietly said to himself, "I wonder what makes a man follow a dream for almost half a century?"

"Not a dream, Mr. Armac, a promise," he heard in reply.

Startled, Tom turned to see Carl standing in front of one of the sinks, laying out his toiletries on the countertop. "Sorry, Doctor, I didn't hear you come in. Couldn't sleep either?"

"I slept quite well actually," Carl replied, as he lathered his face and began to shave. "I have always been an early riser, I must admit."

"So tell me, Doctor, how does it feel to be on the verge of finally achieving the goal you've spent your life working to accomplish?"

Carl momentarily stopped and a frown crossed his face. Somewhat hesitantly, he said, "As you would expect, Mr. Armac. Satisfied. I feel ... very satisfied," and then resumed shaving.

"I would think so," Tom said, as he finished dressing. "Well, I'll see you at breakfast then," he concluded, as he turned to leave.

"Indeed. I'll see you there," Carl replied. After Tom left, Carl put his razor down and gazed calmly into the mirror for a moment, Tom's words echoing in his mind. *Finally achieving the goal you've spent your life working to accomplish ...*

Shaking his head briefly, he finished shaving, picked up a towel, and slowly wiped the remaining shaving cream from his face.

***

After showering, Tom stopped by the conference room again, and promptly lost himself in observation of the final launch preparations. A monitor displayed a live video feed from the mission control center at Space Dome in Long Beach. He had watched Jean run her team through numerous training drills, but today was the real thing. The other members of the crew individually drifted in and out to see for themselves how the countdown was progressing.

After several hours, Marcus said, "Shouldn't you be at the crew brunch about now, boss?"

"I guess you're right," Tom said, startled by the time. "I can't really say I'm that hungry though."

"Well, I don't really think it's about the food, it's more the tradition and making sure you all get a good send off. Think of it as your bon voyage party."

"I just hope no one is expecting a speech," Tom said as he looked one more time at the monitor and then turned to leave.

"At this point, I think you can leave all the speechifying to Robbie. He's the mission commander. You're just a passenger, remember? What, do you think you're important to this mission or something?"

Tom laughed. "Thanks for keeping me grounded, big guy."

"Don't mention it, boss. I'll be down shortly. I heard there's cake."

Tom reluctantly left the room and descended the stairs to the first floor.

"*There* he is!" Tom heard as he pushed open the door to the ground floor staging area. Entering the room, he was startled by the number of people present and the volume of noise they made.

"Mr. Armac, the Senator sends her best wishes for a safe journey," Daniel Brooks said, extending his hand. "She's sorry she couldn't be here today, but she'll be following your progress very closely from Washington."

"Mr. Brooks," Tom replied, shaking Daniel's hand. "Please thank the Senator for helping this come about. How have you been? We haven't seen you since the day you helped with our negotiations for access to the complex."

"Things are good. I'm the Senator's chief of staff now, so I haven't had much time to visit. I love what you've done with the place," Daniel said jokingly, looking around the room.

"Well, we told you we'd make better use of it than Rainier Aerospace was."

"Mr. Armac," Bob Brock nodded as he approached. "We were beginning to worry whether you were going to miss your own send off."

"No, I'm sure Nicole would have come looking for me."

"Are you talking about me behind my back?" Nicole called from a short distance away where she stood with Will Daisy and Keith Barton.

"Thank you both for coming," Tom said, joining the group.

"You're most welcome, son," Will said with a smile, clapping Tom on the shoulder. "You know, if you'd told me that first day in my office that this was what you were planning to do, I'd have thrown you out on your tail."

"Not me," Keith said cheerfully. "I'm loving the chance to see Atlantis fly again, and besides, we've got almost half our people back to work now, which are a hell of a lot more than we would have had without your program."

"No hard feelings?" Tom asked the Congressman.

"Oh hell no, son, I've long since come around to your side. Best of luck to you and your crew!"

"Thank you, Congressman."

Moving toward the buffet to grab something to eat, Tom was interrupted by Mark Rutherford. "I'll never forget the day your folks told me about this crazy plan of yours," Mark said, picking up a plate.

"Me neither," Tom agreed. "I thought Dr. Heinel was certifiable."

"Well I'm damn glad you called me. Next time you're in DC, swing by my office and let me show you the sweet ride you bought me."

"I'll do that, Mr. Rutherford."

"Oh, I almost forget, I'm supposed to give you something," Mark said, setting his plate down and retrieving a file folder from a nearby table. "The crew at the Gagarin Training Center asked me to give this to you."

Opening the folder, Tom found a group portrait of the training center staff, everyone giving a big thumbs up. Each member of the staff had signed the picture, and several sentences were written at the top in Russian.

Tom looked at the picture for a moment, a smile spreading across his face. "What does this say?" he asked Mark, indicating the Russian phrase.

"It roughly says 'Best wishes for a safe journey. Remember us and please visit upon your return.'"

"Mr. Armac, could we get a shot of you and Mr. Funk holding the picture?" Bruce Trunly asked, waving his video crew over.

"Well, here we are," Elton said, standing next to Tom while Bruce's crew shot video.

"Yep," Tom replied simply.

"Are you ready for this?" Elton asked.

"Nothing else on my schedule for the next few weeks," Tom replied. Then he added, "Sorry about some of the things I've said."

"No, I owed you the apology, but I tell you what, this is the last time either of us mentions it again, OK?"

"Deal," Tom said, shaking Elton's hand.

"Now let's go fly," Elton said.

"Hey Tom, there's someone here I'd like you to meet," Robbie called out, waving to him. He and Stephanie were talking to a person that Tom didn't recognize.

"Tom, this is James Leon. He's the one who's made it safe for us to fly today."

"Oh?" Tom asked, confused.

"He's the Chumash medicine man that lifted the curse on the pad," Robbie exclaimed, patting James on the back.

"There was no curse," James commented, reaching to shake Tom's hand. "And I'm an 'antap, not a medicine man."

"Still, he made it OK with the spirits for us," Robbie said cheerfully.

"A pleasure to meet you," Tom said, shaking James' hand. Then, spotting Vivian sitting with Carl and Mike, he headed their way.

"Good luck up there," Jim Arnold said to Tom as he passed. "Make us proud of the old girl. We always knew she had a lot more to give then was asked of her."

"Colonel," Tom nodded. "I hear you've put your retirement papers in?"

"Yep, submitted them earlier this week," Jim replied. "It appears I'll be looking for a new job in about sixty days, if that position you mentioned is still open."

"You know it is," Tom said warmly. "We look forward to having you on the team."

Tom heard Marcus' voice booming across the room, and he turned to see him entering along with Dale Jeffers, the man who had replaced him as

CEO of Altered State Software.

"Why didn't you tell me Dale was here?" Tom asked Marcus with a grin while shaking Dale's hand. "How's the company?" he asked Dale.

"I just got in," Dale replied. "We're doing well. The new owners had the sense to not interfere in our internal processes too much, and we have several new products close to release. Can't say we're that crazy about New Jersey, but what are you going to do?" he said with a shrug of his shoulders.

"I was glad to see that the board made you Chairman," Tom said. "It made me feel better knowing someone would be looking out for my people. Well, the company's people."

"Well, we sure miss you, Tom, but I have to say, I can understand why you wanted to step up to this challenge," Dale said, looking around the room.

A scattering of applause started at the far corner of the room and then spread through the crowd. Turning to see what the commotion was about, Tom spotted two members of the launch support crew carrying a large sheet cake toward a table in the center of the room. Placing it on the table, they stepped back so everyone could gather around. The center of the cake displayed a representation in colored frosting of the official mission patch. It showed the RRI flaming roadrunner running across the moon's surface, with Tinkerbell spreading pixie dust in the background and the distant Earth hovering above. In a semicircle above the design was the phrase "Sic Itur Ad Astra," while in an arc below it, it said "Palus Putredinus De Integro."

"Let's get the entire flight crew to gather around the mission cake, please," Tyler called out, herding everyone together to take pictures.

"They did a nice job on the cake," Robbie noted approvingly. "What's the motto mean?"

"The phrase above literally translates as 'Thus You Shall Go To The Stars,'" Carl said. "It's a quote from Virgil's *Aeneid*. I believe it also has a more poetic meaning."

"What would that be?" Tom asked.

"Thus Is Immortality Gained." Carl smiled. "I'd take it to mean that we shall live forever in history."

"Very nice," Robbie noted. "Two entirely appropriate mission mottos for the price of one. Did you come up with that?"

"I may have been consulted," Carl replied with a grin.

"What about the lower one?" Tom asked.

"Ah, it describes our mission," Carl observed. "It says 'The Marsh of Decay a Second Time.'"

From somewhere, copies of the official crew photo appeared, and were passed around for signatures. It had been taken after their final mission rehearsal. In it, they were all wearing their launch and reentry pressure suits, their helmets lined up in a row on the floor before them, a large image of the moon suspended behind them.

Marcus stepped up to the cake, spatula in hand. "OK, if everyone is done gawking, let's cut this bad boy! These people need to get out of here and go get dressed or they're going to miss their flight." Digging in, he started carving large pound sized portions of cake for distribution.

Nicole's phone rang. Setting her cake down and glancing at her screen, she took the call. "Yes? Who? Did they say why? I see. OK. Where are they now? All right, go ahead and escort them to my office, I'll be up in just a few minutes."

She motioned to catch Tom's attention, and then shook her head and pointed up stairs.

"Are they trying again?" Tom asked as he made his way over.

"Apparently so," she replied. "The state is requesting that we delay the launch."

"On what grounds? They don't have jurisdiction."

"Environmental issues."

"Can you handle it?" Tom asked.

"Of course," she said with a smile. "When I think of all the cards they could have played, I'm almost disappointed they made it so easy."

"Well don't get cocky, the last thing we want right now is a lot of drama. Should I tell them?" Tom asked, nodding toward the rest of the crew.

"No, this won't take long. Ten minutes tops. Here, hold my cake."

***

Nicole found two people waiting in her office, escorted by a member of the site security force. Nodding to the officer, she said, "Thanks, I'll take responsibility for them."

"Please have them sign out when they depart," he said as he left.

Turning to her two visitors, she said, "Good morning. I'm Nicole Ferry, head of certification and compliance, among a list of other things."

"Ms. Ferry, I'm Dean MacKenzie with the California Air Resources Board, and this is Jan Caldwell from the Santa Barbara County Air Pollution Control District."

"Can I ask what this pertains to?" Nicole asked, gesturing for everyone to be seated. "As you can see, we're extremely busy at the moment."

"Well, Ms. Ferry," Dean explained, "I received a call from our agency director, who had received a call from the Governor's office. The Governor is concerned that this launch may be in violation of this facility's air operating permit. I'm afraid we're going to have to ask you to postpone the launch until a proper determination is made."

"That's nonsense," Nicole replied impatiently. "You have our Environmental Assessment on file. Our emissions are all below de minimis thresholds and well within the goals for attainment."

"As it was explained to me," Dean said, "your Environmental Assessment applied to your original booster design." Thumbing through a stack of paperwork and finding the relevant information, he added, "Your Hot Wax oxygen and paraffin fueled system."

"Yes, that's correct."

"Well according to the information you have made public, your launch today is actually that of a space shuttle. The space shuttle Atlantis, I believe?"

"Correct. So?"

"So that represents a deviation from the system configuration for which you submitted your Environmental Assessment. According to the information we've obtained, a space shuttle launch produces significant quantities of aluminum chloride, which is an emission that was not identified in your original submission. Along with nitrogen oxide and trace amounts of hydrochloric acid and some other regulated emissions."

"What are you talking about?" Nicole asked.

"You may not be aware that the chlorine released could have a measurable impact on stratospheric ozone levels?" Jan said, speaking for the first time. "So naturally we're very concerned."

Nicole looked at them incredulously, and then said, "I think you may both be terribly misinformed."

"How so, Ms. Ferry?" Dean asked.

"Yes, we're launching a space shuttle today. But we're launching it with two of our paraffin and oxygen fueled Big Brother Hot Wax system boosters. Which have been certified by the appropriate state regulatory agencies as meeting all applicable emissions standards."

"But our information ... " Dean began, before Nicole cut him off.

"Your information is wrong, because it is apparently based on the mistaken assumption that we would be launching the shuttle using a pair of shuttle solid rocket boosters. But let me say this slowly so you'll understand. We're not using them. We're using the approved rockets."

"What about the shuttle itself? Doesn't it have its own propulsion system?"

"Seriously? Do you even know what the emissions are from a shuttle main engine?" Nicole asked.

"Well not offhand, but ... " Dean began, shuffling again through his papers.

"Shuttle main engines burn hydrogen and oxygen," Nicole explained. "I'm no rocket scientist, but even I know that the only thing you get when you burn hydrogen and oxygen is water vapor. That's it. The space shuttle qualifies as a zero emissions vehicle. Even California doesn't try to regulate water vapor. Not yet, anyway."

The two regulators were momentarily speechless. Then Dean said, "Yes, well, regardless, it should still be stated in your Environmental Assessment."

"It *is*," Nicole said firmly. "We clearly identified the intent to incorporate zero emission propulsion systems for system payloads. In fact," she said, opening her desk drawer and pulling out a file folder, "these aren't even required, but to show that we are good stewards of the environment, we purchased them anyway." She dropped the folder on the desk in front of them.

"What are those?" Dean asked, looking apprehensively at the folder.

"Carbon credits. For the small amount of CO_2 our Big Brothers produce. Now if there's nothing else, I'm afraid I have a launch to attend."

***

"How'd it go?" Tom asked, handing Nicole back her piece of cake.

"Nothing I couldn't handle. We're all set," she replied as she took a bite.

"That actually took over ten minutes," Tom smirked. "Close to fifteen."

"Yes, well, I had to escort them back to security to sign out."

***

Stewart's desk phone rang. "Yes?" he said, picking it up. "You sent who? Well were they able to find anything we can use? I see. Nothing at all? Fully compliant with all environmental regulations. No, it's a little late now. Thanks for trying. Yes, Merry Christmas to you as well."

Well that's that, he thought, as he turned off his computer and put on his coat. *The Associate Director is just going to have to get over it.* Glancing at his watch, he realized if he hurried he could probably make it home in time to watch the launch.

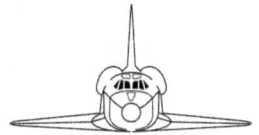

CHAPTER THIRTY–NINE

Marcus and Nicole escorted the members of the flight crew and the technicians who would help them board the spacecraft as they walked the short distance from the crew prep room to the doors that exited the Integrated Processing Facility. Stopping at the end of the hallway, Robbie paused before the doors and turned to address the crew.

"All right everyone, this is it. As soon as we go through these doors, the mission starts. Listen to the instructions from the close-out team, and remember your training. Once we're strapped in, Steph and I will be pretty busy, but if you see anything that concerns you, make sure you let us know immediately. OK. Is everyone ready? Let me see a thumbs up from everyone."

Their faces beaming, everyone pointed skyward with their thumbs toward the direction they hoped to soon be heading.

"OK then, let's do this," Robbie said. Turning to shake Marcus' hand, he added, "See you in a couple of weeks, brother."

"Take care, my man, bring 'em all home safe."

"You know it."

While Marcus shook each person's hand, Nicole reached up and grabbed the neck ring of Tom's suit. Pulling him downward, she kissed his cheek.

"This is as far as I go," she said quietly. "Please come back in one piece."

Two of the technicians pushed open the metal doors, allowing the bright mid-afternoon sun to stream into the hallway. The crew heard a cheer and a swell of applause from outside.

Setting his helmet bag down and unzipping it, Robbie pulled out a purple and gold LSU Tigers cap and tugged it on his head.

"Seriously?" Stephanie asked with a laugh.

"Just having a little fun," Robbie replied, zipping his helmet bag and standing up. "Now I'm ready to go. OK folks, it's show time!"

***

"And as we continue with our live coverage of today's launch of the first commercial moon mission, the countdown has resumed at T minus three hours and we are on track for this afternoon's scheduled liftoff at five PM local time. Here again is our chief science editor Marshall Wheeler, to explain what comes next. Marshall, what's happening right now?"

"Well, Dan," Marshall began, referring to his notes, "at this point, fueling should be finished on Atlantis' external tank, and the launch pad closeout team should be conducting their final inspections."

"And what about the crew?"

"I believe they should be completing their pre-flight preparations, and by now will be suited up in their launch and reentry suits. These suits are designed to … "

"Wait Marshall, just a moment, I think they may be coming out now," Dan interrupted.

Turning to look at the monitor, Marshall saw a set of doors swinging open, followed by an eruption of cheering and applause. "You're right Dan, I believe this is the crew. It's only a few hundred yards to the launch pad, so they will be walking to the rocket instead of taking the traditional van ride. Wait, what's this? Why, I don't believe I've ever seen anything quite like this before."

The camera zoomed in on the flight crew as they exited the building and made their way through the cordon of launch pad support personnel who cheered and shook their hands as they passed. Their pressure suits were covered from collar to calf with emblems and logos of major corporations.

"Why, they look like NASCAR drivers," Dan observed.

"Well I imagine this is just one of many changes we're going to see as we witness the birth of commercial space exploration," Marshall commented. "With us today to provide commentary on the flight is Mr. Tyler Allen, media liaison with Roadrunner Rockets. Tyler? What can you tell us about the suits the crew are wearing? These aren't the familiar orange crew escape suites we're used to seeing from previous shuttle flights."

"Thank you, Mr. Wheeler, and let me just say what a pleasure it is to be here with you on this historic day," Tyler began, turning to face the camera. "Most of the crew are wearing the Orbital Environmental launch and recovery pressure suit. It provides protection to the crew in the event of a sudden cabin depressurization during liftoff and landing."

"You said most of the crew?"

"Yes. Ms. Lee, our flight engineer, is actually too petite to fit the standard OE suit. She's wearing a prototype space activity suit, which is a compressive garment that provides spacesuit-like protection. She's actually wearing a coverall over it for, well, modesty reasons I guess you'd say."

Marshall's eyebrow arched. "And the advertising?"

"The crew members' suits are displaying the corporate logos of our Interplanetary level mission sponsors, without whose generous support today's flight would not have been possible."

Marshall heard the voice of his producer on his earpiece announcing an upcoming break: "Commercial in ten. Five. In three, two, one and we're clear." Turning to Tyler, Marshall said, "A compressive garment?"

"Think spandex body stocking," Tyler smiled.

Marshall placed his finger on his earpiece to call his producer. "Tony? Can you hear me? Yeah, get someone from Orbital Environmental on the phone. Tell them we want some photos of whatever this thing is Ms. Lee is wearing. Yeah, I think our viewers would like to see it."

***

The flight crew and the members of the closeout team escorting them gathered at the base of the mobile service tower to ride the elevator the fifteen stories to the orbiter access level. They had already sorted themselves into two groups, as the elevator was too small to carry everyone at once. The first group to ascend and board would be those seated on the flight deck: Robbie, Stephanie, Tom and Elton, escorted by the closeout support team. The mid-deck passengers, Vivian, Mike, Carl and Nikki, would then ascend and board.

Turning to Tom, Elton nodded toward Nikki, who was tapping away on her smart phone. "You'd think she'd have more important things to think about at the moment," he observed.

"Oh, that's part of her endorsement deal with AT&T. She's supposed to tweet the entire mission. @NikkiMoonGirl has over four million followers."

"Really? How's that supposed to work?"

"You really should have attended more of the preflight briefings," Tom replied, as they boarded the small elevator. "AT&T provided Vivian with two complete micro-cellular stations, which she integrated into the onboard communications systems." Pressing himself against the rear of the elevator, he added, "Please turn your phone to vibrate during launch so as not to distract the pilot."

"You're joking, right?" Elton said, crowding in next to Tom.

"Nope, they're a major mission sponsor, and I never joke about money," Tom replied. "If you brought your phone, you'll be able to use it."

"It never occurred to me," Elton said with a smirk.

The elevator started upward with a slight jerk. Looking through the cage as it rose, Tom could see Mike and Vivian smiling and laughing, while Nikki continued tapping away at her phone. Carl stood to one side, displaying a serene but distant expression. As he disappeared from view, Tom noticed that Carl held his helmet bag to his chest with both arms in a close embrace.

"I sure hope he's up to this," Tom said.

"He who?" Elton asked.

"Dr. Heinel. He seems a bit overwhelmed today."

"Oh, he's a tough old bird, I wouldn't worry about him. Just preflight nerves."

"Yeah, I'm sure you're right."

Bumping gently to a stop at the orbiter access level, the elevator gate was pulled open from the outside by Mitch Donegan, head of the orbiter closeout team.

"Good afternoon, Commander. Atlantis is prepped for flight and ready for crew boarding," Mitch said to Robbie.

"Thanks, Mitch," Robbie nodded as he stepped out of the elevator cage. "Let's get everyone onboard and strapped in quickly. I want them to have some time to calm down before launch."

"Roger that," Mitch nodded, walking beside Robbie as he lead the crew to the orbiter access hatch. "Fine day for a lift off, don't you think?"

"Beautiful. Absolutely beautiful," Robbie replied, stopping beside Atlantis and gazing out at the brilliant blue sky filled with fluffy white clouds floating placidly above the distant Pacific Ocean as the closeout team members tugged at his suit straps and removed his boot covers. "Try and arrange the same weather for touchdown, would you?" Robbie joked.

"I'll see what I can do," Mitch replied, while pointing at Robbie's LSU hat. Robbie removed the hat and handed it to Mitch, who in turn passed Robbie his snug fitting communications cap to don.

"Please make sure that gets on board," Robbie said, nodding toward his hat as he tugged the tight cap onto his head.

"Will do," Mitch replied, shaking Robbie's hand. "Good luck, sir."

"See you in two weeks," Robbie replied. Reaching up and patting the side of Atlantis, he then dropped to his hands and knees and crawled through the orbiter hatch.

"Safe travels, Stephanie," Mitch nodded, as she moved to enter the orbiter.

"Thanks, Jellybean," Stephanie replied, reaching out to awkwardly hug Mitch, calling him by the nickname his crew had given him due to his fondness for the candies. "Don't work too hard while we're gone," she said, knowing how busy he'd be in the next week supervising the reconfiguration of the pad for the first Space Train launch. Technicians began tugging and adjusting her suit as Mitch handed her her communication cap.

"Just going to sit on the couch and watch the flight coverage on TV," Mitch said.

"Good plan," she smiled, tucking her hair under the edges of her snug cap. "Well, here goes," she added, ducking down to crawl aboard Atlantis.

Mitch turned next to Tom and Elton. "OK, gentlemen, just like we've rehearsed," he said, as the closeout team began checking the adjustments on their suits.

***

"All right, Doctor, looks like you're ready to board," Mitch said, giving the shoulders of Carl's suit one last tug. "Just like at practice, once you're inside, please move to seat seven so the techs can strap you in and hook up your air and comms.

"Yes, well, I have this one thing I need to do first," Carl replied, bending down and removing a pale gray slate box from inside his helmet bag.

"Ah. Yes. All right then, I believe they have a locker space for you on the middeck. Just let the tech know that you need your, umm, package stowed."

"Thank you," Carl said gratefully. "Could you hold this a moment for me, please?" he asked, handing the box to Mitch.

"Umm, sure," he said, gingerly accepting the package. Two technicians held Carl's arms and helped him to his knees so that he could crawl through the orbiter access hatch. Once inside, he turned and reached back out.

"I'll take her now if you please," Carl said quietly.

Stooping down, Mitch handed the box to Carl, who then disappeared inside the spacecraft.

"Well that's a first," Mitch observed as he stood back up. Then, turning to Vivian, he added, "OK, you're up, last but not least."

***

"How're we doing on the middeck?" Robbie called out, looking up from his checklist.

"Ms. Lee is still waiting to board. We're assisting Dr. Heinel right now," one of the technicians replied.

"What's the holdup?"

"They have to get Dr. Carl's wife stowed first," Mike called up from below.

"Ah, uh, OK then," Robbie said. *I guess that's one thing we didn't practice during launch rehearsals,* he thought.

The technician assisting Nikki with her seat harness paused to open the locker on the bulkhead in front of her and remove the foam spacer that reserved the spot for the urn. Everyone waited respectfully while Carl carefully reached up to place it in the space and secure it with a Velcro strap. He then gently touched two fingers of his right hand to his lips and

281

then reached out and touched the urn. "Here we go, love," he said quietly. As the technician secured the locker door, Carl added, "She never did like to fly, you know."

"All right, Doctor, let's get you strapped in," the technician replied, helping Carl climb into his seat.

***

" ... and that's how we came up with the name Hot Wax," Tyler said, concluding the bit of historical commentary.

"I see, and a very appropriate name it is," Marshall noted. Turning toward the camera, he then said, "For those of you just joining us, we are at T minus one hour twenty minutes and holding. This is a planned hold to allow for closeout of the spacecraft crew compartment now that the entire crew has boarded." Looking up at the clock, he added, "We're now just a little less than two hours away from liftoff of the world's first commercial moon mission."

***

Jean called Robbie from mission control in Long Beach for a communications check. Much discussion had gone into the call signs to be used. CDR for mission commander and PLT for mission pilot still seemed appropriate, but the traditional name for the launch controller dating all the way back to the Mercury program was NASA Test Director, or NTD. Since this was no longer a NASA operation, they had settled on Roadrunner Test Director, or RTD. Likewise, it seemed inappropriate to use the title of mission specialist for the flight's six passengers, as they were actually just human cargo. "Crew member" seemed more appropriate, and so Atlantis' six passengers were officially designated CM1 through CM6.

"CDR, RTD, how do you read, over?" Jean asked.

"Loud and clear, Jean, and good afternoon from high above beautiful downtown Vandenberg," Robbie said.

"Good afternoon to you too," she replied with a chuckle. "I trust you all had a hearty lunch?"

"It was awesome, it's a shame you couldn't make it," Robbie answered.

"Yes, well, you may have heard, we're a bit busy here in Long Beach," she replied. "By the way, I wanted you to know that Patty brought the launch cake."

"Really? Carrot cake?"

"Affirmative Atlantis, we have carrot cake," Jean said with a smile, looking over at the cake with anticipation.

"Outstanding, all's right with the world," Robbie beamed.

Resuming her professional demeanor, Jean said, "CDR, RTD, Mission Control is resuming the count."

"Roger RTD, the count has resumed."

***

Marshall looked quizzically at Tyler. "For the benefit of our audience, would you be able to explain the significance of that exchange?"

"The carrot cake, you mean?"

"Yes, is that some sort of personal code?"

"No, not at all," Tyler chuckled. "Patty Oarlok was a NASA flight controller who baked launch cakes for shuttle flights for over twenty years, and we just thought it was a tradition we'd continue. Actually, we found out that flight controllers are quite superstitious, and we were sort of directed to make it happen, or else. I believe the words they used were 'no cake, no launch.'"

***

Marcus watched on the monitor as the mobile service tower that had sheltered Atlantis slowly rolled the one hundred yards to its launch position. The rocket now stood exposed on the pad, ready for liftoff.

Marcus keyed his mike. "Atlantis, this is site operations."

"Is that you, Hollywood?" Robbie replied.

"10-4. The MST is in launch position, and we're gonna clear the pad now and get the hell out of Dodge."

"Roger that, site ops, clearing the pad. You all go find yourselves a nice place to watch from now. We expect some good pictures when we get back. Don't make us have to do it a second time."

"No worries, my friend. I think every camera in the state is pointed in your direction. We're pulling the plug here, we'll see you in a few weeks. Site ops clear."

Marcus reached up, flipped off his communications link and monitor, and turned to the handful of people in the room. "OK folks, let's get up to the safe zone at Slick Four."

***

"We're now at the T minus 20 minute hold," Marshall explained to the viewers. "At this point, the people responsible for the final systems checks will have completed their jobs and will be evacuating the site and joining us here at launch complex four, a little over three miles from the launch pad. Although the pad facilities were designed to be manned during launches, the launch control team felt it would be safer to move everyone away from the complex. We're now just a little over an hour from launch."

***

"Oh man," Mike said with apparent distress.

Strapped into the seat next to him, Nikki reached up to rotate her helmet toward him and asked, "What's wrong?"

"I really need to pee."

"Didn't they tell you to take care of that before we boarded? They warned us it could be four or five hours before we'd have a chance to use the space toilet thingy."

"I only had a Coke at lunch. Well, two, maybe. But now I really need to pee."

Nikki twisted her helmet back to the front and settled back into her seat. "Well, use your diaper then."

"Oh man, I did not want to have to do that."

"Suck it up, spaceman. A real astronaut wouldn't care."

"And to think that I used to believe you were a sweet girl," Mike said dejectedly.

***

Jean listened to the rapid flow of communication over the launch control circuit. There was a rhythm to launch operations, and she could mentally ride its flow and sense when things were properly progressing.

"Backup flight system to OPS 1 transition complete."

"Copy."

"OMS/RCS crossfeed valves configured for flight"

"OMS/RCS crossfeeds configured, roger."

"Fuel cell purge complete. Adjusting fuel cell loads."

"Adjusting loads, acknowledged."

Jean took a deep breath and keyed her mike. "The countdown clock will hold at T minus nine minutes. Attention all personnel, this is the RTD conducting a launch status check verifying readiness to resume count for launch." She visually scanned the room as she called out each controller by station and received their reply. "OTC?"

"OTC go."

"TBC?"

"TBC go."

"PTC?"

"PTC is go."

"LPS?"

"LPS go."

"STM?"

"STM go."

"Safety console?"

"Safety console go."

"SPE?"

"SPE go."

"LRD?"

"LRD is go."

"SRO?"

"SRO go.

"CDR?"

Jean thought she heard a touch of excitement in Robbie's voice as he replied. "This is CDR, the crew of Atlantis is go and ready for launch."

"Roger Atlantis. Range weather?"

"Range weather is go."

"Thank you all," Jean said. "The launch team is ready to proceed at this time. There are no constraints to launch." She could hear a burst of muffled applause from the observers in the viewer's gallery behind her.

***

"And what about the lunar materials the crew will be collecting?" Marshall asked Tyler. "Can you tell us what you intend to do with them once they return to Earth?"

"Well, obviously we'll have much of it on display at the Aerospace Museum of the Pacific, and we'll make representative samples available to researchers," Tyler explained. "Beyond that, we really aren't sure. We have promised some souvenirs to a few key personnel and supporters," he said with a smile.

"Really?" Marshall said, wondering how he might become a valued mission supporter.

***

"The automatic ground launch sequencer has started," Jean heard.

"Copy, standby to retract service arms."

"Standing by to retract arms."

Jean keyed her mike. "CDR, this is RTD, you are go to start APU's."

"Roger RTD, we are clear to start auxiliary power units," Robbie answered. Atlantis came fully alive as the APUs began generating the hydraulic pressure necessary to operate the orbiter's control surfaces and orient the main engines.

"And we have three good APU's," Robbie reported, confirming the readout visible at mission control.

"Roger Atlantis, you are go for aero surface profile test," Jean announced.

"Roger RTD," Robbie replied, as he began operating Atlantis' flight controls to cycle the orbiter's rudder and elevons.

***

"As we approach the final minutes of the countdown, it looks like barring a last minute problem, we will soon see the launch of Atlantis on its history making journey to the moon," Marshall said. Turning to his co-anchor, he added, "Dan, I don't think I can recall another countdown going quite as smoothly as this one has."

"You're right, Marshall," his co-host replied. "And you couldn't have asked for better weather either."

"Fortune has definitely smiled on them today," Marshall observed.

"Indeed it has," Dan replied.

***

"Fuel cells to internal, 02 pressurization complete," Jean heard. Keying her mike, she said, "CDR, RTD, looks like it's time to go."

"Roger that RTD," Robbie answered. Speaking to the crew, he said, "OK everyone, lets close and secure visors and initiate O2 flow and give me a comm check when you're ready."

The members of the crew began pulling their helmet visors down and fumbled with the locking bails to secure them.

"PLT ready," Stephanie announced.

"CM1 all set," Tom said.

"CM2 ready," said Elton.

"CM3 is ready," Robbie heard Mike's voice from the middeck.

After a brief pause, they heard Nikki's voice announce "CM4 ready."

After ten seconds of silence, Robbie asked, "CM5? Are you ready? Doctor Heinel?"

Vivian, seated next to Carl, reached up to rotate her helmet and look to her right. She saw Carl, helmet visor open, head back, gently snoring.

"Umm, believe it or not, I think Dr. Heinel is taking a little nap," Vivian said, and then reached over and shook Carl's shoulder.

"Humph, what, what?" Carl said, startled.

"It's time to go, Dr. Heinel. If you'd like to join us we need you to close your visor, initiate O2 flow and check in," Robbie said.

"Oh, yes, yes, of course," Carl said, latching his faceplate closed and switching on his oxygen flow. "All right, I'm ready."

"OK, that's an affirmative on CM5," Robbie said. "CM6?"

"CM6 ready," Vivian answered, settling back in her seat.

"All right, everyone, make sure any loose items are secure and hold on, it's going to be a bumpy ride," Robbie announced. "RTD, CDR, the crew of Atlantis is ready."

"Copy Atlantis, switch to internal power."

"Switching to internal power, roger," Robbie acknowledged. Then, glancing out the corner of his eye to Stephanie, he added, "I'm going to say it."

"Please don't say it, Robbie," Stephanie implored.

"Atlantis, you are go for auto sequence start," they heard Jean announce.

"I'm going to say it," he reiterated.

Stephanie let out a deep sigh. "Fine," she said with resignation.

Robbie beamed. "Go for auto sequence start, 20 seconds, Long Beach, this is Atlantis, let's *light these candles!*"

Mike's sudden involuntary laugh caused him to finally lose his desperate fight to control his bladder.

***

The monitor behind Marshall showed a close-up view of the shuttle's main engines. He had ceased his explanatory narration and let Jean's broadcasted voice from mission control provide the commentary for the viewing audience.

"Go for main engine start. 10 seconds."

The image showed the sparklers igniting below the main engine nozzles to burn off any excess hydrogen that may have vented from the rocket. The three engines quickly ignited in sequence and then swiveled into launch position as they reached full power.

"Main engine start, go for SRB ignition. Five, four ... "

The Hot Wax boosters were technically not solids, but they'd continued using the old term SRB, or solid rocket booster, for clarity. The two boosters each ignited and smoothly throttled up to full power.

" ...three, two, one."

The flight control computers verified that all five engines were operating at full rated thrust and then fired the pyrotechnics to fracture the bolts holding Atlantis to the launch pad.

"And *liftoff* of space shuttle Atlantis as she and her crew depart on the first manned mission to the moon in forty-three years!"

***

From the main viewing gallery and press area at launch complex four, the deep rumbling sound of the launch, like thunder from a distant storm, arrived almost twenty seconds before the rocket slowly climbed into view, rising above the intervening hillside.

"And there goes Atlantis, departing Earth on her journey of a quarter million miles!" Marshall gushed enthusiastically to his viewers.

"Um, actually, that would be a journey of a half million miles," Tyler corrected. "They're coming back, you know."

***

"Max-Q," Robbie heard Jean announce.

"Max-Q, copy," he replied.

Having reduced the thrust of Atlantis' five rocket engines as the vehicle passed through the region of maximum dynamic force, the flight control system now automatically increased engine thrust to maximum.

"Atlantis, you are go at throttle up."

"Go at throttle up, roger," Robbie replied, the vibration of the rocket clearly audible in his voice.

The crew could feel the forces building as the vehicle accelerated, pushing them deeper into their seats, while it rolled onto its back in the "head's down" position. Tom, sitting directly behind Robbie and Stephanie on the flight deck, was startled by a sudden blow to his right shoulder. Turning toward the blow, he saw Elton grinning widely.

"Now *this* is an E ticket ride!" Elton shouted, punching Tom in the shoulder a second time. "Woohoooo!"

***

Virtually the entire population of southern California stopped what they were doing and parked their cars or went outside, watching the sky to the west. For almost an hour, the California Highway Patrol received not a single accident report. From Santa Barbara to San Diego, and on down the coast of Mexico, launch parties were being held on the beaches and hillsides. A church group that had gathered on the Santa Monica pier suspended a large banner that read "God bless Atlantis and her crew." Almost every household in the nation was tuned in to the live broadcast, which was being watched by over a billion people worldwide.

***

The shaking aboard Atlantis began to diminish. The crew suddenly felt a large bump, as if they had hit a pothole in the sky.

"Holy crap, what the hell was that?" Mike exclaimed.

"SRB separation," they heard Robbie coolly reply. "Relax, everything's under control. Get ready for some gees now, they're going to start piling on."

"Man, I almost peed my pants again," Mike noted.

***

The conditions at Big Sur were very good today, and a large group of surfers were taking full advantage. The slender young woman felt the wave giving out underneath her and spun her board for a controlled fall backward into the ocean. Surfacing and pulling her hair back from her face, the long pale streak in the sky caught her attention.

"There it is!" she called out excitedly, pointing to the trail Atlantis left as it accelerated toward orbit. The riders paused and sat on their boards in a rough line, bobbing gently on the swells facing westward as they followed the ascent of the rocket.

"Man, that would totally rock," one said with cool understatement.

***

"How are you doing, Dr. Heinel?" Robbie asked through pursed lips. The crew was now being subjected to three times their normal weight, and simple efforts such as talking and breathing became difficult.

"I am just fine, thank you, although I wouldn't mind if this were to end soon," Carl replied in a thin voice.

"Any moment now, Doctor, we're almost through the worst."

After building for another 30 seconds, the crew could suddenly feel the gee forces start to relent, and then shortly after, cease altogether.

"Main engine cutoff," Stephanie announced.

"Atlantis, Long Beach, copy MECO, we show you in orbit."

The crew could hear a series of muffled bangs as the computers cycled the large fuel disconnect valves and umbilical doors and prepared to separate Atlantis from the external tank. With a jolt, the pyrotechnic fasteners fired, releasing the orbiter from the tank.

Robbie and Stephanie monitored the separation maneuver, and then verified that guidance had properly converged and they were where they expected to be. Satisfied with the results, Robbie turned to Stephanie and said, "Man, that was one sweet ascent."

"Roger that," she replied, as she started working on her on-orbit checklist.

Releasing the locking ring on his helmet, Robbie lifted it off his head and removed his communications cap. Unbelting his harness and reaching down to the storage bag under the seat, he retrieved the LSU ballcap the closeout team had stowed there and tugged it onto his head. Then he loudly announced, "For our six new astronauts onboard, I'd like to welcome you to space!"

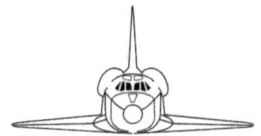

CHAPTER FORTY

"Cargo bay doors coming open now," Stephanie announced from the control station on the aft flight deck.

"So where are they?" Nikki asked, floating beside Robbie and peering out the starboard side windshield.

"Where are who?" Robbie asked, looking up from the checklist he was reviewing.

"Wendy and Tiger Lilly. Where are they?"

Robbie glanced out the windshield. "They're out there."

"Where? I can't see anything."

"Ahead of us about 50 nautical miles."

"I don't see them," Nikki said.

Robbie glanced out the windshield again. "Trust me, they're there, they're just too far away to make out right now."

"So tell me again how this is supposed to work," Nikki asked.

"What do you mean?"

"They're out in front of us, right?" she asked.

"Yep, about 50 miles."

"So how are we supposed to catch up with them by slowing down?"

"I already explained this."

"Well explain it again please."

Robbie closed the cover on the checklist and strapped it to the center console. "We need to catch up with the fuel modules to load them on board."

"Yes, I know," Nikki replied.

"Well things happen a little differently on orbit," Robbie patiently explained. "The lower the orbit, the faster we move in reference to the ground. For example, at our current orbital altitude we circle the Earth about once every 100 minutes."

"OK," Nikki nodded.

"And something orbiting farther out takes longer to go around the planet."

"That's what I don't get," Nikki said with a frown.

"Well, you know that something that's orbiting way out at 22,000 miles takes a full day to go around the Earth."

"Yes, like communications satellites, they stay over the same place constantly," she said. "Geosynchronous?" she asked hesitantly.

"Yes, that's it. And something that's in a lower orbit, like the GPS satellites at 12,000 miles, goes around the Earth in about 12 hours."

"So in order to catch up with the modules ... " Nikki began.

"We need to drop into a lower orbit to overtake them, and then pop back up to match orbits once we're in range."

"And to drop into a lower orbit, we have to slow down. In order to go faster," she concluded.

"Well, sort of," Robbie replied. "Orbital mechanics is a bit more complicated than that, but you're basically right. But if we just pointed ourselves at the modules and hit the gas, instead of catching up with them, we'd end up climbing above them while they pulled further away from us."

"Well I'm glad you're driving, because it doesn't make a lot sense to me," Nikki said. "It's not very intuitive at all."

"That's true of a lot of things up here," Robbie observed. Turning to Stephanie, he asked, "How are we doing?"

"Cargo bay doors are open, deploying the radiators now," she replied, reaching out to operate several switches to her right.

"Let me know when the radiators are online and the evaporators are secured so I can notify Long Beach that we're reducing cabin pressure for the EVA."

"Aye aye, captain," Steph replied humorously.

Robbie floated to the mid-deck access and stuck his head into the lower level. "It's OK to come up now when you're done. The view is amazing."

Tom and Elton were on the mid-deck helping the rest of the crew secure their suits and equipment. Everyone was moving carefully and deliberately to avoid the onset of space sickness, or free fall induced nausea. Robbie noticed that Mike looked particularly pale.

"Are you wearing your patch, Mike?" Robbie asked, referring to his transdermal anti-nausea patch.

"Yeah, I got it on but I'm not sure it's working so well," Mike replied, reaching up to touch the small patch on his neck.

"Talk to me. Where are you at?" Robbie asked.

"I guess about a third of a Garn right now," Mike replied, referring to the measure of space sickness called the Garn scale. It was named after Senator Jake Garn, who flew the first political junket in space. On the scale, one Garn amounted to complete incapacitation, in recognition of the extraordinary level of disability the Senator exhibited during his flight.

"Well tighten up, man, I'm going to need you on the EVA. I can't land those fuel modules without you," Robbie observed.

"Don't worry, I'll be ready," Mike replied, wishing he felt the level of confidence he tried to project.

"Let's hope," Robbie said. "You do *not* want to puke in your Orlan." Shaking his head for emphasis, he added, "Nope, you definitely do not," as he returned to the flight deck.

***

Robbie and Stephanie had trained for spaceflight for years, and for them it was just another day at the office. For the six novice astronauts, though, it took a light meal, an extended rest period during which they grabbed some fitful sleep, and then another and somewhat heartier meal before they started to adapt. While the amateurs adjusted to space, the professionals performed the necessary maneuvers to rendezvous with Wendy and Tiger Lilly.

"See them now?" Robbie asked Nikki, as they stood on the flight deck looking through the overhead windows. One OMS fuel module hung 100 feet above Atlantis, while the other was visible as a distant point of light traveling rapidly across the background starfield.

"That's going to fit in there?" Nikki asked, pointing first to Tiger Lilly, and then the cargo bay. "It looks too big."

"Same size as the ones back at Space Dome, so unless she got fat while waiting for us to arrive, she should fit just fine," Robbie observed. Turning to Stephanie, who was busy at the aft control station exercising the remote manipulator system, he asked, "How's the arm?"

"Everything checks out OK," she replied, releasing the controller and flicking several switches. "Ready whenever you are," she added.

"OK, Mike and I will head to the airlock to pre-breath and prepare." Turning and dropping head first down to the mid-deck level, he said, "Mike, let's saddle up, it's time to get busy. How you feeling by the way?"

"Better now, thanks," Mike replied.

"Well let's go suck some oxygen and get our suits on."

It took forty-five minutes of breathing pure oxygen to purge their bodies of nitrogen so that they would not suffer from decompression sickness while in the reduced pressure of their spacesuits. It took another 15 minutes to finish donning their suits. "OK Steph, we're ready to cycle the lock and enter the bay," Robbie announced.

"Copy that, I'll go ahead and commence grappling the lander propulsion unit while you egress," she replied.

"Roger, going out," Robbie answered. Turning to Mike, he said,

292

"Ready?"

"As I'll ever be," Mike said.

"OK, just like in the pool, we stand by while Steph grabs the lander's propulsion unit and repositions it on top of Tinkerbell. Then we help guide in the first fuel module and do the hook up, followed by the second after she repositions. Questions?"

"No, let's do it," Mike said confidently.

"OK, here we go," Robbie said, venting and cycling the airlock and then opening the outer door. "Don't look down," Robbie joked as he pulled himself out the airlock door and into the short tunnel joining Atlantis' crew compartment to Tinkerbell. Once in the tunnel, he stood up and opened the overhead hatch to the cargo bay.

To his right, the Earth filled most of the field of view, blue and gold and white and breathtakingly beautiful. Above him, Tiger Lilly floated in formation patiently awaiting capture, the sun reflecting brightly off her polished frame and spherical tanks. In front of him, he saw the remote manipulator arm extending toward the lander's propulsion unit in the aft cargo bay as Stephanie reached to grapple it.

Once outside, Robbie clipped his safety line to a rail on the exterior of the tunnel and moved aside to allow Mike to exit. Shortly, Mike's head emerged from the hatch.

"Whoooooaaaa," Mike said with wonder, looking at the nearby Earth. *"that* is *awesome!"*

"Yeah, no amount of looking out the window ever prepares you for the view," Robbie observed, turning to look at their home world. "Not many people have had the privilege of seeing her this way."

"This is worth the trip right here," Mike said, continuing to stare at the world below, enraptured.

"There'll be time for sightseeing later, for now let's focus. Get your line clipped off before you clear the hatch," Robbie instructed.

Stephanie expertly grappled the lander propulsion unit and deftly guided it to its intended location on top of Tinkerbell's crew compartment. Vivian hovered nervously at her side, watching intently as Stephanie aligned the mating pins on the propulsion unit with the crew compartment and then pushed downward to engage the latching mechanisms and join the two. A wave of relief washed over her when the green capture light illuminated.

"OK, we're showing positive capture," Stephanie announced. "Go ahead and square her away while I line up for Tiger Lilly."

"Copy that, we'll finish the job," Robbie replied. He and Mike slowly worked their way hand-over-hand to the now reassembled lunar lander. While Mike plugged together the electrical cables that connected Tinkerbell's upper and lower units, Robbie removed the hand crank from the storage bracket on the frame of the propulsion unit and inserted it into the locking ring gearbox. Four full revolutions on the crank and Tinkerbell's two parts were now firmly locked together.

"OK, we're done," Robbie reported. "We're heading aft to receive Tiger Lilly."

As Mike and Robbie worked their way aft, Stephanie gently nudged Atlantis upward with a few brief bursts from the reaction control system. Once the fuel module was within range, she reached up with the remote arm to capture it and pull it down into the aft cargo bay.

"Watch your arms and legs," Robbie cautioned Mike, as he guided Stephanie the last few feet. "Down two. Now down one. Hold it. OK, down a half. Just a skosh more. Gently. One more quick bump. Latch! Ok, that should be it."

Stephanie and Vivian had noted that the capture light on the indicator panel was shining brightly. "That's a roger, we confirm positive capture and latch," Stephanie announced.

"OK Mike, help me get these fuel interconnects hooked up," Robbie directed, as he leaned into Tiger Lilly to reach the lines. "Good. OK, let's not just stand around here, we have another module to go catch."

***

"Well I'd say that was a pretty good day's work," Robbie noted, as he and Mike exited the airlock.

"I'm definitely glad that's done," Mike observed, exhaustion evident on his face. "That just about wore me out."

"Yeah, working in zero gee is a lot tougher than you would think," Robbie observed. "The pool training helps, but there's no substitute for actual experience."

"Nice job out there," Stephanie observed, floating down from the flight deck to congratulate them. "Since that went so well, Jean wanted to know if you'd like to move the trans-lunar injection up a few orbits," she asked. "They've recalculated the trajectory and there's no energy penalty. Commander's prerogative, she said."

Robbie thought for a moment. "No, I'd rather just stick to the original schedule and have a few extra orbits of downtime here in Earth orbit. It will give everyone more time to adapt and relax and just look out the windows some before the next major evolution."

"OK, I'll let Long Beach know," Stephanie said, returning to the flight deck.

"Man, I'm getting kind of hungry," Mike said, rubbing his stomach. "Satellite wrangling works up quite an appetite. Any way a spaceman can get some lunch around here?"

"It's not quite mealtime, but I'm sure we can find something," Vivian said, floating over to the galley area.

***

As the crew ate and relaxed, Atlantis circled the planet every 100 minutes. For each orbit, it spent half that time being warmed by the direct rays of the sun, and the other half radiating that heat back out into the depths of space as it passed through Earth's shadow. While the crew remained comfortable in the conditioned environment of the crew compartment, the contents of the cargo bay were alternately baked and frozen. Inside Tinkerbell's number three landing support strut, still folded into its launch position on the bottom of the lander's propulsion unit, a small volume of rainwater trapped deep inside the strut latch assembly slowly froze solid and expanded, exerting tremendous pressure on the latch mechanism welds. As the sun then warmed the vehicle, the ice would partially melt, allowing liquid water to creep into newly formed stress cracks. The cycle continued over and over as Atlantis continued to orbit.

Freeze. Thaw. Freeze. Thaw.

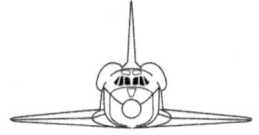

CHAPTER FORTY–ONE

The first of the two planned burns of the OMS engines necessary to break Atlantis free from Earth's orbit and start her on her journey to the moon acted as the shakedown test of Vivian's modifications to the orbiter. Failure of the modified fuel system supplying the engines from the extended fuel reserves in Wendy and Tiger Lilly would have required the crew to abort the mission and deorbit the shuttle.

As the first burn concluded, Carl nodded and said, "Very good," with a subtle smile.

Vivian turned and asked, "Did you have any doubt, Doctor?"

"Oh, not about your system modifications," he replied. "I carefully reviewed your design and found it quite adequate, and the installation was well executed." Settling back in his seat, he added, "No, I was merely concerned about whether the engines could withstand the prolonged operation."

"Wait, what?" Mike asked with alarm. "You were worried why?"

"While the OMS engines were designed for fifteen hours of cumulative operation, the designers never intended their use for such an extended continuous firing. My colleagues and I talked at length about whether they would be able to withstand such use. So naturally I was interested in seeing how they would actually perform."

"Well you should tell your colleagues that they did a terrific job," Tom commented.

"I would, but unfortunately they have all passed away," Carl said.

"It's one of the things we looked at," Elton noted. "When Bob Brock first turned up your plan, I had my engineering team analyze the entire mission profile. They were highly confident that the engines would be up to the job. Otherwise I wouldn't be here."

"Highly confident," Mike repeated. "Well doesn't that just put our minds at ease?"

Robbie heard Jean's voice from mission control. "Atlantis, Long Beach, we show a nominal burn and guidance reports a successful orbital elevation. You are go for trans-lunar injection."

"Copy that Long Beach, go for trans-lunar injection," Robbie replied.

The first burn had modified Atlantis' orbit from a circular one to a highly eccentric egg shaped one. They were now nearing the pointy end of the egg, and the Earth appeared noticeably smaller in the cockpit windows.

"All right everyone, this is your last chance to change your minds," Robbie announced as the flight control system counted down to the second engine firing. "After this next burn it's five days to the next rest stop."

"Let's go to the moon!" Nikki called out enthusiastically.

"Indeed," Carl quietly agreed.

Atlantis fell off the top of the egg and dove down to just over one hundred miles above the Earth's surface, accelerating rapidly, whipping around the planet just above the edge of the atmosphere. As the OMS engines fired, the engine thrust and additional momentum gained though the fall from higher orbit boosted the vehicle to escape velocity. Atlantis whipped out from behind the Earth and broke free of the planet's gravitational pull, beginning its long lazy arc to the moon.

"Atlantis, Long Beach, we show nominal velocity and track. Looks like you're on your way. Good luck and safe travels, congratulations from all of us here on the ground."

"Roger Long Beach, it's an awesome feeling to finally be on our way," Robbie replied. To the crew, he added, "Well boys and girls, you just joined a very exclusive club. There have only been twenty-four human beings who have left Earth orbit. I think you should give yourselves a round of applause.

As the crew clapped and cheered, the moon slowly rose in the orbiter's windshield, filling the cabin with its pale white light.

***

Everyone quickly settled into a daily routine. There were a few science experiments on board to operate, but not many. Mike and Vivian took turns shooting video of Nikki as she held, wore or consumed various sponsor's products, her blonde hair floating like a halo around her head. There were the daily sessions with morning news shows around the world, during which the crew had to smile and wave and answer the same questions from yet another reporter for five or ten minutes. Robbie ensured Tinkerbell was prepared for their excursion, paying particular attention to the stowage of the six Orlan spacesuits that they would wear once on the surface. Stephanie tended to Atlantis, monitoring its systems and their course, ensuring all was well with the spacecraft. It was a relaxing time.

The cabin lights were dimmed and most of the crew peacefully slept. The ship was quiet other than the soft sigh of the ventilation system and the occasional hum of a servomotor. Tom sat loosely strapped to the pilot's seat on the flight deck, where the cold white light of the approaching moon provided ample illumination to see the screen of his e-book reader. There had been little time to read on the ground, and he had loaded several volumes on his reader prior to the flight that he now leisurely worked through. Noticing a reflected motion, he looked up to see Carl floating slowly toward the commander's seat to look out the window.

"Can't sleep, Doctor?" Tom asked.

"Oh, I don't sleep as much anymore, and even less up here it seems," Carl replied as he gazed at the moon. Turning to look at Tom, he said, "And you, Mr. Armac?"

Tom held up his e-book reader. "Just got to a good part, and I wanted to see how it turned out before retiring." Nodding toward the window, he asked, "So did you ever think you'd be on your way to the moon like this?"

"Oh, at one time, as a young man, I was quite certain of it," Carl replied with a touch of sadness. "But then the dream ended, and hope failed, and I gave up on the belief that it would ever be possible."

"And when was that?"

"Oh, long ago. Too early—even before my wife died I knew it was no longer likely." Looking out the window again, he added, "Not like in the early years, when we thought that all things were possible. Dr. Von Braun had such a compelling vision."

"So tell me about your wife, Dr. Heinel," Tom said, turning off his reader.

Carl look wistful for a moment. "Marta? Oh, she was an amazing woman. Strong and confident, but loving and supportive." Looking at Tom, he said, "Her father was a German scientist brought to the US as part of Operation Paperclip. It's a wonder what a sweet girl she turned out to be considering the things she had seen."

"Operation Paperclip?" Tom asked.

"It was an intelligence program at the conclusion of World War Two to bring German scientists and engineers to the United States so that the Soviets could not obtain their knowledge. My father worked in the program, which is how I ended up meeting Marta and her parents."

"I see," Tom said.

"She appeared like an angel in my high school physics class one day, and I loved her from the outset. I knew from our first hello that we were destined to spend our lives together."

Tom smiled. "Love at first sight?"

"For me, yes. For her, maybe it took a little longer," Carl smiled softly. "But we fell in love, and married, and had two beautiful sons. And I had a wonderful career doing exciting, historic work."

"Until, well … " Tom said, knowing the basic details of Carl's story.

"Yes, until. Until the end of the lunar exploration program. Until the tragic death of our sons. Until the loss of my dear Marta," Carl said, tears slowly welling in his eyes.

"Well, I have a question I've been meaning to ask you," Tom said, changing the subject.

"And what would that be, Mr. Armac?" Carl asked, struggling to regain his composure.

"Back at the beginning, when we were still putting our team together, we ran background checks on all of our proposed team members," Tom explained.

"Yes?" Carl asked curiously.

"We learned something, something about you, that we couldn't quite determine how to handle. So we decided to just wait and see."

"And what was that, Mr. Armac?"

"Your tenure at Jacksonville Community College, the period after you were laid off from the Apollo program … "

"Yes?"

"We learned that you were fired. For 'failure to maintain good moral character' the records said. We assumed it meant you were an alcoholic."

"Yes, that's correct," Carl said matter-of-factly.

"Well, we watched you, Doctor. We had eyes on you nonstop for months. And not one member of our team ever saw you take a single drop to drink. You were the soberest, hardest working person any of us had ever seen."

"That's because I had been through my personal trial and salvation," Carl said.

"Doctor?"

"I did get fired from my job as an adjunct professor," Carl explained. "I missed too many classes and showed up for too many others unfit for work. Yes, I drank heavily. We all did in the early days of the program—we drank and smoked and worked very hard. But after the layoffs, and then the deaths of my sons and my wife, I lost myself to alcohol and despair."

"A very understandable reaction," Tom said sympathetically.

"Not really," Carl said, "but I did it just the same. For four years I raged inside and tried to numb my anger with alcohol, until finally it became unsustainable. The college could no longer overlook my shortcomings, regardless of how 'understandable' they may have been."

"So what happened?" Tom asked.

"The day I was fired, I cleaned out my desk. I put everything into a trash can outside the faculty building. Then I went to the closest liquor store and bought a fifth of bourbon and drove out to a deserted stretch of Amelia

Island. I sat on the beach alone as the sun set and drank and cried and tumbled to the darkest depths of despair."

Tom listened intently.

"As the night wore on and the level in the bottle diminished, the moon came up, large and full and deep blood red. And I stood up and shouted *'How dare you!'* at the moon. I shook my fist and bellowed my rage and felt for all the world like I was being taunted by our celestial neighbor. And I decided I could take no more pain and failure. I downed the remainder of the bottle, stripped off my clothes, and waded into the Atlantic waters intent on drowning myself. I walked toward the moon until I could walk no longer, and then swam until my strength gave out. I watched the moon, staring at it as I slid under the water. I remember the way the moon's rays reflected from the bubbles escaping my mouth as I exhaled what I believed was my last breath."

"My God," Tom said quietly. "What happened?"

"I was rescued by my angel," Carl said quietly. "As I closed my eyes and relaxed into the ending of my existence, I felt a sudden warmth, as if I were being hugged by pure love. And then her voice—my darling Marta's sweet voice—saying 'No Carl, not at this time, and not in this place. Live. Live for me!'"

Carl sat quietly for a moment and then looked out at the moon. "And I felt myself pushed to the surface. My next conscious memory was of waking on the beach as the sun came up." Turning to Tom, he added, "And I haven't had a single drink since. Nor did I ever again lose hope."

"Hope?"

"Hope that the opportunity to fulfill my promise would someday arrive. It was the following day that I received the call from NASA offering me a position with the shuttle program."

Both men sat quietly for a moment. "And you never remarried," Tom stated.

"No, I had no desire to," Carl replied. "I had experienced true bliss, and I felt it better to live with its memory than settle for less with another." Looking again at the moon, he said, "No man finds it twice in one lifetime."

"I suppose not," Tom nodded.

After a brief pause, Carl turned and asked, "How about you, Mr. Armac? Has there not been someone in your life to be your partner and companion?"

"No, not really," Tom shook his head. "Oh, there have been women, definitely, but no one I really loved and respected enough to want to spend my life with." Looking at Carl, he added, "I guess I've just been too busy building businesses to make time for a relationship."

Carl smiled warmly. "I thought that possibly Ms. Ferry ... "

Tom suddenly missed Nicole very much. "Actually, Doctor, you may be right. It wasn't something I sought, it sort of slowly snuck up on me, but yes, the only thing I truly want right now other than walking on the damn moon is to see her again."

"Well I hope you have found your bliss, Mr. Armac," Carl said with a twinkle.

"We'll see, Doctor. We'll see."

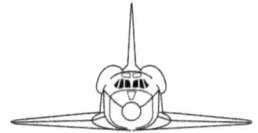

CHAPTER FORTY–TWO

"Man I've been looking forward to today!" Robbie exclaimed.

Stephanie chuckled as she paused from eating her breakfast. "Finally get to take your toys out and play with them, eh?"

"*Yes!* It's been nothing but computer simulations for almost two years. I finally get to let Tinkerbell try out her wings. Let's get going," he said anxiously.

"All right, all right, I'll go man the aft station, you go ahead and power up the lander," Stephanie said, depositing her tray in the waste bin. Turning to Vivian, she asked, "Coming?"

"Right behind you," Vivian answered excitedly, following Stephanie up to the flight deck.

Robbie pulled himself though the short connecting tunnel to Tinkerbell's crew compartment. Entering the lander, he had to reorient himself as he turned to close the lander's door to seal the cabin. Tinkerbell sat upside down in the shuttle's cargo bay, and up and down were reversed from Atlantis' crew compartment.

The access door secured, Robbie settled into the pilot's seat, latched the safety harness, and flipped down the lander's control pod from the right armrest. Donning his headset, he began flipping switches on the panel above his head to energize the lander's systems. "Are you there, Steph?" he asked.

"Standing by," she answered, looking out at the lander from the aft control station. "Give me a minute to make sure the arm is clear," she said as she energized the remote manipulator arm to move it away from the side of the lander.

"Roger that," Robbie answered. Studying the overhead display, he said, "I'm showing good volts on both buses, batteries are at 100 percent."

"Copy Tinkerbell," Stephanie replied as she slowly moved the arm to ensure it wouldn't interfere with the deployment of the lander's undercarriage. "OK, arm's clear, you're go for lander strut deployment."

"Struts coming out," Robbie announced, reaching up to toggle the deployment switch. "OK, baby," he said quietly to himself, "time to stretch your legs."

One of Vivian's biggest challenges had been to design an undercarriage for the lander that would fold compactly for stowage in the shuttle cargo bay, but which could easily deploy once in space, while keeping the weight as light as possible. The system she and her team ultimately created had combined the lander's maneuvering thrusters and landing legs into four articulated strut assemblies that coiled together in a compact bundle around the exhaust bell of Tinkerbell's main engine. To deploy them, pressurized nitrogen was applied to the cylinder for each strut, which would unfold and extend it from the stowed position. As it reached full extension, a spring latch would engage, locking the strut into place. Simple and elegant, and more importantly, lightweight.

Robbie lifted the cover on the switch and flipped it. He heard the hiss of pressurized gas as four solenoid valves cycled open allowing nitrogen to flow into the strut cylinders.

"Positive movement on all four struts," Stephanie announced.

"Isn't that beautiful!" Vivian said proudly, watching over Stephanie's shoulder as the articulated struts unfolded like latticework flower petals.

"Yep, nice job," Stephanie said as she watched the lander.

"We spent over a month playing with soda straws and toothpicks before we had something we could begin to model on the computer," Vivian observed.

"Uh huh," Stephanie nodded absently, concentrating on the motion of the deploying legs, watching for signs of binding or interference. The four legs all slid smoothly to their fully deployed positions and stopped.

"OK, looks good from here," Stephanie observed. "I see four deployed strut assemblies."

Robbie frowned as he examined the indicator lights above him. Three were brightly glowing green. One was still dark. Reaching up, he wrapped on the offending light with his knuckle.

"Steph, we may have a problem," he said with concern. "I'm not showing a latch light on number three."

"I see no issues from here," Stephanie said, leaning forward and pressing closer to the cargo bay viewing windows.

"Well we need to figure this out pronto." Thinking for a moment, he said, "Viv, is there some way I can retract the strut and then extend it again?"

Vivian shook her head. "No, there's no reversing valve in the system, it's a feature we did without for simplicity. One opening, one time. That's all they're designed to do."

"How did you retract them during ground testing?" Robbie asked.

"With a forklift," Vivian replied.

"Damn, and we forgot to bring one. OK, Steph, is there some way you could reach across with the arm and push the strut?"

"Robbie, we don't have a procedure for that," she replied. "I don't know what it's OK to push on, which direction, how hard or for how long. Maybe if the strut were on the port side, but since it's on the starboard side, I'm going to have to reach up over the bottom of Tinkerbell to get to it. I'm not sure if I'll be able to get a good angle."

Robbie continued thinking furiously. "OK, tell Mike to suit up. I'm going to need him to go EVA and wrap that latch with a hammer."

Stephanie's brow furrowed. "Are you sure? He's never done an EVA unassisted, and besides, it's going to take at least an hour before he'd be ready."

Robbie frowned deeply. Then a thought occurred to him. Reaching over to the engine systems panel, he started flicking switches to activate the lander's maneuvering thruster system.

"OK, I have an idea," he announced. "I'm powering up the thrusters now. I'm going to pulse number three aft and see if I can jog the strut into latching."

"Robbie, again, we don't have a procedure for that, or an engineering analysis on thrusting against an unlocked strut ... "

"*Damn* it Steph," Robbie interrupted her. "This is not NASA anymore. We don't have a thousand engineers on the ground running simulations on solutions. Like the Russians, remember?"

Stephanie pursed her lips tightly, and then said, "You're the commander. What do you want to do?"

"Like I said, I'm going to fire number three aft briefly and see if I can jolt the strut into latching. Can you confirm that there's nothing that would be in the plume?"

"The thruster cluster is fully extended, so there's nothing that the exhaust plume would impinge on," Stephanie confirmed.

"Do you see any problem with my plan, Viv?"

"No, not really," Vivian replied tentatively.

"Roger that, firing a pulse on number three aft." Robbie aligned the system to isolate the specific thruster, and then nudged the hand controller briefly to quickly fire it. He felt a mild vibration.

"Looks good," Stephanie observed.

"Still no latch light," Robbie replied. "OK, one second burst this time," he announced, pushing the hand controller again.

The cylinder of the latch assembly had been blocked by the plug of ice contained within the frame, preventing the latch from engaging. As the thruster pushed against the end of the strut, pressure against the ice plug greatly increased. The surrounding weld, already compromised by numerous microscopic cracks induced by repeated freezing and thawing of the ice, suddenly yielded, hinging open, but remaining attached by a sliver of material. The ice plug, released from its enclosed space, slid deeper into the frame, allowing the latch mechanism to engage.

"That's got it!" Robbie announced triumphantly. "I show four green lights!"

"Copy Tinkerbell, congratulations," Stephanie answered.

"Thank God!" Vivian intoned.

***

Robbie flew Tinkerbell in a wide loop, circling Atlantis at a distance of a mile. Brief firings of the main engine and thrusters verified that all propulsion systems were functioning properly.

"Just like at home on the simulations," he said, looking in various directions to test the view through the 3D goggles he wore. He was particularly amused to look down and see Atlantis a mile below, where his brain expected to see his lap.

"Time to bring it home, Tinkerbell, you're going to deplete your batteries unless you're planning to start your fuel cell," Stephanie called.

"Roger Atlantis, fun time's over, bringing her back to the barn." Robbie flew the lander back to rendezvous with the shuttle, where Stephanie reached up with the remote arm and pulled it the remaining few feet into the cargo bay.

"Welcome back," Stephanie said warmly.

"So I was thinking," Robbie mused.

"What now?"

"Once the collar is engaged and the tunnel is pressurized, how about having everyone on the landing team join me over here and we'll do a little dry run."

"Robbie, you need to recharge, you're down too many amps for any more joy-flying today."

"Oh, we're not going anywhere, I just thought it would be nice if everyone could join me on the patio for a moment."

"What the hell are you talking about?"

"Just please have everyone on the landing team join me on Tink."

"Roger, on their way."

***

The ventilation system could barely cope with six people packed into the confined space once the lander access hatch had been secured. "OK," Robbie said, "since we don't have anything major on the schedule for the next six hours, I'd like to do one last landing and suit up practice."

Everyone groaned. Six people and six Orlan space suits made it extremely crowded in Tinkerbell's cabin, and the process of donning their suits felt like playing an hour long game of Twister in a phone booth.

"Just get in your spots. Trust me, I think you're going to like this."

Tom, Elton and Carl joined Robbie, strapping into the seats they had been assigned for landing. Nikki and Mike squeezed into their designated spots against the bulkhead between the crew's spacesuits, belting themselves in securely. They weren't comfortable locations, but they were the best solution that Vivian had been able to provide when directed to accommodate two additional passengers during the design of the lander.

"OK, Steph, deflate the collar and depressurize the tunnel," Robbie requested. "Then I'm reducing cabin pressure and switching to O2."

"I thought you said you're not going anywhere?" Stephanie protested.

"We're not leaving, we're just going outside for a bit."

"Say again Robbie, you're going outside? You mean everyone is going EVA?"

"With the exception of Mike and me, no one has any experience with their suits in vacuum," Robbie explained. "With the thousand and one things I'm going to have on my mind after landing, having to reassure everyone to trust their equipment is the last thing I want to think about. These aren't professional astronauts, you know."

Stephanie shook her head as she operated the controls to deflate the docking collar and depressurize the connecting tunnel. "You're using a lot of oxygen," she said, disapprovingly.

"It's OK, we brought enough," Robbie answered.

Vivian said, "You know, it's probably not a bad idea when you think about it, having them use their suits in space to get more comfortable with them."

"Probably not," Stephanie replied, "but I'm still getting used to this whole 'make it up as we go along' way of doing things that we operate under now."

"All right everyone, listen up," Robbie announced. "We're going to spend the next hour doing a landing rehearsal, so talk quietly among yourselves while Steph and I run the checklist. Then I'll want you all to suit up."

***

Robbie was the first to exit, and Mike brought up the rear in case anyone needed assistance. One by one, each member of the landing team exited Tinkerbell and joined Robbie, who had tethered himself to one of the port lander support struts. Like birds perched on a power line, the six crew members sat in a row along the length of the strut.

The moon was larger than the Earth now, having grown with each passing day as their home world shrank in size. The enormous white orb reflected brightly from each of their faceplates.

"So what do you think?" Robbie asked quietly.

"Best. Day. Ever." Nikki said softly.

"Thank you, Mr. Robichaud," Carl agreed gratefully. "This is truly glorious."

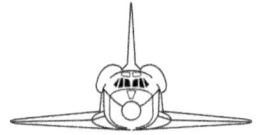

CHAPTER FORTY–THREE

Atlantis' OMS engines fired strongly and steadily as the spacecraft whipped around the far side of the moon, and then shut off as Wendy's fuel supply was exhausted.

"Ready for module one release," Robbie recited from the checklist.

"Copy that, standby," Stephanie responded, toggling the switches that unlatched Wendy from the cargo bay and ejected her into space. "Module one released," she reported, as the ejection springs pushed Wendy out of the cargo bay. On its current course and speed, the empty module would swing by the moon, ultimately looping into solar orbit.

"OMS fuel cross connect switch to module two," Robbie next read.

"Roger, OMS cross connect switched to module two," Stephanie replied, activating the appropriate switches to feed Atlantis' engines from Tiger Lilly.

"Commence module two pressurization."

"Roger," Stephanie answered, flicking several more switches, and then after a moment, adding, "Pressures are nominal."

"Copy that, commencing lunar orbit insertion," Robbie announced, restarting the engines to slow the spacecraft further and allow it to be captured by the moon's gravity.

***

Jean reviewed the data showing that the burn had put Atlantis on target to enter the highly elliptical lunar orbit called for in their minimum energy expenditure plan. "Atlantis, Long Beach, we show you on target for HELO. Looking very good, we're all cheering for you down here."

"Copy that Long Beach, looking good here as well," Robbie replied with satisfaction as he scanned his cockpit displays. The windshield was filled with a view of the lunar surface rapidly skimming by below.

"Atlantis, Long Beach, recommend you launch your remotes before loss of signal."

"Roger that Long Beach, launching remotes," Robbie replied.

Attached to the framework of Tiger Lilly, Atlantis carried three nano-satellites about the size of softballs. Their purpose was to act as communications relays to ensure that the spacecraft could stay in continuous contact with both the Earth and the lander once it left for the surface. They were called remotes in a nod to Star Wars, as they resembled the small floating droids by that name that appeared throughout the series.

"Release initiated," Robbie reported.

The three remotes were ejected in a computer controlled sequence timed to ensure that they would settle into lunar orbit spaced equidistantly from each other.

"Oh, by the way," Jean radioed, "Patty baked a moon cake." She traditionally brought a different type of cake for each major mission milestone, but there had never been a shuttle in lunar orbit before.

"Oh really?" Robbie said, turning to smile at Stephanie. "We've never had one of those before. What kind is it?"

"Oh, it's wonderful, it's a … " The channel turned to a quiet hiss as Jean was cut off. As Atlantis looped around the far side of the moon, communication with Earth was blocked.

"Damn, now we'll have to wait half an hour to find out," Robbie scowled.

***

"Atlantis, Long Beach," Jean called at the appropriate time. Waiting thirty seconds, she tried again. "Atlantis, Long Beach, do you copy, over." For another thirty seconds she waited, and then tried yet again. "Atlantis, Long Beach, over."

"Long Beach, Atlantis, we copy, over," they heard Robbie's voice from the depths of space.

Jean glanced quickly at the navigation console, whose operator had been studying his data. He turned and gave her a quick affirmative nod.

"Roger Atlantis, we confirm you in orbit, welcome back."

"Copy that Long Beach, we also show positive orbit. So what type was it? You have us all in suspense up here."

"Say again Atlantis?" Jean asked.

"The cake. What type was it?" Robbie asked.

Jean laughed and looked over at the cake sitting on the corner of her desk. "Cheese cake of course," she said. "With green cream cheese icing."

Robbie burst out laughing. "Of course, what else could it be!"

***

"Atlantis, Long Beach, we have positive squawk from all three remotes,"

309

Jean reported. "We have continuous comms, so there are no further constraints. You are go for a landing attempt at next perilune."

"Roger Long Beach, good to hear." Looking at the mission elapsed time clock, Robbie did a fast mental calculation. "Looks like we'll be in position in about nine hours. We're going to take a rest period, let's put a wakeup call in for six hours from now."

"Copy that Atlantis, we'll call you back in six hours," Jean confirmed. "Don't spend the whole time looking out the window now, make sure you all get some rest," she cautioned.

To save energy and thus fuel, Atlantis had entered a highly elliptical orbit around the moon. At its closest point, they skimmed just sixty miles above the surface. At its highest, they were over five thousand miles in altitude. It took just under twelve hours to complete one orbit. The lander had to depart for the surface while they were at the lowest point. If they missed the upcoming perilune, they could make one more attempt on the following orbit twelve hours later, but if they were unable to depart for the surface by then, they were out of time and would have to return to Earth.

The entire crew crowded onto the flight deck to watch the lunar surface scroll by. They gazed in amazement and awe as each moment revealed a new portion to view.

"It's a shame we whipped around the back side so fast," Vivian observed. "I would have liked to have seen more of the dark side."

"It all looks pretty much the same when you're this close," Robbie noted.

"Maybe so, but we'll never have another chance to see it after we return," she said.

They each quietly contemplated the fact that they were experiencing something that was truly once in a lifetime, never to be seen or done again.

Finally, Robbie spoke up. "Well I hate to spoil your fun, but we've been watching the moon go by for over an hour now. We have a full day coming up, so I want you all to get some rest."

Everyone reluctantly drifted off to their quiet spots to get a few hours of sleep.

***

"Time," one of Jean's controllers announced, gently shaking her awake.

She opened her eyes, nodded, and sat up on the edge of the cot in the Space Dome conference room, being used as a quiet space where the control team could grab a quick nap. Pulling on her shoes, she headed back to mission control. Entering the room, she quickly scanned the status panel and then sat at her console.

"Let's see how they like this one," she said. "Mr. Robbie isn't the only one around here with a sense of humor."

Keying her mike, she pressed a button on the mp3 player she had plugged into her communication panel. The squeaky tones of an electronic synthesizer began to play a bouncy tune as a nasally voice sang:

We're spending Christmas on the moon this year,
It's all arranged, so have no fear,
We'll see if Santa can find us here,
We're spending Christmas on the moon this year.

Robbie jerked awake from a sound sleep. "Good *God*, what the hell is that!"

"Good morning, Atlantis, this is your Christmas morning wakeup call," Jean cheerfully announced.

"Make it stop!" Robbie demanded.

"You're free to suggest your own titles for wake up calls if you don't like ours," Jean taunted.

"I'd prefer something that sounds like music!" he protested. "I thought the master alarm was going off!"

"Stop grousing and get your crew ready, you have a little less than three hours to perilune."

"Roger that. I think you've killed my mood though," he said, firing off one last complaint.

While Stephanie ensured everyone was awake, Robbie quickly ate and then re-entered Tinkerbell to carefully go over the vehicle one final time. An hour before their intended departure, he rejoined the crew as they finished their breakfast.

"OK, everyone who's going with me, last chance to use the toilet," Robbie announced. "There are no porta-potties on the moon." Turning to Stephanie, he added, "You have the ship. See you back here in twelve hours."

"I'll be here," she replied. "Don't make me wait," she added with a smile.

Tom gave Vivian a hug. "I wish you were going with us."

"It's OK, I'm having a great time, and Stephanie and I will enjoy the extra space while you all are gone." She hugged each of the other team members in turn. "Pick me out a nice rock while you're down there."

The members of the landing team once again crawled through the tunnel to the lander, secured the hatch and strapped into their assigned positions.

"Running fuel cell startup sequence," Robbie announced, enabling the flow of liquid oxygen and hydrogen within the fuel cell that would combine to provide the electricity they needed to operate the lander.

"Copy Tinkerbell," Stephanie announced, assuming her position at the aft control station, Vivian right behind her.

"My board is green, DC bus volts nominal, AC steady at 400 hertz, switching to internal power." Robbie switched the lander to its own internal power supply. Now that the fuel cell was operating, the clock was ticking, as there was only slightly over twenty-four hours of cryogen onboard to operate the cell. The plan was to return to orbit on Atlantis' next pass in twelve hours. If for some reason they missed that rendezvous, they had enough power generation capability to wait for the next opportunity twelve hours later. If they missed that one as well, they weren't coming back.

"OK, depressurize the tunnel and deflate the collar," Robbie ordered.

"Depressurize the tunnel and deflate … " Stephanie began.

"Wait!" Carl suddenly called out. "Marta! I've forgotten Marta!"

"Standby, Atlantis," Robbie announced. "Dr. Heinel?"

"My wife. I must retrieve my wife," Carl said frantically, fumbling with his restraints. "In this morning's haste, I forgot to retrieve her urn."

"Atlantis, Tinkerbell, can you please ask Vivian to retrieve Dr. Heinel's package from the mid-deck locker and bring it to us?" Robbie asked. "Clock's ticking," he added.

"Roger Tinkerbell, she's on her way," Stephanie replied.

Robbie looked up at Mike, strapped to the bulkhead nearby. "Would you please undog the hatch and take the package from Vivian?"

"Got it," Mike said, already unstrapping himself.

Vivian retrieved the urn from its storage location and then reopened Atlantis' outer airlock door to enter the tunnel. She arrived at the lander's hatch just as Mike pulled it inward and swung it aside.

"I believe someone forgot this?" she said, passing the slate box to Mike.

"It's the first time I've ever seen Dr. Carl rattled," Mike observed. "I'm glad he remembered before we undocked, I think he would have freaked if he hadn't realized until we had landed."

"Go easy on him," Vivian pleaded. "You know how emotional this must be for him."

"Don't worry, I'll watch out for him," Mike reassured her. "I always do."

Closing and dogging the lander access door again, Mike slide past Nikki and showed Carl the urn. "Here she is, Dr. Carl. I'm putting her right here in the stowage net," he added, reaching between Carl's legs and tucking the urn into the netting below.

"Thank you," Carl said, visibly relieved. "I don't know what I would have done if I had forgotten … "

"No worries, Dr. Carl," Mike smiled, turning to return to his station.

"OK, is there anyone else?" Robbie asked, looking around. "All right then, let's proceed. Atlantis, Tinkerbell, please depressurize the tunnel and deflate the collar so we can be on our way."

"Roger Tinkerbell, depressurizing the tunnel and deflating the collar," Stephanie replied, as Vivian again joined her.

Robbie donned his goggles and looked about to verify that the external visualization system was operating. "OK, Atlantis, we are go at this end, awaiting your confirmation."

"The collar is deflated and retracted," Stephanie confirmed. "You are go for undocking."

"Copy, Atlantis, we are undocking now." Robbie pushed slightly on the hand controller to fire the maneuvering thrusters and gently ease Tinkerbell up and out of Atlantis' cargo bay.

Stephanie watched closely as the lander rose before her. "You are clear, Tinkerbell."

"Copy that Atlantis, I'm going to take her up about one hundred yards, and then translate for deorbital burn." Robbie let the lander drift upwards for several minutes and then maneuvered to orient Tinkerbell parallel to the shuttle, her engine pointing in the direction they were both traveling. "I show four minutes to deorbital burn," Robbie announced.

"I confirm, three minutes fifty seconds to perilune," Stephanie answered.

"We cut that one a little close," Robbie said. Reaching up to engage the flight control system, he added, "Guidance to automatic."

"Guidance to auto, copy. Seriously, would you have rather just hung out there for half an hour waiting?"

"Some things are supposed to be boring," Robbie observed. "Like deorbital burns. If you're excited, you're not doing it right."

"Let's hope the remainder of the flight is extremely boring," Stephanie said.

"Let's hope. 30 seconds."

"Roger Tinkerbell, good luck and safe journey."

"Thanks, Steph. And five, four, three, two, one."

Tinkerbell's flight control computer fired the lander's Wizard engine to slow the vehicle and allow it to start dropping from orbit. Robbie intently monitored the system's operation, but he was only a backup to the automatic system. The craft shook gently from side to side, randomly jumping slightly in various directions. Tom leaned over to Elton and said, "So what kind of guarantee does your engine come with?"

"The best," Elton replied. "Guaranteed to get you home alive or your money back. Provided you return defective units to the manufacturer for inspection."

"And I suppose we pay the freight?"

"Of course," Elton grinned.

"Fifty miles," Robbie announced for the benefit of the passengers. With no view ports, there was no way for them to determine their proximity to the moon. After a pause of several minutes, he said, "Forty." The gentle shaking and lurching continued. After several more minutes he said, "Thirty miles. Range looks good." The geographic features he observed matched what he expected to see. "Twenty miles. Starting to pick up some nice surface detail now."

"I'm really starting to rethink the decision to skip the windows," Tom muttered.

"That's all right, you'll be seeing it up close shortly," Robbie noted.

"Well next time I want some goggles too," Tom said.

"That actually would have been a good idea, I wonder why no one suggested it," Robbie commented. "Fifteen miles."

"Concerns about vertigo," Mike explained, speaking up to be heard over the vibration. "Multiple sets of goggles would have had to be slaved to your master pair, which means when you turned your head, everyone else's field of view would also change."

"Ah, good point," Robbie observed. "Ten miles."

"We thought by the time you made the surface, everyone else would be hitting the barf bags."

"Yeah, that would have been pretty ugly," Robbie agreed. "No way would I have cleaned that up. Five miles. Picking up the Apennines now. Christ they're big! I sure hope we clear them."

"Not helping," Tom said.

"No worries, guidance is dead on, we're going to clear them with yards to spare and drop down on the other side."

Turning to Elton, Tom said, "Did he say 'yards?'"

"I'm trying not to listen," Elton replied.

"Three miles, six miles downrange. Yeah, we're definitely going to clear the mountains," Robbie said. "Pretty sure anyway." He suddenly heard Stephanie's voice on his headset.

"Robbie, quit tormenting the passengers."

"Yes, mother. Two miles. Mile and a half. Two miles down range. Starting to translate. OK, I believe I see the landing zone. Holy crap, I can see the Falcon's descent stage clear as day," Robbie said, spotting the bottom half of the Apollo 15 lunar lander sitting on the surface. "Well what do you know, I guess we really did land on the moon. Suck it, conspiracy theorists. One mile. Continuing translation. Slowing forward motion. We're over the landing zone. Dropping now. Two thousand feet. Fifteen hundred. One thousand, drifting down range. Five hundred feet. I can see a few rocks and boulders. Looks like we're lining up nicely, should be less than 500 yards from the Falcon. Two hundred feet, descending. Drifting left. One hundred. Picking up some dust. Fifty feet. There's a boulder in the landing area. Switching to manual."

Robbie reached over and toggled off the automatic guidance system and took over manual flight control. "Sliding right. Closer to Falcon. Fifty feet. Thirty. Lots of dust now, but good view of the surface. Twenty feet. Looks like a great spot. Ten feet. Contact light. Engine off."

Tinkerbell slowly fell the last five feet, bouncing lightly as she contacted the surface and then settling firmly on her support struts.

"Long Beach, this is Tinkerbell from Palus Putredinus, we're down."

"Roger Tinkerbell, we copy you down on the surface, congratulations," Jean replied. Robbie could hear cheering in the background. He next heard Stephanie's voice.

"Tinkerbell, Atlantis."

"Go, Atlantis."

"Did you really see a boulder or did you just want to stick the landing yourself?"

"Do you think I'd come all this way and then let the computer have all the glory?" Robbie replied.

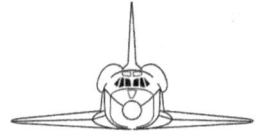

CHAPTER FORTY–FOUR

The crew spent little time in celebration. They had less than ten hours to spend on the surface before they would have to lift off again to rejoin Atlantis, and had a long list of activities to accomplish. While Robbie shut down Tinkerbell's guidance and landing systems and prepared the vehicle for egress, everyone had an opportunity to briefly don his pilot's goggles and take a quick look outside before downing an energy bar and drinking some juice. Then it was time to get dressed. They had long since learned to get over their feelings of modesty, as it was impossible for six people in such a confined space to don urine collection devices and fluid cooled undergarments and maintain even a modicum of personal privacy. The best approach, they had determined, was to just not think about it.

"Check your partner," Robbie ordered, as he turned to examine Carl's gear. Tom and Elton verified they were each properly outfitted, as did Mike and Nikki. She had elected to wear her prosthetic leg, thinking it would better help her manage the loping hop that was the most efficient gait on the lunar surface.

"OK, let's suit up."

They each turned to their respective spacesuits, mounted around the perimeter of the ship with their backpack access hatches facing inward. After a bit of bumping, some elbow jabs and quite a few "excuse me's," they all managed to slide into their respective suits.

"All right, everyone give me a status," Robbie directed. After reporting that their suits were functioning properly, he said, "OK, if anyone has a problem or an alarm, let me know. Long Beach, Tinkerbell, we're depressurizing the vehicle for lunar surface excursion." Turning to Carl, he added, "Don't forget your wife, Doctor Heinel."

"I have her right here," Carl answered, patting the nylon gear bag at his waist.

"Copy Tinkerbell, we're all really anxious to see your smiling faces out on the surface," they heard Jean say from mission control.

It took several moments for the cabin pressure to vent away. Suddenly, Robbie remembered there was still a decision to be made.

"Umm, lady and gents, do we have any kind of a consensus on who's going first?"

Everyone looked at each other for a moment. Although it had been brought up in casual conversation, it was a question that had never been ultimately decided. They had each just assumed it wasn't them. Finally, Mike offered, "Don't you think it should be Dr. Carl? He's the reason we're all here, after all."

"No, no my boy, I have no interest in being first," Carl chuckled. "I'll most likely fall off the ladder if there isn't someone outside to assist me. These suits are quite heavy after all."

"I think just being here is enough, I don't deserve to go first just because I got a lucky ticket," Nikki said.

"I wouldn't feel right either," Elton observed. "I agree with Nikki, we didn't make this happen, we were just lucky enough to be able to ride along. In my case, people would say that I bought the privilege of being first."

"If not Dr. Carl, I think it should be Mr. Armac then," Mike said. "He's the one who sold his company and took the biggest personal risk. The rest of us really didn't have anything to lose if we didn't make it."

Everyone murmured assent and looked at Tom.

"Me?" he said. "That's your decision?" Tom asked.

Everyone agreed.

"OK, well, if you all think it should be me, then I have the right to assign the privilege to someone else. And I choose you," Tom said, looking at Robbie.

"Me? Why me?"

"Because I don't particularly care to spend the rest of my life as a celebrity—that guy who was the first private citizen on the moon. But I think you might actually enjoy it," Tom said with a smile. "You'd probably never have to pay for another beer again as long as you live."

Robbie's smile was visible though his faceplate. "From space shuttle pilot to coonass sewer engineer, who then goes on to be the first private moon walker. Sort of a riches to rags and back again story. Yeah, I like that. I'll take on that burden."

"OK then, that's that," Tom concluded. "Any idea what you're going to say?"

Robbie's face fell. "Crap. Haven't a clue."

"Good luck with that," Tom laughed.

"Tinkerbell, Long Beach, how are you progressing up there? We thought we'd be seeing some pictures by now," Jean radioed impatiently.

"Ah, Long Beach, Tinkerbell, we just had to take a moment to draw straws," Robbie answered. "Looks like I got the short one."

"Really. Well congratulations. Meanwhile, tick tock tick tock," Jean replied.

"Roger, Long Beach, the crew of Tinkerbell is egressing for lunar excursion. We'll be using individual call signs from here."

"Copy that Robbie. Get a move on."

Mike once again undogged the lander's door and pulled it inward, swinging it on its mounting arm to one side of the opening. Robbie took a quick look around.

"All right, in order after me. I want Mike to egress last in case anyone needs assistance, just like our last practice," he said. "See you outside." Turning his back to the access hatch, he dropped forward onto his hands and began backing out of the crew compartment.

Crawling backward into the short tunnel that had connected Tinkerbell to Atlantis, he reached the portion that had opened upward to the shuttle cargo bay. It faced downward toward the lunar surface now, since Tinkerbell was finally right side up. Dropping down into the small vestibule, he reached down and rotated the mechanism that opened the hatch. It slowly swung open, revealing a view of the moon's surface six feet below. Robbie gazed at it for a moment in mild disbelief, and then shook his head to clear it and unlatched and lowered the ladder assembly that ended a foot above the surface.

"Here I go," Robbie announced, as he began to descend the ladder. Hesitating for a moment on the lower rung, he took a deep breath, and then said, "Stepping off now."

Robbie dropped the twelve inches to the surface and then ducked slightly and moved away from the ladder to be clear of the tunnel. Standing up, he gazed out across the brilliantly lit lunar surface. "Like Aldrin said," he muttered quietly to himself. "Magnificent desolation. Well, well, well." Technically, those were his first words.

"Ah, Robbie, Long Beach, you might want to speak up, you have half the planet listening right now."

"OK," he said louder, shocked out of his reverie. "Well, it's been a long, long time. But we're back. And hopefully it won't be as long the next time. Oh yeah, and we came in peace and all that."

Back at mission control, Jean hung her head and shook it slowly.

"Oh, and one more thing. Go Tigers!"

***

The crew set up an American flag, and finally, over two years after Mike first created his animation for Carl's initial presentation, unfurled a Roadrunner Rockets flag on the moon. They then gathered in front of the lander to take their group portrait, after which they split off to perform their individual tasks.

Robbie lowered the collection bin from its stowed position underneath the lander and extracted two collapsible shovels. "Here you go, gentlemen, start digging," he said, handing them to Tom and Elton. "We need this bin full before we leave, we have bills to pay you know," he joked.

As Robbie began an inspection of the lander, Nikki set up a video camera to record herself holding postcards of various commercial products. The sponsors had requested that their actual products be flown to the moon, but Vivian had been insistent that for weight management, it was a picture or nothing.

While Tom and Elton shoveled, Mike opened a small briefcase he had retrieved from beneath the lander and extracted a toy monster truck. Placing it on the surface, he pulled the truck's remote control out of the case and extended its antenna.

"What in the hell is he doing?" Elton asked between shovel loads.

"You really should have attended more of the preflight briefings," Tom chided. "I know you've heard about the WebSearcher Lunar X Prize?"

"Of course. Twenty million dollars to the first team to successfully land a remotely controlled rover on the moon," Elton answered.

"And another five million dollars if they return live video of equipment from an Apollo landing site," Tom said.

Elton stopped shoveling and turned to look at Mike. "Oh, you're joking," he said.

"Nope," Tom said. "We checked the rules, and nowhere does it say from how far away the rover has to be operated."

"Long Beach, this is Mike, powering up the rover now."

"Copy that Mike, don't forget to turn on the video camera."

"Oh yeah, thanks," Mike replied, reaching down to flip on the small HD camera that was duct taped to the toy truck's roll bar. "OK, here we go." The truck took off in a cloud of dust, bouncing wildly as it zigzagged in the general direction of the Falcon, Mike clumsily chasing after it.

"This is just nuts," Elton said, shaking his head.

"Yeah, are you done?" Tom asked. "Because this bin isn't going to fill itself."

Finished with the product photos, Nikki now positioned the camera to record herself making the first mobile phone call from the moon. Holding the phone in her gloved hand so that it was clearly visible, she zoomed in to capture the phone's logo along with her face through her suit faceplate.

"Call Mom," Nikki said. Her suit radio transmitted the message via Bluetooth to the phone, which used its voice recognition app to dial the appropriate number.

"Calling Mom," the phone replied in a soft female voice, routing the call through the micro-cell base installed in Tinkerbell, then to one of the orbiting remotes, and then to Earth. "Hi Mom! Yes, fine thanks, how are you?"

AT&T had won the bidding war for the right to determine who would receive the first cellular call from the moon. They requested that she phone a close family member, as they intended to use the video to launch their new campaign, "Stay Close. Even When Far, Far Away."

Robbie finished his inspection and returned to check on Tom and Elton. Leaning over the bin, he said, "That's enough for now, we'll get the rest later, we just needed to make sure we don't leave empty handed if we have to bug out sooner than we planned."

"I can't believe I paid two hundred million dollars to shovel dirt," Elton said, returning his shovel to the bin.

"You paid two hundred million dollars to shovel dirt on the *moon*," Tom pointed out.

***

Carl was free from the responsibility to shill for sponsors or shovel soil. After the group pictures were taken, he started slowly shuffling toward the distant Falcon, picking up speed as he worked out the mechanics of the hop and skip that lunar gravity required. It was tiring though, and he stopped periodically to rest and catch his breath. Noticing a large object to his left, he headed toward it. Imagery had shown it to be the location where the Apollo 15 astronauts had parked their lunar rover. Carl stopped and gazed at the vehicle. He fondly remembered several of the engineers at Huntsville who had worked with Boeing to design the machine. Sadly, they were gone now. He would have liked to have brought back a memento for them, some small piece from the control panel possibly. He had been proud once of how young he had been, working as an equal alongside so many older and more experienced engineers. Now it just meant he was alone, one of the very few still remaining. He sighed deeply.

Carl was startled from his melancholy reflection by Mike's toy truck suddenly smacking into one of the rover's tires and falling on its side. Its wheels continued to spin, throwing up fountains of dust.

"Sorry, Dr. Carl, it's a bit tricky to handle," Mike said, bounding into view. Turning the truck upright, he turned to look at the rover. "Cool! The moon buggy. If I caught it in the video, we just added another five million bucks to the bank. Hey Dr. Carl, take my picture, would you please?" he asked as he climbed into the driver's seat.

Carl felt a flash of anger, as if Mike were violating the rover and the memory of his friends. Taking a deep breath, he calmly told himself, *It's just an abandoned derelict. There are no ghosts in this machine.*

"All right young Mr. Patrick," Carl said, raising the digital camera

320

mounted on his left wrist. "Smile now." Carl took several pictures.

"Thanks, Dr. Carl!" Mike said, leaping out of the seat. "Do you want me to take your picture?"

"No, my boy, that's all right."

"OK then, I'll see you in a bit." The toy truck sped off toward the distant Falcon, Mike bounding along behind.

Carl watched Mike depart, and then shook his head and started searching the terrain to his left. *It should be close by*, he thought. He almost stepped on the small memorial, its dull aluminum color blending with the surrounding gray surface. The Fallen Astronaut was a vaguely human figurine measuring just over three inches, lying on the lunar surface. A small plaque bearing fourteen names was wedged into the soil next to it, listing the men who had died during the exploration of space prior to the flight of Apollo 15. Two Russian cosmonauts had been left off, as their deaths had remained a secret of the Cold War for some time after the flight. Two Americans astronauts who had perished in aircraft accidents were also missing. Carl intended to remedy the oversight.

Reaching into his gear bag, he extracted a small metal plate. On it were listed the four names of those who had been overlooked. In addition, it included the crew of space shuttles Challenger and Columbia, as well as the crew of the International Space Station who had perished in the station disaster. In all, the plaque listed twenty-four more men and women who had died in pursuit of the dream. Carl pushed the plate firmly into the soil next to the existing one. He had personally known many of the people whose names he had carried to the moon, as well as several who were listed on the original plaque. They had all been extraordinary people. Standing and staring sadly at the lists, he said softly, "We remember."

"Is that you, Dr. Heinel?" Carl heard Robbie ask. "Are you doing the memorial now?"

"Yes, Mr. Robichaud, I am," Carl replied with a soft sigh.

"Hey everybody, let's all stop what we're doing and go join Dr. Heinel for a moment," Robbie said. "Nikki, bring the camera."

Carl wished he had had more time for private remembrance and reflection.

***

"A bit closer," Robbie said, reaching with outstretched arms and bringing his hands together. Everyone shuffled into a tighter group. "OK, that's good," he said, and then bounded over to join them. They posed as the camera recorded them standing behind the small memorial.

"That should do it," Robbie announced. "OK, let's go visit the Falcon and see if we can collect some artifacts."

The group started hop, skip and jumping toward the Apollo 15 descent

321

stage. Carl lingered a few moments, noting how the soil around the plaques was now roiled by multiple boot prints.

And so it shall be for all eternity, he thought sadly.

"Are you all right, Dr. Heinel?" Tom asked, returning to rejoin Carl.

"Yes. Yes, I'm fine Mr. Armac."

"Why don't you come on over to the Falcon and point out the pieces that you may have worked on."

"All right," Carl said numbly, turning and following Tom.

As they arrived, they found the group standing before the descent module ladder that astronauts David Scott and Jim Irwin had used to climb to and from the surface. Their portable life support system backpacks and boot covers lay beneath the ladder where the two astronauts had discarded them prior to leaving the moon.

"Let's make sure we get these back to Tinkerbell," Robbie directed, picking up one of the backpacks. "These will look great in the museum."

Carl felt a stabbing pain in his chest for each item they touched.

"Where's the flag?" Mike asked, looking around. The group moved away from the Falcon, searching.

Carl reached up to run his hand along the edges of the open Modularized Equipment Stowage Assembly. He had designed much of the equipment that had been stored there, and had personally touched this unit almost forty-four years ago. He vividly remembered how anxious he had been, sitting with Marta on the couch in their living room, tightly gripping her hand as they watched the shadowy figure of Neil Armstrong descend from the Eagle, the image being broadcast from the camera mounted in that lander's MESA. *Mounted here*, Carl thought, his hand touching the corresponding spot the camera would have been mounted in on that first lander. *A long time ago ...*

"Here it is!" Carl heard Tom say.

Joining the group, Carl found them standing around the faded remnant of the American flag. It had been knocked to the surface by the thrust of Falcon's ascent engine as it had lifted off. The colors of the fabric had faded to white from exposure to the sun's ultraviolet radiation, but the stitched outlines of the stripes and stars could still be discerned.

"Yes, that's it," Carl confirmed.

"What do you think?" Tom asked. "It's not in very good shape."

"One of the mission's science goals is to see how materials held up through extended exposure," Robbie noted. "I say let's gather it up and take it home for analysis."

As Tom lifted the flag, it began to fall apart in his gloved hands. With Mike's help, he gathered up the fragments.

A tear formed in Carl's eye and rolled slowly down his cheek.

***

The crew finished their exploration and gathered up their artifacts. "OK," Robbie announced, "let's get these items back to Tinkerbell." Turning to Carl, he asked, "Are you coming, Dr. Heinel?"

"No," Carl answered, "not just yet. I'd like to stay here a while longer if you don't mind. I have something I'd like to do."

"That's fine," Robbie replied. Checking his timer, he added, "We're over three hours in, we only have about two and a half hours left before we all need to be back at Tinkerbell."

"Yes, I understand," Carl replied.

"All right, let's go." Robbie led the group as they began hopping back toward Tinkerbell. "I think we ought to get some samples from over there," he said, pointing to the left.

Carl stood silently watching as the group receded. He then turned back toward the Falcon and surveyed the scene.

"We're looters," he said softly. "Oh Marta," he sighed deeply.

"Dr. Carl? Is everything all right?" he heard Mike ask.

"Yes, yes, just fine," Carl replied. He then reduced the volume of his suit radio to silence the continuous chatter. Reaching into his gear bag, he removed his wife's urn. He smiled at it sadly, and then held it closely to his chest.

"I promised, my love," he whispered, as he began slowly turning in time to music that only he could hear. "I'm sorry it took so long."

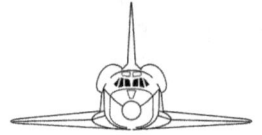

CHAPTER FORTY–FIVE

Carl stood in front of the Falcon's descent stage, looking up at the small platform at the top of the ladder. Called the "porch," it had been the Apollo astronauts' staging area as they exited and entered the lunar module's crew compartment. He was consumed with a desire to climb up and sit there and look out over the surrounding terrain.

Grabbing the ladder firmly, he crouched down to leap up onto the bottom rung. It took several attempts and left him quite winded, but eventually he succeeded. Climbing to the top, he turned and sat down on the porch. Looking out over the beautifully barren landscape, his thoughts drifted to memories of the people and places from his past, when the prospect of man landing on the moon was still a distant uncertainty. His promise to his wife finally fulfilled, his soul was lightened, and he smiled as he recalled his happier times, in love with his wife and his life and the possibilities the future held. He thought again of the day they had first met, the teacher introducing the new student to the class. How gentle her smile was; how badly he had been smitten. He recalled as if it were yesterday that long ago day when the entire country had been consumed by fear and dread as word of Sputnik spread. Closing his eyes, he could envision himself again in that one magic moment, when so many things had suddenly become clear …

***

October, 1957
Carl lay next to Marta on the blanket, the coolness of the damp grass penetrating the weave of the fabric, a brisk chill in the evening air. They looked upwards, watching the night sky above.

"Why does it really matter?" Marta asked, rolling onto her side to look at Carl. "Who cares who was first?"

"Because that was supposed to be *us*!" Carl protested angrily. "The Reds were not supposed to be able to do something like that."

"So?"

"So if we were wrong about that, what else are we wrong about?" he asked. "Don't you see? If they can put a satellite in orbit above us, why couldn't it be an A bomb to drop down on us? Or a camera, constantly taking our picture?"

"Humph," Marta said, rolling onto her back again. "Well, I don't like that."

"There! There it is," Carl said, pointing to the northwest.

"Where? I don't see anything," Marta replied.

"Right there," Carl emphasized, stabbing at the sky. "Wow, look at how fast it is."

"Oh, I see it," Marta said excitedly, spotting the rapidly moving star speeding toward the southeast.

The two lay unspeaking, watching the Soviet satellite traverse the sky. Finally, it disappeared from view to the south.

"It's like they're rubbing our faces in it," Carl finally said, visibly agitated.

"Well what can we do?" Marta asked, rolling on her side again. "There's not much you or I can do about it."

"I know what I'm going to do," Carl said with determination. "I'm going to get Mr. Pierce to write a letter for me to the University of Alabama. He knows people there in the science department. I'm going to be an engineer and work on rockets." Turning to face Marta, he added, "I'm not going to let some Red bastards beat us into space."

Marta frowned deeply. "Carl! Watch your language," she scolded. Then, reaching up to gently stroke his hair, she said, "You could, you know. If you really wanted to."

"Could what?"

"Be an engineer. A rocket scientist. You're the smartest man I know, after all. After my father, of course," she added with a twinkle.

Hearing her call him a man warmed Carl's soul. "You believe I can do it, don't you?" he asked, uncertainly.

"Of course I do," she reassured him, continuing to stroke his hair. "I think you can do anything you put your mind to. Because I love you."

Carl's eyes widened. At that moment his entire future snapped into focus. He knew what he was going to do with his life with absolute certainty, and who he was going to do it with.

***

"Dr. Heinel? Can you hear me? Dr. Heinel?" Carl was snapped back to reality by Robbie's faint but urgent voice on the radio. Turning the volume up, he replied. "Yes, I can hear you, Mr. Robichaud."

"You had me worried, Dr. Heinel, I was about to send Mike to get you. Time, Dr. Heinel. You need to head back. We're going to have to start winding down the excursion shortly."

"All right, Mr. Robichaud, thank you."

Their time on the surface was up. Carl once again pulled the small slate urn from his gear bag and held it in his lap. *What do I do with you now?* he thought, looking at it forlornly. He considered that here might be a suitable final resting place, the Apollo lander becoming a monument to his dear wife. Glancing around the top of the Falcon, he searched for a place to tuck the urn. Then a conversation from a week ago suddenly sprang into his mind. *What was it that Tom had said?* They were standing in the restroom on the morning of launch day. As he was leaving, Tom had turned to Carl and asked, "How does it feel to be on the verge of finally achieving the goal you've spent your life working to accomplish?"

Carl had simply answered, "Satisfied. Very satisfied." Reflecting on that conversation, he realized that everything in his life, his entire existence, had led to this place and time. Looking ahead to the future, he saw … nothing. Everyone he had ever loved had been taken from him. Few if any friends and acquaintances remained, and those few were not long for the world. The biggest challenge he had ever faced in his life was now behind him. And he realized that the thought of leaving Marta here alone was unbearable. His place was here with her. Forever.

"Mr. Armac," Carl quietly said, "I just wanted to thank you for helping this foolish old man fulfill his final dream."

Startled, Tom turned from assisting Mike with the loading of rock samples and faced the distant Apollo lander. "What's that, Dr. Heinel?"

"And Mr. Robichaud, I want you to know that this is indeed my desire," Carl next said.

Robbie also stopped and turned to face the Falcon.

"I just want you all to know how very satisfied I am," Carl said softly. He then turned off his suit radio.

Robbie turned to Mike in alarm. "Mike, let's go, now!" he called out, breaking into the fastest lope he could manage. "Dr. Heinel, we're on our way, wait for us," he shouted. "Dr. Heinel!"

Carl couldn't hear Robbie's shouts. Reaching up, he switched off each of the systems for his suit, securing the oxygen flow, the pressurization system, the circulation of cooling water. Taking one long, deep breath, he spun open the suit's pressure relief valve, allowing its bubble of life sustaining atmosphere to bleed out into the vacuum. As the pressure escaped, he exhaled deeply to save himself the agony of ruptured lungs.

Curious, he thought, as a seltzer-like bubbling began in his mouth and sinuses as the moisture in his body began to boil away. "Oh Marta," he mouthed silently, his vision darkening and fading as consciousness fled. He squeezed the urn between his hands one last time, wanting the reassurance of knowing that she was there with him.

And then Carl felt the familiar warm embrace once again. A light caress on his cheek drew his attention. Looking up, his wife stood smiling gently before him bathed in radiant light, her hand moving from his cheek to reach up and lightly stoke his hair. "My love," she said passionately.

"Marta!" Carl said, enraptured. His attention was then drawn to movement beyond her. Peering into the light, he saw his sons Alan and John. His beautiful, beautiful children. "The boys!" he said joyfully, rising and reaching toward them.

"In a moment, love," Marta said, placing her arms around him. "First, dance with me."

***

"Robbie? Robbie, this is Long Beach, what's going on?" Jean called urgently.

"Robbie? This is Atlantis, what's happening? Is everyone OK?"

"All stations all stations please be *quiet*," Robbie gasped, breathing hard as he struggled to cover the remaining distance to the Falcon, with Mike following closely behind. "We don't know, it's something with Dr. Heinel, we're almost there."

Robbie spotted Carl sitting on the Falcon's porch, his suit slumped forward. He leaped off the ground as he approached the lander's ladder, smacking hard against it, but managing to grab hold and getting a boot on the second ladder rung. Hauling himself quickly upward, he climbed rapidly to the porch and peered through Carl's faceplate. Robbie could clearly see he was dead.

"What did you do," Robbie muttered, quickly scanning Carl's suit, finding that he had turned off all of the life support systems. He quickly toggled the row of switches to reenergize and repressurize the suit. Carl appeared to sit upward as pressure in the suit climbed. Robbie could see the red under-pressure alarm blinking inside Carl's helmet. Looking again at the suit, he found the opened pressure relief valve and closed it.

Mike arrived at the bottom of the ladder. "How is he? Is he OK?" he asked frantically.

Robbie delivered the sad news. "Dr. Heinel is dead," he announced. "He appears to have turned off his suit and depressurized it."

"What? Get him down, let's get him back to Tinkerbell!" Mike exclaimed, leaping up in an attempt to grab the boot of Carl's suit. "We can do CPR. Let's get him back in the lander!"

"Mike! He's gone," Robbie said sternly. "It would take us twenty minutes to carry him all the way back to Tink. And how are we going to get him back inside?"

"Do you want us to come help?" Robbie heard Tom ask.

"No point, stay there. Besides, didn't you hear what Dr. Heinel said?"

"What do you mean?" Mike asked, dejectedly.

"He called me, and said 'this is my desire'. He clearly wanted me to know that this was intentional."

Robbie looked back at Carl. He paused for a moment, and then turned Carl's suit systems back off again.

"Dr. Carl," Mike sobbed gently. "I was supposed to watch out for you … "

Robbie put his hand on top of Carl's helmet. "Thank you for all you've done, my friend," he said sincerely. "Rest peacefully."

***

The crew went joylessly through the motions of stowing their remaining gear and re-boarding Tinkerbell. As Atlantis swooped down toward perilune, they glumly strapped themselves in to prepare for liftoff.

"Long Beach, Tinkerbell, we are in position and standing by," Robbie reported.

"Copy that Tinkerbell," Jean acknowledged. It seemed distasteful to offer up congratulations on conclusion of the surface excursion.

"Tinkerbell, Atlantis, the porch light is on, ready to receive you back home," Stephanie radioed from orbit.

"Roger Tinkerbell, I think we're all about ready to return," Robbie said, speaking aloud the feelings they all felt.

Everyone waited patiently, alone in their individual thoughts, while the seconds counted down. At the appropriate time, the lander's guidance system restarted the Wizard engine, and the crew departed the surface.

Robbie turned his head to watch the Falcon as they began the boost into orbit. He continued watching until it disappeared from view.

***

The automatic guidance system flew Tinkerbell to within a thousand yards of Atlantis. Taking manual control of the lander, Robbie then began closing the distance, aiming to park just within reach of the shuttle's remote arm.

"Nine hundred yards," Stephanie called out, talking Robbie in. "Still nine hundred. Eight fifty. Eight hundred. A bit slow Robbie, you might want to pick up the pace a little."

"Roger, Atlantis," Robbie answered, applying a quick burst with the maneuvering thrusters to increase their closing rate.

"Seven fifty. A bit left. That's better. Five hundred. Now you're looking a bit hot," Stephanie warned, indicating that the lander was approaching a little too rapidly.

"Copy that, I'll slow her down," Robbie replied, applying some reverse thrust.

"Three hundred. Two hundred. One fifty. I'd slow her just a bit more," Stephanie suggested.

"Roger, Atlantis." Whether it was due to fatigue or the shock of Carl's death, Robbie momentarily lost focus and forgot that Tinkerbell was once again upside down in relation to Atlantis. He moved the thruster hand controller in the direction necessary to slow the vehicle for a surface landing, which was the opposite direction from the one he intended, actually accelerating it toward the shuttle.

"Robbie!" Stephanie called out sharply.

Instantly recognizing his mistake, Robbie coolly applied a sustained burst of reverse thrust to slow the lander's approach. "Got it," he said. "Sorry, I lost it for a moment."

Each burst of the thrusters caused the support struts they were attached to to flex slightly, stressing the strut's welds. As Robbie fired the sustained burst to slow Tinkerbell's too fast approach, the fractured weld on the number three strut finally failed completely, allowing the strut latch to release. In an instant, the force of the firing thruster folded the strut upward around the base of the lander. The now off-center thrust still being applied from the other rockets caused Tinkerbell to roll rapidly to starboard.

In horror, Stephanie and Vivian watched as the lander quickly rolled counterclockwise and smashed into the open cargo bay doors on Atlantis' starboard side. Instantly, a large vapor cloud formed and quickly expanded, as the impact crushed the doors and breached the orbiter coolant system lines that ran through the door mounted radiator panels. "Collision! Robbie!" Stephanie shouted.

Robbie felt the lander roll suddenly, followed by the sudden jolt of the collision. The view in his goggles became a confusing jumble. Pulling them from his face, he anxiously scanned the lander's displays.

"Atlantis, Tinkerbell, we're OK, no hull breach," he reported. "What the hell happened? Could you tell?"

"One of your starboard support struts folded up, and the thrust imbalance threw you into the side of the cargo bay."

"Is Atlantis damaged?" he asked anxiously.

"Don't worry about us, let's concentrate on getting you back on board," she replied.

He knew instantly that they were in big trouble. Otherwise she would have simply said "No."

"Roger, Atlantis. Can you reach us with the remote arm?"

"Negative, you're too high, and drawing slowly left. I can't reach you from here."

Robbie put his goggles back on and tried to make sense of what he was seeing. "I'll see if I can nudge us back into range." He shut down the number three thruster cluster and tried to use the remaining ones to fly the ship.

"Robbie, stop, whatever you're doing, you're making it worse!" Stephanie called out sharply.

"I can't figure out what's going on, this doesn't make sense," he replied with frustration as he looked around. "Everything looks distorted and I'm seeing double in areas."

Vivian recognized the problem. "Robbie, your number three support strut is folded up over the bottom of the vehicle, but the visualization software doesn't know that. The camera on the strut is still working, and the software is still blending the image from that camera into your goggle display, which is messing up the visual field."

"OK. What do we do about it?"

Vivian bit her lip. "Nothing. We'd have to rewrite the source code to delete the video stream from that camera and build an image with just the remaining three."

"Then how am I supposed to fly the vehicle?" Robbie asked angrily. Thinking for a moment, he yanked the goggles off his head. "Steph, you're going to have to talk me down."

"Are you sure, Robbie?"

"I don't see any other option. Remember I don't have number three cluster, you're going to have to fly me back without it."

"Copy," Stephanie said, determined. "OK, half second burst on one A."

"Roger," Robbie said, toggling the appropriate switches and pushing briefly on the hand controller.

For the next fifteen minutes, they learned through trial and error how to fly as a team to maneuver the lander back within range of the remote arm.

***

"This isn't quite the Christmas I was expecting," Robbie said glumly, as he and Stephanie looked out the aft flight deck windows and studied the damage to the cargo bay doors. Turning to face her, he said grimly, "You know we can't land her with that damage."

"I know, I just haven't fully absorbed it yet," Stephanie replied.

"I guess we should tell the others," Robbie said.

"I'm sure they know. Vivian was standing here watching and she knows this vehicle inside out."

"Well, let's see what the ground has for us," Robbie said. "Long Beach, Atlantis, have you analyzed the imagery?"

"Atlantis, Long Beach, yes, I'm afraid we have. I can't say we're encouraged," Jean replied.

"Your recommendation?" Robbie asked.

"We're going to need more time to study the situation, Atlantis. In the meantime, conduct your trans-Earth injection burn and let's get you back here closer to home where we might be able to assist better."

"Roger, Long Beach," Robbie answered. Turning to Stephanie, he added, "We're in big, big trouble."

"I know," she said quietly, looking again at the damage in the bay.

CHAPTER FORTY–SIX

Robbie and Stephanie joined the rest of the crew on the middeck. "Here's where we are right now," Robbie explained. "With the damage to the bay doors, we won't be able to close the bay."

"So we won't be able to land," Mike observed.

"We have the ground looking at it," Robbie replied.

"Do they think they may be able to suggest something?" Tom asked.

"Don't know," Robbie replied. "Like I said, they're looking at it. We hope to know more in a day or so."

"Do we have any idea how this happened?" Tom asked.

"Just that apparently number three strut folded up during approach, and the thrust imbalance threw us into the starboard bay doors," Robbie answered.

"I am so sorry," Vivian said, distraught. "We checked every single weld! I can't understand how this could have happened."

"Doesn't matter," Robbie said, matter-of-factly. "Knowing won't help our present situation one bit. Our only concern is what we do from here."

"What DO we do from here?" Nikki asked.

"For now, we're planning on conducting the trans-Earth injection burn on schedule to start for home," Robbie answered.

"Why bother," Mike said dejectedly. "We can't reenter and land. Maybe it would be better to just stay here … "

Everyone stared at Mike in disbelief.

"Look," Robbie said, "I understand. With Dr. Heinel's death and now this, things suck right now. But if we're going to have any chance at all, it means getting back to Earth orbit where someone might be able to help us."

"Help us how?"

"They're looking into whether anyone is in a position to launch a rescue mission."

"A rescue mission?" Elton asked. "How are they going to take the seven of us off a crippled orbiter?"

"Like I said, they're looking into it," Robbie said again encouragingly.

"Well I know EtherX doesn't have anything ready to launch," Elton observed. "And our Minotaur capsule doesn't have a functional life support system yet."

"NASA has nothing," Tom noted. "I think the Russians and the Chinese are the only ones who could possibly launch some form of rescue." Turning to Robbie, he asked, "how much time will we have left once we reach Earth orbit?"

Robbie frowned. "We project about twelve to sixteen hours of oxygen. If we could stretch that some, the cryogens for the fuel cells would be gone after twenty-four hours, so no more power."

"That's not much of a window."

"Yeah, I know. We were already pushing the outer boundaries of the ship's endurance with this mission. I'm really kicking myself for the O2 we wasted on unnecessary training on the outbound leg."

"As you said, it doesn't matter now," Stephanie chided him. "The past is past, only what we do next matters."

Everyone was quiet for a moment, digesting the information.

"So if someone isn't able to come rescue us within a day of reaching Earth orbit..." Mike asked.

Robbie shrugged his shoulders and shook his head. "I'm sorry."

***

Atlantis again fired its OMS engines, this time freeing itself from the moon's gravitational hold. Four hours after breaking orbit, Jean called Robbie. "Atlantis, Long Beach, over."

"Go Long Beach," Robbie responded.

"I'm afraid we don't have any good news," Jean said sadly.

"Truthfully, I wasn't expecting any."

"With the degree of damage the starboard doors sustained, it's extremely unlikely the centerline latches are functional, and you won't be able to lock them shut."

"Concur," Robbie agreed. He had already reached the same conclusion.

"We've analyzed every possible entry angle, and we can't find a single profile that would allow you to reenter without the vehicle sustaining catastrophic damage."

"So if we try, we're Columbia all over again," Robbie said. Jean was silent. Robbie then asked, "What would our chances be?"

"Less than two percent chance of survivable reentry with the bay doors unlatched and ajar," Jean replied precisely.

"Well, two percent is better than nothing, I suppose," Robbie said glumly. "How about a rescue? Is there anyone available to come pick us up?"

"Negative. The Russians say they're at least a month away from being able to launch a vehicle. Even if they could, a Soyuz would only have room for two passengers."

"Well, two would have been better than none. How about the Chinese?"

"They haven't even responded to our request."

"Well wasn't that neighborly of them," Robbie smirked.

"We asked the Pentagon if they had any assets," Jean continued. "The Air Force claims they could configure the payload bay of an X-37B to act as a lifeboat for seven passengers."

"Really?" Robbie asked, feeling the first glimmer of hope.

"Unfortunately, they say if they moved heaven and earth, they thought they could get one on the pad by this time next month."

"Which will be four weeks too late for us," Robbie said with a grimace.

"We even called all the commercial aerospace companies, hoping maybe one of them had something they might be working on under the radar that could do the job."

"How did that go?" Robbie asked.

"Let's just say that only works in the movies," Jean replied.

"And we were so hoping for a happy ending," Robbie sighed.

"Sorry, Robbie," Jean said.

"OK then, I have something I'd like you to do for me," Robbie asked.

"What's that?"

"I'd like you to run the numbers and see if we have enough fuel to do a mid-course that would let us match orbits with the ISS."

"You want to rendezvous with the space station?"

"Affirmative. Run the numbers, see if we have enough fuel to rendezvous with the ISS."

"But why? It's a derelict. Or are you thinking … "

"Yeah, I'm thinking. There's still a Soyuz docked there. It could possibly get three of my crew home safely."

"Robbie, it's been abandoned on orbit for over two and a half years. It's long past its shelf life."

"A drowning man will grab at anything that might float," Robbie mused. "Just run the numbers, tell me if it's possible."

"And if it is?"

"I'll present it to the crew and see which odds they like better—the small chance of being able to fire up the Soyuz and get three people back to their loved ones, or the even smaller one of trying to bring Atlantis down intact with everyone on board."

***

"So you're saying … " Tom asked.

"I'm saying we can do nothing," Robbie explained. "In that case we're all guaranteed to die within twenty-four hours of reaching Earth orbit when our air is exhausted."

"Not a fan of that outcome."

"Or we can try and fly Atlantis back, and have a ninety-eight percent chance of ending up as a really nice meteor."

"Still looking for an idea I can embrace."

"Or, we can alter course and rendezvous with the space station, where I hope it may be possible to use the Soyuz capsule that's still docked there."

"You won't be able to get everyone on board though," Elton noted.

"No, we won't. Only three of us. But I figure that's better than options one or two."

"You'd be one of the three, so I can see why you'd favor that plan," Elton said. "You're the only one trained to fly a Soyuz."

Robbie bristled. "Actually, I thought Stephanie would fly it. She received Soyuz familiarization training for her ISS crew certification. The reentry process is automated enough that she can handle it."

Stephanie started to object, but Robbie held up his hand and said, "End of discussion."

"Option three sounds like the way to go then," Mike said.

"But that Soyuz will be stone cold dead after almost three years in space," Elton objected.

"We don't know that," Robbie argued. "Spacecraft are built very conservatively. There's a chance it might still power up."

"So if only three people could be saved," Nikki asked quietly, looking at everyone, "how would we decide who it would be?"

"I don't know. Rock-paper-scissors, maybe. I'd wait until we saw whether the capsule was still flyable before making that decision."

Everyone nodded. The prospect of spending days drifting toward Earth burdened by the knowledge of who would have a chance at survival and who would almost certainly die was too terrible to contemplate.

"So are we agreed then?" Robbie asked. "All in favor of rendezvousing with the ISS, raise your hand."

The vote was unanimous.

"Good," Robbie nodded. "One more thing. Mission control calculates that we have just barely enough fuel to alter our course and match the station's orbital inclination. But we'll need to lighten the ship by jettisoning Tinkerbell to be sure."

"But all of the lunar material we collected! We'll lose it!" Vivian objected.

"Do you want to be alive, safe on the ground, or dead in space, but with a really nice rock collection?" Robbie asked. "Simple as that."

"It's just, we've lost so much," Vivian said somberly. "Can't we do an EVA and remove at least some of the lunar samples?" Vivian implored.

"No time," Robbie replied. "It wouldn't be quick, it would take three or four hours minimum. We're closing quickly on L1, and we need to be ready to do our course correction burn by then to have any hope of matching orbits with the station."

"L1?" Nikki asked.

"Lunar libration, the point where we leave the moon's gravity well and enter the Earth's," Robbie explained. "It's where we can accomplish the largest course change with the least amount of fuel. If we miss it by too much, then we won't have enough fuel to slow down when we get back to Earth. Then it's bye-bye us as we just sail off into the black." Turning to Stephanie, he said, "Steph, you go ahead and get set up to push Tink overboard. Mike and I are going to go pull the Orlans into Atlantis."

"Do you think we'll need them?" she asked.

"Maybe, not sure yet, but it gives us options. I'd hate to find out later that we should have kept them and be totally screwed."

***

Robbie and Mike passed the spacesuits from the lander back into Atlantis, where Tom and Elton stowed them. As they finished, Stephanie grappled Tinkerbell with the remote arm.

Everyone gathered on the flight deck to say farewell. With a slow smooth motion Stephanie lifted the lander out of the cargo bay, and then with a quick flip of the arm pushed Tinkerbell overboard to drift off into space. As they watched, the large graphic of the lander's namesake on the side of the vehicle rotated slowly into view.

"It's like losing another member of the family," Vivian said sadly.

"She was a good ship," Robbie said with a nod. "Right up to the point where she let us down."

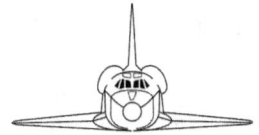

CHAPTER FORTY–SEVEN

"Atlantis, Long Beach, that's a good correction, we show you on track," Jean reported.

"Copy that Long Beach," Robbie answered. The burn had succeeded in altering their trajectory enough to allow them to match the orbital inclination of the space station.

"How's everybody holding up?" Jean asked.

"Good under the circumstances. It's not Joyville, but everyone's keeping their heads about them. Any chance you've been able to pull a rabbit out of your hat since yesterday?"

"Negative, no change in the situation here. Still haven't heard from the Chinese, but we're not really expecting an answer at this point. I wish I could offer more hope."

"Well, at least we have three more days to pray for a miracle," Robbie noted. "Thanks, Long Beach. Atlantis out."

The next three days were the longest and grimmest of their lives.

***

Tom approached Robbie as the rest of the crew slept. "Can I talk to you a minute?" he asked.

"Sure, what's up?" Robbie said, turning off his e-book reader.

"I wanted to ask you what you really believe the chances are that we'll be able to use the Soyuz on the station to get three people home."

"Well, they're not good, but they're a hell of a lot better than trying to fly Atlantis back," Robbie replied honestly. "So far we've been pretty lucky. Maybe our luck will hold a little longer."

"Lucky? What the hell do you find lucky about this?" Tom asked in amazement.

"Well, for starters, Tinkerbell could have punched a hole in the crew compartment, and then we wouldn't be sitting here having this conversation. Next, we could have come up short on fuel. It wouldn't have taken too many more degrees of deviation from the station's inclination to have put it beyond reach. Most importantly, there's the fact that the station is even still orbiting."

"What do you mean?"

"If the sun hadn't been in a good mood lately, the station would have probably dropped from orbit by now. But after the accident they were able to remotely raise its orbit using the Progress supply ship that was still docked there, and the quiet solar cycle means the atmosphere isn't all bloated, creating more drag."

Tom nodded. "OK, so maybe we're a little bit lucky then, although I think we're still suffering from a major deficit. In the event that our luck holds, I'd like to point out that Vivian is really small."

"I've noticed," Robbie replied with a smile.

"I think she could be squeezed in as a forth passenger, possibly even ride in somebody's lap if she had too."

"I've thought the same thing," Robbie nodded. "She and Steph together would equal one large male, so maybe. I don't want to get anyone's hopes up though until we see if we're going to have a capsule to work with."

"I understand," Tom said, relieved. The thought of four of them surviving rather than just three was comforting. "When the time comes, I don't think we need to draw straws or anything."

"Why's that?"

"It's my fault we're all here," Tom replied.

"How do you figure?"

"The only people who had the ability to say, "No, not going to happen," were Dr. Heinel and me. No one else could have pulled the plug on the entire project. But it was really just me, because Dr. Heinel was consumed by the need to fulfill an obligation and had no other choice."

"Well I don't know if I completely agree with you, but what of it? Any of us could have changed our minds about coming."

"But you're all here because I convinced you, or inspired you, or somehow enabled you to believe it was possible," Tom said guiltily.

Robbie looked at Tom for a moment, and then shrugged his shoulders. "OK, it's all your fault, if it makes you feel better. So what exactly are you trying to say?"

"I'm saying I intend to stay here onboard Atlantis. Stephanie and Vivian should fly the Soyuz back, along with Nikki and Elton."

Robbie considered for a moment. "Well, I'm chivalrous enough to agree that the women should go, but I think maybe we should let Elton and Mike sort it out from there."

"I think I know Mike well enough to know how he'd feel. Elton is a guest. He's a paying passenger, but he's our guest, and we owe him a chance to survive our screw up."

Robbie nodded. "Ok, well, I'd still rather hear it from them, but let's not worry about it anymore until we see if the Soyuz is even an option."

"Agreed," Tom said. "But if it is, then afterwards ... "

"Yes?"

"If we can get the Soyuz to work and they get off OK, well, I think we should try and land Atlantis. At least it would be a chance."

"I've thought that too," Robbie agreed. "If it were just me, well, I'd probably just suck it up and accept the hand I'd been dealt, because asphyxiation sounds a hell of a lot less painful than incineration, and I guess I'm kind of a coward that way."

Tom cringed.

"But as the commander of the mission, I owe it to the rest of you to at least try and get you back alive. So that's probably what I'll recommend. But it might not even be possible."

"Why is that?"

"Fuel. We'll be sucking fumes at that point, so if I can't nail the rendezvous with the station on the first try, there's no guarantee we'd even have the fuel left to attempt a deorbit burn."

"OK then, I guess we'll just have to see what happens. Thanks for the talk," Tom said.

"Don't mention it. By the way ... "

"Yes?" Tom asked.

"You're a good man, Tom Armac. Just thought I'd point that out."

***

The Earth grew steadily in the cockpit windows until it once again dominated their view. Atlantis fired its OMS engines to slow the spacecraft and allow it to drop into orbit. Swinging rapidly by just above the limits of the atmosphere, Robbie watched Earth's surface pass by with a melancholy sense of despondency. *So close*, he thought. *So very, very close.* After a journey of a half million miles, the mere sixty or so miles of atmosphere that separated them from the planet below presented an impenetrable barrier that would wreck fatal destruction upon them if they attempted its traverse. They were supposed to return as triumphant explorers. Instead, they were castaways, adrift in the infinite ocean of space, the safe shores of home within view but just beyond their reach.

***

With the Earth orbit insertion burn successfully concluded, Robbie gingerly piloted Atlantis toward a rendezvous with the wreckage of the International Space Station. "My God," Stephanie softly muttered as they slowly drew closer.

Robbie whistled. "That is a mess, for sure," he said, shaking his head as he examined the station, the Dreamlifter unmanned vehicle embedding in its side like a giant dart. "It looks like the entire side of Destiny and Unity are shredded where the ship hit it. They never had a chance."

"Where do you want to place us?"

"I'm going to park right there, below the radiators," Robbie said, pointing to an area below the station's primary truss. "From there you can grapple the S1 truss with the arm so that I'll have a bridge to work across to make my way to the Quest airlock."

"OK," Stephanie acknowledged, unstrapping from the pilot's seat and drifting to the aft control station. "Let me know when you think you're set."

"This looks good right … here," Robbie said, releasing his controller. "Take it and see if you can get us in range to grab hold."

Stephanie flew Atlantis the remaining few yards from the aft control station and then activated the remote arm to reach up and latch on to the anchor point on the station's truss above them. "OK, there we go," she said, as she pulled Atlantis closer to the station.

"Good job. OK, I'll go get ready," Robbie said, heading to the mid-deck to begin preparing to board the station.

"So we're there?" Mike asked, as Robbie descended from the flight deck.

"Yep, did pretty well on fuel also."

"So how long before we know?"

"It will take me an hour to get ready, then maybe thirty minutes once I clear the airlock to work my way up the arm to the truss and then across to Quest. Provided I can get it open OK, then it's not far from there to the docking module where the Soyuz is located. As soon as I can enter it I'll know within five minutes whether we have a viable spacecraft or not. I want you to come suit up with me, in case I end up needing some help. I'd like you to be sitting in the airlock ready to go."

"OK," Mike replied, as they headed for the airlock together.

***

Entering the cargo bay, Robbie glanced briefly to his left at the damaged bay doors. For a moment he felt compelled to make a closer inspection, but then shook his head. "It doesn't matter," he told himself, and turned toward the remote arm, which reached up from the bay to the station above. Moving slowly and deliberately, he used the handholds on the arm as a ladder to work his way upward.

"OK, I'm on the truss, I'm going to start making my way across now," he reported.

"Be careful," Stephanie cautioned.

"Yeah, wouldn't want anything to happen to me, that would be terrible," Robbie chuckled.

"Stop it," Stephanie said.

"Sorry, you're right, it's not funny." A moment later, he said, "OK, I'm across, making my way down to the airlock now."

Robbie worked his way along the length of the Quest airlock module and carefully reached out to grab the circular handrail around the crew lock door. Pulling open the insulated door cover, he read the interior pressure on the lock's gauge.

"No pressure in the lock. Tell Tom we just had another bit of good luck."

Onboard Atlantis, Tom looked quizzically at Stephanie.

"If the inner doors had been closed and the lock had remained pressurized, he might not have been able to get it vented," she explained. "The door opens inward and there's no way to open it with pressure inside." Tom nodded.

"OK," Robbie said with a grunt, "trying to cycle the mechanism now." With a mighty yank, the latch released, allowing the door to open inward an inch.

"Got it," Robbie said, pushing with his shoulder. The door slowly swung inward. Pulling himself through the open hatch, he entered the dark interior of the lock. Switching on his helmet lights, he turned toward the inner equipment lock and the Unity node beyond.

"Geeze Louise!" he suddenly yelled.

"Robbie? What's wrong?" Stephanie called.

Floating in front of Robbie was the body of one of the station crew, illuminated in the beam from his helmet lights.

"I just got met by the welcoming committee," Robbie replied. "Looks like one of the Russian crew members."

"Can you tell who?" Stephanie asked. They knew many of the Russians from their years of working and training together.

"No, and I'd rather not stop to take a look, if that's all right," Robbie replied, a shiver running up his spine. Gently pushing the corpse aside, he started working his way toward the main body of the station. Entering the Unity node from the Quest airlock, he glanced to his left toward the mating adapter that connected to the Zarya module and the direction he needed to go.

"Things look really different with the lights out," he commented. "It's easy to get turned around." Pulling himself along, he floated above the entry to the Leonardo module below, which had been used as a storeroom for the station. As his helmet lights briefly illuminated the module's interior, a subtle movement caught his eye. Backing up slightly, he shone his lights down into the module. He saw several more bodies drifting slowly about the compartment.

"Looks like I found more of the crew," he said grimly. "They were probably working in Leonardo making room for the gear that was supposed to arrive on the Dreamlifter."

"Can you tell how many?" Stephanie asked.

"Not really, no, and I'm heading to the Russian section now," he replied. "I'll stop on the way back to check."

It was a tight fit squeezing through the mating adapter connecting the US and Russian station segments in his Orlan. Once through, it was much easier to navigate the length of the compartment. Finally, he reached the service module, to which the Poisk docking adapter was attached.

"OK, I'm entering the docking adapter," he reported. "Looks like I found another one."

Above him was the circular access hatch to the Soyuz capsule. A pair of legs extended from the open port. Reaching up to grab the body's left foot, he slowly extracted it from the capsule.

"It's Gennady," Robbie said, reading the name 'Usarov' on the corpse's jumper. "He must have been trying to make it to the capsule when he lost consciousness." He gently pushed the body against the bulkhead of the module.

"Sorry buddy," Robbie said, as he squeezed past and into the capsule. His backpack caught on the hatch frame, and it was with great effort that he was able to finally struggle through the hatch and into the Soyuz's orbital module, the upper of the vehicle's two compartments. Turning himself around, he then repeated the process, squeezing feet first through the interior hatch into the lower descent module.

"OK, I'm in," he reported. "Everyone cross your fingers."

Reaching up to the electrical distribution panel, he briefly studied the Cyrillic labels to refamiliarize himself with the switches. Choosing what he believed was the correct set, he switched on battery power to the main bus. Nothing happened. Hoping he had misread the labels, he tried several other switch combinations, and then began furiously toggling every switch on the panel.

There was no effect. He punched the panel in frustration. Taking a deep breath and exhaling, Robbie felt the last vestiges of hope flow from his body. "Steph?" he said.

"Yes?" she answered anxiously.

"No joy, Atlantis. This bird is dead." *And so are we*, he thought with great sadness.

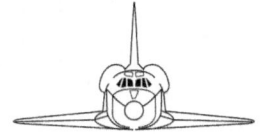

CHAPTER FORTY–EIGHT

Robbie slumped deeply into his spacesuit in defeat. For a moment, he considered whether he had it within him to emulate Carl's final act. How simple it would be to just turn everything off and bleed away his suit's atmosphere to the vacuum, quickly joining in death his former colleagues here on the station. But while he couldn't save his crew, his obligation to them as their commander would not allow him to abandon them to their fates.

"OK, Steph, I guess I'm coming back," he said.

"All right, Robbie," she replied. He could hear the sorrow in her voice.

"I'll go ahead and do a sweep of the station to see what happened to everyone before I return."

"Robbie?" she said tentatively.

"Yes?"

"It's not your fault."

"Oh hell, Steph, I know that, we gave it our best shot, we just ran out of luck is all."

Climbing from the Soyuz capsule, Robbie scanned the remaining volume of the service module, and finding no one, pulled himself back to the station's US section. Taking a deep breath, he dropped down into the Leonardo module, where he knew he'd find many of the crew.

"OK, Steph, I'll give you the names," he said. "You already got Gennady, he was in the Soyuz."

"Yes, I wrote it down," she confirmed.

Robbie grasped the closest of the floating bodies. The postmortem swelling from exposure to vacuum had distorted the face, making it difficult to identify. He depended instead on the name patch on the jumper.

"OK, the first one is Uri Veselov." Gently pushing the body aside, he reached for another. "The next one is Tom Reynolds," he said, pushing it away in turn. As they drifted, the corpses bumped into the numerous unsecured stowage containers drifting about, setting off a morbid chain reaction.

"There's a lot of loose gear in here," Robbie radioed. "They must have been rearranging the module to stow the new cargo." As he spoke, a white fiberglass cylinder shaped like an oversized beer keg bumped the side of his helmet.

"What the hell," he said, pushing the object away. His push imparted a rotation to the container, and large Cyrillic labeling spun into view as he reached to grasp the next body.

Robbie froze. Turning around, he chased after the floating object, seizing it and studying the labeling on the container. Then, looking rapidly around, he started searching frantically to see if he could find any others.

"Steph, I'm afraid there's no time to finish this," he said excitedly, as he located another of the floating kegs deeper in the module. "Tell Mike I need him to join me at the arm, I have some gear to pass to him."

"Say again, Robbie?" Stephanie asked, confused.

"I need Mike to get his ass outside and up the arm and meet me at the S1 truss *now!*"

***

Robbie had three of the large white cylinders staged in the Quest airlock. He'd searched exhaustively for more, but he could only find three. Taking a tether from the gear rack, he secured it to one of the containers, and then attached the other end to his spacesuit.

"How are you coming, Mike?" Robbie asked.

"I'm just reaching the top of the arm now," Mike answered.

Robbie exited the airlock and retraced his original route, climbing up onto the main station truss. He could see the helmet of Mike's spacesuit sticking up beyond it. Meeting him at the top of the arm, he unclipped the tethered cylinder from his suit and attached it to Mike's.

"Take that down to the cargo bay, and tie it off really good," Robbie directed. "Then come back here. I have two more to pass over to you. Once they're all tied down, I want you to go back inside."

"What is it?" Mike asked, looking at the white cylindrical object.

"That, my friend, is your ride home."

Mike's eyes grew large with astonishment.

***

"Robbie, what's going on," Stephanie demanded.

"A miracle, I think," he replied, as he checked to ensure that all three cylinders were securely strapped to the cargo bay forward bulkhead.

"Tell me what you found," she demanded.

Robbie spoke rapidly. "Steph, I have three Russian paracones here. I

344

found them in the Leonardo module. If one hadn't smacked me in the helmet, I'd have never seen it. I looked everywhere, and I could only find three. That's OK though, three's OK."

"Russian paracones?" Stephanie asked uncertainly.

"Don't you remember? We were briefed on them. When shuttle stopped flying, there wasn't a way for the station crew to get large cargo and completed experiments back on the ground. So they developed an inflatable reentry module."

"Oh, you mean the MOOSE clone," she said.

"Yes! That's it. I heard the tests went pretty well, so they made several for operational deployment. But I guess they hadn't started using them yet."

Standing beside Stephanie on the flight deck, Vivian asked, "What's 'MOOSE'?"

"Man Out Of Space Easiest," Stephanie answered. "It was a design from the sixties for a quick and dirty way to get someone down from orbit in an emergency. Like a lifeboat. NASA never built it, but the Russians did some experiments."

"Wait, what now? I've never heard of this."

"The design was very simple. It was a Nomex and nylon fabric shell coated with an ablative layer. It inflated into a large shuttlecock shape. An astronaut would climb in and pull the ripcord, and the MOOSE would inflate, fire a solid rocket to deorbit, and then open a parachute once it had completed reentry."

"And this works?" Vivian asked, incredulously.

"We don't know, it was never tried." Looking back out at the cargo bay, she said, "So Robbie, what are you thinking?"

"You know damn well what I'm thinking, Steph. This is your ticket home. We're going to put you in them and light 'em up and get you down on the surface."

"But they've never been tried," Stephanie protested.

"You're seriously going to tell me you're worried they might not be safe?" Robbie laughed. "Steph, we're all going to be dead in less than twelve hours. If they don't work, what difference does a few hours one way or the other make?"

"What makes you think they'll even operate? Their batteries are probably completely dead."

"I'm sure they are, but you really didn't pay attention to that brief, did you? They're Russian—they use the same batteries as the Orlans! And we have five of those onboard. Well, four, because you can't have mine. Look, here's what I need you to do. First, I want you to pull the batteries out of all the Orlans, and stack them in the airlock. Next, get everyone into their launch suits. Get them all on oxygen and ready for EVA. Don't let anyone touch their suit O2 supplies—make sure they're breathing ship's oxygen.

They're going to need every breath of their suit air when the time comes."

"Robbie, those suits aren't designed for use on orbit," Stephanie objected. "They're not for total vacuum. And Vivian doesn't even have one, just her activity suit."

"There you go again," Robbie said. "They *should* work, and if they don't, you won't be any deader. OK, I need to get the ground on the phone. Long Beach, Atlantis, are you copying this conversation?"

"Roger Atlantis, hanging on every word," Jean replied.

"I need you to find someone who's familiar with these units who can talk me through changing the batteries and then operating them. I need to know what their rated load capacity is. And I definitely need to know how many were onboard the station."

"Roger Atlantis, we're on it."

Robbie released the latches on the first fiberglass cylinder and opened it, pulling out the compact bundle within. He began intensely studying the instructions printed on the inside of the container. "Damn it, I wish I'd practiced my Russian more," he swore as he puzzled through the text.

***

"Atlantis, Long Beach, Robbie, we have some answers for you."

"Go, Long Beach, let me have it," Robbie replied, as he finished unpacking the third container.

"The good news is that one of the paracone designers is here in town for a conference at the Jet Propulsion Lab. He's on his way over as we speak."

"Hallelujah," Robbie said. "What else?"

"He tells us that the units were designed to safely handle up to two hundred kilograms. More than that and they'll burn up on reentry."

Robbie did a quick mental conversion. "OK, that's enough. What else?"

"I'm afraid there were only three on board."

"Damn. I was afraid you were going to say that. Oh well, it saves me another trip to the station. When can we start with the batteries?"

"He should be here in less than half an hour."

"Robbie, everyone is suited up," Stephanie reported. "We're going to go on ship's oxygen and close visors."

"Did you put the batteries in the airlock like I asked?"

"Affirmative."

"Great. Now listen to me. Once everyone is on oxygen, I need you to reduce pressure to 3.9 psi. The lowest you can go and still keep everyone alive."

"But Robbie … "

"Listen—those suits have barely thirty minutes of oxygen built in once you disconnect from the ship's supply. If you reduce the pressure as low as you can go, maybe we can stretch that to forty minutes. I have a feeling you're going to need every second."

"OK," Stephanie replied.

"Keep an eye on everyone, make sure they all stay conscious. Now when I tell you, you're going to depressurize the vehicle and open both lock doors."

"You want me to completely depressurize the crew compartment?"

"It will take too long to cycle you in groups through the airlock. Once I'm ready out here, you'll need to disconnect from ship's air and get your butts outside as fast as possible."

"Robbie?"

"Yes Steph?"

"You're not coming, are you?" she asked plaintively.

"You heard the lady. Two hundred kilos per unit. We're going to pair up Elton and Vivian, Mike and Nikki, and you and Tom. That should work out just about right. Plus they're not big enough to hold three people."

***

The Russian engineer finished his instructions. "That should do it, Commander. Now secure the battery compartment cover. On the side of the compartment, you should see a test switch."

"I see it," Robbie replied, studying the paracone's small control panel.

"Hold that switch for ten seconds. You will see a blinking red light. It will conduct a test of all the device's systems. When the light stops blinking, let go of the switch."

"And then what?"

"The light should turn green. If it does, that will mean that the descent rocket, arming system and guidance element are all operational."

Robbie held his breath and pushed the switch. When the light stopped blinking, he released it. The light turned green.

"Thank God it works!" Robbie exclaimed. "Man I love Russian hardware. Now how do I operate it?"

"It is most simple, Commander. Once energized, the guidance system initiates through GLONASS to determine its location. Simply enter the coordinates of the desired target destination, and then press the arming button."

"The big red one?"

"Yes, that is it. Once you arm the unit, the system will determine if the target is within range. If so, the display will show the remaining time until the unit fires."

"That's it?"

"Yes, that is it. Then simply stand back. Or in your case, I would suggest you eject the unit from the cargo bay, so that it does not collide with the vehicle when the rocket fires."

"Yeah, we've had enough of colliding vehicles for this man's lifetime."

"Commander?"

"Yes?"

"I understand that you will be using the paracones to transport your crew?"

"That's the plan."

"I might point out that the devices are spin stabilized. They were intended for cargo and not crew. You will need to ensure that when the individuals are placed in the unit, their heads are to be as close to the center as possible to prevent negative effects."

"Roger that, thank you. Jean?"

"Yes, Robbie?"

"Tell me if it's possible on our next orbit to drop these so they land off the coast of California. After all everyone has been through, I don't want them to have to wait days to make it home once they're on the ground."

"OK Robbie, we'll take a look."

***

"All right everyone, listen up. This is how it's going to work," Robbie instructed. "When I call you, you'll activate your suit oxygen flow and unhook from the ship's O2. Then I want you to join me in the cargo bay as rapidly as possible. You're going to curl up, and I'm going to push you into a big nylon bag. I want you to each tuck your helmets into the other's stomach and snuggle in tightly. Understand?"

Everyone acknowledged their instructions.

"Once you're both in position, I'm going to zip the enclosure shut around you and then I'm going to chuck you out of the bay. Then just hang on and wait for the rocket to fire. I'm told the unit will be spun up to stabilize it. Try not to get sick. It would suck to get you this far and then have you choke on vomit on the way down. Once the rocket fires, then you're on your way and you'll start reentry.

"You might run out of air before you make it all the way down. Don't panic. Suffocation sucks, but once you're down into the atmosphere far enough, your helmet anti-suffocation valves will let you start breathing outside air, so you should be OK. If you feel yourself passing out, don't fight it. You should come to just fine once you're in denser air. You'll feel the chute open. It should be a nice yank. Once you hit the surface, you can pull the release and open the bag. Any questions?"

Everyone sat in stunned silence.

"You can do this. I saw you all handle worse at the Gagarin training facility. Just try and stay calm, because there's nothing you can do until you hit the ground. OK, let's go. Team one. Vivian first."

"Now?" Elton asked uncertainly.

"NOW!"

Elton and Vivian disconnected themselves from Atlantis' oxygen supply and gently launched themselves through the open airlock doors.

"Curl up like I told you," Robbie directed. Grasping Vivian, he gently pushed her into the cargo compartment of the paracone. "OK Elton, now you."

"You're sure about this?" Elton asked as he curled up, his eyes revealing fear.

Hell no, Robbie thought. "Yes, I'm sure. This will work, I'm certain of it. Now come on, we're wasting time."

Robbie pushed Elton into the compartment alongside Vivian. "OK, tuck in tight. Head to stomach, like I said. You want to keep your heads as close to the center axis as possible."

Satisfied with their placement, Robbie zipped the heavy nylon compartment shut, ensuring the zipper lanyard dangled inside where they could reach it. "OK, you two are first, so I'm afraid you have the longest wait. Looks like you have," he glanced over to the timer on the second unit, "about twelve minutes to retro fire. Try not to think about it, just breath easily and try to conserve your oxygen. OK, I'm going to toss you clear of the bay now."

Robbie crouched down and reached under the white nylon bag in which he had placed Elton and Vivian. Standing up rapidly, he tossed it upward, clear of Atlantis' cargo bay. It continued sailing slowly past the station's main truss and out into space.

"OK, team two, let's go."

Robbie repeated the process with Nikki and Mike. As he finished securing the compartment, he said, "Good luck you two."

"Thanks, Robbie," they both replied gratefully, as he heaved them into space.

"All right you two, let's go, we're running out of time," Robbie said to Tom and Stephanie. They both shortly appeared at the outer airlock door.

"Ladies first," Robbie said, as he reached to help Stephanie into the paracone cargo compartment.

Stephanie looked in anguish at Robbie, tears in her eyes. "Robbie, please, there has to be a way … "

"No time, Steph, this is your only chance. Let's go, don't blow it," he said.

She awkwardly hugged his space suited form. He smiled at her to try and ease her grief.

"It's OK, Steph. Don't worry about me. A captain is supposed to go down with his ship, remember? Now curl up, we're under four minutes."

Stephanie curled into a ball, and Robbie inserted her into the last paracone unit. Turning to Tom, he said, "I have something for you."

"What?" Tom replied, startled.

Reaching down to the cargo pocket on his left thigh, Robbie extracted a golf ball sized rock that he had picked up on the lunar surface. Extending it to Tom, he said, "Give this to Nicole."

Tom took the rock, looking at it, then at Robbie, and then back at the rock again, completely at a loss for words.

"Tom, dude, put it in your pocket already, you need to go now," Robbie emphasized.

"Thank you … " Tom began, struggling to convey the scope of his gratitude.

"You're welcome. Now get in!" Robbie gently pushed Tom into the cargo compartment next to Stephanie. "Have a beer for me when you're down," he added as he zipped the compartment closed.

Robbie pushed their paracone out of the cargo bay and on its way. He watched as it drifted toward the other two, satisfied to see that all three would safely clear the station.

After several moments, he looked around the now empty bay. "Well," he said to himself softly. "What am I gunna do now?"

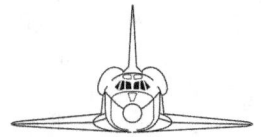

CHAPTER FORTY–NINE

The paracone guidance computers counted down the time remaining. After verifying their location with GLONASS, all three declared "Now!" within a second of each other. With a loud pop, a pressurized cylinder released, forcing quick setting polyurethane foam into each cone's folded fabric ribs. Like giant umbrellas, they quickly unfolded, forming large Nomex and nylon disks—each cone's ablative coated heat shield. The foam quickly hardened into a firm structure, supporting the shield for reentry.

From Atlantis, Robbie could see three large white flowers suddenly blossom in space above him. "Now that's a pretty sight," he said with happiness and relief to no one in particular.

Mounted on the rims of the deployed heat shields, small thrusters fired, spinning the fabric discs like tops. The motion would stabilize the cones during firing of their reentry rockets and their descent through the upper atmosphere.

"Oh my God," Vivian muttered, as the spinning induced vertigo, which was accentuated by the darkness inside the compartment.

"Yeah, now I know how my laundry feels," Elton replied.

As the spin rate stabilized, the reentry rockets now fired. They each felt a gentle push, which grew into a strong shove for thirty seconds and then quickly ended.

"Long Beach, Atlantis, I see three good burns, it looks like they're on their way," Robbie reported.

"Copy that Atlantis. We have assets moving into place to receive them, and the Coast Guard is standing by to assist," Jean replied. "Great job up there, you should feel very good about what you've done for them."

"I have to admit I'd feel better if I could have joined them," Robbie said, suddenly overwhelmed by fatigue. "But yeah, I'm feeling pretty good about it overall. Please let me know when they're down."

"Roger that, Atlantis."

Slowed below orbital velocity, the paracones fell rapidly from space. The passengers believed they could feel a gentle pressure as the discs began to encounter the thin upper reaches of the atmosphere. They could clearly hear a faint sizzling sound transmitted through the cone's fabric structure as the ablative thermal layer began to burn away. Three brilliant shooting stars blazed their way across the North Pacific Ocean in tight formation.

As the air density increased, the guidance systems made subtle adjustments to the flight path of each cone. Pneumatic actuators flexed the ribs of the heat shields, altering the flow of ionized air across their surfaces, controlling their paths through the upper atmosphere.

A member of Jean's team maintained continuous contact with Air Force Space Command, which was tracking the cones as they made their ballistic reentry. His periodic reports of "three targets, on track" gave everyone hope.

The cones buffeted heavily as they tore across the sky at hypersonic velocity. The sizzle grew to a loud ripping sound that convinced the passengers their cones were being torn to shreds. They imagined they could feel the intense heat radiating from the inferno that enveloped them. They were sure they were about to die. There was little time to dwell on it though, as they began to exhaust their small oxygen supplies. They slowly lost consciousness.

Having little mass, the cones slowed rapidly, and their angle of descent increased. As the heat of reentry diminished, a canister on each cone actuated, inflating a set of extensions to the ribs of the heat shield, doubling the size of the fabric disk. Shortly after, each cone deployed a small drogue chute to orient and stabilize the craft.

As they fell below forty thousand feet, the anti-suffocation valves in their helmets began to allow outside atmosphere to enter their suits. Although they remained unconscious, most began spontaneously breathing again.

"Three targets, still on track," the controller again reported to the team in mission control.

At twenty thousand feet, the drogue chute on each cone was released. Each then deployed a larger parachute to continue slowing the craft. The chutes contained radar reflectors to increase their visibility.

"Air Force reports three radar blooms!" Jean's Air Force liaison announced. A small cheer swept through the control room.

"Quiet!" Jean shouted. "They're not down yet!"

At five thousand feet, each cone fired a cutting mechanism that released additional parachute canopy, doubling the size of the chute and continuing to slow their descent.

***

Aboard the Freedom Star, Captain Meyers stood on the port bridge wing anxiously scanning the sky to the west with binoculars. The ship had rapidly rushed to the anticipated impact point six miles off the coast of Los Angeles with a fleet of smaller vessels close behind.

"There!" he heard his first mate shout, who was scanning the sky further north. Looking in the indicated direction, he spotted first one, then two, and finally three large orange and white parachute canopies drop from the broken cloud layer above. Reaching for the VHF microphone, he reported, "Long Beach, this is Freedom Star, we have all three packages in sight."

Leaning his head into the pilothouse, he gave directions to the helmsman. "Full throttle, course three one zero."

"Full throttle, course three one zero," the helmsman acknowledged, pushing the throttles forward and spinning the wheel. The ship churned the ocean into froth as it accelerated.

***

Tom became aware of an intense light that hurt his eyes. Fluttering his eyelids, he tried to turn his head to avoid the painful brightness. Somewhere to his right, he heard a voice shout, "I have a pulse! I need oxygen, now!" Shaking his head, he attempted to lift his arm. After several tries, he succeeded in reaching up to his faceplate. Surprised to find it open, his gloved hand brushed his nose. He struggled to open his eyes.

"It's OK! Breathe! Breathe!" he heard the voice to his right say. Finally, he managed to pry open his eyes. He saw a blurred vision of bright blue sky, white clouds, and a silhouette of a head directly above him. It appeared to be facing the direction of the voice. He heard loud coughing.

"Ugh," he mumbled, attempting to speak. The face turned toward him and smiled. Nicole smiled. She smiled down at him with a huge grin.

"Welcome back, spaceman!" she said, and then looked over her shoulder. "Can someone give me a hand here?" she called out.

Tom felt hands under his shoulders, lifting him into a sitting position. He felt something supportive pushed against his back to help him stay upright. More hands rotated his neck ring and removed his helmet.

"Here, use this," Nicole said gently, pushing a small blue oxygen mask onto his nose and mouth.

Tom held the mask to his face with his left hand. As his vision focused, he scanned his surroundings. He was on a ship. The deck of a ship. Then he spotted Vivian. She was waving at him. She was sitting upright, propped against a bale of some kind, holding an oxygen mask to her face and waving. Tom lifted his right hand and attempted to wave back. Continuing to scan his surroundings, he spotted Mike and Nikki. Mike was sitting. He was a member of the oxygen mask club as well. Nikki was standing, and

353

wasn't using a mask. She had her hand on Mike's shoulder. Next he saw Stephanie. She was looking to his right. She looked concerned. He heard the voice again. It said, "OK, he's going to make it." Looking to his right, he saw several people. They were standing around something. Standing around someone. They were standing around Elton. Elton was coughing. He was coughing and they were holding an oxygen mask to his face. "He's going to make it," the voice said again. It was the person who held the mask to Elton's face.

"Is, is everybody OK?" Tom asked weakly.

"Yes, we got all six of you," Nicole said with a grin. "You're all safe. We're on the Freedom Star, and we're heading back to Long Beach as we speak."

"So everyone is OK?" Tom asked again, still fighting a mental fog.

"Yes," Nicole said again. "You all landed within a mile of each other. You were all unconscious except for Nikki—she was actually standing up in the paracone waving at us when we pulled up."

"Really?" Tom asked, fuzzily.

"Yes, she was. She was very worried about all of you." Turning toward Elton, who was now being helped into a sitting position, she added, "Elton was the worst, he was cyanotic and not breathing. But they did CPR and brought him around." Turning back to Tom, she smiled radiantly. "You all made it!" Reaching out and taking Tom's head in her hands, she kissed him gently on the forehead. "Don't you ever do that again, understand?" she scolded, as she hugged his neck.

"Don't worry, I think our space traveling days are over," he said, attempting to smile back. "Oh, here, I brought you something," he said, fumbling for his thigh pocket.

"You brought me something?" she said incredulously.

"Yes. Robbie gave it to me. He wanted you to have it."

Nicole's mouth dropped open as Tom placed the moon rock in her open hands.

***

"Can I tell him?" Marcus asked, reaching for the microphone.

Jean hesitated for a moment, and then handed it to him. "Sure, that's a good idea."

Marcus paused for a moment, and then keyed the mike. "Atlantis, Long Beach, do you read?"

After a brief pause, they heard Robbie's voice. "Hollywood! Is that you? How you been brother?"

Marcus took a deep breath. "Yes, it's me. I'm fine man, just fine. I wanted you to know you did it. We have all six of them back on the ground safe. You did it, man. You saved them all."

***

Robbie looked down at the Earth from where he sat atop the main truss of the space station. The view was better from here than down in the shuttle's cargo bay.

"Well that's fine, I'm damn glad to hear that. Thank you for that news."

"Robbie," Marcus said, "you know, when I told you to bring them all home safe, I sort of thought you'd be coming home with them."

"Well my friend, sometimes things just don't work out like you planned," he replied. "Life's funny that way."

They were both silent for a moment. "Is there anything we can do for you?" Marcus finally asked helplessly.

Robbie smiled. "Not a thing I can think of, brother," he said quietly. "One thing though. I know what happened. I've been sitting here thinking about it, and I've figured it out."

Marcus gave Jean a puzzled look. "What's that, Robbie?"

"We were too sure of ourselves. We thought it was easy. But it's not. It's actually really hard, all this spaceflight stuff. I'm not saying the NASA way is the way to do it. I still think there's way too much bullshit in their approach. But we didn't take it seriously enough. *I* didn't take it seriously enough." He paused and took a deep breath. "I just thought you should know. Pass that on to Stephanie for me, would you?"

"I'll do that."

Robbie continued to gaze at the Earth passing silently below. After a moment, he said, "You know what? There is something you can do for me."

"What's that, Robbie?"

"I'd like some music. A view like this deserves some music. Do you think you could do that for me?"

Marcus looked at Jean again, who nodded. "Sure thing brother, what would you like to hear?"

"I dunno. Something majestic. Holst's *The Planets* maybe?"

"OK, give us a minute, it's not something I think anyone here has on their player, but we'll sure find it."

"No worries, I'll be here," Robbie replied, settling back to get more comfortable. "I'm not going anywhere." After a moment, he changed his mind. "You know what? Scratch that. I want Pink Floyd. I want some 'Shine On You Crazy Diamond.'"

"That I think we can do," Marcus replied.

Robbie smiled as the haunting opening strains of the melody began. On the Earth below, it was night, and he was transfixed by the lights of the passing cities, sparkling like jewels on the black velvet surface. The thin band of atmosphere on the distant horizon began to brighten from royal purple to deep red as one more sunrise began, the brilliant yellow sun climbing regally above the edge of the planet.

Reaching into his gear bag, Robbie pulled out the Chumash Indian rattle he had carried with him to the lunar surface. *For luck*, he thought wryly, examining it briefly. Returning his attention to the dawn below, his smile broadened. Drawing a deep breath, he slowly exhaled, as the music swelled and the sun rose.

"Man, it truly doesn't get any better than this," he sighed contentedly.

The End

EPILOGUE

As the credits scrolled upward across Quan's visual field, he removed the temporal arch from his head and returned it to its storage location in the seat's armrest. Leaning back in his seat with his eyes closed, he basked for a moment in the joyful sadness of the story. Shortly, a soft bell tone rang, pulling him back to reality. Glancing at the elevation display, he realized that the climber capsule would soon be arriving at the station.

Retrieving his gear from beneath his seat, Quan joined the queue of people slowly shuffling off the climber. Approaching the reception security center, he extended his forearm for the scanner to read his identichip and opened his gear stowage bag for the nanoscreener to process the contents. Receiving a green light, he gathered up his gear.

Right on time, he thought with satisfaction, as he headed for the Celestial Bar to join his friends. Entering the club, a breaking news story on the holoviewer caught his eye. "Major New Water Ice Discovery at Heinel City Reported," the headline read. *That will definitely affect the lunar mining stocks when the markets reopen*, he thought, his mind never wandering far from business.

Spotting his friends already seated in a corner booth, he headed over to join them. "Ah, you couldn't wait for me to start the party?" he chided, pointing to the drinks before them.

"Hell no," Jie Lin laughed. "Hurry and sit down, you're behind." Jie had introduced Quan to diving several years previously, and they tried to make a jump together at least once a month. "Another round, this time on him," Jie shouted, signaling the serving system and pointing at Quan.

The group drank and laughed and caught up while they waited for the departure of the next shuttle to the Central Himalayan dive platform. Their mood was briefly interrupted when a white robed group slowly threaded past the noisy bar, led by an orange clad monk softly chanting and wafting incense.

"Tā māde!" Jie swore. "Why can't those zealots hold their ceremonies somewhere else!"

"There are no dedicated platforms for orbital cremation, you know that," Quan chided his friend. "Besides, the noble one does not take up much room on the shuttle," he added, referring to the urn of the deceased that the mourners had brought to be dropped into the atmosphere to become a glowing golden meteor. "It is how I think I would want to join my ancestors when the time comes," he added thoughtfully.

"Bah, enough," Jie gestured dismissively. "How many rounds do we have time for before our shuttle?"

"I was thinking," Quan said. "We have all jumped the Himalayan platform several times already. What would you think of catching the Trans-Pacific shuttle and diving from Robichaud platform instead? We would have ample time to catch the stratolink from Los Angeles back to Singapore."

"That old dump? Why would you ever want to jump that?" Jie asked.

"It was the first dive platform, and it just seems like something we should all do at least once. Besides, it has been a long time since I have been to California."

"You want to pay homage to the first jumpers," Jie said, nodding thoughtfully. "Yes, you are right. We should all do that once. What do you think?" he asked of the others.

No one among them had a specific objection.

***

The shuttle that had brought them undocked and prepared to depart as Quan and his friends crowded into the confined space of Robichaud platform. They had arrived just barely in time, as it was less than thirty minutes until the next dive arm rotated past. They quickly familiarized themselves with the navigation markers that would guide them through their reentry corridor over the Pacific Ocean, and then donned their exoatmospheric dive gear. As they stood before the boarding door for their dive capsule, Quan noticed the unusual static visual mounted to the wall above them. It showed eight smiling people dressed in antique fabric spacesuits, the large orb of the moon behind them. Above them was written "Sic Itur Ad Astra."

"The crew of the Atlantis expedition," Quan said to his friends, pointing to the image.

No one heard him. As the long dive arm measuring almost a hundred miles in length swept toward the platform, it required the quick performance of a series of choreographed steps to successfully transition into the pre-dive. As Quan made his remark, the door to the dive capsule snapped open, and his comments were lost as they all pushed rapidly inside, completely filling the small space. As the arm approached closer, it reached out to magnetically engage with the capsule, locking fields and snatching it from the platform. They felt the smooth but powerful push as they were quickly accelerated away.

Because the direction of the arm's rotation was opposite the platform's orbital path, the velocity at the end of the arm was below that necessary to remain in orbit. Once the arm completed its rotation and swung back toward Earth, they would simply step out into space and begin their dive. They waited patiently

The translucent surface of the capsule's portal changed from red to yellow. "Don protective gear and acknowledge readiness," an invisible voice announced in Chinese, English, and Spanish. Quan touched the collar of his dive suit, and his diama-glass crystalline carbon helmet snapped into place and sealed. Looking around the capsule, he received a thumbs up from everyone in the group. He reached up and pushed the glowing "Ready" button.

The portal's color now changed to green. The invisible voice spoke again. "Readiness acknowledged. Dive will commence in five, four, three, two, one. Enjoy your dive."

The capsule quickly depressurized, and the portal snapped open. They each quickly stepped out into space and began their fall to the surface.

Quan actually found the exoatmospheric portion of dives somewhat dull, although the view was quite spectacular. The fun really began once they entered the atmosphere. As he encountered the first tenuous layers, he activated his suit's reentry mode. Although he could set it for automatic activation, as an experienced diver he preferred to select it manually, waiting until he actually began feeling the heat starting to build around him.

Immediately, the molecular nanofiber shell of his suit sprang into a compact parabolic shape, his diama-glass helmet extending through the center. He could see the ionized plasma start to build on the surface of his helmet and run in rivulets along the outside of his suit.

Engaging his aerosurface controls, Quan began swooping and twirling through the upper atmosphere, inscribing enormous flaming arcs in the sky. Looking downward, his suit projected a small glowing circle on the inside surface of his helmet that showed his target location on the ground—an area along the waterfront of Los Angeles known as Long Beach. Turning his head to look behind him, he saw the multiple blazing meteor trails of his companions. Laughing gleefully, he arced upward, as he and several others began spiraling around each other, creating brilliant luminous corkscrew patterns in an intricate aerial ballet.

"It truly doesn't get any better than this!" he shouted with great joy.

AFTERWORD

The basic idea for this story, a voyage to the moon utilizing a space shuttle, occurred to me about ten years ago. It percolated quietly in the back of my mind, occasionally pulled to the forefront by some random news event or stray science article that caught my attention. When I finally sat down to start seriously researching this book, I learned that NASA's Langley Research Center had actually studied the concept, producing NASA Technical Memorandum 104084 of June, 1991, entitled Feasibility Analysis of Cislunar Flight Using the Shuttle Orbiter. Many of the technical details in this book originated from that report. It made my job much easier, as it demonstrated that a concept that I had initially assumed would be purely fantastical was in fact somewhat plausible. A copy of the report can be easily found online for those interested in seeing the original NASA concept for such a mission.

Paraffin fueled hybrid rockets, inflatable reentry vehicles, an alternate shuttle launch site at Vandenberg Air Force Base; these and other things central to the story do in fact exist or have been proposed. The more scientifically minded among you may have noticed that while I tried to maintain a basic allegiance to the fundamental laws of physics and adhere to the realm of the possible, I did occasionally take a few liberties with some of the science and technology in order to spin a good tale. I hope you can forgive me, but if not, well, let me remind you that as it says in the beginning, this story plays out in what could be an alternate universe, where such things may in fact be possible.

ABOUT THE AUTHOR

Robert Sapp lives in Pensacola, Florida, a town whose unofficial motto is "Where Thousands Live As Millions Wish They Could." His background as a former nuclear submariner and lifelong aerospace enthusiast along with his degree in Engineering Technology from the University of West Florida gives him the comprehensive grasp of science and technology that is a hallmark of his writing. When not working to pay the bills, he and his wife Rhonda sail the local bays and bayous on *Eagle*, their 34 foot sloop. After receiving numerous compliments on the "darn fine Christmas letter" he wrote each year, Robert finally decided to see if he had what it took to become a professional author. You're holding the result of that endeavor. Currently, Robert is considering a short list of topics to develop for his next novel.

www.ingramcontent.com/pod-product-compliance
Lightning Source LLC
Chambersburg PA
CBHW051446260626
47162CB00001B/273